Run to Ground

Also by D.P. Lyle, M.D.

NONFICTION

Murder and Mayhem: A Doctor Answers Medical and Forensic
Questions from Mystery Writers

Forensics for Dummies

Forensics and Fiction: Clever, Intriguing, and
Downright Odd Questions from Crime Writers

Howdunnit: Forensics: A Guide for Writers

More Forensics and Fiction:
Crime Writers Morbidly Curious Questions Expertly Answered

FICTION

The Dub Walker Series
Stress Fracture
Hot Lights, Cold Steel
Run to Ground

The Samantha Cody Series
Devil's Playground
Double Blind

The Royal Pains Media Tie-In Series
Royal Pains: First, Do No Harm
Royal Pains: Sick Rich

Anthologies
Thrillers: 100 Must-Reads:Essay: Jules Verne, Mysterious Island
Thriller 3: Love Is Murder: Short Story: Even Steven

DVD
Forensic Science for Writers

Run to Ground

A Novel

D.P. Lyle

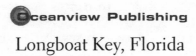
Longboat Key, Florida

ISBN: 978-1-60809-057-0

Published in the United States of America by Oceanview Publishing,
Longboat Key, Florida
www.oceanviewpub.com

2 4 6 8 10 9 7 5 3 1

PRINTED IN THE UNITED STATES OF AMERICA

Acknowledgments

A special thanks to my wonderful agent, Kimberley Cameron, of Kimberley Cameron and Associates.

Another special thank you to all the wonderful people at Oceanview, particularly Bob and Pat Gussin, Frank Troncale, and Susan Hayes.

To my longtime and dear friends Charles Pike, Lewis Brinkley, Paul Haley, and Ronnie Boles for the use of their names.

To Paige Baker, Arthur Dunn, and Sandy Sechrest for their generous library donations in exchange for their names appearing in this book. Their support for their local library is essential for the existence of all libraries.

Lastly, a big thank you to my sister Victoria Cunningham, who, after reading the short story from which this novel sprang, asked the simple question: What happens next? The answer is in these pages.

About the Author

D.P. Lyle, M.D. is the Macavity Award-winning and Edgar Award-nominated author of many nonfiction books (*Murder & Mayhem*; *Forensics for Dummies*; *Forensics & Fiction*; *More Forensics & Fiction*; *Howdunnit: Forensics*; and *ABA Fundamentals: Understanding Forensic Science*) as well as numerous works of fiction, including the Samantha Cody thriller series (*Devil's Playground* and *Double Blind*); the Dub Walker thriller series (*Stress Fracture*; *Hot Lights, Cold Steel*; and *Run To Ground*); and the Royal Pains media tie-in novels (*Royal Pains: First, Do No Harm* and *Royal Pains: Sick Rich*). His essay on Jules Verne's *The Mysterious Island* appears in *Thrillers: 100 Must-Reads* and his short story "Even Steven" will appear in the International Thriller Writer's anthology *Thriller 3: Love Is Murder*.

He has worked with many novelists and with the writers of popular television shows such as *Law & Order*, *CSI: Miami*, *Diagnosis Murder*, *Monk*, *Judging Amy*, *Peacemakers*, *Cold Case*, *House*, *Medium*, *Women's Murder Club*, *1-800-Missing*, *The Glades*, and *Pretty Little Liars*.

He was born and raised in Huntsville, Alabama, where his childhood interests revolved around football, baseball, and building rockets in his backyard. The latter pursuit was common in Huntsville during the 1950s and '60s due to NASA's nearby Marshall Space Flight Center.

After leaving Huntsville, he attended college, medical school, and served an internship at the University of Alabama; followed by a residency in Internal Medicine at the University of Texas at Houston; then a Fellowship in Cardiology at The Texas Heart Institute, also in Houston. For the past thirty years, he has practiced cardiology in Orange County, California.

Website: http://www.dplylemd.com
Blog: http://writersforensicsblog.wordpress.com

Run to Ground

Chapter 1

"I can still smell him." Martha Foster inhaled deeply and closed her eyes.

Tim stood just inside the doorway and looked down at his wife. She sat on the edge of their son's bed, eyes moist, chin trembling, as were the fingers that clutched the navy-blue Tommy Hilfiger sweatshirt to her chest. It had been Steven's favorite. He had slept in it every night the first month, until Martha finally pried it away long enough to run it through the wash.

Behind her, a dozen photos of Steven lay scattered across the blue comforter. A proud Steven in his first baseball uniform. A seven-year-old Steven, grinning, upper left front tooth missing, soft freckles over his nose, buzz-cut hair, a blue swimming ribbon dangling around his neck. A playful Steven, sitting next to Martha at the backyard picnic table, face screwed into a goofy expression, smoke from the Weber BBQ rising behind them. Tim remembered the day he snapped the picture. Labor Day weekend. Just six months before — that day. He squeezed back his own tears and swallowed hard.

Martha shifted her weight and twisted toward the photos. She laid the sweatshirt aside and reached out, lightly touching an image of Steven's face. The trembling of her delicate fingers increased. She said nothing for a moment and then, "I'm taking these."

Tim walked to where she sat and pulled her to him, her cheek nestling against his chest, her tears soaking through his tee shirt. He kissed the top of her head.

"He's gone," Martha said. "Everything's gone. Or will be."

Tim smoothed her hair as details from a room frozen in time raced toward him. A Derek Jeter poster, a photo of Steven's Little League team, and his Student-of-the-Month certificate hung on the wall above his small desk. A crooked-neck lamp spotlighted a history text, opened to the stern face of Thomas Jefferson. His baseball uniform draped over the chair back, sneakers haphazard on the floor. Exactly as it had been the day their lives jumped the track.

They had been through this dozens of times. What they could safely take. What must be abandoned. What could be traced back here. They had scrutinized everything they owned. Their marriage license, birth certificates, engraved wedding bands, the calligraphed family tree Martha had painstakingly drawn and framed, and boxes of family keepsakes. Any photo that showed their home, cars, neighbors, family, Steven's friends, teammates, or school, had to be abandoned. As did Steven's Little League uniform. Each of these could undo everything if seen by a curious eye.

Tim had always won these what-to-take-what-to-leave arguments, but now, with the end so close, he knew he could no longer resist her.

"It's okay," he said.

"Thirty-six hours." She eased from his embrace, looked up at him, and swiped the back of her hand across her nose. "I can't believe it's here."

"We can back out. Stay and risk it."

She shook her head. "No. We can't. Not with him around."

"He might've just been blowing off steam."

"You don't believe that."

No, he didn't. He knew better.

"Besides, that's just part of it. We can't let that animal—" She screwed her face down tightly, suppressing another sob.

Tim touched her cheek, catching a stray tear with his thumb. "It'll be okay. Keep the pictures." He walked to Steven's desk, lifted the uniform from the back of the chair, and returned to her side. "The uniform, too."

"His uniform?" She took it from him as a sob escaped her throat. "He was so proud of it." She swallowed hard and then dabbed her eyes with her shirtsleeve. Her voice broke as she asked, "Are you sure?"

"I'm sure."

"Thank you," she whispered.

"But nothing else. Nothing that leads back here. This life is over. Finished. Tomorrow night Tim and Martha Foster no longer exist. But Robert Beckwith and Cindy Strunk will get a chance to live yet again."

She shook her head, uncertainty lingering in her eyes. "What if they find out Robert and Cindy have been dead for a couple of decades?"

"Not likely."

"Still—"

"It'll work. We're not the first to rummage through old obituaries and cemeteries. Lots of people have done it before us."

"Most get caught."

"Only the ones you hear about. Most just move on. Become someone else."

"Let's hope."

He brushed a wayward strand of hair from her face and lifted her chin with a finger. "You'll make a perfect Cindy."

She smiled, weak and tentative, her face tear streaked, her nose reddened, but it was still a smile. There hadn't been many of those lately.

"It's not like we have another option," Tim said. "We can't simply move. We have to disappear. Become completely untraceable. Be reborn."

She took a deep breath and let it out slowly. "It will be like dying."

"Except that we'll have another chance. A new life." He looked down at her. "And Steven will live on in our memories."

"It's not fair." She hugged the uniform to her chest.

"Can you live with this? What we're doing?"

She sat silently for a moment as if considering his question. The question that had plagued them for the past six months. Even as they pressed ahead with the planning, with getting the documents in order, with building their new life, their new identities, the question hung out there on the horizon. A horizon whose sharp edge dropped into an abyss. A horizon that rapidly approached. Could they do this? Could they really leave everything and everyone behind?

She sighed. "I'll have to."

"We'll both have to."

She swallowed against another burst of tears. "What now?"

He retrieved his to-do list from his shirt pocket and unfolded it. "You have the new passports and the North Carolina driver's licenses. Right?"

"In my purse."

"The money from the house sale and our accounts is in the North Carolina bank."

They'd luckily found a buyer willing to pay cash for the house. At a big discount. He bought the story about them needing to sell quickly and head west to Arizona. Ailing mother. That was lucky, but also easy. The hard part was closing down all their accounts, selling the bonds, and emptying his pension plan without raising too much suspicion. You can't simply take a couple of hundred thousand in cash from a bank without triggering scrutiny. Shutting down a pension plan is even more difficult. Tim had managed to move the money around to several banks and investment houses, each time bleeding off a chunk of cash.

"The rental house there is ready," Tim said. "Tomorrow we'll empty the last bank account."

She stood. "I'll finish packing and then we can take all this over to the new car."

Tim turned the SUV into the mall's parking garage and wound up to the roof. At eleven p.m. only a handful of cars remained on that level. He pulled into the space next to a blue sedan. The one owned by the newly minted Robert Beckwith.

He had purchased and registered it in North Carolina a month earlier and driven it back here. They had moved it around among parking lots and garages all over the city, never leaving it in any one place more than a couple of days. Someone might notice. Might think it was abandoned. Might involve the police. They avoided the airport and any other place that had video cameras. It had been in this spot less than twenty-four hours and would be gone in just over twenty-four more.

Tim stepped into the lazy night air where thousands of stars peppered the clear sky. A perfect Alabama spring night. May was a good month here. The damp chill of winter gone and the heat and humidity of summer still a couple of months away. He would miss this. He'd never lived anywhere else. Neither had Martha. This was home.

For another day anyway.

He popped the SUV's rear hatch. They loaded the four suitcases into the sedan's trunk and then wedged three cardboard banker's boxes into the backseat. Amazing that an entire life can fit into one car. But when cutting loose everything that came before, that's the way it was.

Chapter 2

I parked my 1983 911SC Porsche in the front lot of Walker Lumber. My company. The one I inherited when my parents died. Drunk driver, rain-slicked Governors Drive—a dangerous road under the best conditions. A weave, a skid, a bang, and that was that. Here one minute, gone the next.

I'm Dub Walker. My real job is writing books and consulting on criminal cases not supplying lumber to construction companies and do-it-yourselfers. In the past, I had busted out of med school, been a Marine MP for a couple of years, spent some quality time with the FBI's Behavioral Science Unit, and for six years worked as a criminalist at the Alabama Department of Forensic Science here in Huntsville. Turned out I had a knack for connecting the evidence dots and for understanding how criminals think. Not sure where all that came from, but it lead to a new career. Not one I had ever envisioned but here I was and I had to admit, it wasn't a bad place to be. I've written eight books on evidence and criminal behavior and consulted on dozens of cases all over the country, so people think I'm sort of an expert in these areas. True or not, writing books and giving lectures will at least create that illusion. I keep the lumber company going because it pays the rent and because it carries on my father's work. He built it, he lived it, he loved it. My duty is to keep it going.

Mondays were for bill paying. When I pulled into the front lot, I saw

Milk inside the office, talking on the phone. He gave a half wave. Milk never wasted movement. His real name was Bertie Jackson but everyone called him Buttermilk, a great Southern nickname. Close friends simply called him Milk, his nickname for his nickname. Only in the South could that happen.

My dad's age, Milk had worked here for over twenty years. When the company dropped in my lap, I needed help running it. I had worked here many summers during high school and college, but I didn't know all the ins and outs of making it tick. Milk did. I gave him a chunk of ownership and turned the day-to-day stuff over to him. It worked out well.

Inside, a stack of bills sat on my desk. I scribbled out checks for each while Milk continued his call. Talking to one of our hardware providers. Apparently a late-delivery problem. Milk hung up.

"They late again?" I asked.

"Yep. Just a couple of days and we got enough to make it through the week. Just don't want to fall too far behind."

He knelt and twirled open the lock to the large safe that squatted in the corner. He pulled out a zipped banker's bag and handed it to me. "Last week was a good one. Very good."

The bag felt heavy. "How much?"

"A little over sixty-two thousand." His eyebrows gave a couple of bounces. "Home prices going up so much around here, people staying put and fixing things up. Good for us."

With the increased activity at the U.S. Army Redstone Arsenal, NASA's Marshall Space Flight Center, the Cummings Research Park, and about every other high-tech industry in the area, property values in Huntsville had jerked upward more than a little bit. People moving to the area snapped up the homes in the many new subdivisions almost as fast as they popped up. Locals hunkered down and remodeled.

"Amen to that," I said. "Other than getting this over to the bank, you need anything else?"

"Nope. It's all copasetic."

I got back into my car. I called Claire. Claire McBride. *Channel 8 News's* top reporter. My ex-wife. Our brief, eighteen-month marriage was sandwiched between med school and my time with the Marines.

Didn't work out because we are both bull-headed. Especially Claire. True story. Woman can drink anybody under the table, melt down most people with a glare, and can crack a rib with a single elbow. Personal experience here. But she's beautiful, sometimes charming, and, along with T-Tommy Tortelli, my best friend. Actually we're more than friends. We still love each other, still occupy the same bed from time to time, just can't hang our toothbrushes side by side.

She, T-Tommy, and I met in the fourth grade. Became fast friends. But it was after Jill disappeared that our relationship changed. Claire helped me survive what was impossible to survive.

It was a cold drizzly October night in Birmingham, and I was a senior med student, nearing the end of a two-month ER rotation. I had planned to meet my younger sister Jill at my car in the med staff parking lot at six p.m. but just as I was leaving, the medics rolled in with a major trauma case. One that required opening the chest in the ER. Not a common thing, so I hung around. To help. To learn. Made me an hour late meeting Jill. She wasn't there. Only one shoe and her purse, strap snapped, laid on the rain-slicked asphalt.

She was never seen again.

Med school evaporated as I sank into depression, drinking too much, and feeling sorry for myself. Along with a generous dose of guilt. It was my fault. Had I been there like I said I would, this would never have happened. The spark of life would never have drained from my parents and I would be a doctor now.

Amazing how a simple choice can rip up your life. But Claire was there. She picked me up, dusted me off, and married me. Of course she was coming off a bad breakup so our timing couldn't have been worse. Led to a divorce and my stint with the U.S. Marines.

Claire answered on the first ring.

"Still on for lunch today?" I asked.

"Starving."

"It's the food, huh? And I thought you wanted to see me."

"You, I tolerate. Food, I crave." She laughed. "T-Tommy coming?"

"I'm heading over to pick him up now, then the bank, and we'll see you at Sammy's by noon."

Chapter 3

MONDAY, 11:01 A.M.

Tim and Martha Foster held hands while they waited for Anne Marie Bridges to finish helping another customer. When she waved a good-bye to the elderly lady and turned her smile toward them, they walked up to the teller's window.

"How're you two doing today?" Anne Marie asked.

"Fine," Martha said. "You?"

"Other than my arthritic knee acting up, I suspect okay."

Anne Marie had been with the bank for at least fifteen years. Longer than Tim and Martha had been coming there. Maybe sixty, with neatly styled gray hair and an open smile, she was their favorite.

Tim worked his left hand, balling and opening it a couple of times. "I understand."

"Young man like you? Just wait a few years." She laughed. "What can I do for you today?"

"Time to close the last account."

"Is it May already?"

"Afraid so."

"We're so sorry to be losing you as customers," Anne Marie said. "How long has it been? Ten years?"

"Longer," Tim said. "We'll miss you and everyone else here."

"You're moving out west? California?"

"Arizona," Martha said. "Phoenix."

"I hear it's hot there."

Martha smiled. "They have air-conditioning."

"And ice cream," Tim added.

Anne Marie laughed. "Your balance is seven thousand six hundred thirty-two dollars and forty-four cents. You want a cashier's check?"

"Cash," Tim said. "Need some traveling money."

"That's a lot to carry around."

"We'll be okay."

"I don't have that much in my drawer. I'll have to run to the vault. It'll take a few minutes. Why don't you have some coffee?" Anne Marie pointed toward the corner table that held a large coffeepot and a stack of Styrofoam cups.

T-Tommy Tortelli. His mother called him Thomas, but most folks use either Tommy-T or T-Tommy. I use the latter. Have since grade school. Since we met at football practice the first day of fourth grade. T-Tommy was a linebacker and the toughest person in school. Still the toughest person I know. Still a linebacker at heart. An attitude that serves him well as a homicide investigator for the Huntsville PD. Boy's a bulldog, and once he gets his teeth into a case he can shake all the bad guys out better than anyone. "Relentless" would be the word.

I picked him up at his office at the South Precinct and we drove to the bank. As we walked from the parking lot toward the entrance, I saw Tim and Martha Foster through the front window. They stood, sipping coffee, wearing the same sad expressions they had worn the last time I saw them. When was that? A year at least.

I had consulted on the abduction of their son Steven and had interviewed them a couple of times, but I couldn't say I really knew them. Not much more than anyone else in town. They had a certain celebrity. Not the kind anyone wanted. More the tabloid variety. The kind that nosed into the recesses of your life and ate away at your soul. Lately, with the impending release of Walter Allen Whitiker from prison, their faces had reappeared on TV almost hourly. Not them, not live, but tons of what they call "file footage." The Fosters had apparently declined all interviews, even from Claire, refusing to be dragged back into the limelight.

The only fresh quote from them for at least a year was in the

Huntsville Times a couple of months ago. A Blaine Markland story. It was from Tim, if I remembered correctly. Something to the effect that they remained angry that Whitiker hadn't been tried for murder in the first place and were disappointed that the judge granted him an early release on his perjury and obstruction conviction.

Sentiments I completely agreed with.

T-Tommy and I pushed through the double-glass doors. Tim Foster looked up, dropped his gaze away for a beat, and then looked back toward us. He nodded. We walked that way.

"Mr. and Mrs. Foster," T-Tommy said.

"Investigator Tortelli." Tim looked at me. "Mr. Walker."

"I understand you're moving away," I said. A statement, not a question.

"We have to," Martha said. "We can't stay in a community with that animal."

T-Tommy shoved his hands into his pockets, the butt of his gun now visible. "Because he threatened you?"

"That's part of it," Tim said.

"You don't think we can protect you?"

Tim shrugged. "Maybe. Maybe not. It's the *not* that's the problem."

"It's mostly talk," I said. "Just messing with your head. Doubt he'll actually try anything."

"He killed our son," Martha said. "And got away with it. Why wouldn't he try to kill us?"

"He hasn't exactly been repentant," Tim added.

T-Tommy rattled the keys inside his pocket and rocked back on his heels. "When you heading out?"

"Tomorrow."

"I take it that's because he's being released in the morning?" I asked.

"We don't want to breathe the same air he does," Martha said.

I nodded. "Can't say I blame you. Where're you going?"

"Phoenix," Tim said.

"Been there. Nice place." When Tim didn't respond I went on. "Anything we can do for you, just give a call."

Chapter 4

Sammy's Blues 'n' Q. Great music and the best BBQ this side of just about anywhere. You could tell that a block away. Aligned like sentinels along the rooftop, three thick metal pipes, painted crimson to match the wooden building, pumped smoke and the sticky-sweet aroma of charred beef and pork into the sky. Made your stomach grumble. Grabbed you by the scruff of the neck and pulled you inside.

T-Tommy and I spent way too much time there. Claire, too. Ate too much BBQ. Drank too much whiskey. He and I did, anyway. With Claire you never knew. Could be whiskey, could be wine, but whatever it was, the woman could drink us both to the floor. She had a liver built to handle alcohol. Too much alcohol dehydrogenase—the liver enzyme that tears up alcohol. I remembered that from med school. Or maybe she had the proverbial wooden leg. Either way, when we got sloppy, Claire seemed unaffected. Gave her an advantage. Not that she needed one. She was probably smarter than we were, and definitely didn't play fair.

The front screen door clacked shut behind T-Tommy and me. We beat most of the lunch crowd. By a few minutes anyway. The tables weren't yet packed and the bar stools were empty, except for Claire. She wore tan slacks and a dark-green silk blouse, her long red hair pulled back and bound with one of those wadded-panty looking deals.

I hadn't seen her in a few days. Her hair color had changed. Again.

Not unusual, always a moving target. Last week's lighter, redder color had become this week's deep mahogany. She looked hot, but then she always did.

She sipped from a glass of red wine and chatted with Sammy Lange, the owner. A good friend. Sammy nodded in our direction and Claire spun toward us.

"It's about time," she said.

"You are hungry, aren't you?" I said.

"No breakfast and a hard workout at the gym this morning." She lifted her wine glass. "If I don't eat something soon, this is going to do me in."

Not likely.

We flanked Claire at the bar.

Sammy popped open a pair of Buds for T-Tommy and me and then swiped the bar with a towel. He looked at me.

"What was El Cid's real name?" Sammy asked.

Sammy and I had this trivia thing going. Had for years. We kept score. Sort of. Whatever the true score was, I knew he was far ahead.

But this one I knew.

"Rodrigo Díaz de Vivar."

"Damn. Thought I'd get you with that one." He looked at me expectedly.

"Who did Hitler dictate *Mein Kampf* to while he was in prison?"

Sammy gave the bar a swipe and smiled at me. "Rudolf Hess."

We went back and forth for a couple of more questions each, neither of us missing.

Finally, Claire broke it up. "As much as I'm enjoying this little education in worthless information, I'm starved."

"Got some fresh crab in today. Looks mighty good. How about crab cakes and cole slaw?"

Claire and I went for that, T-Tommy for a pair of pulled pork sandwiches, toss in some onion rings. Sammy headed toward the kitchen.

"I hear you got a new boyfriend," T-Tommy said to Claire.

"Shut up, Tortelli."

"Just asking."

"When do we get to meet this guy?" I asked.

Claire sighed and shook her head. "That's a dynamic that's doomed to fail."

"Why would you say that?"

She twisted toward me. "You want to meet the guy I'm dating?"

Though neither of us dated much, too much BS was Claire's take on it, I knew she had met this lawyer type from over in Athens, and they'd been out a few times.

"Sure," I said.

"What? So we can all be friends?"

"Why not? We're not married anymore."

"We were, Dub. That makes a difference." She pushed her fingers through her hair. "Besides, you wouldn't like him."

"Why's that?"

"I'm not sure I do."

"I like him better already."

She laughed. "Of course you do." A sip of wine. "Anyway, I'm thinking of kicking him to the curb."

"Too bad."

"Liar."

"But—"

"But nothing. Talk about something else."

I did. Not that I didn't want to keep harassing her, but she gave me that look. The look. The one with eunuch written all over it. Fear is a great motivator, so I backed off and told her about seeing the Fosters at the bank instead.

"They're leaving tomorrow," I said. "Heading west."

Claire nodded. "I stopped by their place and spoke with them earlier this week. Wanted to get them on the show." She ran a finger around the rim of her wine glass. "They refused. Said they just wanted to get to Phoenix and put all this behind them."

"Don't blame them."

"Me either." She looked up and smiled at me. "Still, an interview would've been a good piece."

"You still doing the release tomorrow?" T-Tommy asked.

"Wouldn't miss this one. Whitiker back on the street's a big story."

"We'll be there," I said.

"To protect me from the big bad wolf?"

"Maybe to protect him from you."

She nodded. "After what he did to Steven Foster he might need it. If I thought I could beat him to death with my microphone, I just might try it."

T-Tommy grunted. "I just might help you."

"You're on." Claire took a sip of wine and then turned her head toward me. "Why do you think they're leaving?"

"Said they were afraid of Whitiker."

"You believe them?"

"No reason not to. I mean, I think they're wrong, but I'd take them at their word."

Claire shrugged, but didn't say anything.

"What?" I asked.

"*What* what?"

"Something's going on in that head of yours. What is it?"

"You can read my mind now?"

"I know you. Better than anyone."

She couldn't argue with that. She knew it was true.

She looked into her glass. "When I spoke with them the other day, they didn't seem scared. Sad, even resigned, but not scared."

"Maybe they've moved past that."

Sammy appeared with our food. "Anything else?"

Claire and T-Tommy shook their heads.

I pulled the small bottle of Tabasco I always carried from my jacket pocket. "Got what I need." I splashed some on my crab cakes. I didn't bother to offer any to Claire or T-Tommy. I knew the answer to that one.

"What do you mean, 'moved past it'?" Claire asked.

"You know, denial, anger, fear, revenge. All the things that come up when the pain is acute. The abduction was more than three years ago. Maybe they're simply worn out."

She didn't seem convinced.

"Or maybe you're just looking for a story," I said.

The elbow in my ribs hurt. "Bite me, Walker," she said.

"All I'm saying is that you're a good reporter. You see conspiracies in everything."

"Because they're usually there."

"This poor couple's had a ton of crap to deal with. Their only child kidnapped and murdered. The killer dodges the big fall and goes up for some lesser bullshit. Slap-on-the-wrist stuff. He spends his prison time harassing and threatening them. Now he's getting out and they feel the need to uproot their entire lives—leaving friends, family, work—and move across the country. Seems to me that would dump a little resignation on anyone."

"Now I'm depressed." Claire dropped her fork and pushed her plate away. "Lunch with you is a great weight-loss plan."

Chapter 5

MONDAY, 9:34 P.M.

Tim and Martha consumed the entire day, working through their to-do list, making the final painful decisions on what to take and what to leave, wanting to take everything of Steven's, knowing they couldn't. His baby clothes, a stack of his crayon pictures that had once hung on the refrigerator, a half dozen child-sweet letters he had written to Martha over the years, the dark blue Tommy Hilfiger sweatshirt, and his baseball glove and uniform made it into one of the remaining two boxes; his school and team photos, school notebooks, and other sports uniforms didn't.

They loaded these final two boxes and the few other things they thought they might need into the SUV. Tim knew that adding this to the three banker's boxes that already sat in their new car's backseat would be tight, but they would manage. They would have to.

They then went over the list for what seemed like the hundredth time, checking off each item and playing the "what-if" game, finally deciding that they'd done all they could. Planned for all the contingencies. All they needed now was a little luck and everything would work out.

Tim wasn't a big fan of luck, but if they were going to pull this off, luck would have to be part of the equation.

They ordered pizza and ate at the kitchen counter. Both quiet now, knowing this was their last night in the only house they had ever lived in together. There was the furnished apartment they had rented when they first married, but that didn't count. This was home.

Tim remembered the day they had moved in. Martha had been three months into her pregnancy, barely showing. He'd carried her across the threshold. They'd laughed and made love on the new carpet in the furniture-free living room. Afterward, they laid there, staring at the ceiling, talking and giggling, excited about this new phase of their life, about their coming child, until a chill drove them to the warmth of the bed, the only real piece of furniture they owned.

The lump in his throat made swallowing the pizza difficult.

After they finished, Tim cleaned the counter and ferried the empty pizza box and the paper plates to the outside trash can. When he came back inside, he found Martha standing at the door to Steven's room, arms crossed, one shoulder pressed against the doorjamb. Not an unusual position for her. Over the past three years she'd often stood there. Silently staring. As if waiting, more likely praying, for Steven to appear. Their tow-headed son in his baggy pajamas, sitting at his desk doing homework, or sprawled on his bed in exhausted, innocent sleep, or listening to his iPod.

Tonight was different. She was no doubt soaking in memories, knowing that in a few hours they would walk out of here forever. It was as if she wanted to burn the room's image into her mind.

The lump in his throat grew.

He left her to her reverie and went out into the backyard. The sky was clear and the fresh, clean air carried a hint of the honeysuckle that grew along the back fence. He made a couple of laps around the yard, smelling the flowers and touching the thick shrubbery, remembering when they had planted them. Now they towered a good foot above his head, but then they had been scraggly little things that he feared would never survive. He could still see Martha's dirt-smudged face, glistening with sweat. Could still hear six-month-old Steven squealing in his nearby playpen, a quilt draped over the top to block the sun from his delicate skin.

He migrated to the swing set. Steven's fifth birthday present. He'd put it together with his own hands. Took twice as long as it should have, but he managed. Probably should have read the instructions, but what's the fun in that? He sat on one of the swings and began to slowly rock. The rusty chain creaked in protest. He could almost hear Steven begging to go higher and higher as he pushed him from behind. Tears blurred his vision.

Martha came out. He stood and they hugged tightly. He felt her tears against his neck. God, he hated this feeling. His life ripped apart again. As it had been three years ago. A wound that would never heal.

"You look hot," Tim said.

Martha turned from the mirror. "You like it?" Her shoulder-length blonde hair was now clipped short and dyed a deep black. The transition from Martha to Cindy. She laughed. "Look at you. I love the military cut."

He ran a hand over his newly buzzed head. It made a raspy scraping noise. "It'll take a bit of getting used to."

She handed him a plastic trash bag, filled with empty dye bottles and wads of her hair. "Put these by the gym bags. Don't want to forget and leave it here." She began scrubbing her hair with a towel.

"Will do. Then we need to get some sleep. Big day tomorrow."

Chapter 6

TUESDAY, 4:00 A.M.

Maple Hill Cemetery is the oldest and largest public cemetery in the state of Alabama. A hundred acres and 100,000 graves. A city of the dead. At this hour, the trees and the larger grave markers such as the ten-foot crosses, thick obelisks, winged angels, and broad mausoleums, created even darker shadows against the dark sky. To most these deep shadows might seem ominous and threatening like a scene from a Stephen King novel or a Freddy Krueeger movie, but to Tim and Martha they were simply extensions of the sadness they carried every minute of every day.

Now they knelt silently next to Steven's grave, a soft, grass-covered bump and a gray marble headstone. Martha traced her fingers over the inscription. Too dark to read the engraved words but Tim knew them by heart: STEVEN JAMES FOSTER. A SHORT, SWEET LIFE. NOW RESTING IN THE ARMS OF OUR SAVIOR, JESUS CHRIST.

A soft northerly breeze rustled the oak leaves above their heads. Tim reached out and placed his hand over hers. Her fingers seemed as cold as the marble. Martha turned toward him and they held each other.

After several minutes, Martha spoke. "I can't believe we have to leave him here."

Tim broke their embrace. "He's not here." A flash of light caught his gaze and in the distance he saw a car move along McClung, turn onto California Street, and disappear. "He's with God. And with us. He'll always be with us."

"I'll never see his grave again, will I?"

"Never is a long time. It might be a while, a long while, but not never."

They had come here faithfully over the past three years. Every Sunday. Sometimes other days too. Whenever either of them needed to.

"Really?"

"Down the road. When we're forgotten, we'll find a way."

Martha reached out and ran her fingers through the thick grass that covered the grave. "Goodbye, Steven. Mommy and Daddy love you. We'll always love you."

Tim stood and brushed a few grass blades from the knees of his pants. He looked out over the hundreds of tombstones, only their outlines visible in the dark. Who were they? These buried people. How old were they when they died? What took their last breaths? Heart attacks and strokes? Pneumonias and kidney diseases? Auto accidents and old age? A winding down of existence. Natural things. Common things.

How many had been murdered?

He turned the other way. More tombstones. Were any of them children? Did any of them die at the hands of a monster? Had other fathers stood over one of these graves asking why?

He helped Martha to her feet. They walked to the car, his arm around her waist, her head against his shoulder.

Sometimes life sucked. Big-time sucked.

Fifteen minutes later they were out of the city on a two-lane road that wound through gently rolling farmland and patches of pine, maple, pecan, sweet gum, and a wide variety of trees Tim couldn't identify. Dawn lightened the eastern sky, only a handful of the most stubborn stars now visible.

He turned the SUV onto a rarely used dirt-and-gravel road. Rocks pinged against the undercarriage as he navigated over the ruts for nearly a mile. He then eased off the road a good twenty feet into the trees, the vehicle consumed by the thick brush and no longer visible. He parked near the clearing he had found a month earlier.

He set up the tent. Not exactly set it up since it was one of those self-contained jobs. Floor, walls, ceiling, figure-of-eight support cable all in one. He simply removed it from its flat storage sleeve and dropped it on the ground. The cable unwound and a tent appeared.

He crawled inside and, using his Swiss Army knife, cut a dinner-plate-sized hole in one end. Roughly eighteen inches from the bottom. He then piled three pillows near the opening.

It was five thirty a.m. An hour and a half to wait. Then they could get this done, stuff the tent and everything else into plastic trash bags, and drop them into the industrial Dumpster over by the packing plant where they would ultimately disappear into a landfill. Then back to the mall parking garage, pick up the new car, and finally curb the SUV on the west side. Keys inside. Easy for the crack dealers to snatch and chop. After that, goodbye. The transformation of Tim and Martha Foster into Robert Beckwith and Cindy Strunk would be complete.

He actually looked forward to Robert and Cindy getting married. Martha/Cindy would make a perfect North Carolina blushing bride. He looked at her. She lay on her back, eyes blank, staring at the tent's roof.

"You okay?" he asked.

"Nervous."

"Me, too."

"Look." She held up a trembling hand.

"It'll be okay."

"Are we doing the right thing?"

"We have to." He rolled onto his side and looked into her face. "For Steven."

Chapter 7

Stone Gate Prison, a dreary gray concrete and river rock structure, stood along a two-lane black-top county highway in the rolling wooded hills twenty miles northwest of Huntsville and just a handful of miles from the Tennessee border. To offer Walter Allen Whitiker a not so friendly welcome back into the free world, fifty to sixty citizens gathered in the prison's parking area, a gravel patch that extended between the twenty-foot-high chain-link fence that surrounded the facility and the road. Derrick Stone and a half dozen other HPD uniforms were there for crowd control, if needed.

Stone walked toward where T-Tommy and I stood near the fence, sipping the now-cold remnants of the coffee we had picked up before leaving Huntsville. The morning was crisp and clear, a northerly breeze making it a bit cooler than was usual for May.

Stone stood around six feet and went one eighty, still fit from his days as a cornerback at Huntsville High School. He was smart and destined for the homicide division once he had a few more years under his belt. I'd worked with him on a couple of cases in the past, including the Talbert/Kincaid nightmare. He had done a good job and been instrumental in bringing down the bad guys.

"The crowd seems a little tense," Stone said.

"Anyone in particular?" T-Tommy asked.

"No. Just a general anger."

True. The tension in the air was evident in the crowd's murmurings. They carried an angry quality, like a swarm of bees. Two people carried signs, both white cardboard, CHILD KILLER written in black on one and a bright red BURN, WHITIKER, BURN in block letters on the other. I heard someone say, "If he'd done that to my kid I'd torture and kill him." No one offered any disagreement.

"Have you seen any sign of JD?" I asked. JD Whitiker was Walter's brother.

Stone shook his head and then swiped his light-brown hair back from his forehead. "Figured he would be here though."

"I suspect he'll be along shortly," T-Tommy said. "Unless he's going to make Walter walk home as payback for the shame he brought on the Whitiker clan."

"Looks like Claire's ready to do her setup piece," I said.

Claire had staked out a position near the prison's rolling chain-link gate. A hundred feet beyond the gate, the gray metal double doors that led to the facility's interior stood quietly. Inside you could find the worst of the worst. Rapists, murderers, child molesters, you name it. And, of course, Walter Allen Whitiker.

Claire faced the *Channel 8 News* camera that rested on Jeffrey Lombardo's shoulder and waited for the signal. Jeffrey, her favorite cameraman, gave her a countdown, finger after finger folding from sight, until only his fist remained.

"This is Claire McBride reporting live from Stone Gate Prison. We are just minutes from the release of Walter Allen Whitiker. Nearly two years ago he was tried for the murder of eight-year-old Steven Foster, whose body was found six months after he went missing in a wooded area just three miles from his home. Murder charges were brought based on DNA evidence obtained from what were believed to be tear stains in the back of Whitiker's van.

"The murder charges were dropped when Judge Ben Kleinman disallowed this evidence on a technicality. Several weeks of legal wrangling followed, but the judge stood firm. Walter Allen Whitiker was then convicted of obstructing a police investigation and perjury. He received a three-year sentence, and now, nineteen months later, he is being released for good behavior."

She turned and looked back toward the prison where several guards had gathered near the metal doors.

"I see some activity, so Whitiker might come through those doors very soon." She turned back to the camera. "As we have reported here in the past, Whitiker remained in the public eye for making what many believe were not-so-subtle threats toward Martha Foster, young Steven's mother. Whitiker has repeatedly stated that she lied about seeing him drag Steven into his van on the day he disappeared. Many feel that these threats should preclude Whitiker's early parole, but the parole board ruled that he was safe for release and Judge Kleinman agreed."

Chapter 8

Tim lay prone on the floor of the tent, Martha next to him. Before him, a Browning BAR Safari .308 rifle rested on the pillows. He had snapped off two branches of the brush, giving them a clear view of the prison gate.

Through the rifle's scope, Tim saw reporter Claire McBride, a local news celebrity, talking into a handheld microphone while staring into a camera. With three hundred yards separating them he couldn't hear her, but he knew what she was saying. Had heard it too many times. Over and over. From every newspaper reporter and TV news anchor in North Alabama. Particularly now that Whitiker's release had rekindled the story. That's all it was to them. A story. To him and Martha, it was life. Their life. Their misery.

Like everyone else who had reported on this tragedy, Claire McBride's face remained impassive as she told viewers that Whitiker had been charged with murder but wiggled free by the machinations of his slick lawyer and a corrupt, touchy-feely judge. How he had been a model prisoner. How those parole board clowns believed the threats he had made against Martha weren't real. Merely the imaginations of distraught parents and the anger of homicide investigator Tortelli who felt that the judge had trashed his reputation. Which is exactly what that nut-job Kleinman had done.

Whitiker a model prisoner? Maybe him saying he would "get that lying bitch" and "even the score with those that falsely accused him" weren't really threats.

Get real.

He wiped his damp palms with a towel.

"You okay?" Martha asked.

"Anxious to get this over with and get out of here." He raised his right hand. A fine tremor danced through his fingers. "Look."

She grabbed his hand and kissed it. "You'll be fine."

"Unless I miss and hit someone else?"

"You won't." She squeezed his hand. "That's why we did all that practicing."

"That was tin cans and tree stumps. This is a little different."

"Easier. Whitiker's a little bigger than a beer can."

"True."

"I just hope the tent dampens the noise enough," she said. "I have visions of everyone turning and pointing at us."

"You can't watch *Invasion of the Body Snatchers* anymore."

That got a half smile from her. It only lasted a second though. "Our lives are about to change forever," she said. "We can never undo this."

"You getting cold feet? Want to back off and leave right now?"

She shook her head. "I'm just nervous. I have visions of them hearing us. Seeing us. Dragging us inside that prison."

"We're a long ways away," Tim said. "They couldn't see us even if they knew where to look. The tent will work just fine. If they hear anything, it'll be so soft they'll have no idea where it came from. By the time they figure it out, if they ever do, the Fosters will no longer exist, and we'll be halfway to North Carolina."

"I hope so."

"The worst thing right now would be to miss. Let this animal survive. Then all of this would be for nothing."

Martha sighed.

"You got the tissues?" Tim asked.

She pulled two tissues from her pocket and handed one to Tim.

They each tore off pieces, rolled them into wads, and wedged them into their ears. The sound might be muffled out there, but in here it would be painful.

Once he stuffed his ears, Tim looked through the scope again, moving it back and forth across the crowd. He saw Tortelli and Dub Walker, just behind and to the right of Claire McBride, leaning against the fence, talking with a uniformed officer. Tracking back to his left he saw the prison doors swing open and Whitiker walk out. With arrogant strides and that permanent smirk on his face, he moved toward the chain link gate.

Tim took a couple of deep breaths and tried to will his heart to slow its fluttering as he settled the crosshairs on Whitiker's chest, following his movements.

Chapter 9

A commotion behind me caught my attention. I turned. Escorted by two uniformed officers, Whitiker came through the prison's metal doors and walked toward the chain-link gate.

Claire positioned herself to intercept Whitiker as he came out, smoothed her jacket, parked a wayward strand of hair behind her ear, and slapped on her reporter's face. With his camera balanced on his shoulder, Jeffrey moved to one side so he could capture her in profile.

The gate rattled open. Whitiker walked through. A free man. The two prison guards turned and headed back inside, their duties completed. Whitiker no longer their problem.

Jeers rose from the crowd. "Baby killer," a woman yelled. "Animal," came from somewhere. "You ain't safe out here," a man in overalls shouted.

Stone and the other uniforms formed a line between them and Whitiker. No one challenged them. The citizenry didn't really want to get too near Whitiker, they just wanted to get in their verbal shots.

Claire pushed the microphone forward. "Mr. Whitiker, how does it feel to be out of prison?"

At six two he looked down at her, his eyes dark, hooded beneath heavy brows. He had lost weight since I last saw him, prison food not the best, but was still thick through his torso. I moved along the fence. Wanted to be closer to Claire. Just in case.

"Should never have been there," Whitiker said. "I never lied to the police. They lied about me. Especially that one." He poked a finger toward T-Tommy.

T-Tommy pushed away from the fence and took a step forward. I put my arm out and blocked him. I could feel his entire body coil.

"Let it go," I said.

Whitiker looked back at Claire. "I never hurt that child. I never done nothing to nobody."

"What about the DNA evidence?" Claire asked.

"They set me up. When I wouldn't confess—even after they beat on me—they got their lab folks to plant evidence. Just that simple." He again glared at T-Tommy.

Claire wasn't one to let the interviewee take control of things. She nudged Whitiker's arm with her free hand, dragging his attention back to her. Did I mention she was the ballsiest woman I'd ever known?

"Isn't it true that the lab results were never questioned?" Claire pressed him. "Wasn't it the method by which the evidence was obtained that was the controversy? A probable-cause issue?"

"Here's what I think of their probable cause and their corrupt lab." He grabbed his crotch. A big smile split his face. "What're you doing after this? I'm going to get myself a cheeseburger and a bunch of beers. Want to come along?" He looked her up and down. "Been a long time since I had me some—"

I heard a flat thud and a soft pop. Almost simultaneously, as if the two sounds had melted into one another. The pop from far away, the thud very close. Then another thud-pop sound, the pop louder this time, the blended sound followed by a twanging of the chain link fence behind me.

A ragged red blossom erupted on Whitiker's back. His body jerked. He staggered back a step. Then another. He spun slowly toward me, surprise in his eyes. His hands came up and he seemed to be clenching the air as if looking for an anchor. A pair of crimson splotches spread across his chest, one upper right, the other just left of his sternum.

I looked at Claire. She too took a step back, eyes wide. A spatter of red on her right cheek. I tried to move toward her, but my feet seemed frozen and heavy. Everything slowed. I saw the gathered crowd scatter,

many of them dropping to the ground, others running. Lots of screaming, but the voices seemed muffled as if cotton filled my ears.

Then I was moving, toward Claire, looking for some sign that she
had been hit. My ears cleared and sharp screams came from every direction. I reached Claire, wrapped my arms around her, and pulled her
tightly against me. I spun so that I was between her and the direction
the shot must have come from. The microphone fell from her hand.

From the corner of my eye, I saw Whitiker's eyes glaze over. He wavered as if rocked by a breeze. His legs folded and he spiraled to the
ground.

"Are you okay?" I ran my hands over her back, down her arms, but
felt nothing. I touched her cheek. Wet, warm blood. "Are you okay?" I
repeated.

"I think so."

I grabbed her arm and tugged her toward the Channel 8 van. "Get
inside." She hesitated, so I pushed her toward the rear cargo area. "Inside. And stay down."

I turned. Everyone was either on the ground or had ducked behind
the cars in the lot. Jeffrey Lombardo huddled behind the news van,
camera on his shoulder, still capturing the scene. T-Tommy knelt behind a patrol car, gun resting on the hood, scanning the forest across the
road. I hurried in that direction and squatted beside him.

"See anything?"

"Not yet."

Wheezing and gurgling came from behind me. I spun on my
haunches. Whitiker's body convulsed and bloody foam drizzled from
his mouth.

Chapter 10

It wasn't going to work. Knew that from jump street. I'd done this hundreds of times during med school. Sometimes things worked out, sometimes they didn't. The amount of blood that leaked over my hands from Whitiker's chest wound and foamed from his mouth with each compression told me that CPR wasn't going to save him. The blood that pumped from his back each time I leaned into him soaked into the dirt and coated the gravel in an ever-increasing circle.

Didn't take long to figure what had happened. I'd seen it before. Two bullets. Two entry wounds, one exit wound. One bullet still in his chest, the other passing completely through. A through-and-through gunshot wound in medical jargon. Judging from the blood and the location and angle of the wounds, there was little doubt that one bullet had ripped through his heart and his left lung in the process. A deadly deal. Particularly out here miles from surgical help.

The crowd that had scattered when Whitiker went down now crept back, forming a circle around me and the dying—make that dead—man.

Curiosity is an odd thing. It will sometimes override shock and horror. I suspect movies and TV are to blame. People seemed to mix up real tragedy with TV tragedy. Like this wasn't real. Like we were shooting a movie or something. Here I was straddling a dead man, his warm, sticky blood coating my hands, frothy blood gathered in his mouth, and these people thought it was an episode of *CSI*.

Ten minutes into it, blood no longer bubbled from his chest, and Whitiker took on the blue-gray color of the dead. His eyes, glassy and black, stared straight ahead. I kept the compressions going anyway.

"Can I help?"

I looked up to see an elderly woman with blue-gray hair, a deeply lined face, and a wide-eyed expression of concern.

"I'm a retired nurse," she said.

I shook my head. "This isn't going anywhere." I stopped my compressions and checked Whitiker's neck for a pulse I knew wouldn't be there. I stood. "That's it."

Claire handed me a wad of paper towels she had retrieved from the Channel 8 truck. I wiped the blood from my hands. The uniforms began easing the crowd back, protecting what had now become a crime scene.

I walked to where T-Tommy stood near the roadway. He was scanning the wooded hillside across the county road. I knew he had heard the same sounds I had. A pair of soft pops. Gunshots from a distance. Muffled by the trees.

"Anything?" I asked.

He shook his head. "There're a half dozen or so old fire roads that crisscross up that way. I sent Stone and a couple of other guys on up. Shooter's probably in the wind by now. Would've had an escape route worked out. Might get lucky though. Stone called the Chief and he's got more officers on the way." He turned and looked at me. "Want to head up that way and see what the deal is?"

"Let's look at Claire's video first. See if we can't figure out the trajectory. Maybe narrow down the search area."

Chapter 11

I asked Jeffrey Lombardo to cue up his video to where Whitiker took the bullet. He plugged the camera into the Macbook mounted in the rear of the van and began working the keyboard. The progress bar inched along as the video downloaded to the hard drive.

The crunch of gravel attracted my attention and I turned. A pickup, red with oversized dually tires, slid to a stop behind two patrol cars. The late Walter Allen Whitiker's brother JD jumped out. Like Walter, JD didn't leave behind many table scraps. Maybe six two and a good two fifty. He waded through the crowd, pushing people aside with his chest and meaty arms. T-Tommy and I tried to intercept him before he reached his brother's corpse. Didn't make it.

"What happened here?" His deep voice churned up from his thick chest. He looked down at his brother's body, stared for a beat, and then raised his head, his gaze traveling from face to face, his jaw pulsing. "What the Goddamn hell happened here?"

"Mr. Whitiker?" I asked.

He whirled toward me. He had his brother's deep-set, dark eyes and right now they flashed with anger. His gaze cut to T-Tommy.

"You," he shouted. He jabbed a finger toward him. "You did this."

"No," I said. "The shot came from somewhere back there." I jerked my head toward the hillside.

His gaze never left T-Tommy. "Never would have happened if you hadn't planted evidence on my brother."

He shouldered me aside and rushed toward T-Tommy. Bad idea. T-Tommy met him with a forearm across the chest. Did I mention that T-Tommy was still a linebacker at heart? Using his own massive shoulders and forearms, T-Tommy could easily shed any offensive linemen unfortunate enough to venture between him and the ball carrier. He handled JD the same way. His forearm struck Whitiker with a solid thud, stopping his charge in mid-stride. Air whooshed from JD's lungs and before he could suck in a breath, T-Tommy grabbed his wrist, spun him to his knees, and locked a forearm across his throat.

"You want to go inside?" T-Tommy nodded toward the prison. "That can be arranged."

"You killed my brother," JD said.

T-Tommy leaned down and placed his lips near JD's ear. "You know that ain't so. The only question now is how you want to play this."

"Fuck you."

T-Tommy motioned to one of the HPD officers. "Cuff him."

The officer pulled one of JD's arms back and attempted to place cuffs on his wrist. JD jerked his arm away.

T-Tommy locked JD's throat in the V of his elbow, levered his forearm with his other hand, and waited for the choke hold to work. Maybe half a minute and JD's head fell forward. T-Tommy lowered him face-down on the ground. The deputy easily cuffed him.

JD began to wake up. We rolled him onto his back.

T-Tommy knelt next to him. When JD's gaze finally focused on him, he said, "You want to smooth out or you want me to haul your ass in and have this chat there?"

"I'll sue you for brutality."

"You can try."

Two officers helped JD to his feet and led him to a patrol car. They settled him on the edge of the backseat, JD's legs extending out the open door, his boots planted on the ground. T-Tommy leaned on the door; I stood beside him.

"You ready to answer a couple of questions?" T-Tommy asked.

"Get the fuck away from me."

"Why are you here?" T-Tommy asked.

"Came to pick up my brother, genius. Why the hell else would I drive out here?"

He had a point.

"Where were you when he was shot?"

"Driving here. Got a late start." He thrust his jaw toward T-Tommy. "Where were you?"

T-Tommy ignored his question. "Anybody see you in the last hour?"

Whitiker glared at him. "I don't got to talk to you."

"No, you don't. But I suspect that'd be the easy way. If you want, I'll book you right now for assaulting an officer or I can let that little deal slide if you cooperate. That make any sense to you?"

"My wife. Call her. She'll tell you I left home about an hour ago. Had to drop by the shop. Bo was there. You can ask him too. Then I drove here. Takes a good forty minutes to get out this far."

That was true. Only twenty miles from Huntsville, but over a narrow two-lane blacktop that wound through the hills it would take at least forty minutes to drive from JD's shop to out here.

"Any idea who might've done this?" T-Tommy asked.

"You mean besides you?" JD thrust his jaw at T-Tommy. "My brother's attorney humiliated your ass in court. Bet that really pissed you off. Sounds like a motive to me."

T-Tommy shoved his hands into his pockets and rocked back on his heels. "You're right, JD. I'd've killed your brother without hesitation." He looked down toward the man. "Just not this way. Too easy. After what he did to that child I'd have tortured him for a week first."

"That a confession?"

"Statement of fact. Mind if I snoop around your truck?"

JD glared at him. "Mind if I look inside your car?"

"You want to do this the hard way? I can tow it in and have it taken apart bolt by bolt."

JD sighed, apparently realizing most of the cards weren't on his side of the table. He nodded toward his truck. "Go ahead. I ain't got nothing to hide."

"Then we can swab your hands for gunshot residue?"

"What? You think I killed my little brother?" His eyes flashed dark and he started to stand. Hard to do with his hands cuffed behind his back. Oh, yeah, and with T-Tommy's palm flattened against his chest, pushing him back onto the seat.

"Not saying anything like that," T-Tommy said. "Just doing my job."

JD's glare softened. "Have at it."

T-Tommy turned to one of the uniforms. "Swab him for GSR."

We searched JD's truck. It was a mess. Fishing gear, an empty cooler, and dirt-caked work boots in the bed. A folded map on top of a stack of papers in the passenger seat. The papers were letters and invoices for his business. A half-full gallon jug of water, a roll of paper towels, and two wadded Hardee's bags—wait, make that three—on the floorboard. A couple of empty and crushed Dr. Pepper cans down there, too. Receipts inside dated the burger bags from two to five days earlier. A pack of Marlboros, a book of matches slipped inside the cellophane wrapper, rested on the dash. No weapons. No boxes of bullets or shell casings.

"Cut him loose," T-Tommy said.

JD stood and turned his back as a deputy removed the cuffs.

"Why don't you head on home," T-Tommy said. "Tell your family what happened before they hear it on the news."

JD massaged his wrist and glared at T-Tommy. "Mr. Fucking Compassion. What do you care about my family?"

"I'm trying real hard to play nice, but you ain't making it easy. Leave this area now. It's a crime scene. You interfere and I'll truss you up again and haul you downtown."

JD hesitated as if considering his options, but then walked toward his truck, taking a last shot over his shoulder. "This ain't over, Tortelli. Not by a long shot."

Chapter 12

With T-Tommy helping me move and roll his corpse, I examined each of Whitiker's wounds. The first entry wound was anterior, upper-right chest, maybe ten centimeters right of the sternum. Bullet would have hit the upper lobe of the right lung. No exit wound here. The second entry wound was mid-chest, three centimeters left of the sternum, right over the heart. The exit wound posterior, just lateral to the inferior tip of the left scapula. Meant the bullet approached from almost straight on, maybe a degree or so off perpendicular and with a few degrees of downward angle. It had to have penetrated the heart and the left lung.

All this meant that his heart and both lungs had been damaged. Meant his fate was sealed the instant the bullets arrived. Meant that the CPR I tried was doomed to failure before it even started.

Jeffrey Lombardo now had the video loaded onto his computer and had located the frame where the first bullet struck Whitiker. Nothing had registered on his face yet. His expression still defiant, eyes down and to his left, gaze on Claire's cleavage. Pervert. I know it's not nice to say nasty things about the dead, but this is Walter Allen Whitiker we're talking about here.

Claire held the microphone, only inches from where the bullet struck. She was looking at Whitiker's face, a reporter's fixed half smile on her face. I knew she actually wanted to claw his eyes out, but Claire was a pro. The job came first. Even if it meant smiling at this animal while he leered at her.

Lombardo printed the image and handed it to me.

I stepped around Whitiker's corpse and moved to where Lombardo had stood filming. I held the photo up. Using the chain-link fence and its gate and support poles, the walkway back to the prison door, and the prison building itself as reference points, I guided Claire back to where she had been standing, making sure her shoulders adopted the same angle as during the interview. I noticed a slight tremble to her hands.

"You okay with this?" I asked.

"Of course."

"I can get someone else. One of the officers."

She frowned. "Dub, I'm not a ninny."

I knew better than to argue.

T-Tommy stood in for Whitiker. It was eerie seeing Whitiker's body behind them, stretched out in a fan of bloody dirt and gravel, where he had staggered backward and fallen.

Satisfied with their positions, I moved behind T-Tommy. Looking over his shoulder, I imagined a line through his torso that mimicked the first bullet's path. Crude at best and definitely not as accurate as a laser rig, which of course wouldn't work so well out here in the open and in broad daylight. But this would at least give us a ballpark point of origin.

The county road that wound past the prison snaked its way through a narrow valley that sliced through the bumpy terrain of North Alabama. The wooded slope across the highway from where I stood was dense with pine, maple, and sweet gum trees. Reminded me of any of a number of places that I had squirrel hunted with my dad. This particular bump was maybe two miles in length, what I could see of it anyway, and rose several hundred feet to the horizon. The imaginary line through T-Tommy's chest settled in an area almost directly across from where we stood, and three hundred to four hundred yards up the slope.

I walked around and faced T-Tommy and Claire, now imagining the second bullet's path. The through-and-through one. If it stayed on a fairly straight trajectory as it passed through Whitiker, it might have embedded in the ground of the prison yard just beyond the fence and short of the prison wall. Problem was that bullets do funny things inside the body. They twist and turn and tumble through tissues of differing densities and strike bony things and can be easily knocked off course. Sometimes way off course. I had to hope that this one didn't stray far.

I followed the imaginary trajectory to the fence. It took a couple of minutes, but I located where the bullet struck one of the links. The twanging sound I had heard. A bright silvery groove in the age-dulled metal. The good news: the bullet passed through Whitiker in a fairly straight line. The bad news: the fence could have deflected it in any direction.

I turned to one of the patrol officers.

"Grab a couple of the prison guards. Don't let anyone else inside that area until the forensic guys get here." I indicated the large grassy area where I hoped the bullet might be. "Sidau and his people might be able to find the bullet in there somewhere."

"Will do."

Chapter 13

Like much of rural North Alabama, gravel, dirt, and overgrown roads crisscrossed this area. Many were more recent and still in use, while others were long-abandoned wagon and Indian trails. Mostly Chickasaw, Creek, and Cherokee. I remember as a boy walking just such paths with my father, collecting flint arrowheads and ax and knife blades. I had always marveled that these pieces of rock were hundreds of years old and had been chipped into shape by real Indians. I could picture them sitting around a campfire, striking pieces of flint rock together with sharp clicks, launching sparks into the night air. An old cigar box filled with these relics still resides in my dresser's top drawer.

One of the uniforms handed me a map of the area. I unfolded it on the hood of a patrol car and T-Tommy and I studied it. I saw that two nearby gravel roads spurred off the county highway and led up into the wooded hillside. One, a mile north of where we stood, up toward Tennessee; the other, a half mile south, back toward Huntsville. Each connected with a network of roads that mostly wound eastward, over the wooded hillside, and hooked into other paved county roads. No doubt one of these served as the shooter's escape route. The problem was that once he reached one of the county roads, he could go anywhere. Back toward Huntsville, west toward Mississippi, or loop to the north and disappear into rural Tennessee.

T-Tommy and I climbed into my car and headed south until I hung a right on the dirt-and-gravel road that led up into the trees. Small rocks pinged off the undercarriage as the Porsche's stiff suspension gyrated over the uneven and rutted surface. After an up, down, and swerve to the right, we came upon a patrol car angled off on the shoulder. I pulled up behind it and we got out.

Derrick Stone stepped from the woods.

"What've you got?" I asked.

"Probably nothing here." He looked back toward the woods. "Some tire tracks on the shoulder, but this area is thick and there's no clear view of the prison front gate."

"The angle's wrong anyway," I said. I knew we hadn't driven far enough along this road to put us across from the prison.

"Got some better options down that way," Stone said. "Follow me."

We followed his car a half mile before he pulled to a stop. A uniformed officer stood along the side of the road.

"Got some big tracks here," Stone said. "Look like truck tires."

I saw a pair of wide depressions, arcing off the road and then back on. The problem was the grass that grew along the road here. Unlike dirt or mud, grass doesn't hold tire impression detail. Made these tracks mostly worthless.

"Found some shoe prints in there." He pointed through the trees and moved that way. "They're not going to be helpful either."

I followed Stone. We pushed maybe fifteen feet through some trees and came to an opening. Not really a clearing, but an area where little brush grew beneath two mature cedar trees. He pointed out a pair of shoe prints in an area of soft soil. Looked like generic work boots. No tread pattern, which meant they would be of little value. We could get size, but determining the manufacturer would be impossible. I hate it when evidence teases you this way. Almost useful but in the end not.

I moved close to the two cedar trunks. Between them and through a small opening in the branches, the prison gate was easily seen. Maybe three hundred yards away. The angle was in the ballpark. The trees would have muffled the sound.

"Find anything other than the shoe impressions?" I asked

Stone shook his head. "No shell casings anyway. We're waiting for the crime-scene guys to do their thing. Maybe they'll find something." He scratched one ear. "Got two other places to show you. Both close by."

One was only twenty yards farther down the road. Turned out to be nothing, just some tracks on the shoulders. They were casted in what was once mud, but now only dry, crumbling relics of tire impressions remained. Edges and details rounded and fading. Had to be weeks old. This area got some traffic since it was popular with hunters and hikers and even though this wasn't hunting season, the good old boys didn't really care. They'd hunt whatever, whenever. Up here, probably squirrel and quail. I suspected most of the hunters in this area were the prison guards coming out here on their days off.

The next place, forty yards farther down, was more promising. Two sets of deep, wide tire tracks led a good twenty feet off the road and into the trees. Looked like one set going in, the other backing out. These impressions were fresh and clearly visible in the soft soil. I carefully avoided them as I followed their path through a stand of pine trees to a small clearing. Any car parked here would not be visible from the dirt road. Or anywhere else.

Down the hill, three hundred yards away, the prison gate was front and center. I saw that the coroner's and the Forensic Science vans had arrived. Two techs knelt next to Whitiker's body. Sidau Yamaguchi, head criminalist at the Alabama Department of Forensic Science, stood near the open door of his van talking with a HPD officer. Sidau had been my mentor during the years I worked there. Taught me a ton about forensic evidence. Maybe everything I know.

The grass and leaves in the small clearing were mashed flat, some blades broken, some leaves crushed. Even a clump of crabgrass lay bent and broken.

"Something was spread out here," I said. "A tarp or sheet of plastic. Something like that."

"Good way to take your trace evidence with you," T-Tommy said.

"The killer probably watches *CSI*," Stone said.

"Or reads Dub's books," T-Tommy added.

I looked at him. "Funny."

"Just offering possibilities."

"Maybe he's a cop," I said. "Bet I could name a dozen that wanted Whitiker dead."

T-Tommy grunted. "Including me."

Then I noticed the broken shrub. I walked toward it. Two branches had been snapped off. They lay on the ground. The breaks were fresh, the exposed pulp still pale and moist.

T-Tommy stepped up behind me. "Looks like the shooter cleared a path."

I nodded. "The angle here would work. In fact, the last two places we looked at would. I mean just an inch or two of shoulder turn by Whitiker could change the shooter's location by a hundred feet or more."

"This changes things though, don't it?" T-Tommy nodded toward the broken shrub.

"Sure does. A hunter or hiker wouldn't have a reason to break these branches on this shrub on this day. Someone aiming at the prison would."

"Got a weapon."

The voice came from below us. Earlier, Stone had instructed a pair of officers to do a radial evidence search out from where we stood. Apparently one of them had sidestepped down the hillside and found something.

"Where are you?" Stone shouted.

"Here."

I saw a hand waving above the brush about one hundred feet down the slope and two hundred feet to our right. T-Tommy, Stone, and I moved that way.

A rifle. Laying in a tangle of brush. Looked clean and new. No dirt or rust. Hadn't been there long.

I turned to Stone. "Let's back away and get Sidau and his guys up here."

Chapter 14

"A Browning BAR Safari 308," Sidau said. "Good deer rifle." He held the weapon in one latex gloved hand. He had photographed it in situ and then gently extracted it from the brush, careful to avoid any smooth surfaces that might hold fingerprints.

T-Tommy and I followed Sidau back up the hill to where he had parked his crime-scene van. One of the techs spread a plastic sheet on the van's floor. Sidau rolled the gun inside.

"When I get it back to lab, I'll fume it for prints and then test fire it," Sidau said. "Got a couple of guys with a metal detector looking for the bullet down there." He nodded toward the prison. "Maybe they'll get lucky."

"Hopefully, either it or the one still in Walter's body will be in good shape," I said.

"We'll know as soon as Drummond or Cooksey dig it out."

Lou Drummond and Becka Cooksey were the two medical examiners at the Alabama Department of Forensic Science. One of them would cut open Walter and see what damage the bullets did, and of course retrieve the bullet still buried inside.

Sidau lifted a gray plastic box from the back of the van and walked to where we had found the tire tracks angling off the dirt road toward the clearing. He placed the box on the ground and unlatched its lid.

Inside were the materials for making tire impressions: a plastic bag of dental stone, a premeasured bottle of water, and a stiff cardboard frame.

The tracks were fresh, with clear tread detail, and appeared to be from a truck or an SUV, judging by their width and depth. If this was indeed the shooter's site, these tracks certainly came from his vehicle. Determining the manufacturer and size would be easy. Maybe even the make and model of the vehicle. Maybe. If the tires were standard issue and if they hadn't been replaced. Big ifs.

After photographing the tracks and mixing the casting material, Sidau settled the frame over the clearest section of the impression. Looked to me like it had been laid down by the right front tire. He steadied it while I poured the dental stone slurry into the frame.

While the cast set, we thoroughly searched the clearing and the surrounding brush, but found nothing. No shoe prints. No shell casings.

We then moved to the next most promising area. The one with the gap in the tree. The one where we had seen the boot print. Sidau and I casted it too. We found nothing else. No broken branches or hair or fiber or shell casings. We walked back toward the road.

Sidau's cell phone chimed. He answered and listened for a minute and then said, "I'll be right there." He looked at me. "They found the bullet."

Took us five minutes to drive back down to the prison.

Under normal circumstances a crime-scene bullet is a gold mine of info. Type of gun used. Type of ammo used. Markings that could be matched to the weapon that it came from. Not so straightforward here. This bullet was damaged and fractured into two parts. After it passed through the late Walter Allen Whitiker, it struck the chain link fence and spilt in two. Half skidded across the rocky ground beyond the fence and came to rest near a metal power pole. The other piece slammed against the prison's stone wall, flattened, and fell to the ground.

I held up the two plastic evidence bags, a bullet fragment in each. "These are trashed."

Sidau gave me a raised-eyebrow look, implying that I was stating the obvious. "Maybe I can find something under the microscope." He took the bags, examining the one that held the largest fragment. "Looks like a bit of a surface on this one. Maybe some of the striations survived."

"Looks to me like it's something in the thirty-cal range," I said. "Which would match the weapon we found."

Sidau nodded. He handed the bags to one of his techs. "I'll know once I get it back to the lab and weigh it."

Chapter 15

After Tim and Martha had scooped up everything, raced away from the prison, bouncing over several dirt roads, jumped on a time-and-weather-chewed county two-lane blacktop that carried them back to Huntsville, visited the Dumpster to dispose of the tent and pillows, picked up the new car, and dumped the SUV, they had sped northeast on Highway 72 toward Tennessee. Martha had reminded Tim more than once to slow down, that a speeding ticket might not be the best thing. They had been too scared and too wound up to stop for food, but now, after putting seventy miles between them and Huntsville, hunger reared its head.

They stopped at Gladys's Roadside Diner, a weathered, white clapboard building with a sloping, faded-green metal roof. Two gas pumps out front, a hand-painted sign over the front door that said, Home Cooking and Friendly Folks, and a gravel parking lot along one side that appeared to wrap around the back. Tim pulled into the side lot and parked, nosed up to a bank of windows. Thankfully, the restaurant didn't appear to be very busy. He killed the engine, and they sat in silence for a minute.

Tim sensed Martha's apprehension. "Are you going to be okay?"

"I feel like I have a scarlet letter on my chest."

He took her hand. "You want to keep going? The interstate is just a few miles ahead and there'll be plenty of places there where we can drive through and not get out of the car."

She sighed, shaking her head. "No. We have to do this. Have to get on with this new life."

"You don't have a scarlet letter and your new look makes you unrecognizable."

"I just don't want to see our faces on TV, or in a newspaper."

"You know that's going to happen. Sooner or later."

"I'll take later."

"You'll be fine." He released her hand and pushed open the car door.

Inside they found a deli case filled with prewrapped sandwiches, muffins, sweet pastries, and a tempting array of pies, and beyond, a dining room that had four booths and a dozen tables. After one of the waitresses breezed by, coffeepot in hand, and told them to take any table they wanted, they settled in a booth that snugged up against the wall of windows, their car just outside.

A stack of laminated menus nestled against the window, held in check by a glass sugar dispenser and squeeze bottles of catsup and mustard. Tim handed one to Martha and then thumbed through the six-page tome until he found the two pages devoted to breakfast.

"Coffee?"

The waitress was middle aged, cantaloupe round, and with gray-streaked brown hair stuffed beneath a hairnet. She wore a catsup-and-grease-stained white apron over an oversized formless blue dress. She gripped a coffeepot handle in one fist, while dangling two cups from a finger of her other hand.

"Sure," Tim said.

She placed the cups on the faded-yellow Formica tabletop, filled both, and then turned and put the pot on the table behind her.

"Where you folks from?" she asked.

Tim felt Martha stiffen. He did too for a beat, before he realized that a place like this would be mostly populated with locals and that new faces would stand out.

"North Carolina," he said. "We've been on vacation in New Orleans and we're headed home."

She pulled a pad from her apron pocket and a pencil from just above her right ear. She looked down at him over half glasses. "Don't like the freeways I guess."

Tim smiled. "Prefer the back roads. On the freeways you miss places like this."

"Ain't it so? But it seems like everybody's in a hurry nowadays." She tapped the pencil against the pad. "What can I get you?"

Martha closed her menu. "Pancakes and bacon."

"I'll have your Country Boy Special," Tim said. "Eggs over easy. Bacon crisp."

"Toast or biscuits?"

"Biscuits."

"Good choice." She settled the pencil back in her hair, turned, and headed toward the swinging door to the kitchen.

"I'd better call Paige," Martha said. She pulled the prepaid cell phone from her purse. They had purchased it three months earlier, cash of course, and had not yet used it.

"Any trick to using this thing?" she asked.

"Just open it up and dial the number."

"I'll be right back." She left the table and stepped outside. Tim saw her walk into the parking lot, away from the gas pumps, out of earshot. She dialed the phone and brought it to her ear. As she talked, head down, she kicked at some loose gravel and aimlessly paced back and forth.

Beyond her, Tim saw a police car round a bend in the highway, slow, and turn into the lot. His heart fluttered a beat. What the hell?

Martha didn't see the cruiser, which hesitated as if waiting to see which way she was going to meander next. Finally, she seemed to hear the idling engine and turned toward the two officers who smiled at her through the windshield. She moved out of the way, her wide-eyed gaze snapping around toward Tim.

The patrol car slid by her, parked next to their car, and the two officers stepped out. The driver headed toward the front door, his partner following, glancing over his shoulder toward Martha a couple of times.

The waitress that had waited on Tim and Martha waved at the officers as they came in and greeted them with by saying, "How're you boys doing today?" They were obviously regulars.

Martha ended her call and came back inside, eyes locked straight in front of her, walking stiffly past the cops, who had taken a table near the front. She sat down, dropping the phone in her purse.

"What are we going to do?" she whispered.

Before Tim could respond, their food appeared.

"Anything else?" the waitress asked.

"Not that I can think of," Tim said. "Smells good."

"It is," the waitress said. "I'll check back shortly." She headed toward the kitchen.

Martha looked past Tim toward the officers and then lowered her gaze to her plate. "One of them is looking at me."

"The young one?"

She nodded.

"He checked you out when you were in the lot."

"What?"

"I think he thinks you're cute."

She frowned at him. "What are we going to do?"

"Nothing. They have no idea who we are."

"How do you know?"

"Either of them have his gun out?"

"Don't be ridiculous."

"They're here for breakfast. Don't get all goofy."

"I'm not. I just feel like everyone is watching us."

"I suspect we'll both have that feeling for a while. It'll pass."

"When?"

"Once we get to Asheville and get settled."

"I hope so." She smeared butter on her pancakes and drizzled them with syrup.

Tim heard the two cops laughing with one of the waitresses.

Martha looked up at them again and then said, "Okay. I'm just being spooky."

Tim dug into his eggs and then, his voice low but not exactly a whisper, asked, "How'd it go? What'd Paige say?"

"She heard about Whitiker. On the news."

"And?"

"I acted surprised. Told her we hadn't heard."

"Good."

"I hate lying to her."

"I know, but we talked about this. The less she knows, the better."

Martha nodded. A quick glance toward the cops.

"Sooner or later the police will visit her," Tim said. "If she knows nothing, she won't have to lie to them."

"I told her I'd call again in a few days. Once we got settled."

"Anything else?"

"Wanted to know where we were and, that since Whitiker was dead, if we might abort this whole thing and come back."

"What'd you tell her?"

"That we'd think about it."

Tim raised an eyebrow.

"I didn't want to get into a long discussion right now."

Tim nodded as he sopped up egg yolk with a piece of biscuit. "Good idea."

Martha sighed. "I really hate lying to her."

Chapter 16

"You're leaving?" I asked Claire who was standing at the open door of her Mercedes, rummaging in her oversized purse.

"Heading over to the station to edit this footage for my six o'clock report."

"It's been a morning to remember."

"Tell me about it." She settled her purse onto the passenger's seat. "I can still feel that bullet whizzing by."

"Glad it whizzed by."

"But it's going be a hell of a story."

That it is.

"I'll call you later," I said.

She climbed in and drove away. I watched until her car disappeared around a curve and then turned toward the prison. Warden Marshall Alston stood near the prison gate, talking with two guards and a pair of HPD officers. T-Tommy and I walked that way.

"Investigator Tortelli," Alston said as we reached him. "Dub."

We shook hands. Alston was an ex-HPD officer. Went to law school, became political, and had been warden here for the past decade. Mid-fifties, bald crown ringed by graying, curly hair, quick, dark eyes, he always appeared disheveled as if he had slept in his cloths. Today he wore wrinkled tan slacks, a light-blue open-collared shirt, and a navy-blue jacket.

"Ain't this a mess?" Alston asked.

"All that and then some," I said.

"Any idea who might've done this?"

T-Tommy shook his head. "Not yet. But we'll get there."

Alston shoved his hands into his pockets and rocked on his heels. "Let's hope." He sighed and looked out toward the wooded hillside across the highway. "I dread all the investigations and paperwork this'll generate."

"Ain't that the truth," T-Tommy said.

"Can we talk?" I asked.

"Let's head up to my office."

We followed Alston through the gate, the massive metal prison doors, a couple of locked doors, and then upstairs to his second-floor office. It was disheveled too. Alston moved a pile of magazines from one of the two chairs that faced his paper-stacked desk. T-Tommy and I sat. Alston slipped off his jacket, hung it on a wall hook behind his desk, and fell into his swivel chair. It creaked under his weight.

"As if I didn't have enough paper pushing to do." He waved a hand over his desk. "Never-ending stream. It's like they have a conveyer belt from downtown to my desk and they keep shoveling shit onto it." He looked up at us. "What can I do you for?"

"Tell us about Walter," T-Tommy said. "His time here."

Alston scratched an ear. "I got his file right here." He fished a two-inch-thick blue folder from the mess on his desk and flipped it open. "I was hoping to file this for good." He looked up at me and shrugged. "Now I guess I can. It'll just go in the deceased drawer and not the paroled one."

"He have any problems while he was here?" I asked.

"Sure. Mostly his first couple of months. Him being a child killer and all."

Sometimes you say things that you know are stupid but they get out of your mouth anyway. This was one of those. I said, "But he wasn't convicted of child murder."

T-Tommy gave me one of his "Are you an idiot?" looks.

Alston tossed me a half smile. Apparently, he thought I was an idiot, too.

"You think these guys don't know the story?" Alston hooked a thumb toward the window behind him. The window that looked out on the rec yard. "They know more about what goes on out there than I do."

"So, what happened?" I asked.

"A few guys tried to take Walter on. Bad idea. Walter could handle himself. Put one guy in the infirmary for a couple of days. Extracted a tooth with his fist if I remember correctly. There were three or four similar incidents. I looked into all of them, but he was clean. Someone else always instigated it. Walter simply protected himself."

I nodded.

"I kept a close eye on Whitiker," Alston went on. "His case being so high profile I didn't want him doing something or have someone do something to him that would come back on us. Put another pile of paper on my desk." He began rolling up his shirtsleeves. "Anyway, after that first couple of months, he settled in and was a model prisoner."

Somehow Walter Allen Whitiker and model prisoner didn't seem to belong in the same sentence.

"Anyone with a grudge?" T-Tommy asked. "Another inmate or a guard?"

"Just one. Old boy named Charles Pike. Mean SOB if there ever was one."

"What was his beef with Whitiker?"

"Pike had a kid. Killed by a pedophile. Up in Ohio. Years before he came down this way and ended up as my guest."

"He and Whitiker tangle?"

"Just once. That was one of the altercations Whitiker had in those first few months."

"What happened?"

"Pike jumped him. Whitiker fought back. They bloodied each other up a bit but nothing permanent. I moved Pike to another area and they rarely crossed paths after that."

"What's Pike in for?" I asked.

"Armed robbery. He's maybe five years into a double dime."

"What about outside?" I asked. "Are you aware of anyone out there with an agenda against Walter?"

"Not that I know."

"Visitors?" T-Tommy asked. "Who came to see him?"

Alston thumbed toward the back of Walter's file until he found what he was looking for. He spun the open file toward T-Tommy and me. "That's it."

I leaned over and read it along with T-Tommy. Only four people visited, each several times. Mostly his brother JD. Also his sister-in-law Priscilla Whitiker, his mother Lula Whitiker, and someone named Bo Hudson. Bo had only visited a couple of times, the most recent about three weeks earlier.

"Who's Bo Hudson?" I asked.

"Works at Walter and JD's gun shop."

T-Tommy pushed the file back toward Alston. "So you got no idea who might've done this?"

Alston leaned back in his chair and shoved the fingers of one hand beneath his belt. "I'd suspect someone with Walter's attitude toward life and other folks makes a mess of enemies along the way. Apparently at least one angry enough to kill him." He rubbed his nose with the heel of his other hand. "In broad daylight. In front of my prison."

"Can we talk with Pike?"

"Sure. I'll get him down to an interrogation room and pull his file for you."

Chapter 17

The interrogation room was small, sterile, and contained a plain metal table and three chairs. T-Tommy and I sat shoulder to shoulder on one side of the table. A one-way window filled the wall behind us and a ceiling-mounted camera angled down on the single empty chair across from us. While we waited to see Pike, I looked through his file. Robbed a service station out near New Market. Stuck a gun in the owner's face and walked away with all of forty-two bucks. Apparently, the owner wrote down his license number and called the police. They were waiting for Pike when he got home. Some folks just aren't cut out for the criminal life. Can't quite connect all the dots.

Toward the back of the file were photocopies of all his ingoing and outgoing mail and the transcripts of every phone call he made or received. I read through them, finding one of interest. I started to show it to T-Tommy, but the interrogation room door swung open and a guard led a handcuffed Pike to the table where we sat.

Pike was tall, lean, with ice-blue eyes, thinning gray hair, looking older than his stated age of forty-nine. A jagged scar angled across one cheek. Looked like he had lost a knife fight at some point in his chosen career.

"What the hell is this about?" he asked as he flopped into the empty chair, a defiant gaze aimed our way.

"I'm Investigator Thomas Tortelli. This is Mr. Dub Walker."

"Ain't that grand. What the fuck do you want?"

I leaned forward, resting my elbows on the edge of the table. "We want to talk about Walter Whitiker."

He laughed. "I hear someone killed him this morning." He nodded toward the barred windows that faced the prison front. "Right out there."

"That's true."

"Ain't that some shit?"

"You know anything about it?"

"I know he's a scumbag and shooting him was too easy. Motherfucker should've been raped and tortured first."

I nodded.

"What?" Pike said. "Don't tell me you feel sorry for that piece of shit?"

"Actually, I don't think either of us will shed a tear for Walter," I said.

Pike stamped a foot on the floor. "Well, there you go. We're on the same side there." He seemed to relax a bit. "So what can I do for you?"

"Did you have anything to do with Walter's death?"

"Yeah. I snuck out the back door, shot him, and crawled back into my bunk." He shook his head. "And I was startin' to like you guys. Now you come in here and accuse me of this shit."

"No, Mr. Pike, we're not accusing you of anything," T-Tommy said. "We're just asking the questions that have to be asked. The fact that you wanted Walter dead isn't exactly a secret."

"You got that right. I'd've killed him in a minute if I'd of had the chance."

"Did you?" I asked.

He looked at me blankly, hesitated a beat as if he didn't understand the question, and then said, "Are you out of your mind? Where the hell do you think we are? You think I can come and go any old time I want?"

"I was thinking maybe someone on the outside. Someone you might've paid to do it for you?"

"Like who?"

I shrugged. "Maybe Alvin Dixon?"

"My cousin? What the fuck are you talking about?"

I opened his file to the letter I had found. "Let me share something with you. From a letter you wrote a month ago to Mr. Dixon. And I quote 'You take care of that thing for me and I'll get you five grand this week and the other five next month.'" I handed the file to T-Tommy and looked Pike in the eye. "Want to explain that?"

He stared at me, then T-Tommy, and finally back to me. Then he burst out laughing. "You guys are a whole lot dumber than you look and you look as dumb as dog shit."

"Can't say we haven't heard that before," I said.

"Why don't you enlighten us," T-Tommy added.

"Alvin's my cousin. He's picking up a new truck for my old man. A surprise for his birthday this July." He laughed again. "You think Alvin's a hit man?"

"Is he?"

"He's my cousin. We grew up together, but we ain't nothing alike. I'd've killed Walter. Alvin wouldn't've. He's what you might call passive. He don't hunt. He don't like guns. He damn sure wouldn't kill anyone. For me or anyone else." He laughed again. "You guys are a hoot and a half."

Chapter 18

JD and the late Walter owned Whitiker's Rods and Guns. Billy, their father, had opened the shop over fifty years earlier. When he died, the two boys took over. Did all right for themselves. Whitiker's was the most popular shop of its kind in the city.

It sat along Bob Wallace Avenue, half a block from the Big Spring Cafe, home of the greasiest burgers in the world. They advertised them that way. T-Tommy gave it a glance and a grunt as we drove by. He was getting hungry. Me, too, but I wanted to chat with JD first.

When I pulled into the gravel-strewn, pockmarked asphalt lot, I saw JD's car angled up close to the building. I slid in beside it. A bell attached to the door jingled as we went inside.

"Can I help you?" the guy behind the counter asked.

"We need to see JD Whitiker," I said.

"Not a good day," the guy said, his expression flat, his chest and arms thick, bulging against his dark-blue Whitiker's Rods and Guns tee shirt.

"We know. Still need to chat with him."

He rested his palms on the counter, arms braced wide for support. "Not going to happen."

"Yeah, it is," T-Tommy said. He flipped open his shield.

The guy didn't flinch. "Maybe he ain't here."

"What'd he do?" I asked. "Slap his car on the butt and send it ahead?"

Empty eyes stared back.

"Look, Jack—" T-Tommy began.

"It's Bo. Bo Hudson," the guy said.

Walter's prison visitor.

"You visited Walter while he was in prison," I said. "Want to tell us why?"

"Not really."

"Why don't you anyway?" T-Tommy said. "Might save us from digging around in your life."

Bo hesitated a beat and then said, "Business. He had to sign some things for JD."

That made sense.

"Okay, Bo," T-Tommy said. "We're sorry about JD's brother. Him being such a stand-up citizen and all. We really do hate to bother JD, but we have to and we will. Now. So, unless you want a trip over to the lockup for interfering with an investigation, tell your boss man we're here." T-Tommy crossed his arms over his own thick chest and smiled.

Again, Bo hesitated. Like he was going to stand his ground. I almost suggested to him that that wasn't good idea. That T-Tommy wasn't the guy he wanted to play "mine's bigger than yours" with. Apparently Bo got the message.

"I'll see." He disappeared through a door that probably led to JD's office.

While we waited, I rummaged around. Whitiker's shop was well organized. The right side was reserved for fishing gear. Rods, from cheap cane poles to expensive fly rigs, creels, and nets lined the wall above a glass case filled with reels, lures, and hand-tied flies. Nearby racks held clothing, waders, and hats.

The back area was devoted to hunting. A wall-mounted rack displayed a row of rifles and shotguns. Beneath them another glass case held handguns, ammo, and scopes.

JD came from his office, Bo trailing behind. JD finished the Dr. Pepper he held, crushed the can in his fist, and tossed it into a wastebasket behind the counter. He looked at us and a scowl fell across his face.

"What the hell do you two want?" he asked.

"Just a couple of questions," T-Tommy said.

"Today? You guys ain't big on allowing a mourning period are you?"

"Sorry about your brother," I said.

"Yeah. I'm sure you are." His eyes narrowed. "Like you're sorry you harassed my wife?"

We had swung by JD's home before coming here. Wanted to chat with his wife, Priscilla, while he wasn't there. To check out his timeline alibi. She backed up everything JD had said. She obviously had called JD as soon as we left.

"She didn't seem to think it was a bother," I said.

"And she told you when I left the house, didn't she? It was just like I said, wasn't it?"

I nodded. "Yes, JD. It was."

"And I assume Bo here will vouch for you stopping by here before heading out to the prison," T-Tommy said.

"Sure will," Bo said. "Fact is I had to run him off. Afraid he'd be late picking Walter up."

"So there you go," JD said. "You guys can run along now."

"A couple of more questions," T-Tommy said.

"Like hell. Get out of my shop."

"Relax, JD," I said. "This'll only take a minute or two."

JD's face hardened. "I don't have to talk to you."

"We're not trying to add to your pain or harass you," I said.

He snorted. "Right."

"We want to find who did this," T-Tommy said. "I assume you do too."

JD said nothing, which was a good thing. Progress is measured in small steps. Rather than spitting and spewing, he was at least listening. Finally JD sighed. "What do you want to know?"

"Walter was killed with a rifle," T-Tommy said. "A thirty caliber, something like that. I imagine you sell quite a few of those. Any idea how many over the past few months?"

"I know exactly how many. Makes, models, who bought each and every one."

"Could we get a copy of that list?"

He looked toward the back of the store, his gaze locking on nothing, as if deciding what to do. He looked back at T-Tommy. "Sure." He leaned on the counter. It creaked under his weight. "You don't think the killer bought the gun here, do you?"

"It would be a hell of a coincidence," I said, "but I've seen stranger things."

"You and your brother own this place. Right?" T-Tommy asked. "No partners or investors?"

"We own it outright."

"And now you do?"

"What's that supposed to mean?"

"Nothing. Just getting the lay of the land."

JD's eyes narrowed, exaggerating his prominent crow's-feet. "I didn't kill my brother and I don't like you hinting otherwise. All that crap back at the prison. Searching my truck. Checking my hands. I know what you were doing. And why."

JD bent down and pulled open a small refrigerator that sat on the floor behind the counter. He snatched a Dr. Pepper, cracked it open, and took a couple of healthy gulps. He didn't offer us one. Kind of rude. I glanced at the trash can. Four crushed empties that I could see. And it wasn't even noon yet. Boy had a Pepper jones.

"It's common knowledge that you and your brother didn't exactly get along," T-Tommy said. "I seem to remember a knock-down, drag-out at a bar."

"Sure we fought. Did since we were kids. Knocked each other around from the time we could walk. Still do." He swallowed hard. "Did." His jaw flexed. "Yes, I get the company. But don't let all that confuse you. I loved my brother. I want whoever did this found. If you don't, I will."

"I'd advise against those kind of thoughts," T-Tommy said.

"I don't give a shit what you think, Tortelli." He glared at T-Tommy as he tugged his red Whitiker's cap down more tightly on his head. His anger turned toward me. "You either, Dub. Why don't you run on home and write one of your fancy books?"

"I will. As soon as we find the person responsible for your brother's murder."

JD stared at me for a beat and then said, "Want to know what I think? It was that Foster dude that did this. He and his bitch wife framed my brother. Lied about him. And now that he was getting out, they took matters into their own hands and killed him."

"Why would you think that?"

"Where are they? I understand they're pulling out of here today. Maybe already gone. You think maybe they popped a shot at Walt before they headed off?"

Did that make sense? Could Tim and Martha Foster have done this? Were they that afraid of Walter? Nothing I had seen or read about them during the investigation and trial said that was likely. Certainly nothing in the interviews I did with them nearly three years ago indicated they were capable of something like that. But people do some strange and out-of-character things when under pressure. Odds were that they felt pressure from Walter's threats. From the crushing loss of their son. From believing Walter had destroyed their little boy. But enough to do this?

"Look," JD said, "my brother was sick. Had all that child porn shit on his computer. I tried to get him to get some help."

"But he wouldn't listen?" T-Tommy said. "Something like that?"

JD nodded. "A couple of the brawls we had were over just that." He sighed and then took a gulp of Dr. Pepper. "You see, our mother didn't know nothing about Walter's . . . what's the word?"

"Proclivities?" I said.

"Yeah. I kept it secret. It would have killed her." He looked toward the front windows for a beat, his eyes unfocused. "Of course when Walter got arrested, it all came out. She still didn't believe it. Least that's what she said. But I could tell. It ate her up."

I nodded. "Understandable."

JD's gaze caught mine. His hard eyes seemed to soften a bit. He shook his head. "Maybe I should've pushed him harder. Got him into some program. But that would have exposed his secret to Mother and that's the last thing I wanted." Another gulp of Pepper. "Had I known how this was all going to play out, that Walter would be framed for kidnapping and murder, that she was going to find out anyway, I might've done things a little differently. I might've hog-tied him and dragged him into a clinic or something. I'm sure they have clinics for this kind of stuff."

"They do," I said.

He sighed. "A little late now."

"For both Walter and Steven Foster," T-Tommy said

His gaze snapped toward T-Tommy and hardened again. "My brother didn't kill that boy."

"You sure?" I asked.

He looked back at me. "Sure, he liked looking at all those pictures but he never touched anybody."

"These things do sometimes escalate," I said. "From pictures, to staking out schools, to an actual abduction."

"Not Walter."

"But you can't be sure of that, can you?" I asked.

JD stared at me, but said nothing.

Chapter 19

The Fosters' red brick house seemed well maintained. White trim freshly painted, yard lush and recently mowed, shrubs that flanked the front stoop neatly manicured. Whoever they sold it to was getting a jewel.

I parked at the curb and T-Tommy and I walked up the flower-framed walkway. No one answered my knock. The front curtains were drawn, so I couldn't see inside. I flipped open the wall-mounted mailbox, empty.

We moved around to the rear patio. The curtains to the kitchen and breakfast nook hung open. I rapped a knuckle on the window. Nothing. I rapped again, louder.

"Mr. Foster?" I yelled. No response.

Then I saw that the back door was cracked an inch or two. I pushed it inward.

"Tim? Martha?"

Dead air.

"Something ain't right," T-Tommy said. He pulled his gun and moved past me into the house, his head on a swivel. I followed. "Mr. Foster? HPD," T-Tommy shouted. No response. "Wait here."

No argument there. He moved deeper into the house, repeatedly shouting for the Fosters and identifying himself. I loitered in the kitchen.

Salt and pepper shakers and a napkin holder sat on the nook table; a blender, a toaster, and a compact microwave on the tiled counter. Clean dishes filled a drain basket next to the sink. I picked up a plate. Dry. Hadn't been used in at least a couple of hours. I settled it back in its slot.

I opened the fridge. The usual stuff stared back. Milk, OJ, pickles, jellies, mayo, ketchup, mustard, bread, yogurt, even three sealed containers of what appeared to be leftovers. Ice cream and two steaks in the freezer section. I then rummaged through the cabinets, finding glasses, coffee cups, stacks of plates and saucers, cereal and cracker boxes, and a bag of chocolate chip cookies, another of marshmallows.

T-Tommy returned, holstering his gun.

"The kitchen looks like they still live here," I said.

"So does the rest of the house," he said.

Now we both went from room to room.

The living room: Filled with furniture. Ready for use and not wrapped or covered as if expecting a moving company. Pictures still hung on the walls. The TV remote lay on the sofa that faced a big-screen Sony. A stack of magazines and a half-filled candy jar sat on the coffee table.

The master bedroom: The bed unmade, sheets wadded in the middle, a brown comforter bunched near the bottom. Dresser drawers and the closet nearly empty, only a few clothes remaining.

The second bedroom: Obviously a home office. A desk nudged up against a window that looked out on the backyard. The computer on top splayed open, a tangle of wires protruding, the hard drive missing. Desk drawers and the adjacent file cabinet empty. Paper confetti filled a trash can as well as the cross-cut shredder's basket.

"They destroyed a pile of documents," I said.

"Maybe they didn't need them anymore and didn't want to move them."

"Why rip out the computer's hard drive? Why not just take the whole computer? Seems they'd need that."

T-Tommy grunted. Meant he didn't have an answer for that either.

The third bedroom: Steven's room. The bed neatly made, the blue comforter without a wrinkle, corners tucked in. Closet and drawers filled with the boy's clothing. Tennis and baseball shoes on the floor beneath a desk. Open history book on top. Thomas Jefferson looked up at me.

The room screamed shrine. It looked as if the Fosters had changed nothing since young Steven's death. Left it frozen in time. I'd seen this before. Parents preserving a missing child's room, at first hoping the child would return, and after the body is found, after knowing the child would never come back to them, holding onto memories, afraid they would fade and the child would be forgotten. For some people letting go wasn't an option.

I picked up a baseball cap that hung on the back of the desk chair. "Why would they leave this?"

"Maybe the memories are too painful?"

"Yet they kept his room intact? For three years?" I shook my head. "They did that to remember Steven. So why not take his stuff with them?"

"Don't have a clue." T-Tommy waved a hand. "And all this furniture. They going to leave it behind?"

"It's like they left, but didn't."

He scratched an ear. "You think they changed their minds? Maybe decided to stay?"

"They said they were leaving today."

"But if they heard about Whitiker, maybe they altered their plans."

"Like went to the store or a movie? Left the back door open? I don't think so." I looked at him. "This smells wrong."

"You think maybe they have movers coming to pack everything up?"

"No."

People who had a moving company pack for them might leave all the kitchen stuff and the furniture as is, let the movers deal with it, but not personal items like clothes and extra toiletries. Definitely not the shrine they had created for their son. I couldn't imagine Martha Foster allowing strangers to touch Steven's clothing and personal stuff. Allowing them to pack up his Little League team photo or the Student of the Month certificate that hung on the wall. Not a chance.

"Let's check on it anyway." T-Tommy pulled out his cell phone and punched in a number. When someone answered, he said, "I'm over at Tim and Martha Foster's house. Check out the area moving companies and see if they've arranged to have their stuff moved." He listened for a minute. "That's right. Get back to me as soon as you know something." He closed his phone and dropped it into his jacket pocket.

We walked back to the living room. I picked up the TV remote and punched the big screen to life. *Fox News* appeared.

"Cable still works." I clicked the TV off. "Obviously the other utilities do too."

"Maybe they forgot to cancel them. Or maybe they're all scheduled to go off later today."

"Maybe." I picked up a throw pillow. Looked fairly new. I tossed it into the lounge chair beside the sofa. "It's as if they left before they finished packing," I said.

"Or were forced to leave."

"Abducted?"

T-Tommy shrugged. "Just trying to figure all the angles."

Could that be it? Who would take the Fosters? And why? If so, was it connected to Whitiker's murder?

"That might explain the hard drive being ripped out," T-Tommy went on. "Someone took them and the hard drive."

"What could possibly be on Tim and Martha's computer that would lead to an abduction?"

"Don't know."

"Not saying I buy the abduction angle, but any thoughts on who might've snatched them?"

T-Tommy shrugged again, but said nothing.

"So, you have one of Claire's conspiracies working here?" I asked. "Someone whacks Whitiker, kidnaps the Fosters, and then what? What's the payoff?"

"Ask me an easy question."

Chapter 20

"Hello." The woman's voice came from the front followed by a rapping on the door. "Hello."

I opened the door. A middle-aged woman in jeans and an untucked blue work shirt stared at me. Her dark brown hair was pulled back and secured with a red bandana.

"Who are you?" she asked.

"I was going to ask you the same thing," I said.

T-Tommy stepped up beside me and flipped open his badge. "Investigator Tortelli. HPD. This is Dub Walker. And you are?"

"Sandy Sechrest. I live next door." She leaned to her right and tried to look past us into the living room. "What's going on?"

"You know the Fosters I take it?" I asked.

"Of course. For years."

"We're looking for them."

"Why?"

"Need to talk with them."

"They're gone." Now she leaned to her left, her brow wrinkling as she peered past my shoulder. "At least, they planned to leave this morning."

"Did you see them head out?"

She shook her head. "They had their SUV all packed and sitting in the drive last night. It was gone when I went out to get the paper earlier this morning."

"What time was that?"

"About seven." She looked at T-Tommy and then to me. "I know they planned an early start. They were dreading the long drive to Phoenix."

"Did you see anyone else around here?" I asked.

"Like who?"

"Like anyone. Someone or maybe a vehicle that seemed out of place?"

Lines of concern dug deeper into her forehead. "No."

"Hear anything unusual?" T-Tommy asked.

"Why are you here? In their house?"

"You see the news today?" I asked.

She shook her head. "I've been doing housework all morning. Mostly window cleaning. Why?"

"Someone shot Walter Whitiker as he was leaving prison."

"What? When?"

"About seven this morning," I said.

"So did you hear anything?" T-Tommy asked again.

She stared at him, obviously confused. "Like what?"

"Arguing or shouting? Maybe a loud car engine? Anything out of the ordinary?"

"No." She laid an open hand across her chest. "Are they in danger?"

"Why would you think that?" I asked.

"You're here. From the police department. Snooping around their house. Asking all these questions."

She had a point. "No. I don't think they are," I said.

"They ever talk about Walter Whitiker?" T-Tommy asked.

She hesitated a beat and then said, "Sure. How could they not? He killed Steven and destroyed Tim and Martha. Choked the life right out of them."

"They ever express a desire to do anything to Walter?" I asked.

"What do you mean?" Her eyes widened. "You don't think they had anything to do with the shooting?"

"Do you?"

"Of course not. Tim and Martha are wonderful people. They wouldn't hurt anyone. Not even a low-life like Whitiker." She blew a strand of hair away from her face. "Can't say I'd blame them though. I would've hunted him down." She looked at me. "Bet you would've too."

I nodded. "Probably. The question is, would they?"

She shook her head. "Not possible."

"Because?"

"Because they're good and decent people. Churchgoing. Christians. I mean, what happened to Steven knocked them for a loop, but could they shoot someone? No way."

I looked at her, but said nothing, sensing she had more to say, letting her get it out her way.

"They are as loving a couple as you'll ever see. Losing Steven devastated them. Nearly killed Martha. I didn't see her smile or hear her wonderful laugh for nearly a year afterward. She was severely depressed. Lost all kind of weight. Her doctor gave her something, but she only took it a short while. Didn't like it. Thought it made things worse."

"Sounds like you two are close."

"We are. We talk a lot. I'd like to think I helped her get through all that."

"I'm sure you did," I said. "You never heard her or Tim say anything about getting even with Whitiker?"

"Not a word."

"Even though he was harassing and threatening Martha from jail?"

She shook her head. "I mean, she definitely feared him. Dreaded the day he would be released, but never did she or Tim say anything about doing something to Whitiker. Not to me anyway, and I think I would've known."

"Just that they were going to move away when he got out?" I asked.

She sighed. "I tried to talk them out of it. I mean, leave home? Leave everyone behind? Leave their church and Tim leave his job? It didn't make sense."

"Maybe it did to them."

"Still seems drastic to me. And I told them so."

"Did they own guns?" T-Tommy asked.

"No. Hated them. Would never allow them around Steven."

"What about all their stuff in here?" I jerked my head back over my shoulder. "Do they have a mover coming or something?"

Again she tried to look past me, so I stepped aside and let her enter.

She walked around the room, her steps short and hesitant, her gaze traveling over everything. She glanced back at me, wide-eyed, confusion evident. She walked through the kitchen and then down the hall toward the bedrooms. We waited. By the time she came back into the living room, the furrow in her brow had deepened and she appeared a bit pale.

"Well?" I asked.

"This is odd. I don't know what to tell you. I assumed they had packed up everything. I never thought to ask when the movers were coming."

"You know how to reach them?" I asked.

"I know Martha's cell number." She gave it to us.

T-Tommy dialed, waited, and then left a message for Martha to call him back.

"Do you know if they're stopping anywhere on the way? Maybe visiting relatives or friends?"

"No plans. Just motels when they get tired of driving."

"Do you know where they plan to stay once they get there?"

"Martha said they had already closed on a house. In the Phoenix area. Tim has a job waiting. Not sure where."

"You expect to hear from them?" T-Tommy asked.

"They said they'd call when they got settled."

"They have any family around?"

"Martha has a sister in Scottsboro. Her name's Paige Baker. I don't have her number though."

"We'll find it," I said. "Thanks for answering our questions."

She stared at me. "I'm still confused. What exactly is going on here?"

I smiled, hoping to dampen her anxiety. Not sure it worked. "We simply need to find Tim and Martha. Make sure they're okay and ask them a few questions."

T-Tommy handed her a card. "Give me a call if you see or hear from them or if you think of anything else."

"I will." She stepped through the front door, but hesitated on the porch, turning back to look at us.

"What is it?" I asked.

She shook her head, glanced up the street, and then back to me. "Something's wrong. I can feel it." She shook her head again, stepped off the porch, and crossed the lawn toward her house.

Ain't that so. Something is indeed wrong. Just not sure what yet.

I took one more spin through the house but saw nothing that helped. I returned to the kitchen where T-Tommy was just closing his cell phone.

"Got someone checking with the utility companies, and I just put out a BOLO on them," he said.

"How'd you package it?"

"Could be suspects. Could be kidnapping victims. Right now they're only wanted for questioning. Also got some guys working on a warrant to trace Martha's cell phone. Their credit cards, too."

I sat on one of the kitchen stools. "You know what bothers me the most about all this?"

"What?"

"All of Steven's stuff being here, but the computer hard drive missing. The two don't fit. One says they're coming back, the other says they aren't."

T-Tommy nodded.

"Maybe get someone working on a warrant for their ISP," I said. "We don't have their hard drive but we can look at what sites they visited and what files they downloaded. Also their e-mail history. Maybe we'll find something that makes sense out of this."

"Let's hope."

T-Tommy then called Derrick Stone and brought him up to date. Asked him to work on the ISP warrant. He then called Martha Foster's sister. No answer. He left a message for her to call him back.

"Want to take a hop over to Scottsboro?" I said. "See if we can find her."

"Food first."

No argument here.

Chapter 21

We drove over to the Big Spring Cafe. T-Tommy got their famous burgers in his head earlier and wouldn't let go. I didn't argue.

The Big Spring is serious about burgers. Grease, too. Precooked patties soak in a small metal vat of grease beside the grill. When an order comes in, the cook fishes one out and tosses it on the grill for a couple of minutes. An added slice of cheese quickly melts, a few pickles are scattered on top, everything embraced by a bun, and the best hamburger you're likely to eat anywhere slides at you across the counter. That's the way it is there. One table and a counter. If they're occupied it's take-out.

We luckily grabbed a pair of counter stools. A construction worker type exchanged a twenty for a bag of burgers, grease soaking through the white paper sack, and headed out the door.

We each ordered a cheeseburger, T-Tommy adding a chili dog and fries on the side. Took the guy all of three minutes to get our order up.

I heated mine up with a few splashes from my stashed bottle of Tabasco. The first bite was a little slice of heaven and it got better from there. Just as I finished my burger and drained my Double Cola, my cell rang. It was Sidau. He was back at the lab, getting ready to fume the rifle and begin going through all the evidence items they had collected. I told him we'd be there soon and slid my iPhone back in my pocket.

I told T-Tommy what Sidau had said. "We'd better head on over."

"We got time if Sidau's going to do that superglue deal," T-Tommy said. "That'll take a bit." He wiped his mouth with a napkin. "Leaves us just enough time for pie."

The cook turned from the grill where he had a take-out order of twelve burgers working and looked at us. "Did someone say pie?"

T-Tommy nodded. "Apple. Heated. With ice cream."

The cook looked at me. "You?"

"No," I said. "The burger did me in."

Pie never lasted long in front of T-Tommy, so we were back in my Porsche and headed toward the Forensic Science Department ten minutes later. Took another ten before we pulled into the lot off Arcadia Circle and parked near the entrance to the Wheeler-Pruitt Laboratory. As we climbed out of the car, T-Tommy's cell chimed. He answered and listened for a couple of minutes.

"Perfect. I'll let him know and we'll get all the paperwork done." He snapped the phone closed. "Good news. You're now an official consultant."

"How'd that happen?"

"I called earlier and asked them to hire you."

"Thanks. I'm feeling wealthy already."

"Right. With what they'll pay you, you can maybe buy a double latte."

"True."

Once inside, we found Sidau and Derrick Stone, walking down the hallway toward the test-firing room. Sidau carried the rifle in a gloved hand.

"Got anything?" I asked Sidau.

"No prints. Looks like it was wiped clean."

"Expected that."

"The scope on this thing is a good one. A Nikon ProStaff." His eyebrows bounced a couple of times. "Wouldn't mind having a rig like this myself."

"You don't hunt," I said.

"Doesn't mean I wouldn't want to shoot something." He smiled. "Or somebody."

"That'd be a long list."

"So true. Mostly defense attorneys."

Amen to that. "Any cartridges inside?" I asked.

"Six. Remington Core-Lokt Centerfire. A spent cartridge was still in the chamber. Since we didn't find any casings at the scene the shooter must have picked the other one up."

I nodded.

"It gets better." Sidau swung the weapon up and pointed the muzzle toward me. I stopped in mid-stride.

Sidau laughed. "It's not loaded anymore." He pushed the muzzle closer to me. "Look at that."

I immediately saw the problem. The blue-black metal inside the muzzle was scratched and gouged. Someone had damaged it by shoving something into the barrel. That would make matching difficult, if not impossible.

Here's how it works: When a bullet travels down a rifled gun barrel, the lands and grooves inside the barrel add spin to the bullet. Makes it come out like a Joe Namath rocket and not all squirrelly like a Kenny Stabler left-handed lob. Increases the bullet's distance and accuracy. These lands and grooves also cut small surface scratches, called striations, into the bullet and these are the basis for comparing bullets to see if they were fired from the same weapon. Each barrel is microscopically different and this difference is written in the striations. By damaging the inside of the barrel, either up and down its length with a coat hanger or similar device, or simply the terminal portion with a screwdriver or ice pick, the striations are altered and comparing a bullet fired before the damage with one fired afterward becomes problematic.

Unlike horseshoes, hand grenades, and thermonuclear warfare, in ballistics matching close doesn't cut it. It either matches or it doesn't.

This meant that whoever did it knew what they were doing. Knew that damaging the inside of the barrel would leave no way to make a match. Knew the gun would be worthless to us. Better to leave it behind than get caught toting it around.

The test-firing room was long and narrow, with walls of cream-colored cinder block, overhead fluorescent lights, and a series of tall, narrow windows along one wall. It held two types of firing chambers: a large rectangular water-filled gray metal box and a long, bazooka-looking cotton-filled metal tube. Each had a firing port on one end. When the weapon being tested was fired through the port, the water or the cotton slowed and captured the bullet without damaging or altering it in any way.

Sidau opted for the water trap. He fired two shots and quickly retrieved the bullets with a long-handled net. We then walked down the hall to the Firearms Lab, where Sidau sat down at his comparison microscope. After he mounted one of the test-fired bullets and one of the crime-scene fragments on the scope's two platforms, he leaned in, pressed his eyes to the double eyepiece, and began twisting knobs, adjusting the focus, and rotating the two bullets. T-Tommy and I stood quietly for the next few minutes while Sidau worked. Finally, he swiveled around in his chair and looked at me. I could see the frustration in his face.

He moved out of the way so I could sit. I hunched over the microscope. Took a couple of minutes for me to share Sidau's frustration.

The good news: the crime-scene fragment found burrowed in the ground had a single undamaged surface where striations could be seen.

The bad news: the damage done to the barrel made matching impossible.

"Maybe we'll have more luck with the one in Walter," Sidau said. "Drummond is doing the autopsy today, and he'll send the bullet over after he fishes it out."

I slipped on a pair of latex gloves and lifted the rifle off the table where Sidau had placed it. "Got a penlight?"

Sidau pulled open a desk drawer, rummaged around, and then handed me a small metallic light.

I aimed the beam down the barrel, angling it one way and then another. "Looks like the damage is just a half inch or so. Hard to be sure, but that's what it looks like." I laid the rifle down and handed the light back to Sidau. "Probably a screwdriver. The flared end makes it impossible to reach very far down the barrel."

"That's my take," Sidau said.

I peeled off the latex gloves, tossed them into a trash can, and propped one hip on the edge of the table where the gun lay. "I worked on a similar case with the FBI. Couple of years ago. Barrel damaged with a screwdriver. A lot like this one. We considered sawing off the last inch of the barrel and retesting it. Problem was that would alter the evidence and it might get tossed. Not to mention that it still might not match well enough to be sure."

"And?" Sidau said, obviously anticipating there was more to the story.

"We used rubber cement. Made a cast of the barrel and then used that to match to the striations on the bullet. Not a perfect solution since that evidence probably wouldn't be allowed in court, but it helped us determine that the gun in question wasn't the murder weapon in that case."

"Interesting," Sidau said. I could almost hear the wheels turning in his head. "We might be able to rule out this weapon if nothing else."

"Or hopefully rule it in," T-Tommy said.

"That, too," Sidau said. "I'm running a registration search on the serial number."

"If it's registered, it won't be by the shooter," I said. "Whoever dumped it isn't worried about it being traced back to him. It's either stolen, purchased privately, or laundered through a gun show or two. A guy smart enough to damage the barrel wouldn't leave a paper trail."

"Maybe we can find the original owner though," T-Tommy said. "That might lead us to whoever stole it."

Maybe. Probably not.

Chapter 22

Alvin Dixon's white clapboard house occupied a corner lot in a modest neighborhood, shaded by two thick maple trees, whose apple-green leaves wavered in the gentle southerly breeze. A cement walkway split the well-kept lawn and newly planted azaleas hugged the front stoop. A faint aroma of wisteria came from somewhere. The woman who answered our knock had a pleasant smile and brown hair locked into a bun on the crown of her head.

"Can I help you?" she asked through the screen door.

"Is Alvin here?" I asked.

Her smile weakened a notch. "And you are?"

"I'm sorry. I'm Dub Walker. I'm a consultant for the Huntsville PD." T-Tommy rolled his eyes. "This is Investigator Tortelli." I nodded toward T-Tommy.

T-Tommy flipped open his badge and held it out for her to see.

She glanced at it, her smile evaporating, a worry wrinkle creasing her forehead. "Is something wrong?" Her gaze moved past us, sweeping her yard and the street, as if she expected to see something horrible.

"I assume you know Charles Pike?"

Her gaze returned to me and her face hardened. "Why?"

"We need to ask Alvin a couple of questions about him."

"What's he done now?"

"Maybe nothing."

"Or maybe something?" she said.

I nodded.

She hugged herself as if suddenly cold. "He's always up to something and, unfortunately, he often drags Alvin into it."

"Oh?" T-Tommy said. "Like what?"

"Drinking. Staying out to all hours. Gambling. Been that way since they were kids. I know I shouldn't say this, but the last few years with Charles in jail have been a godsend."

"He get Alvin into anything illegal?" I asked.

"Like what?"

"Like anything."

"They stole some stuff as kids. Cigarettes, candy, comic books, that kind of thing. Weren't very good at it since they seemed to get caught a lot. Got tossed out of school a couple of times." She unfolded her arms and began to pick at a cuticle, head now down, shoulders taking a defeated slant. "Alvin's a good man except when he's with Charles. Charles is strong. Alvin is weak." She sighed the last word. She looked up at me, a slight glisten in her eyes. "At least as far as Charles is concerned. He's always followed his lead. Even when he knew it wasn't wise to do so."

"Anything more recent?"

She hesitated. The lines at the corners of her eyes deepened. "What's this about?"

"Do you know Walter Whitiker?"

"The guy that kidnapped and killed that little boy?"

"That's him."

"No. I know he's getting out of prison soon. Read that in the paper."

"He got out today," I said. "For a few minutes anyway. I take it you haven't seen the news today?"

"No. I don't watch much TV."

"Walter was shot and killed outside the prison."

"What? Who?"

"We don't know yet."

"What does this have to do Alvin?"

"Probably nothing, but we'd like to talk with him."

"He's in the hospital. Had a ruptured appendix. Thought it was indigestion or something he ate. I told him to go to the doctor, but he put it off until it ruptured. That got his attention in short order."

"When?"

"Three days ago. Been a rough recovery with all that internal infection."

We thanked Mrs. Dixon and drove over to the Huntsville Memorial Medical Center on Governor's Drive. We found Alvin Dixon in the Progressive Care Unit, sort of a step-down ICU. T-Tommy badged the charge nurse, and she led us to his bedside.

Thin and pale, he looked up as we walked in. Intravenous lines rose from each arm to fluid-filled bags, one clear, the other yellow, and electrode cables stretched from his chest to the cardiac monitor above his bed. He hadn't shaved in a few days and his thinning hair lay plastered over his head.

T-Tommy and I introduced ourselves and told him we had a couple of questions about his cousin Charles.

"When did you talk to him last?" T-Tommy asked.

"A month ago. I drove out and visited him."

That fit the visitors' list in Pike's file. "Nothing since then?" I asked. He shook his head.

"What about letters?"

"We've written a few times."

"About?"

"This and that." He coughed, clutching his belly in the process. A fine sweat lacquered his face.

"You okay?" I asked.

"Hurts like a bitch. Don't ever let your appendix rupture."

I smiled. "I'll remember that."

He took a couple of breaths as the pain seemed to settle. "Why're you asking me about Charles?"

"He pay you some money?" I asked.

He hesitated and then said, "Is he in some kind of trouble?"

"I don't know," T-Tommy said. "Is he?"

"Why do you cops always talk in circles? You got something to ask, just ask it. I ain't got nothing to hide."

"His last letter to you indicated that he was going to give you about ten grand," I said. "Five now and another five next month."

"That's right."

"Why?"

"I'm buying a truck for his dad. My uncle. Surprise birthday present. We wrote about how he was going to pay me back."

Either they had their story well oiled or the truck story was the truth.

"Who you buying it from?" T-Tommy asked.

"Woody Anderson's. Over on Jordan Lane."

"What type of truck?"

"He's got a clean F-150 Ford he's holding for me to come pick up."

We asked Alvin a few more questions but didn't get much and nothing overly useful.

He said he didn't know Walter Whitiker personally but knew Charles had issues with him. Prison issues, he called them. Cons always have little fights, according to him. Yes, he knew that Walter had been killed, heard the nurses talking about it, but that didn't mean much to him. Thought Walter probably deserved whatever he got "after what he did to that kid." Said his cousin couldn't be involved in Walter's murder or he would've known about it. They talked about everything. Always had.

This was a dead end. No way Alvin was the shooter. Hard to pull the trigger when you got a hole blown in your gut and are locked up in an ICU.

I hated dead ends. Like spinning your tires in mud. Messy and it doesn't get you anywhere. But that's what police work is. Walking up blind alleys to make sure they are indeed blind. At least this one meant we could slide Alvin Dixon right off the suspect list.

By the time we reached the parking lot and climbed in my Porsche, T-Tommy had called Woody Anderson's and talked with the used car manager. He confirmed that Alvin Dixon was buying a truck from them. A F-150. Had already put five thousand down and was to pay the other five when he picked it up.

Like I said, this was a dead end.

Chapter 23

TUESDAY, 3:53 P.M.

The city of Scottsboro sits along the Tennessee River forty miles due east of Huntsville on Highway 72, a road that passes through some of the most beautiful land in the country. At times nudging my Porsche up against eighty-five miles per hour, T-Tommy and I slid by cities with such great names as Gurley, Paint Rock, and Rocky Ridge. We reached Scottsboro's Broad Street exit in well under an hour. I turned north and headed toward downtown.

Scottsboro is famous for three things.

It is home to the largest lost luggage retail outlet in the country. Whenever the airlines lose track of checked baggage, the contents are likely to end up here. It's a bargain hunters' paradise.

Scottsboro's second claim to fame is First Monday, an open-air market that sets up beneath the trees that hug the central courthouse on the first Monday of each month. People drive many miles to search for treasures and odds and ends. Depression glassware, handmade quilts, cast iron pots and pans, jewelry, and trinkets of all kinds can be found on the sellers' tables.

But the event that comes to mind when most outsiders mention Scottsboro, and the one most residents wish wasn't so, is the landmark Scottsboro Boys case. It began with the 1931 conviction of eight black teenage males of raping two white female train-riding hobos. Their conviction wasn't the end of the case, merely the beginning. A series of trials and appeals that spanned decades and involved such institutions as the U.S. Supreme Court and the American Communist Party followed. The case remained subject to jurisprudence until 1976 when then-Governor George Wallace pardoned all concerned.

I slowed as we approached the downtown square and the Jackson County Courthouse, the site of the famous Scottsboro Boys trial and the hub of the First Monday market. The courthouse was red brick and topped with a brilliant white four-clock-faced cupola. The clock facing us showed it was 3:53. Brick buildings of tan, gray, and mostly various shades and ages of red wrapped the block and housed a bank, a pharmacy, a couple of cafes, and several antique shops. Today the town was quiet, little traffic and only a few shoppers moving lazily along the sidewalks.

We continued north, then right onto Maple Avenue, left onto Tupelo Pike, and finally found Paige Baker's house in a peaceful, tree-shaded neighborhood. A simple two-story, pale-yellow shingled house with a pitched roof and a pair of upstairs dormer windows, jutting over the porch roof. No one answered our knock.

As we headed back toward the car, a woman came from the house across the street. She picked up a garden hose, twisted a faucet handle just left of the front door, and began watering a collection of thick rose bushes. Red, white, yellow, and a couple of shades of pink. While she worked she eyed us. We walked toward her.

At least sixty, she had silver hair and a round pleasant face. She wore tan shorts that reached her knees and a light-blue tee shirt that boasted "World's Best Grandma" in navy-blue block lettering. She smiled as we approached.

"How are you doing?" I asked.

"Mighty fine." She looked us both up and down and then nodded toward Paige's house. "You looking for Paige?"

"Yeah. Know where she might be?"

"Who are you?"

"I'm Dub Walker. This is Investigator Tortelli. Huntsville Police Department."

"My name's Eloise Frye."

"Nice to meet you. Pretty roses."

"Thanks. They take some work, but I love them." She took a few steps, directing the hose at another bush, letting the water collect in the dirt well that surrounded the base of the plant. "What do you want with Paige?"

"Just a few questions."

"This have anything to do with that shooting over at that prison this morning?"

"Sure does."

"I hear that Whitiker guy was killed."

"That's right."

She nodded and moved to the next plant. "It's what he deserved."

"Can't argue with that."

"What he did wrecked Paige. Her sister, Martha, and her husband, Tim, too."

"Did you know their son Steven?"

Another step and water began settling around the next bush. "Sure. Great kid. He'd always help me with stuff when he was visiting. My husband, before he died, tossed the ball around with him. Steven was a good athlete."

"That's what I understand. So, you know where we might find Paige?"

"You never said why you want to see her."

"We're looking for her sister."

"Last I heard they were moving out west. Not sure when or where though."

"We hoped Paige might know how to reach them."

The roses now soaked, she dropped the hose, walked over to the faucet, and twisted it off, the handle emitting a squeak and then a clunk. She dried her hands on the tail of her tee shirt. "She works over at the Blue Willow Restaurant. Should be there."

Chapter 24

The Blue Willow Restaurant had once been a home. Victorian in style, its walls were pale blue, part clapboard and part scalloped wood, and the trim white as were the columns that supported the roof over the small entry porch. The front yard offered many tree-shaded sitting areas, benches, and even a gazebo, where diners could await their tables. The sign along Willow Street boasted that the restaurant was HOME OF THE BLUE WILLOW BOURBON BUTTER. That couldn't be anything but good.

I turned into the side gravel parking lot and T-Tommy and I went inside. What had previously been a living room, a parlor, and various bedrooms were now dining areas. The decor in each room varied and was severely eclectic, with an assortment of framed pictures on colorful walls, antique pieces with pitchers, lamps, candles, and collectables littering their surfaces, and mismatched tables and chairs. We had beaten the dinner crowd and only a few tables were occupied.

I recognized Paige immediately. I'd never seen her before, and she was a couple of inches shorter than her sister, but there was no mistaking that the woman that approached us was Martha Foster's sister. Same eyes, same face, same walk. She wore a dark-gray dress beneath a crisp white bib apron.

"Table for two?" she asked.

"Paige?" I asked. "Paige Baker?"

"Yes."

"I'm Dub Walker. This is Investigator Tortelli. Can we talk somewhere?"

She took a step back. "What's this about?"

"Your sister."

I detected a flicker of—what? Concern? Anxiety? Whatever she was feeling, it plastered an uncomfortable look across her face. Her gaze hit the wall, the floor, and then back to me. "Is something wrong?"

"Can we go somewhere?"

She nodded. "Sure." She turned to another woman who was arranging plates and flatware on a nearby table. "I'll be back in a sec."

The woman eyed us. "Is everything okay?"

"Yeah," Paige said.

She led us back outside and across the grassy front yard away from the entrance to a shady spot beneath a thick magnolia. She turned toward me. "What's this about?"

"We're trying to find your sister, Martha."

"Why?"

"Do you know where she is?"

"She and Tim headed off to Phoenix this morning."

"Have you talked to her?"

She hesitated a beat and then said, "Not today."

"Expect to hear from her?"

"Sure. She said they'd call from the road." A couple moved past us and headed toward the entrance. She nodded to them and smiled. Then she said, "I'll ask again—what's this about?"

"I guess you heard that Walter Whitiker was shot and killed this morning?"

"Sure. Everyone's been talking about it."

"Do you think your sister knows?"

"I don't know. Maybe. If she and Tim have been listening to the car radio or have seen a TV somewhere they might."

"Any idea what time they left this morning?"

"Not really. But knowing them, it was probably very early. Both she and Tim are early risers. Whenever they go somewhere, they'll leave at four or five in the morning. Always have." She nodded to a family of four that walked by. "Why are you asking me all this?"

I told her what we had seen at Tim and Martha's house and about not being able to reach her on her cell phone. "Any idea why things aren't packed up at their place?"

"I think they had movers coming to do all that."

"When?"

"I thought yesterday."

"The back door was standing open. They sloppy about stuff like that?"

"No. Never. Just the opposite."

"The problem," T-Tommy said, "is that Whitiker was popped, your sister had been threatened by him, and now they're gone and their house looks like they left in a hurry."

"They've been planning for months to leave today. That's hardly in a hurry."

"But with everything they left behind, the back door open, it seems odd."

"What are you saying?"

"Do you know anyone who would harm them?" I asked. "Did she ever say anything like that?"

"You mean other than Walter Whitiker?"

"We know he didn't do anything," T-Tommy said. "Being in prison and now dead and all."

"Do you think something's happened to Martha and Tim?"

"Don't know," I said. "We just want to talk to them and make sure they're okay."

She looked at me, her eyes glassy with moisture. "You're starting to scare me."

"We don't want to do that. We just want to find them and make sure they're okay."

"That's all?"

I nodded.

She looked at T-Tommy. "You an investigator? What type?"

"Homicide."

"Why would a homicide cop be looking for Martha and Tim?"

"Just gathering information on the Whitiker murder."

"You saying they had something to do with Whitiker getting shot?"

T-Tommy shrugged. I looked at her but said nothing.

"That's ridiculous. Not possible. Never in a million years."

Again we waited her out.

"Why would they leave if they knew he was going to be killed? Why uproot everything?" Tears now collected in her eyes. "That bastard tormented them while he was alive and still is after he's dead." She pulled a tissue from the pocket of her apron and dabbed both eyes. "All they wanted was to get as far away from him as possible."

"That's probably exactly what they did," I said. "We just need to confirm that."

She wadded the tissue and returned it to her pocket. "Martha often turns her cell off. Doesn't like the bother. Tim hates them, so he doesn't even have one."

"Do you know their travel plans? What route they're taking? Any stops planned?"

She shook her head. "Not for sure, but I think they were going up through Memphis and picking up I-40."

"Do you have their new address in Phoenix?"

"No. I guess they'll send that once they get settled."

"They've bought a place there. Right?"

"Yes. I'm sure of that. I just don't have the address. I know it's in the Scottsdale area."

"Doesn't that seem odd?" I asked.

"Doesn't what seem odd?"

"That they have a place there but didn't tell you their new address? I mean, if they bought a house they'd know the address. Why not tell you before they left?"

"Well . . . I mean . . ." Her voice trailed off and lines of concern appeared around her eyes. "I guess that is odd."

T-Tommy handed her a card. "If you hear from them, have them give me a call."

Chapter 25

When Paul Twitty entered Whitiker's Rods and Guns, he saw JD ringing up a customer at the checkout counter. Guy was buying a new reel. JD nodded and raised a finger, indicating he'd be done in a minute. Twitty nodded back and made his way to the gun display toward the rear of the store.

He loved cigars. Never smoked them, never even lit them, just liked having one clamped between his teeth. Why light up when the rich flavor of the tobacco and the low-level jolt the nicotine gave him was enough? He preferred Cohibas. Castro's choice. He had unwrapped a fresh one and crushed it between his molars on the drive over and it was just now getting settled, just now beginning to release its juices.

He shifted the Cohiba to the other side of his mouth and lifted a Remington Model 870 Wingmaster from the rack and examined it. Lightweight, twelve gauge, an improved cylinder choke. Great bird gun. He racked the pump a couple of times and then brought the stock to his shoulder. He swung it toward the front window and settled the sighting bead on a telephone pole across the street. The customer, new reel under his arm, pushed through the door and stepped into the sunlit parking lot. Twitty moved the bead in his direction and followed his movements until he disappeared into his car.

He liked this gun. Good balance. Solid feel. He could use a new shotgun before next dove season. Of course, he felt that way every year.

He returned the shotgun to the rack and looked over the others: Moss-bergs, Berettas, Brownings, Marlins, JD had them all.

"See anything you like?" JD's voice, just behind him.

Twitty turned. "Only all of them."

JD smiled. "They're all for sale."

"I like the Remington. Maybe I'll drop back by and pick it up an-other day."

"Maybe I can make you a good deal on it today."

Twitty nodded. "Maybe." He scratched one ear. "You wanted to see me?"

"Let's talk in my office."

The office was small and disorderly. JD introduced Twitty to Bo Hudson who had been hunched over the cluttered desk, examining ledger sheets when they came in. Big guy, big muscles, hard handshake.

"Take the register," JD said. "No calls until we're finished."

Bo nodded and left. JD took the seat vacated by Bo; Twitty a chair facing him across the desk.

"What can I do for you?" Twitty asked.

"I want to hire you. To track someone down."

"Anything to do with your brother's murder? By the way, my con-dolences."

"Thanks. That's exactly what it's about." JD rocked back in his chair. "Not that I don't trust the cops, it's just that I don't trust the cops."

Twitty smiled. "Me either. Not even when I was one."

"Tim and Martha Foster. They're gone and no one seems to know where. I believe they killed my brother. I want you to find them."

"What do you plan to do with this information?"

"That's my business. I only want you to track them down."

"No problem. I'm sure you don't mean them any harm."

"Wouldn't dream of it."

That was a lie and Twitty knew it. Truth was he didn't care what his clients did with the dirty laundry he brought them. Information, pho-tos, voice recordings, videos, whatever they'd pay for. What they used it for was on them. He simply lied, spied, and recorded. "My fee is three hundred a day plus approved expenses."

JD nodded. "I'll even toss in the Remington."

"How could I turn down such a generous offer?"

JD scribbled a retainer check for Twitty and then escorted him from the office. Twitty stuffed the check into his jacket pocket while JD lifted the Remington from the rack. At the counter, JD handed the gun to Bo.

"Wipe this down and slip it into a case for Mr. Twitty while I grab some ammo," JD said.

"The Wingmaster," Bo said. "That's a good one. Got one just like it myself."

"Does it do the job?" Twitty asked.

Bo smiled. "Guaranteed to bag the limit every time."

While JD stuffed several boxes of shells into a paper bag, Bo laid the shotgun on the counter. He grabbed a gun cloth and a yellow-and-brown quart can of Brownells Rust Preventative No. 2 from under the counter, soaked the rag with the clean-smelling oil, and began wiping down the gun, the Brownells adding a rich sheen to the metal.

JD handed the bag to Twitty. "Here you go. Eight-and-a-half shot. Six boxes."

"Thanks."

Bo slid the gun in the case and zipped it closed.

"Tell you what," Twitty said, "I might leave all this here for now. I got a ton of meetings scheduled and I don't want to leave it in the car all day. That okay?"

"Absolutely," JD said. "I'll put it in my office. Come by and pick it up any time."

"Will do."

After Twitty left, Bo asked, "Want me to ring that up now or wait till he comes back?"

"Neither. It's a gift. A partial payment actually."

"For what?"

JD hesitated a beat. Should he tell Bo what was what? The less he knew the better, but JD would likely need him at some point. Besides he knew he could trust Bo. Maybe not completely, but enough. Truth was that Bo would do just about anything for JD. JD had pulled him from a life of hard work, hanging off the back of a garbage truck, dumping foul-smelling, greasy trash into the rear bin. A job Bo had had for two years and would probably have for twenty more if he hadn't stepped up and given Bo this job.

The other truth was that Bo wasn't very smart. Hell, sometimes he didn't even catch the jokes that JD or the customers told. He'd laugh, but JD knew he didn't get it. Saw it in Bo's eyes and in the way he waited for everyone else to laugh before he followed their lead. Some of the customers saw it too. Of course they never said anything. JD was never sure if they were just being kind or were intimated by Bo's size. Probably the later.

"He's going to track down the Fosters."

"Why would you want him to do that?"

JD circled the counter, pulled a fresh Dr. Pepper from the small fridge, popped it open, and took several hefty gulps.

"The way I see this is that it can go one of three ways. The Fosters are never found. Not by the cops, and not by Twitty. Then they'll never face justice. My only hope there is that their guilt eats them up like a dose of cancer or TB. Or maybe the cops'll find them and bring them back here for trial. Probably get off easy since everyone has my brother pegged as a child killer. Their child. That always plays well with juries. Or maybe, just maybe, Twitty might find them and the cops won't have a clue."

"Then what?"

"Plan B."

"What's that?"

"Let's just say it involves our friends over in New Hope."

Bo nodded. "You know anything you need, I'm there."

"I'm counting on that."

Chapter 26

Crows are clever creatures. Inquisitive, relentless, and research has shown that they have at least some rudimentary level of cognitive reasoning. Makes them excellent thieves. I once saw a video of a crow attempting to remove a small, round metal basket from a cylindrical glass container. It was just out of reach so the crow grabbed a piece of wire in his beak and tried to lift it that way. No luck. He then shoved one end of the wire beneath the container, cranked the other end up, and bent a hook into the end. He then easily lifted the basket by its handle. Amazing.

Norton and Kramden, my two crows—I use the word *my* in its broadest sense—were also clever, but mostly just annoying. They terrorized the neighborhood, their neighborhood being the entire city, and managed to drop by at least once a day to harass me. Thieves without equal, I kept a basket filled with shiny trinkets the boys had scavenged over the years. I had rescued them from a pine tree nest in my neighbor's yard after their mother abandoned them, or more likely was killed, and raised them into the obnoxious beings they had become.

Obnoxious, but lovable. Sort of like Claire.

Wait a minute? What did she and the boys have in common? Where did their crossroads meet?

Me.

Don't you hate it when logic works against you?

When the boys showed up, Kramden carrying a watch that he

deposited on the table in front of me, I wasn't surprised. Neither were T-Tommy and Claire. They had seen this all too often.

We were huddled around my patio table, sipping sweet tea and going over everything we had on Walter Whitiker's murder and the Fosters' disappearance. So far, it wasn't much.

I picked up the watch. Old, dotted with rust, crystal broken, its metallic case retained just enough shine to attract Kramden's attention. He stood looking at me, head cocked to one side as if saying, "Now what do you have for me?"

I went inside, filled a bowl from the bag of corn I kept for the boys, and carried it out into the yard. Norton and Kramden followed, squabbling and jockeying for position before I could even settle the bowl in the grass. I got out of their way and returned to the table.

"I spoke with Derrick Stone about an hour ago," T-Tommy said. "No phone or credit card use by the Fosters. We put out a BOLO on them in every state they're likely to go through, whether they use I-40 or take the southern route on I-10. So far, nothing."

"Won't be easy to pick out a single car from a slew of interstate traffic," Claire said.

T-Tommy gulped some tea. "Here's the kicker. Stone checked on home sales in the Phoenix area over the past six months. Nothing was sold to Tim Foster. Nothing currently in escrow."

"Is that right?" I asked.

"According to Maricopa County records. Stone said he still had a couple of things to check out. A private sell, for example. If it didn't go through a realtor and the sale hasn't been documented yet, the county wouldn't have a record of it on their books. He's checking with the county tax assessor and the various community associations in the area."

"What does that mean?" Claire asked. "That they lied about moving to Phoenix?"

"Maybe," I said. "Or they could be leasing until they get settled."

"Everyone's said they bought a place," T-Tommy said. "The sister, the neighbor."

Kramden and Norton had finished tanking up and took to the air, squawking, and twisting, and diving, and chasing each other out over the valley.

"I'm getting a vibe that the Fosters have secrets." I looked at T-Tommy and he nodded his agreement.

Claire pushed the sleeves of her long-sleeved black pullover up to her elbows and rested her forearms on the table's edge. "What kind of secrets?"

"Where they are and where they're going."

"Well, duh. Aren't they trying to hide from Whitiker?"

T-Tommy grunted. "Don't need to hide from a dead man."

"If they left early this morning, they probably know nothing about it." She took a sip of her tea. "To them they're running from Whitiker. It wouldn't make much sense for them to broadcast their whereabouts. If it were me, I'd tell everyone I was going to point A while I hightailed to point B."

I hated it when she was logical. Took the fun out of everything.

"Yesterday, I had the feeling that Paige knew more than she let on," I said. "I just don't believe that she wouldn't know Martha's new address." I looked at Claire. "Even when we suggested that Martha might be in danger, she didn't flinch."

"She definitely knows more than she's letting on," T-Tommy said.

"So what?" Claire said. "Wouldn't her sister help them? Protect them? Not tell anyone where they were? Not take the chance that word would get back to Whitiker?"

"But would she lie to the police?" I asked.

"Wouldn't you? If you were in her position, wouldn't you do the same?"

"I showed her my badge," T-Tommy said.

"Your out-of-her-jurisdiction badge?" Claire shook her head and sighed. "Maybe you should've showed her your gun."

"I didn't think of that."

"How do you two get through life?" Claire asked. "Who dresses you each morning?"

"I can dress myself," I said. "And I have you to undress me at night."

"Button it, Walker." She finished her tea. "All I'm saying is that blood is thicker than anything. Didn't everyone tell you that Martha and her sister were close? It makes more sense that she lied for her than it would if she gave her up."

T-Tommy's cell rang. He answered, mostly listened. "We'll be right there," he said. He closed the phone. "The Fosters' car turned up."

"With them?" I asked.

"Apparently abandoned."

Chapter 27

Tim felt a nudge against his shoulder.

"Wake up, sleepyhead." It was Martha.

He rolled over. She stood beside the bed, a steaming mug of coffee in her hand.

"What time is it?" he asked.

"Almost noon."

He stretched and yawned. "Why didn't you wake me earlier?"

"You needed the sleep." She handed him the coffee as he swung his legs from beneath the covers and sat on the edge of the bed. "But now I'm starving and there's nothing here to eat."

He took a sip of the coffee. Then another.

He had slept poorly. Tossing and turning, repeatedly readjusting the pillow, kicking the covers here and there. The mental movie of the bullet he unleashed splatting into Walter's chest played in a continuous loop. The up-close and personal images he had seen through the scope in real life took on added dimensions in his dreams. He could not only see the bullet tear into Walter's chest but he could hear it, even feel its concussive impact like a sharp burst of air against his face. Dreams were funny that way. It was near sunrise before the loop faded, and he finally succumbed to fatigue and descended into a deep sleep.

He carried the mug to the bathroom where he took a shower, the coffee and the hot water finally shredding the cobwebs. He slipped on

jeans and a tee shirt and then he and Martha drove into downtown
Asheville. On College Street, the red brick facade and green awning of
the Tupelo Honey Cafe caught their eye. They parked and went inside.

Upscale, with a sort of sixties, hippyish vibe, the cafe was spacious
and busy. Most tables were occupied and the hum of conversation filled
the air. Nicole, one of the waitresses, a trim young woman in jeans and
a chocolate-brown tee shirt, dark hair pulled into a short ponytail, wel-
comed them from behind the small check-in counter and then settled
them into a two-top along the wall.

"You guys been here before?" she asked.

"First time," Martha said.

"Well, then I recommend you start with the hot pimento cheese
dip. We make it fresh everyday and it comes with homemade chips. It's
the most popular thing on the menu."

"Sounds wonderful," Martha said.

Tim looked over the menu. Eclectic with a deeply Southern slant.
Too many good things to choose from. Before he could decide, Nicole
returned with the dip, placing it and basket of chips on the table.

"Hmm. Smells good," Martha said.

"It's my favorite," Nicole said. "I have it for lunch most days."

Tim scooped up some and shoved the chip into his mouth. "Wow,"
he said around his chewing, "that is good."

"What else do you recommend?" Martha asked.

She rattled off several of her other favorites, complete with detailed
descriptions of each. Tim opted for the Angus Beef Tupelo Burger
while Martha went for the Tupelo Tomato Sandwich—tomato, havarti
cheese, and mayo on Texas toast.

"Good choices," Nicole said. "That'll leave just enough room for
our famous Brown Butter Pecan Pie."

How could that not be good?

While they munched, they sat silently. They had not talked about
yesterday, both seeming content with avoiding the subject. The three
hundred-mile drive, unpacking their suitcases, opening a few boxes,
beginning to settle into their new place, and not a single word about
Walter Whitiker. As if not talking about it, not saying it out loud, meant

it never happened. As if it had been merely a disturbing movie and not real life.

Tim looked around the restaurant. Tables filled with people. Ordinary people. People who hadn't lost a child. People who hadn't killed anyone. People who slept well, free of guilt.

Was it guilt he felt? Remorse? Was he sorry he shot Walter? Did all the planning and execution—the irony of that word not lost on him— blind him to how he would feel afterwards? Or was he simply exhausted, coming down from the intensity of the past forty-eight hours? A lot had happened. The Walter thing. Dumping their entire lives. For real. Not in theory as it had been for the past few months, but rather in stark reality. With a single act, they had swerved their lives onto an uncharted path. One that no amount of planning could have prepared them for.

A woman two tables away caught his eye, stared at him. Did she know? Was she going to call the police? He felt a tightness rise in his chest. Then she offered a nod and a friendly smile and turned back to talking with her companion. Tim reined in his imagination.

Martha reached across the table and laced her fingers with his. She leaned forward and spoke softly. "You okay?"

"Tired."

"Is that all?"

"Mostly."

"Regrets?"

"Maybe. Maybe just coming down from all that's happened."

"It does seem a bit surreal."

"A bit?"

She laughed. He loved her laugh. "Okay, more than a bit."

"I'm fine. It's just that after all the planning, we're finally here. Sitting in a restaurant like two normal people, enjoying a normal day."

"We are normal people."

"Really?"

"So we have a little extra baggage to haul around. Look around. Everyone does. Everyone here has secrets."

"Probably not these kinds of secrets," Tim said.

"That might be true." Martha squeezed his fingers with hers. "But here we are."

Tim nodded. "Too late to undo it now anyway."

"Would you if you could? Undo it?"

Tim hesitated for a beat, thought about that, and then shook his head. "No. What happened had to happen." Now he cupped her hand in both of his. "We'll be fine. This'll just take a little getting used to."

The waitress appeared with two plates. "You lovebirds break it up. Here's lunch."

Tim released Martha's hand and sat back as the plates were placed in front of them.

"Ketchup and mustard's there. You need anything else right now?"

"This'll do it," Tim said.

"I'll check back shortly."

They ate silently for a few minutes until Martha said, "It really will be okay."

"I know."

Chapter 28

Claire pulled to the curb outside the impound yard, and I slid my Porsche in behind her. She wanted to see the SUV, but then had to get to the station to prep her evening report, so she drove herself and T-Tommy rode with me. We walked through the open chain-link gate. The Fosters' SUV sat in the middle of the lot, the other impounds slotted around the periphery. Sidau Yamaguchi and his crew were working it over. Derrick Stone stood nearby, talking on his cell phone.

The vehicle was dirty, muddy tires, spatters on the side panels and wheel wells, but I didn't see any damage. From what I knew of the Fosters, this seemed odd. Their home and yard were meticulously clean, even in the middle of a move or whatever they were doing. But this? The SUV was a mess. Not sure what that meant, but it didn't fit. And when things don't fit, there's a reason.

Stone closed his cell as we walked his way.

"What you got?" T-Tommy asked.

"Patrol recognized the vehicle from the BOLO we put out. Motoring down University. Pulled it over. Two kids inside."

"Kids?" Claire said.

"Fifteen and fourteen. Brothers. Desean and Tyrell Richards. Said they found it over off Ninth. Windows down, keys inside. Took it for a ride. Said they were going to take it back after they went to the mall and drove through McDonald's. They were eating burgers when they were pulled over."

"Where are they?" I asked.

"Over at the station. Just got a call. Their parents have arrived. Apparently not happy."

"Anything in the car?" I walked toward it.

Sidau was on his knees in the rear cargo area, shining a Maglite beneath the backseat. He saw me and backed out.

"Car's pretty clean on the inside. Not as in scrubbed, but no trash. Except for the McDonalds' bag the kids left." He passed the light to one of his techs. "No damage. No visible blood. We're just starting though. Got to vacuum for trace and dust for prints. That'll take a while. I'll let you know what I turn up." He walked toward the front of the SUV where one of his techs was rolling out two long strips of white paper, while another prepared to ink the front tires.

"It looks like it's been off-roading or something," Claire said.

"Maybe the kids took a little cross-country joyride," Sidau said.

A uniformed officer, standing with two others near his patrol car some one hundred feet away, called to Stone. Stone excused himself and headed that way.

"Do you think the Fosters could've been abducted?" Claire asked. "The bad guys dump their car here and take them away in another vehicle?"

"You been talking to T-Tommy?" I asked.

"What?" Claire said.

"He came up with the same theory."

"Not really a theory," T-Tommy said. "More like a random thought."

"Which you have often," Claire said.

T-Tommy grunted.

"So, isn't it possible?" Claire asked.

"Make a good story, wouldn't it?"

"Don't go there, Walker."

"I'm just saying—"

"And I'm just saying isn't it possible?"

"Yes, it's possible," I said. "But mostly it doesn't wash." I nodded toward the SUV. "No pun intended."

Claire shot me a look but wouldn't be deterred by my feeble humor. "Why?"

"Too complicated. Why wouldn't they simply load the Fosters into the getaway car at their home? Why complicate it with dumping the SUV on a busy street? Expose themselves that way? Doesn't make sense."

"Dub, do criminals ever make sense?" Claire asked.

She had a point. "This waltz would really complicate things," I said.

"Maybe they nabbed the Fosters somewhere else?" Claire said. "Not at their house. Maybe near where their SUV was found?"

"You mean like scamming the Fosters to meet them somewhere and then nabbing them?" T-Tommy asked.

"Something like that."

"What could they offer a couple that's getting ready to disappear?" T-Tommy asked.

Claire hesitated a beat as if thinking, and then said, "Maybe something they needed to pull off their disappearing act? New driver's licenses? Passports? Hell, maybe they told them they won the lottery."

T-Tommy gave her a slow nod. "That's a lot more than simply moving to Arizona. New passports? That would take this to a whole different level."

"Still, what if they did take them from home?" Claire said. "Took them out someplace." Now she nodded toward the SUV. "Someplace muddy, whacked them, buried them, and then dumped their SUV where it was found."

"That does make some sense," T-Tommy said.

"I agree," I said. "But the question is who would kill both Whitiker and the Fosters? Why would they? What's the connection?"

"Whitiker was a child molester," Claire said. "Maybe he belonged to one of those child abduction rings."

"Go ahead," I said.

"I did a piece on them about a year ago. They're huge. Thousands of members. Nationwide."

"How would the Fosters fit into that?"

"I don't know. But as you said, they have secrets."

"You're not suggesting that Tim and Martha had anything to do with what happened to their son are you?" I asked.

"Lord, no," Claire said. "I can't imagine that."

"Then what?"

She hesitated a beat and then said, "Maybe they knew about Whitiker and this ring."

"Wouldn't they have brought that up at Whitiker's trial?" T-Tommy asked. "They wanted him put away for life."

"Or executed," I said.

"Unless they found out about it recently," Claire said. "Maybe they were keeping it as an ace in the hole in case Whitiker ever found them. Something like that."

"And you're thinking Whitiker might've known that they knew—if that's the case," I said.

"Not just Whitiker. The group. These perverts stick together. They share information and photos and all kinds of vile crap. They also help each other stay off the radar. Maybe some members learned that the Fosters knew about Whitiker and, by extension, the group. Or maybe they just feared they might. Either way they would do anything to avoid exposure. Getting rid of Whitiker and the Fosters would be in their best interest."

On a couple of levels that made sense. On a few others, it didn't.

"Back when Whitiker was arrested," I said, "his computer was confiscated and torn apart. They found a batch of child porn on there but nothing that connected him to NAMBLA or any of the other child abuse organizations. Just a few porn sites and newsgroups."

"Why wasn't he charged with that? You know, having child pornography on his computer?"

"The DA thought about it, but in the end no one could testify with any certainty that Walter was the one that downloaded the material."

"It was his computer."

"But he often left it at the shop. Anyone could have used it."

"But not just anyone kidnapped and killed Steven Foster. Walter did."

"True. Still, the DA wasn't comfortable with filing on him for this."

"Too bad." A frown settled over her face. "Do you think Walter hurt any other children?"

"No evidence of that." I shrugged. "But he would have. People with that type of bad wiring can't avoid it. The need eats at them and sooner or later, if they've done it once, they'll do it again. But I believe Steven was Walter's first."

"Why?"

"He wasn't very good. Serial predators in the making occasionally get caught their first time around the block. They're unprepared and inept, make critical mistakes. Thank God. If they get away with it several times, they get better at it. Learn to be a more skillful predator. That makes them very hard to track down. Better to get them early."

"Dub, I know you're pretty good at thinking like a criminal," Claire said.

"Thanks."

"It wasn't a compliment. In fact, it's a bit disturbing."

"And I thought you loved me."

"I do, but that doesn't mean you're not weird."

That definitely wasn't a compliment. I started to say so, but before I could she continued, probably saving me from myself yet again.

"Why do you think Walter was a novice?"

"A handful of reasons. He snatched Steven in the light of day a couple of hundred feet from his home. Where everyone knew Steven and would know that Steven had no business being in a car with a man that wasn't Tim. And on a Sunday when most people would be at home, or going back and forth to church, not at work. Makes for a host of possible witnesses."

"But only Martha saw the abduction," Claire said.

"Only takes one witness. And she did identify Walter and his van." Claire nodded.

"Then old Walter didn't clean the inside of his van, so Steven's DNA was found, and he didn't trash his hard drive, so the files were found. Not very smart. Amateurish."

Claire shoved her hands into the back pockets of her jeans. "Then what do you think's going on here?"

"The scary version?"

"Sure. Why not?"

"If the Fosters dumped their car, they planned it all and had another vehicle waiting. Which means they are definitely on the run and trying to disappear. From what? Either they are truly afraid Walter Whitiker would come after them or something else spooked them enough to leave everything we saw at the house behind." I looked at Claire. "Or they killed Whitiker."

"You don't believe that," Claire said.

"I don't know what I believe yet. But if they did, it sure would explain this disappearing act."

"And the mud on the tires," T-Tommy said. "If this is the vehicle that left the impressions we saw near the sniper site, that'll more or less seal the deal."

We stood silently for a minute, letting the implications of that sink in.

Finally Claire said, "If they did, I can't say that I'd blame them."

"It'd be a ballsy move," T-Tommy said.

You got that right, big guy.

"Let's go talk to the kids," I said. "Maybe they saw something."

Chapter 29

The kids, Desean and Tyrell, turned out to be tall, lanky, black, and scared. They sat at the table in the interrogation room. They wore oversized jeans that bunched around their ankles, oversized tee shirts that looked more like nightshirts on their thin frames, and had the oversized eyes of someone caught in a bad situation.

Their stern-faced parents stood behind them.

T-Tommy and I introduced ourselves.

Jamal Richards, the father, a big man with a shaved head, a scowl on his face, and a crushing handshake, looked me in the eye as we shook hands. Marissa, the mother, a thin, attractive woman, with perfectly cornrowed hair, seemed more embarrassed than angry. She nodded and gave me a half smile but mostly kept her gaze aimed at the floor.

T-Tommy sat down across from the brothers. "Want to tell me about it?"

"We didn't do nothing," Desean said.

His father thumped him on the back of his head. "You tell the truth. Everything or I'll whip your butts right here."

"But, Dad—"

"But nothing. Your mother and I had to take off work and come down here to deal with this—stupidity. You think we can afford that? You know those new sneakers you guys wanted? That's what I was working to pay for. You can kiss them goodbye."

T-Tommy leaned forward and lowered his head to look Desean in the eye. "Well?"

Desean's head bobbed a couple of times. He looked up at T-Tommy. "It was just sitting there. The keys were there like they wanted us to take it."

Jamal thumped him again. "Don't you dare try to justify this, boy. You hear me? You took that car. It wasn't yours. You ain't even old enough to drive. Now you tell the officer what he wants to know and no more BS."

Tears collected in the young man's eyes and he wiped them away with the back of one hand. "We just wanted to go to the mall. We was going to take it back after we was done."

"Did you see anyone there?" I asked. "Near the car?"

His head came up. "We wouldn't of taken it if they was. We watched for a long time. Maybe half an hour. No one came to get it, so we borrowed it."

Jamal's face tightened, but he said nothing.

"Borrowed, huh?" T-Tommy leaned his elbows on the table. "Did you find anything in the car? Throw anything out?"

"No."

"Did you take it anywhere else? Maybe out in a field or something?"

Desean gave T-Tommy a what-the-hell-are-you-talking-about look. "We just went by the mall and then got something to eat. That's all. We was headed to leave it back on the street when we got stopped."

Jamal rolled his eyes and shook his head. I could tell he was struggling to keep his anger in check. I looked at him and smiled.

"I was planning to repaint the house," Jamal said. "Wasn't sure whether to do it myself or hire it out." He laid a hand on Desean's shoulder. "But I think I just found my crew."

Life for Desean and Tyrell just got ugly. Didn't matter whether the police brought charges or not, I could tell by Jamal's tight jaw his boys would pay for their sins.

T-Tommy asked a few more questions but got nothing. These kids simply took a joyride. That's it. They didn't know anything else.

Chapter 30

I sat on a stool hunched over the clean sheet of butcher's paper Sidau had laid out on a metal exam table. Before heading over to Sammy's to meet Claire, T-Tommy, and Derrick Stone, I had decided to swing by the Forensic Science Department to see what Sidau had. I found him here in the Firearm's Lab. The bullet from Walter's autopsy, the bullet fragments found at the prison shooting scene, and the long rubber cement cast of the rifle barrel Sidau had made lay before me.

"After I injected the rubber cement and let it set," Sidau said, "I wasn't exactly sure how to extract it from the barrel without damaging it. I finally put the barrel into the fridge for a couple of hours. The cast shrank enough that I could pull it out without much effort."

"Looks good."

Sidau handed me a magnifying glass. "See what you think."

First I examined the intact bullet taken out of Walter and compared it with the rubber cast, letting my gaze travel up and down each, over and over, back and forth. I saw nothing similar. No striations that even came close to matching. I looked up at Sidau.

"Nothing. Right?" he said.

I nodded. "So this isn't the murder weapon?"

"Not so fast." Sidau pointed to the larger of the two fragments of the other bullet. "Check out this one."

Again, I compared the single intact surface of the fragment with the cast, rolling the latter as I examined every inch of it.

I sat up straight. "Not sure I see anything here either."

"I have a bit of an advantage since I spent an hour with it." He rolled the cylindrical casting back and forth until he found the surface he was looking for. "Start here." He pointed to an area near the breach end. "Follow this land and groove pair to here."

Looking through the magnifying glass, I followed as he trailed his finger along the cast, slowly rotating it to track the spiral of the groove. He stopped about six inches short of the damaged area near the muzzle.

"Now look at the fragment," he said.

I did. Took a few minutes, but I saw it. The land and groove pair could have laid down the striations seen on the bullet. Or not. That was the problem. In court, close wouldn't count. If Sidau couldn't sit in the witness box and state with certainty that this bullet passed down this barrel, then he might as well not show up. A match is a match, and no match is no match. Couldn't be a maybe and carry any weight.

"I see what you're saying," I said. "Unfortunately, close doesn't quite get it."

I placed the magnifying glass on the paper and spun toward him on the stool.

"So the bullet pulled out of Walter definitely did not come from this gun, but the fragmented one might have?"

Sidau nodded.

"But regardless, we have two weapons involved."

"Exactly."

That was a game changer. Two guns. Two shooters. If Tim and Martha did do this, then they both fired a shot. But why leave behind one rifle and not the other? Didn't make sense.

"According to Drummond," Sidau said, "the bullet he extracted at autopsy, the good one, collapsed the right lung and embedded in the back muscles. Not a lethal shot. The fragmented one passed between the fifth and sixth ribs and nicked the heart, actually ripped away the left atrial appendage. Then punctured the left lung, ripped a chunk out of the descending aorta, clipped a posterior rib, and exited the body. It then struck the fence near where you were and cracked in two parts."

It was easy to see why my CPR efforts hadn't worked. With the left atrial appendage torn away and the aorta trashed, he was essentially dead before he reached the ground.

"So the fragment is the killing bullet?" I asked.

"Sure looks that way."

"What else you got?" I asked

He smiled. His eyebrows did a little dance. So Sidau. Saving the best for last. The punch line.

"Come on."

I followed him down the hall to another room. Sidau sat down in front of his computer.

"Grab a chair," he said.

I rolled a chair over next to him and sat. Three photos were on the screen.

"Here," he pointed to the leftmost image, "is a photo of one of the tracks we found near the probable sniper site." He moved his finger to the middle picture. "This is a photo of the cast we made of that track, and this last one is the inked impression I made of the right front tire of the Fosters' SUV."

I leaned closer. The similarities were obvious.

"Look at this gouge here." Sidau pointed out a nick in one of the lugs. "And the sipe pattern here."

Sipes are narrow grooves cut into the lugs and ribs of the tire tread. They add traction for the driver and evidence for the forensic examiner.

"Fairly new tires," I said. "The sipes are pretty clean."

"Exactly. And for good measure." He handed me a photograph. A close-up of a tire tread. "Same tire, different part of the tread." He pointed to a small rock that had wedged into one of the grooves. Again he worked the keyboard. Another pair of images appeared.

I saw it immediately. The photo, the impression left in the soft dirt, and the inked pattern Sidau had made each showed the same stone. Identical in size, shape, contour, and location. Powerful evidence.

Luckily it hadn't been thrown free between the time the impression was left at the scene and the SUV was found. Sometimes, most times, investigations require a slice of luck. This definitely fit.

No doubt the Fosters' SUV left tire impressions at the shooting scene.

Son of a bitch.

Chapter 31

T-Tommy and Derrick Stone were late. Supposed to be here by seven. They'd been off following leads while I swung by to see Sidau. I had arrived at Sammy's around five thirty and sat in with Colin Dogget. I played his 1941 Martin. Loved that guitar. Smooth and strong. We went through mostly old Delta stuff—John Lee Hooker's "Boom Boom" and "Boogie Chillen," Robert Johnson's "Hellhound on my Trail" and "Sweet Home Chicago," Charlie Patton's "Pony Blues" and "Mississippi Bo Weavil Blues," and a few others.

I sang a couple of them but mostly laid back, fell into a groove, and let Colin sing and work his slide over my rhythm. Gave me time to think, let my mind try to get around Tim and Martha Foster, come to some kind of understanding of what they'd done.

They shut down their lives. Closed out their bank account. Took off to who knows where. Haven't used credit cards or their cell phone. Left everything they owned in their house. Dumped their car.

After leaving tire tracks at a murder scene.

I didn't much care for the inescapable conclusion.

Claire showed up around seven, nodded to Colin and me, grabbed a stool at the bar, and sipped wine while she chatted with Sammy, her head nodding slightly in time with the music. Even though I couldn't hear it over our playing, I had earlier seen her six o'clock report on the TV Sammy had mounted high behind the bar. Just to the right of the large Bear Bryant picture that scowled down on the bar as if saying, "Stop drinking and get to work, slackers." No slack in The Bear.

I knew Claire's report had focused on the murder of Walter Whitiker and the now missing Tim and Martha Foster. The faces of all three appeared on the screen at one time or another during the broadcast. Claire and I had discussed her story and decided that it wouldn't hurt to get the public involved in looking for the Fosters. Of course she still assumed this was a missing-persons case. Didn't yet know it was beginning to smell like something all together different.

She'd obviously come directly from the studio since she still wore the same outfit I'd seen on TV. Gray slacks and a dark-green silk blouse, the only difference her red hair, which was now pulled back into a thick ponytail. She spun on her stool and smiled at me as Colin and I finished the set and acknowledged the applause from the crowd that had run right through hump-day happy hour, two for one, and were now soaking up alcohol like it was the weekend, with no regard for tomorrow's workday.

Want people to appreciate your music? Feed them alcohol. Makes everything sound better.

I joined Claire at the bar. Sammy poured me a Blanton's, neat.

"Did you see my report tonight?" Claire asked.

"Saw it. Couldn't hear it."

"It went well. Maybe we'll get some calls on the Fosters."

I felt a hand on my shoulder. It was T-Tommy. He and Stone had arrived.

Sammy splashed a dose of Blanton's into a glass and handed it to T-Tommy, popped the cap off a PBR longneck for Stone, and then moved along the bar wiping its already clean surface.

"We need to talk," T-Tommy said.

The four of us moved to a corner table. One of the waitresses appeared, menus beneath one arm. She was new. Said her name was Tina. She handed Claire a menu, but Claire waved it away, saying she knew it by heart. I added that we all did, so she took our orders and headed toward the kitchen.

T-Tommy started to say something, but I held up a hand. "You better hear this first."

"Sidau?" he asked.

I nodded. "The test-fired bullets weren't much help, but the rubber cement injection was. The match isn't strong enough to stand up in court but to me—Sidau too—it looks like a match. The rifle found at the scene fired one of the bullets."

T-Tommy frowned. "One?"

"The other one, the one Drummond dug out of Walter, came from a different weapon."

"Two shooters?" Stone asked.

"Looks that way."

Stone shook his head. "The rifle was a semiauto. I just assumed it fired both shots."

"Me, too," I said. "Which raises the question—where is the other weapon? Why take one and leave one?"

T-Tommy grunted. Like me, he hates it when things don't make sense.

"I can see tossing the weapons at the scene," Stone said. "If you've wiped them down and there is no chance of them being traced back, then okay. That's better than getting caught with them in the trunk of your car. And I can see taking them and dumping them far away or destroying them. But doing both—or I guess one of each—doesn't make any sense at all."

I shrugged. "I can think of a couple of reasons. Maybe the shooters decided to keep one in case they got cornered and had to shoot their way out. Or maybe they hoped leaving behind a damaged rifle, one that couldn't be matched to the bullets, would hide the fact that there were two shooters."

"So we spin our wheels looking for one dude instead of two?" Stone said.

"Of course, the two bullets wouldn't match each other so we'd know two weapons were involved anyway."

"Unless one or both were so damaged a match wasn't possible," T-Tommy said.

"That was almost the case. But no way they could have predicted that."

"So who are the two shooters?" T-Tommy asked.

I took a slug of bourbon. "There's more."

All eyes turned in my direction.

"What are you?" T-Tommy asked. "A drama queen?"

"Just been around Sidau too long, I guess. Save the best for last."

T-Tommy shook his head. "Please enlighten us, Mr. Wizard."

Claire laughed at that. She can be so insensitive sometimes. Really, she can.

"The tire tracks?" I said. "The ones at the sniper site? They match the Fosters' SUV."

T-Tommy cradled his drink in his massive hands and looked at me over the rim. "You're sure?"

"No doubt." I told him about the nicks and the stone in the treads.

Here's how it works: Almost any item of evidence can be considered to have either class or individual characteristics. Class characteristics put it into a definable group; individual ones separate it from all the other members of the class. For example, a tire track might show a certain tread pattern and this can be traced to the manufacturer: Dunlop, Goodyear, Michelin, or whoever. The width might indicate tire size. So this evidence alone narrows the possible tires that could have made the impression to a certain manufacturer and a certain size. All tires that match those characteristics remain suspect; all others are excluded.

Now add the wear pattern, and cuts, and nicks, and rocks imbedded in the tread and you have individualizing characteristics. No two tires wear the same way or pick up the same cuts, and nicks, and pebbles. If these defects are identical when a crime-scene impression is compared to a suspect tire, then this tire, to the exclusion of all others in the class, left the impression. Like the Fosters' SUV tire.

"Jesus," Stone said. "They did it."

"Sure looks that way," I said. "At least they were at the scene."

T-Tommy spread his hands on the table. "Why else would they be there? In that location? At that time?"

"Couldn't those tracks be old?" Claire asked.

"They were fairly fresh." I said.

"Just not necessarily yesterday morning," Claire said.

I hate it when she's in her smart-ass mode. "True. But if not that morning, shortly before. Couple of days at the most."

"How can you say that?"

"The thunderstorm we had last weekend? What day was that?"

"Friday," T-Tommy said.

"These tracks were laid down since then. They were clean. No erosion of the edges. A good rain'll do that."

"So they were put there sometime between Saturday and Tuesday, the morning of the killing?" Claire asked.

I nodded. "But like T-Tommy said, why else would they be up in the woods across from the prison unless they came for Whitiker?"

"Then there's the whole dumping their car thing," Stone said.

"And this explains the muddy tires," T-Tommy said.

I nodded. "Yes, it does."

"So you're saying that Tim and Martha are the two shooters?" Claire said.

"Maybe."

"And you think they could do that? That Martha Foster could shoot someone?"

"He killed her child," I said. "Her only child."

"If they did it then she must have," Stone said. "Can't see a reason Tim would use two rifles."

Everyone fell silent for a minute and then I asked, "What do you guys have?"

T-Tommy scratched an ear. "Some more shit that don't look so good for the Fosters." He nodded to Stone.

"We interviewed a half dozen neighbors and three of Tim Foster's coworkers," Stone said. "Each of them said there was no way Tim Foster would kill Whitiker. Felt that he might want to, that the murder of his son had knocked him sideways, but that he and Martha had recovered and were simply planning to move away and leave all this behind. Far as anyone knows, they're off to Phoenix. No one knew how to contact them except through Martha's cell phone. Everyone one of them said that the Fosters would send them their new address and phone number when they got settled."

"Sounded almost like a rehearsed bit," T-Tommy said. "Everyone used the same words, same phrases. Like they had huddled beforehand."

"Are you saying that all their friends are in on some grand conspiracy?" Claire asked.

"Everybody we talked to parroted what the neighbor and Martha's sister said. To the letter."

I looked at Claire. "Ooh, a conspiracy. Right up your alley."

She elbowed me in the ribs. It hurt. Claire's elbows are as sharp as her tongue.

"What?" I asked.

"You want some real damage? Keep it up."

I rubbed my ribs. "All I'm saying is that none of this means conspiracy. Not on their friends' part anyway."

"Then what?" Stone asked.

"The Fosters. They probably rehearsed what they would tell everyone. Over and over until it became automatic. Didn't want to send conflicting signals. Wanted everyone to believe they were off to Arizona. These people simply repeated what they were told."

"Makes sense," T-Tommy said.

"It also means that Phoenix is a total head fake," I said.

Chapter 32

Sammy appeared with our food, plates lined up one arm. Tina flanked him with another round of drinks.

"Anything else?" Sammy asked.

Everyone declined and dug in. Sammy headed back toward the bar.

"What else you got?" I asked.

"The money trail," T-Tommy said.

Ah, yes. Money. Always follow the money. It'll tell you where someone has been, and sometimes where they are and where they're going.

"There's been no credit card use," T-Tommy continued. "No mail or magazine subscription forwarding address. No evidence of a home purchase or rental in the Phoenix area. Your head fake idea just might be the deal."

"Why would you ever doubt I was right?"

Claire shook her head. T-Tommy grunted. Neither was very impressed.

"We went by their bank," Stone said. "Jackson Bank over by Five Points. Spoke with Quinton Moore, the manager." He glanced at me. "You know him don't you?"

"Sure. I use the same bank. Known Quinton for years."

"He said Tim Foster had removed fifteen thousand in cash from his account seven times over the past six months. Martha Foster took out another twenty K in five K bites over the same timeframe. Then they took the last seven thousand or so on Monday. No funds were forwarded to another bank."

"That's a hundred and thirty-two K," I said. I'm good with math.

"That's not the creative part," T-Tommy said. "Foster had just over three hundred thousand in a pension account. We talked to his broker. Apparently he closed that account about six months ago, walked out with a cashier's check, and went over to Redstone Savings and Loan."

"When was Whitiker's early release announced?" I asked.

T-Tommy smiled. "About two weeks before Tim closed the account."

Claire drained her wine glass. "So they did plan this for months."

I looked at T-Tommy. "Let me guess, not all the three hundred K made it to Redstone."

"The amount was actually three hundred and twelve thousand. Tim deposited two-fifty and walked out with the other sixty-two in cash."

"The guys at Redstone didn't balk at that?" I asked. "Him walking out with that much cash?"

"He told them he was buying into a land deal over on Guntersville Lake. Seller wanted cash."

"And they were happy to get the two hundred fifty K deposit."

"Exactly."

I took a sip of bourbon. "Bet the rest didn't stay at Redstone very long."

T-Tommy laughed. "No wonder you write all those books."

I shrugged. Claire shook her head and gave me that look. The one that said, "You aren't nearly as clever as you think."

"The money got moved from Redstone to First National, to Cotton States Bank, to Union Bank, and finally to Madison Savings and Loan. Each time the nut got smaller until it evaporated."

"How'd you get the warrants to do all this?" I asked.

"It was a horse race," Stone said. "We had guys running paperwork all over the city, back and forth to Feigler's office."

Judge Andrew Feigler was arguably the most cop/DA friendly judge in the neighborhood. His warrant threshold was fairly low as was his threshold for allowing evidence into a trial. Unlike Ben Kleinman who was at times openly hostile to the prosecution. Of course Kleinman's disallowing the DNA evidence in Walter Whitiker's trial had inadvertently signed Walter's death warrant so there was that.

"Feigler was very helpful on this," T-Tommy said. "Once he saw what we had, he signed off on everything without question."

"We humped from bank to bank," Stone said. "A couple of times we had to wait for the warrant to arrive. We got to Union just before it closed, and the guys over at Madison let us in the back door since we didn't get there until well after closing time."

"Good work."

"Couldn't have done it without Feigler."

"So they've walked away with nearly half a million in cash?" Claire asked. She's good with math, too.

T-Tommy nodded. "Looks that way."

Claire flipped her ponytail from one shoulder to the other. "How do you walk out of a bank nowadays with that much cash? How do you bleed out a pension account without raising eyebrows?"

Stone propped an elbow on the edge of the table. "Only the brokerage firm knew the money was in a roll-over IRA. He told them he was simply moving to another institution. Of course, the withdrawal would be reported to the IRS, but that wouldn't come into play until he filed his next tax return. Then he'd have to show that it went into another IRA account or face the wrath of the IRS."

"Makes sense," Claire said.

"He had a similar story for each bank. At Redstone it was the property over on Guntersville Lake. At First National he showed up with a cashier's check for the two-fifty from Redstone but took fifty-five of it in cash. Supposedly for a down payment on a new house. Owner would carry the note but wanted the down payment in cash." T-Tommy hit his bourbon. "At Cotton States the cash was for a cabin down on Smith Lake."

"And so on," I said.

"Until the pot was empty," Stone said.

Another sip of bourbon and T-Tommy said, "Just before we came over here, we swung by the Fosters' place again."

"No warrant?" Claire asked.

"We were just checking on Tim and Martha's well-being. Like Dub and I did before. Don't need a warrant for that."

"So now you're buying into my abduction theory?"

She can be such an ass.

T-Tommy shrugged. "Wouldn't exactly say that."

"Find anything?" I asked T-Tommy.

"Remember that bag of shredded paper we saw?"

"Yeah?"

"Found another boxful in the closet of his makeshift office and a stuffed garbage bag in the garage. He must've shredded thousands of pages."

"Cleaning house," I said. "Dumping everything. Didn't want to leave any personal papers behind and didn't want to take them."

"Why wouldn't they keep old bank records and business papers?" Claire asked.

"Because they're disappearing," I said. " Dropping off the radar. If they did Whitiker, as it looks like they did, they know they'll have to dig a deep hole. A murder charge never goes away. Need to break all connections back here. If someone stumbled on checks or records or photos or anything with their old names or identities on it, their cover could go up in smoke."

"You're saying they have new identities?" Claire asked.

"That'd be my guess. You can't just whack someone, move to the next county, and live happily ever after."

"How do you do that?" Claire asked. "Create new IDs?"

"It can be tricky, but new IDs can be found on cemetery headstones, birth certificates of anyone who died young, or Social Security numbers of dead folks whose death hasn't been reported to the Social Security Administration. The law says deaths have to be reported to Social Security, but that doesn't always happen. The file gets pushed aside, ends up in a dusty filing cabinet in the basement of some county building, and the years go by. The person's gone, but his Social Security number is alive and well." I looked at Claire. "New identities come from information that slides into bureaucratic cracks."

Claire gave me a slow nod. "Tim Foster worked for the Madison

County License Department. Bet he had easy access to all kinds of information."

"Bingo," I said.

"We're working on that," T-Tommy said. "A warrant to search his office computer." He smiled toward Claire.

"So nice of you to recognize the law."

"Oh, I recognize it. Just think it's a bit sluggish sometimes."

"Good excuse to stomp all over it."

"I prefer to tiptoe around it," T-Tommy said.

"Rationalization."

"I don't remember you being such a stickler when we crashed into Talbert's place."

"That was a hostage rescue."

"And you made a great hostage. Particularly in your birthday suit."

"Can it, Tortelli. Or do you want a subdural hematoma to go with your bourbon?"

Ouch.

T-Tommy raised his palms in defense.

"Doubt he used it," I said.

Everybody looked at me.

"His office computer," I continued. "Probably used someone else's or an off-site one. I'm getting the impression that Tim Foster is a very clever dude."

"Sure looks that way," Stone said.

"That brings up a question," Claire said. "Why shred all those documents if you're changing your ID and disappearing? Seems like a colossal waste of time."

"First of all, they had plenty of time. Six months between when they apparently began planning this and when they pumped a couple of rounds into Walter Whitiker. Secondly, people who try to disappear are often caught because they left behind something that leads to them. You just never know what little bit of info will unravel even the most tightly wound ball. They were just being overly cautious. Pretty impressive actually."

"So how do you find them?" Claire asked.

I sighed. "Won't be easy. If they've planned this for months, destroyed everything that could be a loose end, and managed to dig up clean identities, they'll be a bitch to track." I drained my glass. "Unless they contact someone back here."

"Like the sister," T-Tommy said.

"That'd be my guess."

"On it," Stone said. He nodded toward T-Tommy.

"I called Feigler on the way over. Asked for a warrant on the sister's phones. He said if we made a probable-cause application, he'd sign off on her phone records. Both home and cell. But he wouldn't give us a tap and trace. Said that we had no evidence that the sister was involved, even if the Fosters had pulled some financial shenanigans and disappeared. Said that a tap and trace would violate her privacy rights."

Feigler's threshold might be low but it wasn't nonexistent.

"Did you tell him that the sister might be our only link to them?" I asked.

T-Tommy nodded. "He wouldn't budge."

"Add what Sidau uncovered today and maybe he'll change his mind," I said.

"Let's hope."

"What about their ISP?" I asked. "Anything on that?"

"Feigler signed off on that," Stone said. "I got a guy working on it."

Chapter 33

THURSDAY, 1:14 A.M.

I eased out of bed, careful not to wake Claire. We had stayed at Sammy's until around ten, and then she followed me home. Her idea. I didn't mind. Our divorce didn't preclude spending quality time together. We had showered and made love. Afterward, Claire curled on one side, her back snuggled up against me, and drifted to sleep, her breathing quickly settling into a steady rhythm.

Not me. Not unusual. I rarely slept well when working a case. The committee in my head kept banging gavels and yelling at each other. I couldn't understand half of what was said, voices walking over each other, everything muddied by some weird feedback hum, like a guitar amp that needed new tubes. I hated it when they argued, unable to make a decision. About anything.

I could use a little help here, guys.

I slipped on a pair of shorts, no shirt, snagged a bottle of water from the fridge, and went outside. Stars blanketed the sky and a half moon peeked through the pecan trees in my neighbor's yard. I stepped off the deck and walked to the back of my property. The grass felt cool and lush beneath my bare feet, dew-dampened blades insinuating themselves between my toes. I looked out over the city. Quiet, except for the cars that moved along Memorial Parkway in the distance.

I liked this spot. The dark solitude of my backyard, the grass spongy beneath my feet, the trees above catching the lazy breeze, leaves rustling softly, the city sleeping below. Did some of my best thinking here. Usually in the middle of the night. Usually when a case crawled inside my head and wormed around.

The Fosters did the worming tonight.

Here's what we knew:

> The Fosters split around the same time Whitiker was shot.
>
> They left a ton of personal stuff and furniture at their house.
>
> They had a bedroom shrine to their son, yet walked away from his clothes, books, team photos, academic awards, everything.
>
> They dumped their car where it would be easily stolen and hopefully chopped into oblivion.
>
> Their SUV left tire tracks at the shooting site.
>
> They went through an elaborate two-step, actually more of a jitterbug, to turn their assets into untraceable cash.
>
> They were supposedly driving cross-country but hadn't called anyone or used any of their credit cards. Not even for gas.
>
> They probably had new identities and a new car registered to that name.
>
> The shooters, most likely both Martha and Tim Foster, wiped down one murder weapon and left it behind, while taking the second one with them.
>
> They were smart enough to damage the rifling of the abandoned weapon.

Here's the problems we faced:

> No fingerprints or DNA to connect the apparent murder weapon to the Fosters.
>
> The ballistics weren't all that good.
>
> No proof that they were driving the SUV when it laid down the tracks we found.
>
> No evidence that the Fosters ever owned a gun of any type.
>
> With clean identities, we had no way to track them.
>
> They were not headed for Phoenix.

We had no idea which direction to look.

With a wad of cash they could run to ground and stay low for a long time.

And then there's the gun. Why leave one and take one? Was the damage to the rifling an attempt to prevent matching and make it impossible to prove whether the gun found at the scene fired both bullets? And something that just came to mind, was Tim protecting Martha just in case they were caught? So he could say he was the lone shooter and if the damaged gun couldn't be matched to either bullet there would be no evidence to refute it.

I didn't have an answer for any of these. I did know that luck would be the key to this one. They might drop just the right bread crumbs that would lead us to them. Or might unexpectedly run into someone they knew. Someone from this life and not the new one they had surely created. Maybe contact someone back here, Martha's sister, Paige, being the best candidate.

I hated relying on luck, but sometimes that's the way it was. The problem was that luck had two edges. Could be good, could be not so good. Could look one way yet be the other. Could open the clouds and focus a beam of sunlight right on the Fosters' heads, or crawl up your shorts and bite your ass. You just never knew. Luck could be a fickle bitch.

What really bothered me was the Fosters themselves. Good people as far as I could tell. I had interviewed them after young Steven had been snatched and, even though they were shattered and knocked sideways, I sensed an inner strength in each of them. Was that strength what gave them the courage to kill Whitiker, dump everything, and slide away? Abandon their lives? Did they have the survival instinct and commitment to do all that?

I had watched them in the courtroom and on TV when Claire and others interviewed them. Never did I see any vindictiveness. Anger and sadness, sure, but they had absorbed all of Whitiker's threats and humiliations without flinching. They had trusted the police.

Good people.

The big question was could these good people have kept their anger inside? Hid it so well? Act like any other grieving parents while plotting to kill Whitiker when he next breathed free air?

For me, the answer was yes, they could have. But then I believe everyone has a dark side and given the right stressors anyone would kill. Not just for self-defense or to protect family, but also to protect their self-image, or a nasty secret, or to hide some other crime that could do them in.

And to revenge the murder of a child.

Chapter 34

THURSDAY, 1:59 A.M.

I heard footsteps behind me, soft and muffled by the grass, and then felt Claire's arms snake around me. Hard nipples against my flesh. Skin on skin.

"What are you wearing?" I asked.

"Your favorite outfit."

I reached back and ran my hand up her bare thigh and to her equally bare buttocks. "Is this what you call haute couture?"

"Hot couture."

I laughed. She kissed my back and then pressed her cheek against me. Her breath warm against my skin when she spoke.

"Thinking about the Fosters?"

"Yeah."

"And?"

"And nothing. Can't quite get my head around all this."

"You mean like why would a God-fearing Christian couple do this?" Claire asked.

"Something like that."

"People do odd things when stressed. I'd suspect everyone in their situation would entertain the thought. Revenge is sweet. Of course, thinking it and actually doing it are different sports altogether."

"You would," I said. "Given the same circumstances, I'd bet you could pull the trigger."

"Probably."

"Definitely."

"Like you wouldn't?"

"Of course, I would," I said. "T-Tommy, too."

"That goes without saying."

"But, the real question is: would the Fosters?"

"Sure looks that way."

"Yes, it does."

"To me," Claire said, " the big question is, how do they reconcile popping Whitiker with the stuff they teach at Bible school?"

"It's covered in the Bible," I said.

"So Jesus would approve?"

"Not in his domain. This isn't New Testament turn the other cheek stuff. More Old Testament eye for an eye."

She laughed. "Not sure a jury would buy that."

"They might. Remember that guy in Louisiana? Years ago. His daughter was kidnapped, tortured, raped, and murdered by some miscreant. The dude was arrested in another state and extradited back to Louisiana. The father waited in the airport and shot the scumbag as he walked off the plane. Right in the head. Right in front of the police. Jury let him go. Justifiable homicide. Same thing here."

She was silent for a minute, her cheek still pressed against my back, and then she said, "This isn't personal."

"Sure it is. It always is."

I knew it always would be. My sister, Jill, was my phantom limb. One that had been amputated yet still there. The brain conjuring pain, tingling, and a cold, dead numbness in an appendage that no longer existed. Jill had been amputated from my life on a cold, drizzly night in the UAB Medical Center parking lot. A night I didn't show up as promised. Then she was gone. Just like that. Now only pain and numbness remained.

The Fosters had suffered the same trauma. The same amputation. Steven gone; Steven still there. Always there. Always painful and cold and numb.

A knot arose in my gut and the tears that began forming in my eyes blurred the parade of car lights, far below along Memorial Parkway, into hazy white ribbons. God, I hated this feeling. I was sure the Fosters did too. I swallowed hard.

"It doesn't have to be," Claire said.

"Of course it does. If it's not personal, why get involved in the first place?"

"Maybe that's the answer. Don't get involved."

"What would T-Tommy do without me?"

"He's pretty good at what he does."

"Yes, he is. But he's better when we work together."

"True."

"Then there you go."

"You do this every time," Claire said.

"That's what you love about me."

"That's what I tolerate about you. I love this." Her hand slid down my stomach, beneath the waistband of my shorts, and gripped me.

"What will the neighbors say?"

She laughed, her breath playing across my back. "They're asleep."

"We should be, too."

"I was."

"What would your boyfriend say?"

She squeezed me. "Want to keep this?"

Time to change the subject. "Aren't you cold?"

"Yeah."

"Want to go back to bed?"

She didn't respond but rather turned and pulled me toward the house.

Chapter 35

Last night after Claire pull-toyed me back to bed we made love again and then eased into sleep. I woke at seven thirty to an empty bed, rolled out, tugged on my jeans, and followed the aroma of eggs and toast to the kitchen. Claire stood at the stove, barefoot, one of my tee shirts hanging to mid-thigh. I poured a cup of coffee and sat on a counter stool, facing her.

"Think you made enough?" I motioned to the mound of eggs she stirred in a cast iron skillet.

"I'm starving."

"Good sex will do that."

"Who said it was good?"

"You did. Over and over."

"Dream on."

"So you faked it?"

"News flash—us girls can do that."

"Not you though."

She pointed a spatula at me and laughed. "You know me too well."

Once the eggs were done, she spooned them onto plates, flanking them with two slices of buttered toast, and carried them out to the deck. I followed with glasses of orange juice and my cup of coffee.

Kramden and Norton showed up, fussing and squawking, hopping around the table, investigating what we had. While Claire held them at bay; I gave in. I tore off two pieces of toast, extending them toward the boys. They snatched the offerings and flapped out into the yard to eat.

After we finished, Claire cleared the table while I snapped open today's *Huntsville Times*. The murder of Walter Allen Whitiker still dominated the front page but just below the fold was a two-column story about the Fosters. The byline was Blaine Markland, the city editor. Mostly a rehash of their personal tragedy, the story did raise the question of whether the Fosters knew that Whitiker had been murdered. No hint that they were suspects; even Blaine with all his connections couldn't know that. Yet. The article ended with a note that the Fosters had moved away and could not be reached for comment.

No shit.

T-Tommy had put a lid on what we had uncovered yesterday. Didn't want to spook the Fosters in case they were still in the area. They weren't. No way. If they dropped Whitiker, they were gone. Far and fast. Still, in an investigation like this, it's better to keep your hole cards facedown.

Claire returned, now dressed, placed her purse on the table, and sat down. "Are the Fosters official suspects?"

I looked at her over the paper. "Not official."

"But you think they did it?"

"I think they might have done it."

"I want to go with a story that they could be suspects."

"Isn't that a little premature?"

"Is it?"

I took a sip of my coffee, now lukewarm. "You tell me."

"They were there, at the prison, when Walter was shot."

"Their SUV was there. Doesn't mean they were."

She flashed me that look. The one that said, "Are you an idiot?"

"Okay," I said. "The evidence isn't looking good for them."

"Which makes a story about them being suspects a hot property."

"And you want to break it?"

That look again. "Someone will."

I laid the open paper on the table and pointed to Markland's article. "See, even Blaine isn't thinking that way."

"That's because he doesn't know about the SUV tracks, but he will. He always digs up stuff like that."

"I'll talk to T-Tommy."

"Make sure he knows that if you two tie my hands and someone scoops me, I'll make you both wish you'd taken off with the Fosters."

She could, too. In a dozen ways I could think of and probably twice that many that I couldn't.

"I'll talk to him, but don't get your hopes up. I doubt he'll budge on this."

She stood and picked up her purse. "We'll see."

I walked her around the house to her car and watched as she drove away. I returned to the deck and stretched out on a lounge chair. A few clouds peppered the clear blue sky, drifting slowly to the east, looking like fluffy patches of torn cotton. In them I saw a clown, a horse head, and Mrs. McAllister, my sixth-grade civics teacher. What a hard-nosed bitch. Sent me to chat with the principal three times and once banned me from class for a week. And I didn't do anything. I swear.

And here she was memorialized in the heavens. I'd always assumed she'd go the other way.

While creating these cloud creatures, I went over and over what we knew about the Fosters. If they had clean IDs and stayed low to the ground, they could melt away forever. Unless we got lucky. But relying on luck didn't seem a good strategy. Better to be proactive.

When you're doing a skip trace, it helps if you know who your looking for. Not just name and physical description—the Fosters likely changed both—but really know them. Their habits, their hobbies, the organizations they belonged to, their behavior over the past few months, what they had told friends and coworkers. What things were important to their lives and what they could discard. People can change many things, but not their core values and interests. Those are ingrained for life.

If we were going to find the Fosters, I needed to know everything I could dig up about them. Maybe find some loose thread that would lead us to them.

I called T-Tommy, told him my plan, and asked if he wanted to join me, but he and Derrick Stone were following up on a couple of leads

on another unrelated case. He said that Feigler had given up a warrant
for the Fosters' house and Sidau and his crew had processed it early this
morning. Last he heard nothing earthshaking popped up. For sure,
nothing that would lead to the Fosters. He gave me the names of one
of Tim's coworkers and a couple of his golf buddies. I told him Claire
wanted to run with the suspect angle and that she couldn't be held back
much longer.

"You can't control her?" he asked. He didn't hide the laughter in his
voice very well.

"Want me to send her over there? Let you deal with her?"

"Not a chance."

"Then let's do an interview."

"That her idea?"

"Mine. Just thought of it. An interview would allow us to control
what's said." T-Tommy didn't respond, so I went on. "Getting the public involved just might help find them."

"I don't want the evidence we have floating around out there."

"We don't have to give anything away. Make it look like they're missing. Maybe victims. Ask for help in finding them."

"That's not what Claire wants."

"We'll just have to convince her that that's the best approach."

"Good luck with that."

He had a point. "Let's chat about it at lunch."

"Sammy's at noon work for you?"

"See you there."

After I hung up, I called Claire, told her T-Tommy was going soft,
might let her run with a few things, might even do an interview on
tonight's six o'clock. I told her to meet us at Sammy's for lunch.

I should've felt at least a twinge of guilt about setting T-Tommy up
that way but what the hell. He's a big boy. Why should I be the only one
painted with Claire's crosshairs?

Chapter 36

THURSDAY 8:27 A.M.

I figured that if I was going to dig into the Fosters' lives I would begin near their home with their neighbors and end with a second visit to Martha's sister, Paige Baker. When T-Tommy and I talked with her a couple of days ago, the day Walter Whitiker died of lead poisoning, I felt that she knew more than she let on. Not that I would blame her. Made sense. The Fosters were trying to disappear. She would help them. That's what family does. So when we went back over to Scottsboro for another chat, I wanted to have as much ammunition as possible.

I parked in front of the Fosters' house. Crime-scene tape now angled across the front door. I decided to start with the next-door neighbor, Sandy Sechrest. She didn't answer when I knocked, so I walked around back. I found her on her knees, trowel in hand, packing dirt around a fresh-looking tomato plant. She wore jeans and a work shirt, this one tan and dirt-smudged. I apologized for interrupting her gardening. She was gracious and asked if I wanted something to drink. Said she had some sweet tea in the fridge. Sure. She disappeared into the kitchen and returned with two large ice-packed glasses of rich caramel tea. We settled on her redwood deck at a round table with a furled green umbrella.

"Good tea," I said.

"Sun tea. Made it yesterday."

I took another gulp and placed the glass on the table, sweat already accumulating on and streaking its sides. "Beautiful garden," I said.

It was. Rows of thick hydrangeas flanked the yard and an explosion of azaleas, white, red, and lavender, hugged the back fence. A white gazebo, its lattice sides snaked with honeysuckle, sat between a large rectangular vegetable garden and several rows of multicolored rose bushes. Everything was perfectly manicured.

"Thanks. It takes work." She wiped perspiration from her face with the tail of her shirt. "Have you heard anything from Tim and Martha?" she asked.

"That's what I was going to ask you."

"Not a word." A sip of tea. "Do you really think they could be in danger?"

"It's possible, but maybe they just want to run away and hide."

"But Whitiker's dead now."

I nodded. "Yes, he is."

She looked out over her garden. Not really focused on anything as if she were creating some mental picture. "I'd bet they don't know yet. Probably hasn't made the news out in Arizona. If they've gotten that far." She looked back at me. "When they do hear about it, maybe they'll come back. No need to run off if he isn't around."

The light breeze carried the sweet aroma of honeysuckle. Nothing like it. A memory from my childhood. Growing up we had a thick wall of it along the side of the garage. I remembered plucking the flowers and tugging on the stamens to release a clear drop of sap. As sweet to the tongue as it was to the nose.

"If that's why they took off," I said.

"Why else?"

"That's what I'd like to ask them."

"So how can I help?"

"Tell me about them."

"Like what?"

"Anything and everything. Something that'll help me find them."

She stared at me for a minute.

"Look, you said yourself they could be in danger," I said. "Or they could be running scared from something that's no longer a problem."

"You think they had something to do with the Whitiker shooting, don't you?"

"We have no evidence that that's the case." A lie. A necessary one. "Talking with them would clear everything up."

"Is that why the police were over there this morning?"

"I imagine so."

"There was a mess of them. Three or four cops and I don't know how many of those CSI types. They backed their van right up to the house."

"What time was that?"

"Must have been early. I saw them around seven and it looked like they had been at it for a while." She swirled the tea in her glass. "They put that awful tape up, too. The yellow stuff. Any idea how long that'll stay there?"

"Until they finish their investigation."

"Investigation? They're investigating Tim and Martha?"

"They're investigating all sorts of people."

"They think Tim and Martha were involved, don't they? That's why all this is going on?"

"Maybe." Another lie. "Definitely" would have been a more accurate assessment. "They're just considering all the possibilities."

"I suppose." She looked back over her garden, seemed to focus on her azaleas for a beat, and then returned her gaze to me and sighed. "What do you want to know?"

"I know Tim worked over at the County Licensing Department. Did Martha work?"

"Not really. She did some substitute teaching. Junior high level. Also some volunteer work for the church. More so in the past couple of years. The first year after Steven disappeared, she barely left the house. Except to go to church."

"Where'd they attend?"

"Whitesburg Baptist."

"They were active there?"

"Very. Both taught classes. For middle and high schoolers, I think."

"What about hobbies?"

"Tim was an avid golfer. Martha took lessons. So did Steven. Until—well, after Steven was gone, Martha lost interest in golf. Everything else too. I think she was learning so she and Tim and Steven could do something together. As a family." She took a sip of tea. Another. "It's just so sad. So unnecessary."

I nodded. "Anything else?"

"Martha belonged to a quilting group. They got together every couple of weeks. She made some beautiful quilts. Gave me one for Christmas last year."

I didn't remember seeing any at the house. Must have taken them with them.

"They're both from here, aren't they?" I asked.

"Tim is. Martha was born over in Scottsboro. Her family moved here when she was in grade school. Her sister, the one I told you about the other day, moved back to Scottsboro maybe five years ago. Did you ever find her?"

"Yeah. We chatted."

"I take it she didn't know where Martha and Tim are."

"No."

"I assumed she would. They're very close."

"Did they travel much? Take vacations?"

She shook her head. "Not often. And very rarely since Steven's death."

"Recently? Say the last six months or so?"

"Last winter, just before Christmas I believe, they went to Gatlinburg for a few days. Then last month over to Myrtle Beach, South Carolina. Tim likes the golf there, and Martha loves sitting by the pool with a good book."

"Any trips out west?"

"Not that I know."

"Never mentioned Phoenix before?"

"Not until they said they were moving there."

"Why do you think they chose Phoenix? If they'd never been there."

She shrugged. "It seemed odd to me. They're Southern. Through and through."

I nodded, but said nothing.

"They love it here. Wouldn't have considered raising Steven any-where else. And Tim loved down-home Southern cooking. They prac-tically lived at Cracker Barrel."

Why not? Great Southern food. Of course, there were a couple of Cracker Barrels in the Phoenix area. I'd been to one of them.

We chatted for another twenty minutes, but I learned little else that would be of use. I thanked her and left.

I visited three more houses. A single mother who lived on the other side of the Fosters, a couple on the corner who were close friends, and an elderly woman across the street. The story was the same:

The Fosters were a kind, decent, God-fearing couple.

Good neighbors and good friends.

None had heard from them or knew where they were.

All assumed they were on their way to Phoenix.

All thought the move to Phoenix was odd.

All thought they would never leave the South.

All would miss them greatly.

All, without hesitation or qualification, believed there was ab-solutely no way they could have been involved in Whitiker's murder. Not possible.

Of course, they didn't know what I knew.

Chapter 37

After visiting the neighbors, I returned to the Foster house. Unlike two days ago, it now felt abandoned. Not that in the past forty-eight hours weeds and Johnsongrass had overgrown the manicured lawn, or the paint had curled and chipped from the clapboard, or the roof shingles had split or slid. Nothing like that. It simply felt abandoned.

Probably because I knew it had been. The Fosters had jettisoned this phase of their lives.

The front and back doors were locked, crime-scene tape across each. I don't know why I felt the need to look inside again, but I did. I needed some connection to the Fosters. And right now I didn't feel it. Talking with Sandy Sechrest and the other neighbors hadn't helped much. Each magpied the same story.

I probably should have called T-Tommy or Derrick Stone to come over and open the house up but I didn't. They were busy and I was impatient. Something Claire says I suffer from way too often. I couldn't argue with that. Instead, I used a credit card to nudge the lock of the garage side door. A trick T-Tommy taught me years ago. He would've made a great criminal.

Inside the garage was little of interest: a few boxes of old clothes and books, a canvas tarp, two bikes suspended on one wall, two sets of golf clubs propped in one corner: one women's, one child's, each covered with dust. Family golf outings ended when Steven was taken, the dusty clubs a remnant of the horror that fell on this home three years ago.

I opened the door to the house and entered the kitchen. Fingerprint powder smudged the cabinet and fridge handles. I glanced at my watch. For Sidau and his crew to have finished their work this early they must have started at 0-dawn-thirty. I wasn't surprised. Sidau was an early riser and on most days got more work done before breakfast than anyone I knew.

A pair of discarded latex crime-scene gloves and an empty evidence bag lay on the Fosters' abandoned kitchen table. The thought that the Fosters had sat at this very table and planned the killing of Walter Allen Whitiker crossed my mind. Did they create a to-do list? Make sketches? Did they argue over whether to go through with it or were they on the same page all the way? I'd bet on the latter.

I moved into the dining area and then from room to room. More powder on doorjambs and handles, light switches, phones. I knew Sidau had found no foreign prints. Looking for evidence of an abduction was simply being thorough, as Sidau always was. They weren't abducted. They ran.

None of Martha's quilts were in sight.

In the bedroom Tim had converted into a home office, I saw that the paper-filled trash can and shredder had been taken by Sidau and his crew. Escaped flakes littered the floor. I knelt and picked several of them up. Mostly paper, but some appeared to have been photos.

I imagined the Fosters standing here, shredding their memories. Afraid to take anything that led back here. Not wanting to leave anything behind. Going as deeply underground as they had obviously planned required some painful choices. Photos taken with friends, at family gatherings, on vacations, during Steven's school and sports events. The pictures families keep forever and pass down through the generations, all reduced to confetti.

It must have been like a coyote gnawing off a leg to escape a trap.

A fact that didn't bode well for finding them. It proved their level of commitment. It proved that they had planned this meticulously. It meant that they had probably left few, if any, clues in their wake.

I left the same way I had come in, fired up my Porsche, and headed south. Took fifteen minutes to reach the Madison County License Department, which sat along Bailey Cove Road near Weatherly.

The perky receptionist greeted me with a smile and said that she would take me right back. I had called earlier and asked Noreen Polk, the new manager that replaced Tim Foster, if I could chat with her about Tim. She had readily agreed.

When I entered her office, she shook my hand and offered me a seat opposite her desk. Maybe forties, attractive, professionally dressed in a dark-blue pantsuit and a white blouse, a pleasant smile. I gave her the same explanation I had given Sandy Sechrest for why I was looking for the Fosters. Maybe in danger, maybe running from someone who could no longer do them harm, yada, yada, yada. She seemed to accept it without question. She said she had heard nothing from Tim since his last day a week earlier.

"Is that unusual? Him not calling to say goodbye?"

"Not really. We've known he was leaving for a couple of months. Had a big office party for him, over at the Cracker Barrel on Airport Road. I was promoted to Tim's position, and he spent his last two weeks training me." She picked up a folder and moved it to the credenza behind her desk. "We sort of said our goodbyes then. Besides, I suspect he and Martha've been pretty busy with the move."

"What about his final check? Did he leave an address where he would be?"

"He used direct deposit. Most of us here do. His final paycheck went to his bank last week."

"Did he ask for any letters of recommendation? Ask anyone to make a call on his behalf?"

"Not that I know. Not me anyway."

"What about his car registrations? They had two cars, I understand."

"They sold Martha's Toyota several weeks ago. To a newlywed couple. I did the ownership transfer for them."

"So that left them with only the SUV?"

She nodded. "As far as I know." She turned to face her desktop computer. "Let me check something." She tapped a few keys, read the screen, and then looked back at me. "Nothing else in the database."

"What about new driver's licenses? Any requests from Arizona or anywhere else on either of their driving records?"

Again she worked the computer. This took several minutes. "Not that I see." She looked up at me. "They'll get around to it." She smiled. "Most people wait several months before getting a new license. Usually not a high priority."

That made sense.

"A neighbor, actually several neighbors, told me that they were surprised Tim and Martha chose Arizona and not somewhere else in the South."

She nodded. "Me, too. I asked Tim about it. He said they wanted to be as far away from Whitiker as possible." She smiled. "I teased him about moving to Florida."

"Teased?"

"They both hated Florida. Too many people and too much traffic and crime."

Hard to argue with that.

"I understand Tim didn't take many vacations."

"Not in the last three years anyway. Not since Steven—" her voice trailed off. "Last month they went to Myrtle Beach." She parked a wayward strand of hair behind her ear. "Tim still had three weeks of vacation time on the books when he left."

"Do you know where they stayed over in Myrtle Beach?"

"Not exactly. I think Tim mentioned the Pawleys Island area. Just south of Myrtle Beach. I know he liked the golf courses there."

"Do you remember the dates of this trip?"

"Sure. Just a sec," She slid open a drawer and pulled out a notebook. After thumbing through the pages she said, "Tim took four days off in December. The nineteenth through the twenty-second. I think they went up to Gatlinburg. Then the week of April fourth. That was the South Carolina trip."

"Before that?"

"Nothing for two years." She closed the book.

"They never visited Phoenix?"

"Not that I know."

I thanked Noreen and left.

The Fosters never visited Phoenix and there was no evidence they had moved there, or had ever planned to. It made sense that they would visit their real destination before they packed up and left. Find a place to live, set up bank accounts, get new driver's licenses, under whatever their new names were, scout out new jobs, all the things necessary to start a new life.

As I walked to my car, I called T-Tommy and suggested he check out hotels in the Myrtle Beach and the Gatlinburg areas. I gave him the dates the Fosters were supposed to have been there. Maybe check on real estate purchases in those areas too. He said he'd get someone on it.

More wheel spinning. Necessary to cover all the bases, but it wouldn't amount to anything. I knew the Fosters never visited either Gatlinburg or Myrtle Beach. They visited wherever they've set up their new lives. If it were one of these places, they wouldn't have told anyone they were visiting there. Which means that they went somewhere else. Somewhere within fairly easy driving distance. Somewhere in the South. Their friends and neighbors knew them well.

As for driver's licenses and new homes, the Fosters would have been stupid to do any of that under their real names, and nothing I'd seen so far suggested the Fosters were stupid. Most criminals are, but not these two.

It looked as though they had pulled off the perfect murder and the perfect disappearing act. At least on the surface. The truth is that the perfect crime is a myth. No such thing. Even the best of plans can unravel in a heartbeat. You just have to find the right string to tug on.

Chapter 38

Paul Haley and Lewis Brinkley were an odd pair. Paul, tall, thin, and animated, wore gray slacks and a pink golf shirt, tightly tucked. Sold real estate. Apparently good at it. Lewis, hefty and laid-back, wore tan slacks that could have used a little more room in the waist and a loose Hawaiian golf shirt, blue with red flowers and green leaves. He owned a couple of strip malls and was VP at a local bank.

I did a little research. Rather, Claire did. I asked her to tap into her resources. Took her all of twenty minutes to get the scoop on the two men who sat across the table from me. We were in the dining area of the massive stone-and-wood clubhouse at The Ledges Country Club.

The Ledges, a high-dollar community that hugged the crest of Huntsville Mountain and overlooked Jones Valley, was one of Huntsville's best neighborhoods. One of those where if you have to ask the price, move on down the hill. The dining room carried on that theme. Not exactly your typical golf course lunchroom setup. Double tablecloths, cream-colored over crisp white, turned ninety degrees, equally crisp white napkins, heavy silver flatware, and gold-edged china. Better than most high-end restaurants. Better than Sammy's. Well, not better, just classier.

When I called Paul earlier, he said they had a noon tee time and would be having lunch around eleven. Said he'd leave my name at the guardhouse. He did, so here I sat.

Paul worked on a salad and a bowl of beef stew; Lewis on a club sandwich and chips. They asked if I wanted anything, no thanks, except maybe a cup of coffee, black. Lewis summoned the waiter, and he poured my coffee and refilled their tea glasses.

After the waiter left, I gave them the same song and dance about why I was looking for the Fosters. Neither had an explanation for why Tim and Martha hadn't called anyone. Other than what others had said—they were traveling and would call when they got settled.

"When did you last speak with Tim?" I asked

"We played golf here last week," Paul said as he munched on a buttered roll. "Haven't talked to him since."

Lewis nodded his agreement with that.

"You guys play often?"

"Two, three times a week."

"Did Tim belong here?"

"No," Paul said. "I do. These clowns are just my guests."

"Unless we play over at Hampton Cove," Lewis said. "That's my course."

"Tim an avid golfer?" I asked.

"Oh, yeah," Paul said. "Loved it. A seven handicapper."

"Better than either of us," Lewis said. "Takes us for a few bucks every time."

I asked about the Fosters' decision to move to Phoenix, and told them others had found this odd.

They agreed.

"I didn't think either of them would ever leave Alabama," Lewis said. "But under the circumstances—" He turned his palms up.

"At least Phoenix has some great golf courses," Paul said.

"Any hint that they might have gone somewhere else?" I asked.

"Tim said they were going to Phoenix," Paul said. "Why would he lie about that?"

"That's what I'm asking."

Lewis leaned his elbows on the table edge. "Are you saying they aren't going to Phoenix?"

I shook my head. "What I'm saying is we have no evidence that's where they're going."

Lewis cut his eyes toward Paul for a beat and then his gaze came back to me. "I'm not sure I follow you."

I explained that the Fosters hadn't purchased or rented anything in Arizona or anywhere else we could find. That they hadn't used Martha's cell phone or any of their credit cards since they left town. That even Martha's sister didn't know where they were.

They both gave me blank stares.

"What are you suggesting?" Paul finally asked. "That they took off somewhere and don't want anyone to know?"

"Maybe."

"Why would they do that?"

"To get completely away from that Whitiker dude," Lewis said. "Tim was afraid he might find them regardless of where they went."

"He talk about Whitiker much?"

Guys talk on the golf course. It's like a private den or a treehouse. A place where jokes are shared, lies are swapped, and secrets slip out.

"Sometimes," Lewis said.

"What'd he say?"

Lewis took a gulp of his sweet tea. "Just what you think. He hated the dude. Afraid of him, too."

"Did he ever mention doing him any harm?"

"Whoa." Paul raised his palms toward me. "No way. If you think Tim killed that asshole, you better recalibrate your thinking."

I glanced at Lewis.

He shook his head. "He never said anything like that. He did wish someone would kill him in prison. Dreaded him getting out. Made him and Martha give up everything. Job, home, friends, everything."

"You're making a case for him having done it."

"Not a chance," Lewis said.

"I don't like where this is going," Paul said. His head came up and his chin pointed directly at me. "What you're insinuating. I think we've said about all we're going to say."

"I'm not accusing him of anything," I said. "It's just odd that they took off before the sun came up and no one has heard peep one from them. We simply have to consider everything."

"Consider something else." Paul's finger jabbed the air between us and his jaw flexed a beat or two. He pushed back his chair and stood. "You need to take your bullshit theories somewhere else." He looked down at Lewis. "See you outside." He walked away, head shaking, fists balled at his side.

"Sorry," I said.

"I more or less agree with him."

"More or less?"

Lewis scratched an ear. "Tim told me once that he'd kill Whitiker if he thought he could get away with it."

"Really?"

"He was just talking. It was a day when some shit from Whitiker was on the news. Saying things about Martha. Made Tim angry. Talking don't mean he did anything though."

"No, it doesn't."

He swirled his tea, the few remaining ice cubes tinkling against the side. "I would. No doubt about it."

"Me, too. But would Tim?"

"He loved Steven. More than anything." He took a deep breath and let it out slowly. "Except maybe Martha. He loves her just as much. He'd never risk going to jail and not being with her."

Part of me hoped he was right. The other part said he wasn't.

"You guys ever travel to play golf?" I asked.

"Sure?"

"Myrtle Beach?"

He nodded. "A couple of times."

"Where do you usually stay?"

"Pawleys Island. The Litchfield Resort is our favorite."

"Did you go last month?"

"No. He and Martha did."

"Was that unusual? The two of them going to a golf mecca and Tim not taking his golf buddies with him."

"Not really."

I raised an eyebrow, but said nothing, waiting him out.

"When I heard they were going, I mentioned that Paul and I might tag along. Tim said this wasn't a golf trip. He and Martha needed some time alone together. Away from everything."

"Did you think that was odd?"

"Actually, I thought it was a good idea. Lord knows they needed a break from all this."

Lewis glanced at his watch. "Time to go make some divots."

I stood. "Thanks for your help."

"Not sure I helped much."

"You did." I started to walk away, but stopped. "You might hear some ugly rumors."

"About?"

"Tim and Martha. Saying they killed Whitiker and took off."

"I figured that. Someone would put two and two together and get thirteen and there you go." He shrugged, hesitated, and looked up at me. "But I sense you're telling me this ain't just some rumormonger flapping his gums."

I nodded.

"JD?"

"He's making noises that way."

"Like JD gave two shits about his brother."

"Oh?"

He looked out the window for a beat and then said, "Besides being a pedophile and a murderer, Walter was worthless. Lazy. Drunk more often than not. I've seen him passed out at the gun shop more than once. Wouldn't pull his load. Screwed up the books. Maybe even stole a bit."

"How do you know this?"

He pushed back his chair and stood. "Friend of mine used to work there. A few years back. Said JD and Walter had issues."

"This friend. Mind telling me who it is?"

"Not at all. I'm sure he'd like to chat with you." Lewis pulled out his wallet, thumbed out a business card, and scribbled on the back. He handed it to me. "Hope it helps."

"Thanks."

"Mind if I ask you something?"

"Sure," I said.

"Why are you sniffing around after Tim and Martha?"

"Just being thorough. Making sure all possibilities are covered."

"Don't smell that way to me."

"They disappeared. No one knows where they are. Not even Martha's sister. Seems to me if they were simply moving they would've called her by now. Makes me wonder if they aren't in trouble somewhere. Might need help."

Lewis stared at me for a beat and then said, "You're a pretty smart fellow. I've actually read a couple of your books."

"Thanks."

"Ain't trying to blow smoke up your ass. You know all that forensic stuff. Know how criminals think. But the one thing you ain't is a good liar. So tell me what the Sam Hill this is all about."

"I can't talk about an investigation."

"Bullshit. You ain't no cop." He looked toward the floor and shook his head. "I'm sorry. But you see, I love Tim and Martha." His gaze came back to me. "They're almost family. I have to know what's happening. Does that make sense?"

It did. I could see the pain in his face.

"This goes no further," I said.

He nodded.

"We have evidence that might connect them to the shooting of Walter Whitiker."

"What evidence?"

"Can't say, but it's bothersome."

"It's not true. I don't care what the evidence says. Tim and Martha wouldn't hurt anyone. Not a chance."

"And I want to believe that," I said. "That's why I'm here. Talking to you and Paul. I'm having trouble reconciling the evidence with what I know and what everybody says about them."

He scratched his ear. "Thanks for telling me."

"Not a word. To anyone."

"You don't have to worry about that. Even though I wanted to know, needed to know, I now wish I didn't."

"I'm sorry."

"Like I said, you're a smart guy. I'll just have to trust you'll figure it out." He stood. "And pray the evidence turns in another direction."

I watched him walk away. His shoulders sagged and his steps seemed heavy.

Life can be such a bitch sometimes.

When I got to my car, I called the number Lewis had written on the card. A woman answered. I asked for Bobby Poehler. She told me he was out of town, seeing his ill mother down in Opelika, and would be back either Sunday night or Monday morning. She offered to take a message, but I said I'd call back on Monday.

Chapter 39

"So what's it going to be?" Claire asked. "You going to green-light me going with the story or do I kick your butt?"

T-Tommy grunted.

"Better you than me," I said.

"I'm sorry," Claire said. "I didn't mean to leave you out. I should have said both of your butts."

"How could we refuse?" I said. "With you being so nice and all."

"I was nice last night. This is business."

"Exactly how nice were you?" T-Tommy asked.

"Don't duck the subject, Tortelli." She tried to give him a look, but a smile broke through. "If you want to know ask Dub how nice I was."

I shrugged. "'Very' would be the word."

"Not 'extremely'?" Claire said. "Or 'stupendously'?"

"Those, too."

We were at Sammy's. Corner table on the screened-in porch dining area. Waiting on the Cajun shrimp and dirty rice we had ordered for lunch. T-Tommy and I had beers, Claire iced sweet tea.

She took a sip. "I can't hold off on this any longer. Someone will scoop me. The Fosters being suspects is big news." Neither T-Tommy nor I said anything, so she went on. "Enlisting the public's help in finding them can't hurt."

"They ain't around here," T-Tommy said. "Don't know where they went, but it ain't just over to Limestone County."

"But if I break this news, it'll be picked up by the services. This story has long legs. Whitiker's shooting has already made the *Atlanta Constitution* and the *Memphis Commercial Appeal*. Even the *Houston Chronicle* and the *Dallas Morning News*. It'll be in the *Miami Herald* today."

I nodded.

"I guess I'm not being a good journalist today," Claire said. "Not speaking very clearly. I'm not asking permission. I'm telling you that this will be my piece on the six o'clock. I'm just offering you guys a chance to come on my show and toss in your two cents."

Sammy appeared. "Here you go," he said. He deposited a plate in front of each of us. "Another round?" We declined, so he nodded and headed toward the kitchen.

The aroma was heavenly, the taste even better. The shrimp were fat, juicy, and spicy. Especially after I doctored mine with some of my Tabasco. The rice as dirty as it gets. Mighty fine.

Conversation died for a minute and then Claire said, "Look, it's about time for someone to start asking where the Fosters are. Making the connections. Digging up the evidence against them. This stuff always worms its way out."

I shrugged and looked at T-Tommy. "She has a point."

"How are you going to play it?" T-Tommy asked.

"Not flat-out accuse the Fosters, or reveal any of the evidence. I'll say that they could simply be running away or they could be victims themselves. But I am going to say that it's possible they were involved in Whitiker's murder."

"And you want Dub and I there for credibility," T-Tommy said.

She smiled. "Something like that."

"I feel so used," he said.

She held her tea glass in both hands and looked at T-Tommy over the rim. "The truth is you'll be using me. To help catch your slippery criminals."

He laughed.

"And it's not like it'd be the first time," Claire said. "The Brian Kurtz case comes to mind."

She had another point. She was on a point roll. In the Kurtz case we had sort of set her up. Used her report to poke the bad guys in the eye, bring them out into the open. It worked. She'd get over it. Apparently, not yet, but eventually. Probably. With Claire you just never knew. She had a long and deep memory and wasn't shy about bringing up things you'd long since forgotten. She said it was a woman's thing. Me? I think it's a Claire thing.

T-Tommy took a sip of beer. "We can talk about the weapon, but nothing about the tire tracks or the money."

"I know the game. You know I won't do anything stupid." She looked at me. "Except for Dub, that is."

"Funny."

T-Tommy shrugged. "Okay. We'll go with it."

"Maybe it'll shake something loose," I said. "It's one thing if the public thinks they're on the run and hiding from a killer and another thing again if they could be involved. Maybe someone knows something and will consider it their civic duty to turn them in."

"Be at the studio by five thirty," Claire said.

"Do I have to do that makeup crap?" I asked.

"You need it."

She's funny. Should have her own TV show.

T-Tommy drained his beer and looked at me. "Uncover anything interesting this morning?"

I told him about my chats with the Fosters' neighbors, with Noreen Polk at the Madison County License Department, and with Tim's golf buddies Paul Haley and Lewis Brinkley.

"How do you read all that?" he asked.

"They didn't go to Phoenix. Never even visited as far as I can tell. They won't leave the South and hate Florida, so I'd bet east and north. Just not above the Mason-Dixon. Tim's passion is golf, Martha's is quilting, and both are very active in the Baptist church. Sniffing around those worlds might help."

"Wouldn't they avoid all that?" Claire asked.

I shook my head. "People can change their name, their appearance, even their profession, but they can never completely dump who they really are. Habits and beliefs are difficult to leave behind."

"The golf angle might not help," T-Tommy said, "Too many golfers. The quilting and the church deals might."

"Quilting's bigger than you think," Claire said. "I did a piece on it a couple of years ago."

"Then we'll concentrate on Jesus," T-Tommy said.

"I'm heading over to see their pastor right now," I said. "Want to go?"

"Yeah."

I motioned to Sammy to bring the check, and then to T-Tommy I said, "Anything on Myrtle Beach or Gatlinburg?"

"Nada, and still no credit card or phone activity."

"Those are dead," I said. "But have someone check out the Litchfield Resort in Pawleys Island. That's where Tim liked to golf with his buddies."

Chapter 40

"I thought I might find you guys here."

I looked up from signing the credit card receipt to see Paul Twitty, a local PI. Six three, razor thin, a gaunt face with tight, pale lips, dark, slicked-back hair, intense brown eyes. He wore a freshly pressed gray suit and a crisp white shirt, collar open. As usual, an unlit Cohiba settled into one side of his mouth.

"Paul," I said.

He nodded to Claire. "Ms. McBride. Always a pleasure."

Claire nodded back.

"Is this what you guys pass off as work? Hanging out in a bar and drinking beer?"

"Seems to work out okay," I said.

"Mind if I sit?"

"We were just fixing to leave."

"Only need a minute."

I nodded toward the empty chair.

He pulled it out and sat down next to T-Tommy. He scissored the stogie between his fingers and pulled it from his mouth. "I'm looking into Walter Whitiker's murder."

"For whom?" I asked.

"JD."

"I see."

"He seems to think the police are looking under the wrong rocks."

"Which rocks would those be?" T-Tommy asked.

"Anywhere that isn't aimed at Tim and Martha Foster. JD seems to think they're the ones."

T-Tommy grunted.

"He thinks you can find them?" I asked.

"Yep. I do too."

"I see your modesty's intact."

Twitty had been around the law enforcement block a couple of times. Tried law school but wasn't smart enough. Tried the police but wasn't clean enough. He went through the academy a half decade before T-Tommy. They had actually worked several cases together before Twitty fell under a dark cloud. Something about planting evidence. Never proven, but the suspicions were strong and mostly uncontested. Blew up in the papers and the TV news. HPD wanted no part of the scandal and allowed Twitty to sneak out the back door with his ability to snag a PI license and a carry permit intact. So he went the PI route. A less than stellar reputation. Known for bending the rules. Had had his license pulled more than a few times, but always managed to crawl back to his feet.

"Modesty's for losers." He brushed an invisible something from one lapel and returned the macerated end of the cigar to his mouth. It bobbed as he spoke. "I thought we might be able to help each other."

"How's that?" T-Tommy asked.

"Maybe share information."

T-Tommy shrugged. "Don't see that happening."

Twitty smiled. "I'll even go first. I know the Fosters split. Presumably for Phoenix, but that's not where they're going."

"Where are they going?" I asked.

"That's the money question, isn't it? I know the crime lab has what could be the murder weapon and that tire tracks from the SUV the Fosters abandoned match some found at the crime scene. I know that no one knows where they are. Not even Martha Foster's sister."

"You've been busy."

"I know how to do this job."

He did. He was good at it. That was never the question. It was how he went about it that was usually the problem. I knew he had contacts inside both HPD and the Sheriff's Department and wasn't shy about slipping them a Benjamin here and there.

Twitty spread his spider thin fingers on the table. Perfectly manicured nails, a square diamond pinky ring. "So now what can you tell me?"

"Nothing," T-Tommy said. "That's about all we know."

Twitty stared at him for a beat and then a hint of a smile appeared at one corner of his mouth. "You wouldn't tell me anyway, would you?"

"Nope."

"I'm not feeling the love here, guys."

"What's love got to do with it?" T-Tommy asked.

Twitty laughed and shook his head. "So now you're Tina Turner?" He stood. "I'll catch you guys later." He headed toward the door.

"See what I mean?" Claire said. "If Twitty knows about the evidence against the Fosters, is the rest of the planet far behind?"

Another point. A hat trick. She was indeed on a roll.

We walked out into the parking lot. It had been sunny when I arrived but a few wads of gray clouds, dark bellies filled with rain, had drifted in from the north.

Claire climbed into her Mercedes and eased the window down. "Five thirty. Don't be late." Before I could respond, the window slid up and she pulled away, her tires crunching the gravel.

She always got bossy after scoring a few points.

Chapter 41

By the time I turned off Whitesburg Drive at Sanders Road and swung into the parking lot of the Whitesburg Baptist Church, the thickening clouds had begun to spit a fine mist. The Porsche's wiper blades stuttered back and forth, streaking more than clearing the windshield. Been meaning to change those for a month or so.

The church was over fifty years old. That is, Whitesburg Baptist had served its congregation for that long. The buildings were new and sparkling.

We parked in the visitors' lot, hustled through the drizzle, pushed through the glass doors, and entered the south lobby. High-ceilings, a wall of windows, everything rosy-tan brick and marble, it had an atrium feel. A young woman looked up from behind the marble-topped reception desk and smiled.

"Welcome," she said. "I'm Ashley. What can I do for you?"

"We're looking for Pastor Boles."

"Who should I say is asking for him?"

"I'm Dub Walker. This is Investigator Tortelli."

Her smile flattened. She looked at T-Tommy. A crease appeared in her brow. "The police?"

"Just need a few minutes," I said. "About an ongoing investigation."

Her smile returned. A little forced this time. "Just a sec."

She stood, moved around her desk, and walked down a hallway. She returned in a couple of minutes.

"Pastor Boles is in the Worship Center. Follow me."

The Worship Center was massive and magnificent. An elevated dais and pulpit, flanked by ample choir seating, faced ascending rows of pews and an upper deck of even more pews. Down lights peppered the vaulted ceiling and washed the walls. You could almost feel Jesus and I suspected that when the place was filled with the Sunday faithful that feeling was even stronger.

Pastor Ronnie Boles stood at the pulpit, scanning the stack of loose pages he held in one hand. He looked up and smiled when we entered. He stepped off the dais and walked toward us, hand outstretched. He looked mid-forties, fit, with thick brown hair and sharp blue eyes. His attire, jeans and an untucked white shirt, didn't fit the room.

After introductions, he said, "I was just going over Sunday's sermon." He smiled and when we didn't respond, he continued. "What can I do for you?"

"We need to ask some questions about Tim and Martha Foster," I said.

Concern narrowed his eyes. "In regards to?"

"They're missing," I said. "We're trying to find them."

The concern crept into his forehead. "What do you mean 'missing?'"

I explained the situation. Mostly. I left out the part about the gun, the dumped SUV, and the money.

"They moved to Phoenix," he said. "Left a couple of days ago."

"And if they didn't?" T-Tommy asked.

Now confusion joined concern. "I don't understand. What do you mean?"

"What if they didn't go to Phoenix?" I asked.

"They've planned this move for months." He hesitated a couple of seconds. "Does this have anything to do with Walter Whitiker's murder at the prison the other day?"

"They disappeared around that time."

He looked at me for a beat as if considering what I'd said. "Are they in danger?"

I shrugged. "Possible."

His hand came up to his chest. "Oh, my. I never considered—"

"The truth is, we don't know," I said. "That's why we want to talk with them."

"Of course."

"Let's suppose they didn't go to Phoenix. Any idea where they might have gone instead?"

A thoughtful crease appeared in his forehead. "No. Not offhand."

"They ever mention somewhere they liked?" T-Tommy asked.

"I know they traveled to Myrtle Beach a few times. Tim's a very good golfer."

"Did they ask you to contact another church for them? Maybe introduce them to a pastor you know?"

He shook his head. "No."

"Did you find that unusual?" I asked.

"A little." He massaged one temple. "This is very bothersome."

"Would you know if they joined another congregation?"

"Maybe. When we get a new member, someone who has just moved here, I usually call their old church and chat with their previous pastor. Let them know that they were settled in our church and how things are going. Many other pastors do the same."

"But no one has called about them?" T-Tommy asked.

"No, but it's only been a couple of days. I suspect that when they get settled and locate a new church, I'll hear from them."

That made sense. "Is this contacting a previous pastor a formal program or just something you do?"

"Nothing formal." His face relaxed and a smile returned. "We pastors tend be very close with our church members. Like to know how they are doing—even if they move away."

"So you have no idea where they might be?" I asked.

"Phoenix is all I know."

"Pastor Boles?"

The voice came from behind us, and when I turned, I saw receptionist Ashley at the rear door.

"Sorry to bother you," she continued, "but the Hill family is here."

"Take them down to my office and tell them I'll be there shortly."
"Will do."

"Thanks, Ashley." He returned his gaze to me. "A family meeting."

"We only need a few more minutes," I said.

"Go ahead. Ashley will take good care of them until we're finished."

"We understand the Fosters were very active in the church," I said.

"Oh, yes. They were both very generous with their time. Especially with our youth programs. They taught Bible study classes. The kids loved them."

"I take it you knew their son Steven?"

He sighed. "What a tragedy. It tore them both up. Shook their faith."

I raised an eyebrow but said nothing.

"I counseled them on many occasions. Particularly during the months that Steven was missing. They acted as if they believed he was alive and well. Said all the right words. But they knew."

"Martha Foster did witness the abduction."

"I know. Then after his—he was found—they fell into a deep despair." He looked up toward the ceiling as if recalling something. "I remember going to their home that evening. We prayed. We cried." He looked back at me. "I failed. Couldn't console them. Especially Martha. She seemed to blame herself for what happened. They didn't return to church for six months. I talked with them on the phone and visited them several times, but they said they just weren't ready. That they couldn't have faith in a God that would let this happen to Steven."

"Not an uncommon feeling among victim's families," I said.

That was true. In spades. I'd seen this many times. In virtually every murder case I'd ever consulted on. Seemed particularly prevalent when a loved one was the victim of a serial predator. The loved ones always asked: How could this happen? How could someone like that exist? Why would God make such a creature?

I never had an answer. It always came down to the old argument that if God is God, he's not good, and if God is good, he's not God. If he is indeed omnipotent then he made the predator and if he isn't, well then, he's not God. At least not the one most preachers and theologians talk about. The one that made heaven and earth and everything in be-tween.

"Unfortunately, that's true," Boles said.

"But they did eventually come back?" T-Tommy asked.

He nodded. "They visited me one day. We talked for a couple of hours. More crying and praying but they did find their faith again."

"With your help, I'm sure."

"Mostly with God's help."

"Can you think of anything else that might help us find them?" I asked.

He thought for a minute. "Not that comes to mind right now."

"Everyone we talked to said they didn't believe they would leave the South. That Phoenix seemed an odd choice."

"I must admit it did surprise me."

"Did they tell you why they chose to move so far away?"

"I know they were afraid of Whitiker. Especially Martha. She took all his threats very seriously." He took a deep breath and let it out slowly. "Can't say I blame her."

T-Tommy handed him a card. "If you hear from them, or from any-one who knows where they are, could you give me a call?"

"Sure." He studied the card for a minute, brow wrinkled. "Are they in any trouble?"

"We don't know."

He nodded. "I'll contact the pastors I know. Put a message out through our network. See if they turn up at any of our member churches."

"Do you have any pictures of them?" I asked.

"In our member profiles."

"Can you send the photos out too?"

"Why?"

"In case they changed their names."

Confusion returned. "Why would they do that?"

"So Whitiker couldn't find them."

He glanced toward T-Tommy and then back to me. "But he's dead."

"They might not know that."

"I see." He clasped his hands together. "Our network involves nearly a hundred and fifty churches in eighteen states. I'll send a note and their photos to each of the pastors."

"That would be great."

We thanked Pastor Boles and headed out into a rain.

Chapter 42

We drove back to T-Tommy's office at the South Precinct, the rain now steady, thumping the Porsche's roof, the worn wipers not able to keep up. Did I mention that I needed new blades? Derrick Stone pulled into the lot right behind us. He had news and talked rapidly as we hurried inside and walked down to T-Tommy's office.

"Still no phone or credit card use," Stone said. "No news from Phoenix. They didn't buy and it looks like they didn't rent either. At least nothing listed."

T-Tommy flopped into the chair behind his desk. "The sister's phone? Got anything on that?"

"I talked with Feigler this morning and filled him in on the new evidence we have on the Fosters. The tire tracks and the money trail. He said that had little to do with the sister. Said we had no evidence she was involved in anything criminal, so he still wouldn't authorize a tap and trace."

"And her call records? Anything there?"

"Not much. Home or cell. All the numbers in or out are accounted for. Friends, work, that kind of thing. Except that one she received from the prepaid phone. That phone was sold for cash over in Rome, Georgia. Three months ago. From an outfit called All Things Wireless."

"Registered to whom?" I asked.

Stone retrieved his notebook from his back pocket and flipped it open. "Sam Clarkson."

Prepaid phones. The lifeblood of drug dealers, pimps, and criminals who need to communicate off the grid. The bane of law enforcement. Once purchased and registered, which can be done with complete anonymity, they can't be traced. The numbers called and the locations where the phone is used can be, but that's it. Unless the seller or an in-store security camera can ID the buyer there's no way to track down the user.

"How'd you get that?" T-Tommy asked.

"Got a buddy that works at Radio Shack. He tracked the number. AT&T's the carrier."

"Be nice to get a warrant to trace that phone. Just in case."

"Got it working."

"Never happen," I said. "You won't get a warrant based on a single call that could be a wrong number." I looked at Stone. "How long was the call?"

"Just under four minutes."

"Can your buddy do anything for us?" T-Tommy asked.

Stone shook his head. "Not that. He can check on numbers. Find out who has them. But he can't go into someone's records."

"Didn't think so, I said."

"Anything else?" T-Tommy asked.

"Got all the stuff from their service provider. The ISP. Nothing. Searches and downloads are all local businesses, movies, Amazon books. Some church stuff. E-mails are all to friends or the church folks. A total dead end."

"So why'd they take the hard drive?" T-Tommy asked.

"Same reason they shredded everything," I said. "Just being thorough."

"That Twitty guy came by earlier," Stone said. "Said he was working for JD Whitiker. Said he was helping you guys."

"Get real," T-Tommy said. "Only person Twitty ever helps is Twitty. What'd he want?"

"Asked about the investigation. What we knew."

"What'd you say?" I asked.

"Nothing. Just gave him a dumb smile." He now gave us the same dumb smile.

"You're good at that," T-Tommy said. "You practice in front of a mirror?"

"Yeah. I used it on my mom growing up. Kept me from confessing to all sorts of bad behavior."

Could I ever relate to that. I suspect all kids had used that deflection at some time. A survival of the fittest sort of thing.

"One more thing." Stone flipped a few pages in his notebook, frowned, and flipped a few more. "Here it is. The rifle. Original owner was a guy down in Foley. Bought it three years back. Couple of years ago traded it for a handgun at a gun show in Mobile. Doesn't remember who. Then it drops off the radar. Not reregistered or sold as far as I can tell."

"Figured that," I said. "If it were traceable, the shooter would've ground off the serial numbers."

"The guy?" T-Tommy asked. "The original owner? Anything there?"

"Clean. No record, no nothing."

"How's the suspect list going?"

Stone closed his notebook and slipped it back into his pocket. "Got about forty names on it. Walter made his share of enemies. Mostly minor stuff. A couple of barroom fights. A guy he stiffed on a truck sale. Another had a beef about the way Walter treated his sister. We've worked through about half of them, but so far none look good for the shooting."

"Good work," T-Tommy said.

"Catch you guys later." Stone left the office.

T-Tommy looked at me. "What time we supposed to be at the studio?"

"By five thirty."

He glanced at his watch. "Time to swing by Sammy's and pick up my car." He stood. "Maybe have a drink."

"You saying you need alcohol to face Claire?"

"You said it. I didn't."

Chapter 43

One drink turned into two. And a pulled pork sandwich for T-Tommy. Said he didn't want his stomach growling on air. I let that slide. He'd have had one regardless of what was on the schedule.

We made it to the studio with time to spare and were ushered directly into makeup and from there to the set. The producer wanted us in our place before the newscast opening rolled. The hot studio lights baked the goop and powder Maria Sanchez, Channel 8's best makeup artist, had slapped on my face. I felt like a Kabuki actor. I sat between Claire and T-Tommy behind a desk across the narrow studio from the two anchors. They ran through the top stories and then introduced Claire. The small red light on the camera aimed at us snapped on.

"As I reported last night, the murder of Walter Allen Whitiker remains unsolved and so far the police have few leads." Claire sat erect and looked into the camera. "My guests this evening are Homicide Investigator Tommy Tortelli, who is heading up the investigation, and Dub Walker, noted author and forensic consultant." She turned her shoulders toward us slightly. "Investigator Tortelli, I know you've made no arrests and as yet don't have a suspect, but I understand you've found what might be the murder weapon?"

"At the scene, we located a weapon but aren't yet sure if it is the one used to kill Walter Whitiker or not."

"I understand there was a problem with the ballistics."

"That's right. Both the rifle and one of the bullets were badly damaged so a confident match isn't possible."

"The rifle was damaged? How?"

"Since this is an ongoing investigation I'd rather not say right now."

Claire looked at me. "Mr. Walker, is that your take on it?"

"I examined the bullet, as did lead criminalist, Sidau Yamaguchi, and though it appears it could match the weapon we found, there is no way to be sure."

"What type of weapon was found?"

I smiled. "Can't really say."

"My sources tell me that it was a deer rifle. True?"

"No comment," T-Tommy said.

Claire nodded, a slight smile at the corner of her mouth. "I understand that Tim and Martha Foster, the parents of young Steven Foster, who many believe was murdered by Walter Allen Whitiker, left town on the morning of the shooting."

"That's right," T-Tommy said. "We believe they intended to relocate to Phoenix."

"Because of the threats Whitiker made against them?"

"Correct."

"On that point, it seems to me that making threats against someone from prison would preclude an early release, as was the case with Whitiker."

T-Tommy shrugged, his massive shoulders straining against his navy-blue sports coat. "You'd think so, wouldn't you? The DA petitioned the court on that very point, asking the judge to hold Whitiker until he had served his entire sentence. Said that such threats didn't exactly represent good behavior and an early release should not be considered. The judge saw it differently."

Claire nodded. "Have you spoken with the Fosters since they left?"

"We haven't been able to locate them," T-Tommy said.

"They left rather abruptly, didn't they?" Claire asked. "Left behind many of their possessions?"

"Looks that way."

"Let me ask you this, Mr. Walker. Is it possible that they themselves are victims? Either harmed or abducted? That Walter Whitiker's murder might be more complex than a simple shooting?"

"There's nothing simple about this or any other shooting," I said. "But yes, both of those are possibilities. Or maybe they're just running away from Whitiker as they said they would."

"But if Whitiker's dead, why wouldn't they come back?"

"They might not know about the Whitiker shooting." I was sure my makeup was melting and I imagined my face sliding down and bunching at my chin. "If they're still on the road, they might not've heard anything yet."

She glanced down at her notes and then back up to me. "Could the Fosters have been involved in Whitiker's death? Could they, or should they, be considered suspects?"

Her face remained passive, lips still, but I saw a slight smile buried behind her eyes. She knew this was the money question. T-Tommy and I knew it was coming, so we had talked over how to handle it. What to say. What not to say. Didn't want to say anything that if it got back to the Fosters might spook them, drive them even deeper underground. Better for them to think we weren't focused on them as suspects, only as possible victims. Give them some level of comfort. Maybe they'd get sloppy.

So I did what anyone would do under the circumstances. I punted. "I think Investigator Tortelli could best answer that."

T-Tommy didn't miss a beat. "We have no evidence that would definitely implicate them. But we're keeping an open mind."

"So, it's possible?"

"We haven't ruled anyone out yet."

Claire turned her gaze directly at me. "Did Walter Whitiker have any enemies? Anyone who might have a motive for doing this?"

"Walter was a pedophile and a murderer," I said. "In my opinion anyway. He spent nearly two years in prison. Murderers and pedophiles make more than a few enemies."

"He was never convicted of the murder," Claire said.

"Neither was OJ," I said. "Doesn't mean he didn't do it."

I could see Claire's mouth tighten as she tried to hide a smile.

"Thank you both for being here." She turned to the camera. "If anyone has any information on the murder of Walter Whitiker or the where-abouts of Tim and Martha Foster, please contact the Huntsville Police Department at the number on your screen."

I glanced at the monitor that hung just below the camera. Tim and Martha's faces filled the screen, the HPD number beneath them. Looked like a pair of mug shots.

Chapter 44

The Chapel Creek Baptist Church, red brick with pristine white entry columns and cross-topped spire, sat along a winding two-lane road, in a pastoral cove ten miles north of downtown Asheville. Its three wooded acres backed up to the creek that gave it its name.

Tim and Martha Foster, now Robert Beckwith and Cindy Strunk, parked across the street near a white wooden sign with black letters that said:

Chapel Creek Baptist Church
Sorrow looks back
Worry looks around
Faith looks up

Tim held Martha's hand as they walked up the cracked sidewalk and climbed the front steps, flame azaleas along each side, the aroma of fresh paint in the air. Tim pushed through one side of the double-entry door, holding it for Martha. Down a short corridor to the left they found the church offices where a young woman greeted them. The plaque on her desk indicated she was Debbie Tyson. She had light brown hair, green eyes, and an innocent smile. After they explained that they were new to the area and might be interested in joining the congregation, she said that Pastor Dunn was out back, working in his garden, and would love to meet them.

Debbie led them through the chapel. Much smaller than Whites-burg Baptist, it looked like it held a congregation of a hundred or so. The small pulpit stood front and center, two rows of choir chairs arrayed in a semicircle behind it. A larger-than-life crucifix, flanked by two intricate stained-glass panels, filled the wall above and behind the pulpit. Jesus's head lolled forward as if looking down on the pews.

Debbie continued through a rear door and into the parklike church grounds, which were open and airy and dotted with trees, including two very large oaks, pines of various ages and sizes, and at least two dozen heavily flowered pink and white dogwoods. The pastor's house sat a hundred feet away and beside it Tim saw a man in jeans and tee shirt on his knees, working in the garden.

The man stood, brushed his hands together, and then knocked dirt from his knees. He smiled as they approached. He appeared to be around fifty with soft brown hair, touched with gray, that swept across his forehead just above his intense brown eyes.

"Welcome," he said. "I'm Pastor Arthur Dunn." He extended a hand toward Tim, hesitated, glanced at his open palm, and withdrew it. "Sorry. You caught me playing in the dirt."

Tim smiled. "No problem. I'm Robert Beckwith. This is my fiancée Cindy Strunk."

"Welcome."

"We just moved here and are looking for a church. One of our neighbors suggested we visit here."

"Who is your neighbor?"

"Lauren Corcoran."

He nodded. "Yes, she and Jason have been members here for many years."

Debbie excused herself, telling the pastor that if he needed anything she would be in the office. He thanked her.

"Nice garden," Martha said.

Dunn smiled. "Takes some work, but I love it. Grew up on a farm over in Virginia. My daddy worked that farm his entire life. I love getting dirt beneath my nails." He looked at his hands. "Come on inside."

He led them into his home. Like the church columns and spire, the slope-roofed, white clapboard house was bright white and also smelled of fresh paint. Inside it was small but neat. They sat on the sofa while Dunn excused himself to wash his hands.

"Can I get you anything to drink?" he said when he returned, drying his hands with a towel. "Coffee? Tea? Soft drink?"

"Thanks, but we're fine," Tim said.

He sat in an overstuffed chair. "Where are you folks from?"

"Atlanta. Just moved here a few days ago."

"What church did you attend there?"

Tim glanced at Martha. They had rehearsed this.

"I'm afraid we haven't been very active in recent years," Tim said.

"Life get in the way?" Dunn's smile seemed genuine and caring.

Martha nodded. "You might say that."

"Happens a lot. I hope our congregation can motivate you to be active here. We have a very good group. Nearly two hundred members."

"That's what we want," Tim said. "To start again. Many years ago we taught Bible school. Teens. We miss that."

"We could sure use some experienced teachers. Children and teenagers are the future of any congregation and we're no different. Unfortunately, they have so many distractions today that Jesus seems to be a low priority."

"That's so true," Martha said. "We would love to help out."

His eyes lit up. "That's wonderful. We are in the process of expanding and updating our youth programs and Bible study classes and would welcome your help." He smiled. "And your ideas."

"Count us in," Tim said.

"We have three services a week. Two on Sunday, at eight and eleven, and then every Wednesday evening."

"We're just getting settled," Tim said, "but we'll be here Sunday."

"Excellent. I would love to introduce you to some of our members. I think you'll feel comfortable here."

"I think so, too," Martha said.

"What brought you here? To Asheville?"

Another thing they had rehearsed.

"I had a business," Tim said. "Office supplies and equipment. I sold it recently. We were tired of the city and wanted to find a quiet, pleasant place to live."

Dunn nodded. "Asheville is definitely that. I've been here nearly fifteen years and can't imagine living anywhere else."

"Then there are all the golf courses around here," Tim said.

"Ah. You have the golf bug."

"Big time," Martha said. "He'd play every day if he could." She reached over and patted Tim's arm. "Which is good since it keeps him out of my hair."

Dunn laughed. "I think you two will fit in very well here."

"Which brings up another thing," Tim said. "We want to get married."

Surprise erupted on Dunn's face. "That's marvelous."

"Maybe this Sunday?" Martha asked.

Dunn was silent for a beat as if that's not what he expected to hear. He looked from Martha to Tim and back again. "Seriously?"

Martha laughed. "I guess that does sound sudden, but we've been engaged for three years and decided that with this move, with starting our new lives here, it was time to tie the knot."

"You want me to perform the ceremony?"

"If you would," Martha said.

"I'd be honored. What did you have in mind?"

"Small and simple," Martha said. "We don't know anyone here to invite anyway."

"Sunday it is." Dunn clasped his hands together. "You bring the license, and I'll arrange everything else."

"We already have it," Martha said.

"We can have the ceremony here. Beneath the wedding arbor." He waved a hand toward the large living room window and beyond an ivy-covered white-lattice arch that stood beneath a broad oak tree near one corner of the property. "We have all our outdoor weddings there."

"It's perfect," Martha said.

"We can do it between services or after the eleven o'clock one. Your choice."

"Between," Martha said. "We'll be here for the early service."

Chapter 45

I was securing new wipers on my Porsche when T-Tommy pulled into the drive. I pressed the final clip in place and then released the wiper arm. It slapped against the windshield.

T-Tommy climbed from his car and walked into the garage. "I thought Claire was going to do that?"

The ugly truth was that Claire was better at this kind of stuff than either of us. T-Tommy knew it. I knew it. Claire definitely knew it. She could change oil, gap spark plugs, set timing, all those things that were a mystery to me. And power tools? She had a garage full of them. Me? Never touched them. Call me crazy, but having a tooth-edged metal disk spinning at insane rates near my face or fingers didn't seem all that wise.

"Got tired of nagging her," I said.

"Scared. You got scared of nagging her."

"That too. Anyway, I decided I better get it done. Supposed to rain more today."

"What'd you do? Break down and read the instructions?"

"Just the pictures," I said. "All that tab A into slot B crap didn't make much sense."

"You got that right."

I glanced up at the sky. Pewter clouds slammed a lid on everything and the smell of rain hung in the air. A squirrel, his jaws clamped on a fat pecan, spiraled up the huge oak tree that Old Church Road looped around just beyond the end of my drive. Another intercepted him halfway up and an argument over pecan ownership broke out.

I wiped my hands on a dirty towel. "Ready to head out?"

"Let's get at it."

Yesterday, we had decided to drive back over to Scottsboro and chat with Martha Foster's sister, Paige Baker. I was sure that she knew where her sister was. If Tim and Martha were dropping out of sight that was the one tie Martha wouldn't, or more likely couldn't, cut. Everything I had learned indicated that these two had a tight bond. One that wouldn't snap just because one of them planted a thirty caliber into Whitiker's chest. Blood is thick, especially in the Deep South.

We didn't call ahead and let her know we were coming, wanting to catch her unprepared. Maybe she'd let something slip. Particularly, if we leaned on her a bit.

We swung by the Krispy Kreme on Memorial Parkway near University. T-Tommy insisted. Said his stomach was growling and his blood sugar was low and that if he didn't get something to eat he'd be cranky. I didn't argue. The choice simple. Krispy Kreme donuts or a grumbling T-Tommy. No contest.

Two for me, four for him. Two coffees.

Back on the Parkway, we headed north and hooked up with Highway 72. My donuts didn't last long and after I had two free hands again, I eased the Porsche up to eighty-five.

By the time we reached downtown Scottsboro, a steady drizzle fell. No problem, I had new wipers.

Paige Baker answered my knock. A look of surprise fell across her face when she saw T-Tommy and me standing on her porch. She wore flannel pajamas beneath a terry cloth robe. No make up, hair mussed.

"What do you want?" she asked. I detected a note of hostility.

"Just a couple of questions," I said

"I don't think I should talk with you."

"Why's that?"

"I saw you on TV last night. You said Martha and Tim killed that Whitiker animal."

I didn't respond. Knew she had more to say. Better to let her vent it all. See where it goes.

"My sister and Tim are good Christians. They would never—never ever—kill anyone. Even someone like Whitiker."

"Actually we didn't accuse them of anything," I said. "We were simply airing possibilities. They could be hiding, thinking Whitiker is still alive. Or as we said the other day, they could be victims. We just don't know."

"What do you mean by victims?"

"Their car was found abandoned. Their house was still full of stuff. The back door was standing open. Looked like they left in a hurry—or were forced to leave."

Her face showed no reaction. No shock. No disbelief. Absolutely no concern that my words could be true. Her calmness confirmed several things for me. She knew they hadn't been abducted. She knew they were fine. She knew where they were. She had probably communicated with them.

"Have you heard from them?" I asked.

"No."

"Doesn't that worry you?"

"Not really." A gust of wind blew through the door, dragging a few stray droplets with it. She clutched the neck of her robe. "Please, come in."

We wiped the water from our shoes on the welcome mat and followed her into the living room. It was small and neat with a deep sofa, two high-backed chairs, and several well-oiled oak antique pieces. A screened fireplace with family photos on the mantel. Two pictures were of her with Martha, one from their teenage years, another more recent. A collection of Depression glass filled a hutch against the far wall. A green pitcher; a pink, covered butter dish; and a clear hobnail candy dish that I could see.

T-Tommy and I sat on the sofa; she took a chair across from us.

"Look," she said, "I don't know where they are and I haven't heard a word from them."

"I'm having a hard time with that," T-Tommy said. "Everyone says that the two of you were very close."

"So?"

"Means that she wouldn't just leave you in the dark. She'd let you know where she was and that she's okay."

"Well, she hasn't."

"Yet you don't seem overly worried," I said.

"They're driving to Phoenix. Martha said they were going to take their time. Have a little vacation on the way. See the country."

"Anywhere in particular?"

"She mentioned Santa Fe and Monument Valley. They've never seen either."

I stared at her, but said nothing.

"I'll hear from her when they get settled," Paige said. "That was the plan."

I held her gaze for another beat. "Yet they've not used any of their credit cards and haven't made any calls on their cell." I leaned forward, resting my elbows on my knees. "Doesn't that seem odd?"

"What seems odd to me is that you could even think they might be involved in that man's death. That they might've shot him."

"We never said we considered them suspects," I said.

She glared at me. "Sure you do. I'm not stupid. You wouldn't be here if they weren't suspects."

"We're not sure what they are," T-Tommy said. "But the truth is that we have some evidence that will need some explanation from them," T-Tommy said.

"What evidence?"

"Can't say."

"I don't believe they were abducted or were harmed," I said. "Which means they dumped the car themselves. Chose an area where it would likely be stolen and chopped into oblivion."

"You don't know that for sure."

"No, I don't, but besides not using their cell phone or credit cards, they emptied their bank accounts. Took it all in cash as far as we can tell."

"They're moving. Of course they'd take their money."

"In cash?" T-Tommy asked.

She gave us a blank stare.

"I'd feel more comfortable if they'd transferred the money to a new bank," T-Tommy said. "Walking around with that much cash makes me wonder."

I jumped in, cranking up the heat a little. "There's no evidence they're in Phoenix or ever planned to go there. No home purchase. No bank accounts. No driver's licenses. Nothing in Arizona. No one has heard a word from them. Not even you. You have to admit, it does look suspicious."

"Suspicious nothing. You listen to me—"

The phone on the table beside her chair rang.

"Hello." She listened for a beat. "Can you call me back in a few minutes?" More listening. Her gaze went from me, to T-Tommy, to the floor. She wound the cord around one index finger. "I'm talking with the police." A pause. "From Huntsville. They're looking for Martha and Tim." Pause. "A half hour would be fine." She hung up the phone.

"Look," Paige said, "I don't care what it looks like, they would never do that. Not a chance."

"Because they're active in the church?" T-Tommy asked.

"Because they're good people and good people don't kill other people. For any reason."

"Why'd they run?"

"You know why. To get away from Whitiker."

"Yet they told everyone where they are going," I said. "I've talked to a dozen people who know about Phoenix. Don't you think Whitiker could find that out?"

"Phoenix is a long way from here."

"Not by plane. If Whitiker's threats were real, don't you think he'd hop a flight?"

"What are you saying?"

"I'm saying they didn't go to Phoenix. That was a head fake for Whitiker." I locked my gaze on her. "Or for the police."

"Stop it." She stood. "I won't listen to these accusations anymore. I think you should leave."

T-Tommy and I stood.

"We didn't mean to upset you," T-Tommy said.

"Sure you did. That's what cops do."

She walked to the door. We followed.

"One more question," I said as she pulled the door open. "We've talked with many of their friends. Golf buddies. Coworkers. Neighbors. Every one of them believe that Tim and Martha would not move out of the South. Do you agree with that?"

"They're going to Phoenix."

"Mrs. Baker, they're not going to Phoenix."

"You don't know that. They could still be on the way there."

I shrugged. "You don't think they would lie to you?"

"No." Her answer came quickly. "Martha and I've never deceived each other. Not even when we were kids."

"Couldn't she be protecting you? If you don't know what really happened out at that prison or where she is, you don't have to lie to us."

"I wouldn't lie to you or anyone else."

"Not even for your sister?"

Chapter 46

"What did they want?" Martha asked.

"If I knew where you were." Paige told her of last night's TV interview and the questions Investigator Tortelli and Dub Walker had asked. "They think you did it."

"We didn't," Martha said. "I told you that."

"They said they had evidence against you."

"We weren't anywhere near where Whitiker was shot and had nothing to do with it."

"But the police believe you did."

"They'll never find us."

"Where are you now?" Paige asked.

"It's better that you don't know."

"But—"

"But nothing. If you know and don't tell them then you're breaking the law. We don't want that."

"It's just so hard not knowing."

"Just know that we are well and happy. In fact, I have some good news. We're getting married Sunday."

"Under your new names?"

"Yes."

"You and Tim are already married. In God's eyes."

"Then this will be reaffirming that."

"Can't you at least tell me your new names?"

"Better you don't know that either."

Paige knew that everything Martha said was true, but she wasn't sure she could live with it. Not knowing where they were. Not being able to call and chat any time she wanted. Not being able to drive over for lunch or an afternoon visit. It was just too much. Her throat tightened and tears stung her eyes. "I just hate this. Are you sure this is the right thing to do? Leaving me? Your friends?"

"I know, honey. I hate it too, but it has to be this way."

"Are you sure?"

"Yes, we're sure. We thought about this for a long time. You know that."

"I wish I could be there for the wedding. Wherever there is."

"You will be. In spirit."

"With Whitiker gone, is there any chance you could come back?"

"It's not possible. We broke too many laws. Taking pension money. Things like that."

"Those can be undone. Pay some penalties. That sort of thing."

No answer came for a minute and then Martha said, "We like our new life. Our new city."

"You're there? Your new home?"

"Yes."

"I would feel a lot better if I knew where you were."

"When all the dust settles, you will."

Paige sighed. "Will I ever see you again?"

"Of course. It might be a while, but definitely you will."

"I hate this." Martha closed the phone and dropped it on the side table near the sofa. "Lying to her." She felt tears gather in her eyes and her vision blur.

"It's for her protection," Tim said.

"I know." She swiped the back of her hand across her eyes. "It's just so unfair to her."

"What did she say?" Tim sat down next to her.

"Claire McBride interviewed Investigator Tortelli and Dub Walker on TV last night. They essentially told the world we were suspects."

"We are."

"But—all our friends—what will they think?"

He wrapped an arm around her and pulled her against his chest. "We talked about this. Remember? We knew we would eventually be suspects."

"That was talk. This is real." She sighed. "All of this is real."

He smoothed her hair. "I know. All the planning was like a game compared to now."

She lifted her head away from him and looked up. "What are we going to do?"

"Nothing. What's done is done. We move forward."

"But—"

"But, nothing. We're getting married. We're starting a new life. Just as we planned."

She again pressed her cheek against his chest. "I love you."

Chapter 47

By the time we blew by Paint Rock and Gurley on Highway 72, some twenty-five miles from Huntsville, the rain arrived in full force. It pounded against the Porsche's roof and came up in a rooster tail in our wake. The windshield wipers worked perfectly. At least neither had wiggled free and flown off. My fear wasn't so much losing a wiper blade, but rather Claire finding out—she always sniffed out stuff like that— and then I'd have to live with her harassment. A painful thought. I could hear her: "You should've let me do it. You know you aren't any good with this stuff." Sometimes she can be such a bitch.

T-Tommy: "She was lying."

Me: "Sure was."

T-Tommy: "She knows where they are."

Me: "Sure does."

T-Tommy: "They'll call her or she'll call them."

Me: "Bet that's true."

T-Tommy: "Until then I guess we just scratch our asses and wait."

Me: "Maybe lunch?"

T-Tommy: "That'd work."

T-Tommy's cell chirped. He flipped it open and mostly listened for a couple of minutes, before folding it and dropping it back into his jacket pocket.

"That was Paul Twitty. Said JD has something for us."

I kicked the Porsche up, the needle bouncing around eighty-five. The rooster tail thickened. We made it to JD's shop in forty minutes. Inside we found Twitty and JD chatting over the counter. Twitty had a chewed-on cigar in his mouth and a cup of coffee in one hand; JD his ever-present Dr. Pepper.

"What's the deal?" I asked.

Twitty nodded toward JD.

"Got a call this morning from a friend of mine. Old boy named Dale Bonner. Has a gun shop over in Rome, Georgia. He saw a report on the Fosters on TV. Recognized them immediately."

"From?"

"From a gun show he was at. Over in Rome. Big outdoor event they hold each year." JD crossed his arms over his chest and looked at me. He obviously wanted to stretch the story out a bit. Make us work for it.

Okay, I'll play. "So?"

"He sold Tim Foster a rifle, a scope, and ammo."

I looked at T-Tommy and then back to JD. "When?"

"Three months ago."

"What date?"

"Let's see."

JD turned to the wall behind him where a calendar hung. The top half had a picture of a woman in a sparse, bright-red bikini holding a Sig556 Swat rifle, a thick belt of high-caliber cartridges draped across her as if it she had won the title of Miss Assault Rifle. The lower half displayed the month of May. JD had scribbled variously colored notes into some of the squares. He flipped back three months. Miss February appeared. Her bikini was bright yellow with black polka dots and she clutched a shiny stainless-steel Kimber .45 ACP to her ample chest.

JD tapped the calendar with an index finger. "It was the weekend of February twenty-seventh."

"How come you have that marked on your calendar?" T-Tommy asked.

"This's where I keep my schedule."

"You were there?" I asked. "At this show?"

"Sure. I do about six or seven a year. Either buying or selling. Usually both."

"Did you see the Fosters there?"

"You think I would'nt've told you if I had?" He emptied the Pepper, crushed the can, and dropped it into the trash. "I would've told you, the DA, everyone. That asshole killed my brother. If you still doubt that, then you ain't paying attention."

"Did he register it?"

JD gave me a you're-dumber-than-you-look look. "Most gun shows aren't too big on registrations. And Dale ain't the FB-fuckin'-I. He sells guns."

"Even if that's the law?" T-Tommy asked.

JD snorted. "Right. The Second Amendment don't say shit about registering guns. Just says everybody has the right to one."

I let the fact that I agreed with him slide.

"How many did he buy?" T-Tommy asked.

JD grabbed a fresh Dr. Pepper from the small fridge behind the counter, hissed open the tab, and knocked back a couple of slugs. He suppressed a belch. "He didn't say."

"He say the make and model?"

"Didn't ask. Here's his info." He slid a piece of paper across to me. "Ask him yourself. Ain't that your job?"

I wanted to pull out one of the Glocks I saw beneath the counter glass and shoot him. I was sure T-Tommy felt the same way. Only he was already armed.

Instead, we left.

Chapter 48

I wished we had known this before we drove over to Scottsboro earlier. Would have saved time since Scottsboro is smack-dab on the way to Rome, Georgia. Maybe halfway between. We decided to swing by T-Tommy's office before heading that way.

At the South Precinct, I used a computer in an empty office while T-Tommy made some phone calls. I Googled and then MapQuested Dale's Cheap Guns. Looked like it was just north of downtown. I printed the map and directions, folded them, and settled them in my jacket pocket.

I ran into Derrick Stone as I walked down the hall.

"I heard you guys were here," Stone said. "I was just getting ready to call."

"About what?" I asked as we turned into T-Tommy's office.

T-Tommy was on the phone. I sat down in the chair that faced him; Stone stood to the left.

T-Tommy ended his call, shifted his weight in his chair, and looked up at Stone. "What've you got?"

"The sister's phone. She received two more calls from that prepaid cell."

I sat up straight. This was getting interesting. "When?"

"Both today."

"What time?"

Stone flipped open his notebook and thumbed through the pages. "Last Tuesday's call was at nine fifty-two in the morning. Went through a tower in Tennessee. Near South Pittsburg right about the junction of Highway 72 and I-24."

Nearly three hours after Whitiker was shot. That gave them time to flee the scene, drive back to Huntsville, dump the SUV, and disappear into Tennessee.

"The two today," Stone continued, "were at ten-oh-two and ten thirty-seven. The first was one minute, the second for a little over twelve minutes."

I looked at T-Tommy. "That was them. The call Paige got while we were there. Told them to call back in thirty minutes and apparently they did."

"Where'd the calls originate?"

"Couldn't have told you that a half hour ago, but I got a guy keeping an eye on Paige Baker's phone activity. Not exactly according to Hoyle, but what the heck. It's off the radar so there's no record. He called as soon as the other two calls came in. I got on the phone to Feigler. Faxed him the probable cause and he signed off on a warrant. Just for records but it does allow us to follow her phones in real time. Anyway, I got the warrant over to the AT & T folks and bingo."

"That was quick," I said.

"And who says the wheels of justice are slow?" Stone smiled.

"I thought AT & T was the prepaid phone's carrier?" T-Tommy said.

"It is," Stone said. "Paige Baker's, too. Both her home and cell service."

"So let's have it," T-Tommy said. "Where did the calls originate?"

"The Asheville, North Carolina, area."

"The question is," T-Tommy said, "are they just passing through or is Asheville where they ran to?"

I shrugged. "No way to know. I'd bet Tuesday's call was a pass though based on the timing, but Asheville could go either way."

T-Tommy looked at Stone. "Get someone sniffing around for them in both areas."

"Will do."

"Treat it as a missing persons," T-Tommy said. "We don't want the local PDs getting all excited. If they think it's only a missing couple, they'll be casual. If they think we have homicide fugitives on our hands, they could go all ballistic and spook them."

"Makes sense," Stone said.

"If they do locate them in either city, ask them to hang back and not approach or talk to them if possible," I said. "Any scrutiny could put them back on the road."

Stone nodded.

"Feigler going to give us a tap now?" I asked.

Stone shook his head. "He did say that the three calls to the sister were too much to ignore but only for access to the numbers in and out. We can follow both of Paige Baker's phones. The guy at AT&T said he'd let me know every time either of her phones were used."

"But no tap?" T-Tommy said.

Stone scratched an ear. "Feigler wavered a bit, but in the end, said we didn't have enough to go that far. The same blah-blah-blah about the sister not being a suspect. The usual judicial BS."

I never can understand how judges think. This seems a no-brainer to me. A man is shot dead at a state prison, the two primary suspects haul ass out of town with a bag of money and no known destination, and the sister suddenly starts getting calls from an anonymous cell phone. What was Feigler not seeing?

Could this simply be a coincidence? Sure. Likely? Not a chance. There are very few true coincidences in life and virtually none in criminal investigations. One act leads to another. The behavior of one person alters the behavior of another. If Paige Baker's sister Martha split just before she started getting calls from an untraceable cell phone, the two are related. Cause and effect. Why couldn't Feigler see this?

"What about the other phone?" I asked. "The prepaid one? Maybe we should ask for a tap on it."

"You think he'll give us permission to tap a phone when we don't even know who owns it?"

Put that way it did sound silly. "Probably not."

"Definitely not," T-Tommy said.

"Didn't you say the prepaid was bought in Rome, Georgia?" I asked Stone.

"Yeah."

"What was the purchase date?"

"Got it right here." The notebook pages crinkled as he rummaged through them. "Looks like February, twenty-seven."

The same day as the gun show.

My, my. What a small world.

Chapter 49

The 115-mile trip from Huntsville to Rome, Georgia, took just under two hours, and by the time we settled into an idle near the corner of Broad and Sixth, the overcast sky only delivered a fine mist. Out the side window I saw the rain-slicked bronze statue of Romulus and Remus. A 1929 gift from then-Italian dictator Benito Mussolini, the Capitoline wolf mother and her suckling human twins squatted on a white marble pedestal in front of the two-story, red brick Rome City Hall.

The story goes that Romulus and Remus were the twin sons of the god Mars and the Vestal Virgin Rhea. As feral children they were raised by a wolf-mother. In a dispute over naming rights for a new city, Romulus killed his brother and dubbed the new city Rome. Gave new meaning to the term "sibling rivalry." Romulus became Rome's first king, reigning until his death around 717 BC.

Like the ancient original, Georgia's Rome lay over seven hills. They bore cool names like Myrtle, Blossom, Clock Tower, and Old Shorter. Lush with trees, the hills overlooked rich farmland and the tranquil city of forty thousand. The Etowah and Oostanaula Rivers wound through the valleys before melting into the Coosa River near downtown.

When the light changed, we left the twins to their meal and hunted for a service station, finding one two blocks away. While the tank filled, I looked over the MapQuest pages I had printed. We were only three blocks from Dale's Cheap Guns. Ten minutes later we walked through the front door.

Dale's place looked a lot like JD's, maybe a bit heavier on the fishing gear, but racks of hunting rifles and shotguns filled one wall. Dale proved easy to find. He was the only person in the store.

He was a big guy with a dense black beard, and carried an extra fifty pounds or so. He wore jeans, an untucked red-and-brown plaid shirt, and a white Dale's Cheap Guns cap.

After we introduced ourselves, he said, "You guys made good time. I didn't expect you for another hour."

I had called him just before we left T-Tommy's office to let him know we were going to drive over for a chat.

"Not much traffic."

"Yeah, you never know about that. At least the rain hasn't washed out any of the roads."

T-Tommy slid a pair of photos from the folder he carried and placed the images of Tim and Martha Foster on the counter in front of Dale. Before T-Tommy could even ask, Dale said, "That's them."

"You're sure?"

"Absolutely."

"Tell us about it."

"We have a gun show here every winter. Pretty big deal. Dealers and buyers come from all over. Even had an outfit down from Ohio this year."

"How many people show up?" I asked.

"Over the entire weekend—maybe ten, twelve thousand or so."

"That's a lot."

"Used to be smaller, but over the past few years it's gotten a whole lot bigger. Have to hold it over at the park. Spread out all to hell. Must've been forty tents and twice that many tables and booths."

"Sell many guns?" I asked. "At the show?"

He smiled. "Yeah. We had a good weekend."

"With that many people how can you be sure these are the folks you sold a gun to?"

"Told you I was sure. Wouldn't've said it if I wasn't." He picked up the picture of Martha. "Wouldn't forget a face like that."

"What'd they buy?"

He pulled open a drawer and removed an invoice. "When you said you were headed this way, I pulled out the sales slip." He handed it to me.

At the top next to "Sold To" it said Sam Clarkson. Same name as that attached to the prepaid phone.

The next line revealed an Atlanta address. Wabash Street. No phone number. A list of purchased items came next: a Nikon ProStaff 3-9x40 scope, four boxes of Remington Core-Lokt Centerfire ammo, twenty per, and a Browning BAR Safari .308. Same model as the weapon found at the scene. Same scope. Same ammo. The total was $672.34.

"They paid cash, right?" T-Tommy asked.

"Most do at these shows."

I handed the invoice back to Dale.

"Can I get a copy of this?" T-Tommy asked.

"Sure."

"They only buy the one rifle?" I asked.

"Just what's on the invoice."

"Did they know what they wanted or did you help them pick the rifle?"

"The man, Mr. Clarkson, said he wanted a hunting rifle. For deer and bighorn sheep. I remember he said he had a hunting trip to Wyoming planned in the fall."

I nodded. "I imagine you see all kinds here in your shop and at the shows. People who know about guns and others that aren't so sure."

He shrugged. "Yeah."

"Did this Clarkson guy seem comfortable with it? Know how to handle it?"

"Seemed that way to me. Of course, it's hard to tell those kinds of things unless you're on a shooting range or out hunting."

"But he wasn't a butterfingers? He knew how to handle it, how to work it?"

"Best I can remember."

"Were they with anyone else?" T-Tommy asked.

Dale rubbed his chin. "Not that I remember."

"What about JD? I understand he was at the show. Did he see them or talk to them as far as you know?"

"Not while they were at my booth." Again he rubbed his chin. "I do seem to remember that Bo Hudson stopped by around that time. He works for JD."

"We know him," I said.

"Can't say for sure. I do know this Clarkson dude was there late morning. And it was around that time that Bo stopped by and said he was heading over to the BBQ tent to get a plate. Asked if I wanted him to pick up something for me."

"And did he?"

Dale patted his belly. "I never pass up good Q."

"Did Bo see the couple or say anything about them?"

"Not that I recall."

Chapter 50

We found All Things Wireless a block and a half from the river, hanging to the end of a strip mall next to a bagel shop. Inside we did indeed find all things wireless: computer keyboards, handheld radios, GPS devices, an armada of Blue Tooth and WiFi gadgets, and, of course, cell phones.

The only worker, a middle-aged, pudgy, semi-bald and combed-over guy, stood behind the checkout counter finishing up a sale. The customer was a dude with long, dirty hair and a tattoo of a spiderweb on one forearm. His equally stringy-haired girlfriend held his hand and lolled her head on his shoulder. Her jeans rode low, her cropped tee shirt high, revealing a red script tramp stamp on her lower back that said, "Thanks, Dude."

Wonder who she was thanking and for what? On second thought, I didn't want to know.

I fought to suppress a smile as Mr. Stringy Hair scooped up a boxed cell phone and he and Ms. Stringy Hair moved past me and headed out the door. The odor of marijuana trailed behind them.

The man came around the counter. "Can I help you?"

T-Tommy badged him. "I'm Investigator Tommy Tortelli. Huntsville, Alabama PD."

"I'm Dub Walker," I said. "I'm consulting on a case with Investigator Tortelli."

The man hesitated a beat, concern nipping at the corners of his eyes, and then said, "Name's Wilbert Pitlock. What can I do for you?"

"We need some information about a customer of yours," I said.

T-Tommy handed him the pictures of Tim and Martha Foster. "You recognize these people?"

Pitlock studied each photo carefully. "No. Don't think I've seen them before." He handed the picture back to T-Tommy.

"You sold a phone to a Sam Clarkson back on February twenty-seventh."

"Let me check." He retreated behind the counter, slipped on a pair of glasses, and began working the keyboard of the computer that sat next to the cash register. The keys clicked softly. He frowned at the screen, clicked a few more keys, and then nodded. "That's right. A pre-paid phone. Paid cash." He looked up at me.

"We think the two people in the picture bought that phone," I said.

He looked back at the screen. "Marlin Lucky, one of my employees, made the sale." He looked toward the front door. "He just ran next door to get us a snack. Should be back in a sec."

I nodded.

"What's this about?"

"Can't say," T-Tommy said. "It's an ongoing investigation."

"Did this Clarkson guy leave an address?" I asked.

Again Pitlock squinted at the computer screen. "Sure did. Looks like he lives down in Atlanta."

"Can we get a copy of the sales slip?"

"Sure." He punched a couple of keys and the printer on a shelf behind him hummed to life. Once it spit out the page, he handed it to T-Tommy.

I glanced at it over T-Tommy's shoulder. Wabash Street. Same address he'd given at Dale's Cheap Guns. If nothing else Tim Foster was consistent. Smart move. Consistency made keeping the lies straight easier. We'd check it out, didn't want to assume anything, but I knew the address would be bogus.

I looked up to see Pitlock studying me. I gave him a quizzical look.

"You that guy that writes those books on all that forensic stuff?"

"Guilty."

"I thought so. My wife reads mysteries like there ain't no tomorrow. Watches every *CSI* and cop show there is. She's got a couple of your books."

"That's good to hear. Hope she likes them."

"Oh, she sure does." He hesitated a beat, his eyes glancing toward a closed door to his right. "I think I got one of them here. Been meaning to read it." He looked back at me. "Would it be too much if I asked you to sign it for her?"

"I'd be happy to."

"She's going be be thrilled." He walked through the door, which I assumed led to a back office, and returned in a few seconds, book in hand. *How Bad Guys Think: A Look into the Criminal Mind.* One of my older books. He handed it to me.

"What's her name?" I asked as I pulled a pen from my pocket.

"Eloise."

I opened the book, found the title page, scribbled an inscription to Eloise, and handed the book back.

"Thanks. She's going to love it."

"Glad to do it."

"Mind if I ask what a consultant does?"

"Mostly I keep these guys from running around in circles." I nodded toward T-Tommy.

T-Tommy grunted. "Mostly he goofs off and we pay him to do it."

At first Pitlock didn't react, didn't seem sure what to make of our banter, but when we both smiled, he did too.

I heard the door open behind me and turned. A black teenager came in. He was dressed exactly like Pitlock: blue slacks, a white short-sleeved shirt, and a narrow blue tie. He carried a bag from the bagel store in one hand and a pair of Styrofoam cups stacked in the other.

"Here he is," Pitlock said. "Maybe he'll recognize them."

The kid walked behind the register and placed the bag and coffees on the counter. The aroma of fresh coffee and toasted bagels wafted toward me. I heard a soft grunt from T-Tommy. He smelled it, too. Must be time for his mid-afternoon feeding.

"Recognize who?" the young man asked.

T-Tommy introduced us and then handed the photos to Marlin. "Ever see these two?"

He looked at Tim, then Martha, then back to Tim. His brow furrowed. "Were they in here?"

"We think so."

"When?"

"Three months ago," I said. "February twenty-seventh to be exact."

"Bought a prepaid phone," Pitlock said. "Paid cash."

Marlin nodded slowly. "Yeah, I do remember them. Her anyway. She's very pretty."

"You sure?"

He looked at Martha's picture again. "Yeah. I'm sure."

"Anything unusual about them?"

"Nothing that I remember."

"Just bought the phone and left?"

He looked back at the photos. "That's all I remember."

"Did they say where they were going?"

Marlin shook his head as he peeled the top off his coffee cup and took a careful sip. "Are they in some kind of trouble?"

"They're missing and we're looking for them," I said.

T-Tommy handed each of them a card. "If you hear from them or see them, could you give me a call?"

"Sure," Pitlock said.

"Don't say we were here," I said. "Wouldn't want to concern them unnecessarily."

Marlin smiled. "We'd be like undercover agents?"

"Something like that," I said.

"Cool."

Chapter 51

Last night after T-Tommy and I drove back from Rome, we stopped by Sammy's. We planned to have a drink or two and head home. Make it an early night. Didn't exactly work out that way. Before we finished our first drink, Alison Chapman came in with a couple of her girlfriends. Twenty-five, very pretty, and a waitress at the very upscale downtown restaurant Cotton Row, which sat on the south side of the courthouse square on the original Cotton Row, where countless tons of cotton had changed hands back when cotton was king. She was also T-Tommy's latest . . . I'm not sure what. I know they'd been out a few times, but it certainly wasn't anything serious.

After the third drink, I sat in with Colin Dogget for two sets. T-Tommy and Alison waved and headed out in the middle of the second one. T-Tommy can be such a dog sometimes. Not often, but sometimes. Mostly he worked. Dated rarely. Said real relationships required too much "tending." His word. Not a bad word, though.

I made it home at eleven thirty and found Claire's car in my drive. I knew she had had a date with her new boyfriend. The attorney. The one she didn't really like. He drove over from Athens to take her to dinner. He probably hoped to spend the night, but she sent him home and drove over here. She had used her key to get in, opened a bottle of wine, and was sitting on the back deck, wine glass in hand, when I arrived.

Now, the morning after, with me trying to shake off a hangover,

Claire and I sat on the deck, drinking coffee. I hoped it would rip up the brain cobwebs left behind by last night's alcohol, marathon sex, and fitful sleep. So far, not so much and I was already on my second cup. Or was it third? I'd lost count. I watched an orange-breasted robin do his herky-jerky zigzagging around the yard, stopping to root around for a worm every now and then.

I rubbed my ribs. They were sore from where Claire had slugged me last night. Woman could deliver a rib shot. I had teased her about dumping Mr. New Dude and coming over for a Dub fix. She told me to shut up. I didn't listen and went on about how I must be a super stud and she must be addicted to my hot monkey love. She warned me. I didn't heed it. It was when I started singing "Save the Last Dance for Me" that she hit me. The blow was accompanied by the words "Pig" and "Asshole."

She can be so endearing sometimes.

All was forgiven in bed though.

"Want to go get some breakfast?" I asked.

"I can whip up some eggs and toast."

"Let's call T-Tommy and head over to Gibson's."

"You sure T-Tommy's up and about yet? I mean after a night with that little waitress filly of his?"

I had told her about Alison unexpectedly showing up and she and T-Tommy leaving together. "She's a very nice young lady."

"With young being the operative word."

I didn't respond.

Tending comes in many forms.

Gibson's Bar-B-Q sat along Memorial Parkway near Airport Road. Famous for Bar-B-Q and a competitor of Sammy's, Gibson's was also a local breakfast meeting place and had the best biscuits you'll find anywhere. And pies. Lord, they could make pies.

Booths and tables, mostly four-tops, each topped with a plasticized red-and-white checkered tablecloth, filled the large dining room. As usual, customers surrounded every table, the aroma of eggs and bacon hung in the air, and the murmurs of conversation and the clatter of forks attacking plates filled the room. We luckily found an empty booth near the back wall. Claire and I slid into one side, but the collection of pies in the nearby pie case, things like pecan, chess, coconut, apple, and lemon icebox, distracted T-Tommy so he stopped to have a look before making his way to the other side of the booth.

I had scrambled eggs and biscuits, Claire just biscuits, lots of butter, and T-Tommy everything: eggs, country ham, patty sausage, grits, and a stack of biscuits. He topped it with a piece of chess pie. Even though Gibson's coconut pie won best dessert in town, T-Tommy was always partial to chess.

When Claire asked about the rationale of pie with breakfast, T-Tommy grunted and said there wasn't a law against it. Hard to argue with that logic.

While he ate, Claire began her interrogation. "So tell me about last night."

"What about it?"

"Did you defile that poor young girl?"

"Best I could."

"Pig."

"How can you say that with a straight face while sitting next to Dub?"

How did I get dragged into this?

"Means I have experience with pigs," Claire said.

I had sore ribs to prove it.

After we paid the bill and reached the parking lot, T-Tommy's cell buzzed. He talked for a minute and snapped it shut.

"Pastor Boles. Said he might have something on the Fosters."

Claire and I followed T-Tommy, and ten minutes later we walked into the Whitesburg Baptist Church. We found Pastor Ronnie Boles in his office. I introduced him and Claire, and he graciously told her he was a big fan. Watched her reports all the time.

"I got a call from Pastor Arthur Dunn this morning," he said from his seat behind his desk. "I sent him a note about Tim and Martha and included their photos. He said he had two new members that could be them. Just joined the church yesterday."

"Where?" I asked.

"North Carolina. Asheville."

Well, well, Asheville pops up on the radar one more time.

"It might not be them," Boles said. "All he said was that they looked similar. Different hair but otherwise the photos looked like them."

"Names?"

He glanced at a piece of paper on his desk. "Robert Beckwith and Cindy Strunk."

"I take it Pastor Dunn didn't send along photos of his new members," I said.

"No. I didn't really ask, but I doubt he would have photos of them anyway." He looked up at me. "Want me to give him a call? You can talk to him yourself."

"No. I don't want them to know we found them. If it is them."

"I see." His face sagged as if the force of gravity had suddenly increased. "They're in trouble, aren't they?"

"Maybe."

He sighed. "Could this—whatever it is—simply be a misunderstanding? I mean, I've known the Fosters for years. I can't imagine—" His voice trailed off.

"That's possible," I said. "Once we find them, we can straighten everything out."

"Let's hope."

"He say anything else? Pastor Dunn?"

"Actually he mentioned that this couple is getting married tomorrow."

"What?" That wasn't anywhere near what I expected to hear.

"They stopped by his church yesterday," Boles said. "Told him they had just moved from Atlanta and were looking for a new church and wanted him to marry them. He said he was surprised but pleasantly so. He agreed to perform the ceremony tomorrow."

And now Atlanta rears its head again.

"He say what time?" I asked.

"After the eight o'clock service."

We thanked Boles and started to leave, but I had a thought and turned back toward him. "One thing."

"Yes?"

"I had another thought. Maybe you should call Pastor Dunn."

"Why?"

"If this couple is Tim and Martha, I don't want them to have even a hint that they might have been found. They might take off again."

"I see."

"If he were to mention your conversation to them, even in passing, it could spook them."

"He's going to want to know why. I mean, we pastors are rarely that secretive."

That made sense. I felt suddenly uncomfortable as if Jesus was watching me ask this man and his North Carolina counterpart to lie. Maybe not lie, but close. Close enough that Jesus might not split those hairs. Before I could come up with a cover story that made sense, Claire jumped in.

"Just tell him that some friends want to surprise them at their wedding," Claire said.

She obviously had no problems with asking him to lie. She can be such a Jezebel.

"I'm not sure I'm comfortable with that," Boles said.

"It's for their own good," I said. "People on the run are always looking over their shoulder and not where they're going. Sometimes they run headlong into worse trouble than they're fleeing."

"But—"

I raised a hand. "If they don't know we're coming, they won't run, and we can make all this as easy and safe as possible."

"You're starting to sound as if you believe they might have been involved in Walter's death."

I stared at him but said nothing. His shoulders dropped an inch or two.

"That's what you're saying, isn't it?" Boles continued. "That they were involved."

"We have some troubling evidence," T-Tommy said.

The pain Boles was feeling was in his face. His eyes glistened slightly. "But you're not sure this couple is them. What if it's not?"

"That's not the major concern," I said. "I'm worried that if it is them, they'll get spooked."

"This is all so confusing, and disturbing." He hesitated a beat and then looked at me and sighed. "But, I do see your point. I'll call him and I'll use your story." He offered Claire a weak smile. "Sometimes little white lies are necessary, I guess. Not often, but sometimes."

Back in the car, Claire said, "We're going to burn in hell for this."

"I'm not sure asking a pastor to tell a little fib rises to the burn-in-hell level."

"Sure feels that way." She sighed. "I feel like I need a shower."

"Want me to wash your back?"

"Shut up and drive."

Chapter 52

We swung by the South Precinct. Derrick Stone intercepted us before we reached T-Tommy's office.

"That Atlanta address you asked about," Stone said, "it doesn't exist."

"Figured that," T-Tommy said.

"There's a Wabash Street but not a house number that matches."

"Thanks," T-Tommy said. "We might have a lead on them."

"Really? Where?"

"North Carolina."

"Interesting." Stone glanced at his watch. "I have a witness interview in about five. That homicide in New Hope. I'll check in when I'm finished."

Once we got to T-Tommy's office, he called the Asheville PD and spoke with the duty officer. Asked him to run a DMV check on Robert Beckwith and Cindy Strunk. When the officer asked why, T-Tommy said it was a missing persons case. Wasn't sure these were the folks he was looking for, but their licenses' photos could clear it up. The officer said he would get someone on it and send along the info. How long? Apparently they were a little shorthanded, something about a big accident on I-40 had sucked everybody out of the office. Maybe an hour. Maybe two.

T-Tommy hung up the phone and leaned back in his chair. "Looks like we wait."

"Your favorite thing," Claire said. She looked at me. "Yours, too."

"Don't leave yourself out of that mix."

"I'm the most patient person you know."

She actually said that with a straight face. She should play poker.

"Yeah, right."

She shrugged. "Compared to you two, I'm downright easygoing."

"Not the word I'd use," T-Tommy said.

She tried to give him a Claire look, but I could see the smile buried beneath the frown.

"Atlanta and Asheville," I said. "They keep jumping up on the radar. Sam Clarkson gave an Atlanta address to Dale Bonner when he bought the rifle and to Wilbert Pitlock at the phone store. Now a pastor in North Carolina says his two new members are a couple from Atlanta."

"Big city makes you anonymous," T-Tommy said. "If you're trying to drop off the radar, better to say you came from somewhere like Atlanta rather than some small town where everyone knows everyone. In case you run into someone from your so-called hometown."

"If this is them, it would make sense of the phone calls," I said. "Even the one last Tuesday to Paige Baker. It came from an area between here and Asheville."

T-Tommy rubbed one eye with a knuckle. "Looks like a trip to North Carolina."

"If that's them in Asheville," Claire said.

"It is," I said.

Claire looked at me. "You don't know that."

"Makes sense. A move, but not out of the South. Close enough to check out on their fake trips to Gatlinburg and Myrtle Beach. Two calls from that area on a cell phone we know they bought. Now a local pastor recognizes them." I shrugged. "It's them."

"You're probably right."

"Could you say that again?"

"Cram it, Dub."

"Come on. Humor me."

"I humored you last night. This is business."

"You thought last night was funny?"

"Very."

"Hmm. I seem to remember a couple of 'Oh, Gods' coming my way."

This time her glare was real.

T-Tommy laughed.

Claire's glare turned to him. "Don't jump into this, Tortelli."

T-Tommy raised his palms in defense.

"Do something useful," she said. "Check your e-mail."

T-Tommy glanced at his computer screen. "Nothing."

Claire stood and walked to the window. She separated the blinds and looked out as if checking the weather. "Let's go get some coffee."

We walked down to The Coffee Tree, a coffee shop, snack bar, bookstore combination that made great coffee and sandwiches. We grabbed a table near the counter. Claire and I opted for coffee, T-Tommy coffee and an egg salad bagel. And Mississippi mud pie.

"If you go to Asheville, I'm going with you," Claire said.

"No, you're not."

She gave me a look. One that I knew well. One that said following this line of reasoning probably wasn't the best idea. Especially since I already had sore ribs.

"Really?"

"Okay, you can go."

She rolled her eyes. "Thanks, Daddy."

"That was last night. Today you can call me Mr. Walker."

Another look. This one could singe your hair. I need to learn to shut up.

An hour later we returned to T-Tommy's office. Still nothing. Claire made some phone calls, T-Tommy met with Stone and a couple of patrol officers about the New Hope murder case they were working.

Another hour slid by.

Finally T-Tommy's computer chimed, indicating a new e-mail. He tapped the keyboard. Claire and I moved behind him and looked over his shoulder. He opened the e-mail and then the two attachments.

The faces of Tim and Martha Foster filled the screen.

Chapter 53

SATURDAY, 2:57 P.M.

Claire and I stopped by her place. She packed up a few things, and we headed to my house, where Claire's E 550 still sat in the driveway. T-Tommy turned in just behind us and climbed from his car, duffel bag in hand. I threw some clothes into my own duffel, and we stuffed everything into the trunk of Claire's Mercedes, my Porsche way too small for the three of us to make a three hundred-mile trip.

"Do you need some kind of permission to do this?" Claire asked T-Tommy.

"This what?"

"Arrest a pair of murder suspects in another state."

"Is that what we're doing?" T-Tommy raised an eyebrow and smiled. "I thought this was just a friendly road trip."

"So you didn't tell your chief?"

"Nope. Nothing to tell. Not yet anyway."

"Besides," I said as I closed the trunk, "wouldn't want this to get back to Twitty. He has sources inside. If he learns where the Fosters are, then JD will know."

"What about Derrick Stone?" Claire asked. "He knows."

We had huddled with Stone before leaving the South Precinct and brought him up to date. T-Tommy told him to keep it to himself and to call him immediately if anything new came up.

"Stone's not Twitty's deep throat," T-Tommy said. "He hates the guy."

"There's a story there," Claire said.

"Nothing much. Twitty sandbagged Stone once when Stone was assigned to his squad. Maybe ten years ago. Stone was a rook, Twitty a jerk."

We climbed into the car. Claire drove, I rode shotgun, and T-Tommy lounged in the backseat.

"Are you worried that JD might do something?" Claire asked.

"Don't know," I said.

T-Tommy grunted. "The less JD knows, the better."

"So he could?"

"JD ain't exactly an upstanding citizen," he said. "He's pissed his brother got shot. He's aimed directly at the Fosters. Add that up and I'd suspect he might decide to do something stupid. Stupid seems to run in his family tree. Better he doesn't have a chance."

Claire whipped into a Starbucks, saying she needed coffee if she was going to be cooped up with us all day. She can be so gracious when she really tries. She got a Venti with a couple of extra shots, T-Tommy and I each got a small, which they call "Tall" for some inexplicable reason, and soon we were back on Highway 72.

Again.

Sometimes life is a yo-yo. Or maybe a pendulum. Up and down, back and forth, repeatedly following the same rutted path. We had already been to or by Scottsboro three times this week. Twice to see Martha's sister and again when we flew past on our way to Rome. Now, since Scottsboro was on the way to Asheville, we slid by it yet again.

Claire settled in at a steady seventy-five miles per hour while I eased back my seat and closed my eyes. The Fosters immediately marched through my thoughts.

Here we were driving along like we were on vacation, not a care in sight. Truth was we were going to confront a couple whose life had been ripped apart and our visit would crush what was left. It felt as if we were betraying them.

What really perplexed me though was how a clean-living, God-fearing, Christian couple could plan a murder and their disappearance over several months, maybe much longer. If they had done this in a fit of passion, maybe bursting into the courtroom and blowing him away, or gunning him down on the street as he was moved back and forth be-tween the court and the jail, I could easily understand. Pressure mounts and folks sometime explode in wildly uncharacteristic ways to release it. But to let it simmer for months and then plan it down to the tiniest detail? This was cold and calculated, not hot-blooded passion. Passion can't be carried that long. Time softens pain and heals wounds. Ap-parently not for the Fosters. They had held this venom inside. Used it to drive them to this.

Then they pulled it off with a pair of three-hundred-yard shots that would make any sniper proud, went off to Asheville, and planned a wedding. I just couldn't see this coldness in the Tim and Martha Fos-ter I knew. Throughout the search for their son, the media frenzy that surrounded the discovery of his remains, and at Whitiker's trial, they had appeared broken, resigned to a life of pain, rather than one filled with anger and revenge. Yet, something brewed within them. Some-thing malignant enough to push them along this path.

Still, on some level I got it completely. If I ever found who took Jill, it would get real ugly, real quick. Torture wouldn't cover it. It'd be some-thing much worse. Something medieval. Something Dahmer or Bundy would be proud of.

I looked out the window. A few patchy clouds broke up the clear blue sky. The rich green farmland flew by. In the distance, I saw the vague silhouette of a barn tucked beneath a velvety green blanket of kudzu. A pair of crows spiraled into the sky, apparently fighting over some morsel of food or a pilfered object. Like Kramden and Norton did on a daily basis.

"What is it?" Claire asked.

"What's what?"

"What's bugging you?"

I turned from the window. "Who said anything was bugging me?"

She tossed a frown at me. "Let's have it."

"The Fosters."

"What about them?"

I told her of my musings.

"But we know they engineered their own makeover," Claire said.

"We know they bought a weapon and the cell phone. We know their SUV was at the scene and was later abandoned with the keys in it."

I sighed. "It's just that with everything I remember about them while we searched for their son and at the trial and what everyone has said about them, murder seems to be a huge leap."

"Unless your child's been murdered," T-Tommy said from the backseat. "That'd knock anyone off the path of righteousness."

"I guess I'm just having trouble with them being this far off the path."

"You'd do the same. I would. Bet Claire would."

"In a heartbeat," Claire said.

"The evidence says the Fosters would too," T-Tommy said.

I twisted in the seat to look at him. "How do you want to play this?"

"Maybe just knock on the door."

"Should we notify the Asheville PD?" Claire asked. "Get them involved in this or at least let them know we're coming?"

"Only if we have to," T-Tommy said. "Maybe we can convince Tim and Martha it would be best if they simply came back to Huntsville with us. Save me a world of paperwork and a ton of shit for them."

"Might make their defense a bit easier, too," I said. "Giving yourself up often does. They just might find a friendly jury that understands why they did it."

"You think that's possible?" Claire asked.

I sighed. "Don't know. It's happened before. I do know one thing, I'd be a character witness for them if they asked."

"You got that right," T-Tommy said. "My only regret is that I didn't get the chance to dump Whitiker myself."

"What if they refuse to come back?" Claire asked.

"Then we'll have to bring in the Asheville PD to arrest them and begin the extradition process," T-Tommy said. "Rather not travel that road. Better if the Asheville PD doesn't have a clue we're in town."

JD Whitiker hung up the phone and sat quietly behind his desk for a minute. "Well, well, well, this just might work out," he said to himself.

He drained the Dr. Pepper he held and tossed the empty can in the trash before picking the phone up again and dialing. Kyle Spraggins answered after three rings.

"Remember that job I said I might have for you and Cody?" JD asked.

"Sure do."

"Well, it's on."

"When?"

"You'll need to leave right away."

"Where are we going?"

"Asheville, North Carolina."

"Been there. Nice safe place."

"You and Cody can make it a little less safe."

Kyle laughed. "My favorite pastime."

"There're a few things you'll need to do and few rules you'll have to follow, but it should be a piece of cake."

"We love cake. Tell me."

JD did.

Chapter 54

Tim lay in bed, Martha curled next to him, her back against his side. The new bed, not yet broken in, felt firm beneath his shoulders. The TV flickered from across the room but neither watched. He read a golf magazine; she the latest James Lee Burke novel.

She closed her book and rolled toward him, nestling her head against his shoulder.

"Are you feeling better about things?" Martha asked.

"A little. Time'll fix the rest of it."

"You sure?"

"No." When she didn't say anything, he continued. "I guess the planning of everything was so all consuming that I never really thought about what it would be like afterward. After I pulled the trigger."

"We're in this together. We're both responsible."

He sighed. "I know. It'll just take time. And concentrating on the future and not the past." He smoothed her hair. "Like the wedding tomorrow. I'm looking forward to that."

"Do you think the vows we wrote are okay?"

"They're perfect. Wouldn't change a word."

She snuggled more tightly against him. "This reminds me of when we were dating."

"How so?"

"We're not married. We're lying in bed. We're hiding out."

Tim laughed. "From your parents."

"Only because my father would have killed you."

"For deflowering his little girl?"

Now Martha laughed. "Something like that."

Tim let the magazine slide to the floor. "You have to admit this is a little better than that dump we used to go to. What was the name of that place?"

"The Happy Daze Lodge."

"That's right. Out off the Ardmore Highway."

Martha propped up on one elbow and looked down at him. "Remember the creepy guy behind the desk?"

"Norman Bates?"

"That's the one."

"In his defense, he knew what we were up to and didn't give us any grief."

"Didn't he waive the security deposit even though we didn't have a credit card?"

"That's what I mean." He rolled toward her and took her in his arms. "Of course he probably had hidden cameras in the room."

She poked his belly with a finger and laughed. "If we end up on YouTube, I'll hunt him down."

God, he loved her laugh. He hadn't heard much of it the past three years, Martha's depression crushing any joy she felt. But right here, right now, she seemed relaxed and happy. Was this simply excitement from the move and the wedding or did the killing of Walter Allen Whitiker make the difference? Was she that relieved?

Was he?

He did feel more relaxed. Why? Was Whitiker being alive and Steven dead that heavy a weight? Did the taking of Whitiker's life bring peace to both of them?

How would they reconcile this with God? Would He understand? Would they ever receive forgiveness or had the murder of Whitiker forever blocked their path to heaven?

Murder.

What an ugly word. But that's exactly what had happened. Regardless of what angle you took, it came out the same. Walter Whitiker was murdered. And he had done it.

He didn't want to think about that right now. He only wanted to savor this moment. The first time in years they had felt this relaxed. Comfortable. He didn't want to dwell on the incongruity of it. He only wanted to live in this moment.

He tilted her head up with one hand and kissed her, while his other hand slid down her back. He pulled her against him, trapping his growing erection between them. She reached down and held him.

"Look what I found."

"Don't you hate it when he does that?"

"Totally." She kissed him. "But, Mr. Beckwith, we're not married. I couldn't possibly."

"Well, Ms. Strunk, you woke him up so you'll have to deal with him."

She laughed and rolled on top of him. "I think I can handle that."

"I like this. The honeymoon before the wedding."

"I think most men would agree with that one."

He kissed her. "I'm excited about the wedding tomorrow."

"More than the first one?"

"Can't say that, but it'll be fun. A new beginning."

She laid her cheek against his chest. "I like it here. I think we made a good choice."

"We did. Once we get settled and make some new friends, it'll be perfect."

"I'll miss Huntsville. All our friends there. And Paige, of course."

"Me too, but we'll be okay." He flicked off the bedside lamp and punched the TV remote. His hands cupped her hips. "Now, where were we?"

Chapter 55

I examined the neighborhood while Claire eased her Mercedes to the curb across the street and down a couple of houses from the Fosters' new home. At least the address on their new North Carolina driver's licenses. The ones issued to Robert Beckwith and Cindy Strunk. Derrick Stone had called when we were still a hundred miles from Asheville and said he had tracked down the original Beckwith and Strunk. Both former residents of Ohio. Both deceased. Beckwith twenty years earlier, car accident at age eighteen; Strunk sixteen years ago at twenty-one from melanoma. Apparently the two lived on opposite sides of the state and never knew each other.

Now they were reborn as brand new North Carolina residents and were getting married in the morning.

The neighborhood was sleepy quiet. The Fosters' rented house, a small cottage, light gray with white trim, also appeared quiet. A single porch lamp threw out little light; no interior lights visible. The car registered to them wasn't in the drive. Maybe in the garage.

We had rolled into Asheville a little over an hour earlier and checked into the Marriott just off I-240. We decided to give the Fosters' place a drive-by and see if they were home. Didn't look like it.

"Maybe they're out somewhere," Claire said.

"Looks that way." I glanced at my watch. "Maybe they'll be along soon."

Twenty minutes later they still hadn't arrived and the house remained dark and quiet.

"I'm hungry," T-Tommy said.

Claire laughed. "Gee, I've never heard you say that before."

T-Tommy grunted but said nothing.

"Actually, I'm hungry too," I said.

"We know where they'll be tomorrow morning," T-Tommy said.
"We can chat with them then."

"At the church?" Claire asked.

"Yeah. Doubt they'll cause trouble there. And they probably
wouldn't be armed at their wedding."

Claire swiveled in her seat and looked at T-Tommy. "You think
they're armed?"

"We do have a missing rifle. It just might be inside the house. Better to assume so than to walk in flat-footed and stupid. That could complicate things."

Made sense to me. Confronting them at home at night might not
be wise. Not knowing whether they were armed or not and not knowing the layout gave them home-field advantage. Could cause a ruckus
if nothing else. Wake the neighbors and attract the police. Better to do
it quietly, in public, while the sun's up.

"Let's go grab some chow and catch up with them at the church in
the morning," T-Tommy said.

"Let me check something first." I opened the car door and stepped
out.

"Where are you going?" Claire asked.

"Just a quick look." Before she could protest I closed the car door.

Kyle and Cody Spraggins watched as Dub Walker hurried across the
street. They were a block away, their bland rental car parked beneath a
lush tree that partially blocked the nearby streetlamp. The rental was
JD's idea. Everything was JD's idea. He had told them not to use one
of their own vehicles just in case they crossed paths with Walker or
Tortelli. And now they had.

This changed things.

Damn it. All they had needed was another half hour and this little adventure would have been over. No Fosters, and they would have a pocketful of cash. Then these clowns showed up and trashed everything.

The plan was to use the rental, follow the speed limit, stay low to the ground, pay cash only for gas and food back and forth to Asheville, slip into town at night, whack the Fosters, and get the hell out. Clean and simple.

And they had been so close. Sitting in the shadows, checking their weapons, watching the neighborhood that seemed to be sound asleep, steeling their nerves. In fact, Kyle had been reaching for the door handle when the Mercedes drove by. Kyle recognized it as Claire McBride's. Saw Walker and McBride in front, Tortelli in back.

Kyle and Cody slid low in the seat as the Mercedes cruised up and down the street a few times and then parked just across from the Fosters' house. Then they simply sat there for what seemed an eternity. Doing nothing. And now Walker was out of the car and headed toward the house.

Son of a bitch.

"What now?" Cody asked.

"Sit tight."

"But they'll arrest them."

"Maybe not," Kyle said.

"What? Of course they will. That's why they're here."

"I'm not so sure they will. You see any local cops with them?"

"No."

"Tortelli can't arrest them. Not his jurisdiction. He'd need the locals for that."

"So what the hell are they doing?"

"Why don't you shut up and watch?"

"Don't get pissy, big brother," Cody said.

"Shut up. Let me think."

"Yeah, like you're so good at that."

Kyle glared at him but said nothing. He returned his attention to Walker.

Kyle found it curious that Tortelli hadn't called in the Asheville

PD. Meant he wasn't going to arrest the Fosters. Meant he wanted all this off the radar. Maybe simply talk them into giving up and coming back to Huntsville quietly.

JD wasn't going to like this.

Chapter 56

SATURDAY, 10:17 P.M.

I walked up the Fosters' drive. The garage door had two narrow windows. In the darkness inside, I saw their car. I moved around to the backyard. Nice sized lot, neatly mowed and trimmed. Not unlike their home in Huntsville. No lights glowed inside. I crossed the patio and cupped my hands against one window. Kitchen and dining room. An open cardboard box sat on the counter, another on the dining table. A stack of clothes, mostly dresses, hung over the back of one chair. Not yet settled. Still unpacking.

I walked back around the house and crossed the street. Headlamps from an approaching car washed across me. The car slowed and came to a stop. A white Asheville PD squad car. I knew this because I'm very observant and because of the light bar on top and the huge block letters that read POLICE across the side. The lettering was either black or dark blue. Couldn't tell in the dim lighting.

A young officer stepped from the car. "Can I ask you what you're doing?"

T-Tommy opened the rear door and started out.

"Sir, remain in the car." The officer's hand dropped to his sidearm. He didn't remove it, just rested his palm on it.

T-Tommy stepped out anyway and produced his badge. "Investigator Tommy Tortelli. Huntsville, Alabama PD."

"Investigator?"

"Homicide."

"What're you doing here?"

"Looking for a missing couple," T-Tommy said. "We think they live on this street."

"You call the station and tell them you were running an investigation here?"

T-Tommy walked toward the younger man. "Not yet. We just got in town."

The officer turned to me. "And you are?"

"Dub Walker. I'm consulting on this case."

"Consulting?"

"I have a little experience in skip tracing so the HPD asked me to help."

The officer seemed to relax. His hand fell away from his holster. "These people—the ones you're looking for—are they suspects in a crime?"

"Maybe," T-Tommy said. "Mostly just missing."

"But they could be?"

"Everybody could be," T-Tommy said.

That worked. The officer smiled. "Ain't that usually the case." He looked at me and then back to T-Tommy. "I'm Officer Philip Ponder. This community has a very active neighborhood watch program. Someone called in and said a suspicious car had been cruising the neighborhood."

"Sounds like the program works," I said. "We've only been here a few minutes."

"Now what?" Ponder asked.

"Looks like they're either not home or are already tucked in for the night," I said. "We'll drop back by in the morning."

"Just to chat with them?"

I nodded.

"If you decide you need them arrested, call us."

"You can bet on it," T-Tommy said. "I know the protocol."

"Where're you staying?"

"The Marriott."

T-Tommy and Ponder exchanged cards.

"I'll call if we need you," T-Tommy said.

Ponder studied T-Tommy's card. "I'll have to file a report on this. Be a good idea if you stopped by and spoke with the chief. He likes to know what's going on in his city."

"Will do. First thing Monday."

Ponder nodded and pulled open the door to his car.

"Got a question," T-Tommy said. "Where can we get something to eat around here this time of night?"

"That's an easy one. The Blue Ridge Cafe. Not far from here. I'll scribble down the directions for you."

"What was that all about?" Cody asked.

"Get down."

They ducked low as the Mercedes and then the cop car went by. Kyle twisted in his seat and peered over the seat back. The Mercedes turned left a block down the street, the patrol car made a U-turn and headed back their way.

"The cop's coming back," Kyle said. He shrank lower into his seat. "What do we do?"

"Pray he goes on by." Kyle gripped his nine millimeter, holding it against his chest.

The patrol car did. After it turned left a block away and disappeared, Kyle sat up. "Let's get out of here."

He cranked up the car and pulled from the curb.

"What are we going to do?"

"Wait for another chance."

"Tonight?"

"Tomorrow. Too much going on around here right now."

"We have to let JD know."

"We can't. You know that."

JD had been adamant that they turn off their cell phones and make no calls to anyone and especially not to him until they were back in Alabama. He'd said cops can track cell phone calls and even phone locations when no call was made. JD wanted absolutely no connection between him, or them, and Asheville. If the bodies of Cindy Strunk and Robert Beckwith were revealed to be those of Tim and Martha Foster, any connection between this area and JD would be hard to explain.

JD was smart. He'd thought of everything.

"So what are we going to do?" Cody asked.

"Get some sleep and see what tomorrow brings."

"Shit. I wanted to be home by morning."

"Ain't going to happen."

"Tomorrow's Sunday. Going to be hard to get to them in broad daylight."

"Maybe. But then again maybe all their neighbors will traipse off to church and we'll get a chance."

"Don't you think Tortelli will be back in the morning?"

"Probably."

"Then what?"

"Then we're done. JD said if we can get to them, fine. If Tortelli or the cops get them first, he'd deal with it some other way. The only thing we can't do is leave a trail back to us or JD."

"What about the money?"

"We'll get paid something regardless."

"But more if we finish the job. Right?"

"Yep."

"Let's do something. I want that money."

"Then shut up and let me think."

Chapter 57

Memories are meant to fade. Good ones, bad ones, didn't matter. Maybe it's a self-protective mechanism. Keeps the brain from overloading, from living too deeply in the past. Maybe it's so old psychic wounds, like surgical scars, can heal and fade.

Doesn't always work out that way. Any surgeon will tell you that some scars don't shrink to near invisibility. Some become large and ugly and look as if some alien creature, like a gopher rooting around in an otherwise manicured yard, has burrowed beneath the skin and created a thick, raised, angry-looking ridge. In medical terms these are called keloids. Most are simply unsightly, others bring pain and aggravation.

The memory of my sister, Jill, became an ugly, painful keloid. As if that alien invader had burrowed into my brain and settled in, creating a living, pulsing scar. Constantly reminding me of my failures. The image of her purse and single shoe, lying on the wet asphalt like a pair of accusatory sentinels, refused to fade. And like the hollow pain that settled in my gut that night as I stood in the drizzle unable to move, barely able to breathe, those images have remained as clear and acute as if Jill's abduction had happened only minutes ago, not a dozen years.

If memories were meant to fade, why did this one remain so vivid? Why did this one still visit in the dark of night?

Parts of the dream varied, but the major actors—me, Jill, and her shadowy abductor—and its heart, soul, and distilled essence never wavered. I might chase the abductor or he might chase me. The scene might play out in a thick forest, a cave, or a mine shaft. There might be fog or rain or a bitterly cold wind. Whatever form it took, it invariably ended with me wedged into some tunnel or mine shaft or well casing where sounds were muffled and the air thin.

Jill always there. Just out of reach. Begging for my help. I would twist and turn and stretch but could only brush her fingertips as she faded into the abyss, her fear-dilated eyes locked on mine, her frantic, extended hand clutching only air.

That's when I would wake up.

Like tonight.

I slid out of bed and walked into the bathroom where I splashed water on my face. Cold sweat slicked my chest. A headache throbbed in my temples.

When I climbed back beneath the sheets, Claire propped up on one elbow.

"Jill?" she asked.

She knew me too well. Knew exactly where my head was. She'd seen it many times. "Yep."

"Triggered by this Foster mess?"

"Yep."

"Want to talk about it?"

"Nope."

"Okay."

She laid down. I settled on my back and stared at the ceiling, my brain in full gallop. Not heading in any particular direction. Mostly running in circles.

The real dilemma? Part of me wanted justice served, wanted the Fosters to pay for their sins, while part of me, maybe the biggest part, hoped they'd be gone by morning. Off into the ether. After all, hadn't they done a public service by removing Walter Whitiker from the planet?

For ten minutes I said nothing and then finally, "I feel like we're betraying them."

"The Fosters?"

"Yeah."

"Why?"

"They're like us. Neither Tim nor Martha is some psychopath like Brian Kurtz or a scumbag like Rocco Scarcella. They're good people."

"Were good people."

"Probably still are."

"They killed Walter Whitiker."

"He needed killing."

Claire propped up on her elbow again. "I can't argue with that, but they still committed murder."

"Now we're here to murder them."

"Isn't that a little dramatic?"

"Is it? If they don't get the death penalty, they'll get life without. Same thing."

"Because it was premeditated?"

"Apparently for months."

"A good attorney could argue self-defense," she said. "Walter did threaten them. Maybe knock it down to manslaughter."

"That would get them twenty years. You think that isn't life?"

"Shouldn't they be punished?"

"They already have been. For three years."

"You having second thoughts about this?"

"Some." I rolled over to face her. "We could simply leave. Let them get on with their new lives. Heal from their wounds."

"T-Tommy might not go for that."

"He feels the same way."

"He told you that?"

"Didn't have to."

"You know his sense of duty. He won't let this slide."

"I also know his sense of justice, so he just might."

"And I know your sense of justice, Dub. You won't let this slide either. You'll help them in every way you can but you won't simply walk away."

"You're probably right."

"Not probably, I am."

"Pretty sure of yourself, aren't you?"

"Who knows you better than me?"

That was an easy one. No one. I pulled her to me.

Chapter 58

Tim and Martha stood beneath the ivy-covered white-lattice arch and the broad oak tree behind the Chapel Creek Baptist Church. They held hands and looked at each other. Tears of happiness pressed against Tim's eyes and he could see a glistening wetness in Martha's. God, he loved her.

A soft breeze whispered through the oak leaves and they in turn fractured the warm sunlight, dappling Martha's face. The face he had fallen in love with the very moment they had met. The face that was still as beautiful as it had been on the day of their first wedding. No white dress this time, but the gray skirt and white blouse she wore seemed perfect. Tim had chosen a similar outfit, gray slacks, white shirt, and a navy sports coat.

They giggled like two teenagers who had eloped. In some respects, it felt that way. As if they had snuck away to get married and feared their parents would show up at any minute and stop the ceremony. That edge of excitement made them both giddy.

No pomp and circumstance this time. No organ music or choir or wedding singer. The trickling sounds of the church's namesake creek provided the only wedding music.

Pastor Arthur Dunn stood before them, a Bible in one hand, the ceremony script in the other, a peaceful smile on his face. Earlier, as they walked from the church and across the grounds to this spot, he had told them how much he loved performing weddings. "Renewal and hope" was the way he put it. Tim agreed. He and Martha were renewing their lives. Under different names but a renewal just the same. The past folded away, a hopeful future ahead.

Claire, T-Tommy, and I stood beneath an apple-green leafed maple that hugged the back of the Chapel Creek Baptist Church. Toward the back of the property, not far from what I took to be the pastor's quarters, I saw the Fosters and whom I assumed was Pastor Dunn, standing beneath a white-lattice arch in the shade of an oak tree that must have been a hundred years old.

When we arrived ten minutes earlier, morning services had just let out and much of the congregation milled in front of the church, the adults chatting, the children restless and obviously anxious to get home and out of their Sunday-go-to-meeting clothes. We got a few nods and a couple of "good mornings" as we filtered through the crowd and entered the church.

We found Dunn's office where we met an attractive young woman who said her name was Debbie Tyson. She told us that Pastor Dunn was performing a wedding "out back" and that he would be finished "shortly" and that we could wait in the chapel if we wanted.

We didn't. We walked through the chapel and out the rear door to where we now stood.

The Fosters had their backs to us. Pastor Dunn faced our way, head bowed in prayer. We were too far away to hear more than the faint murmuring of his voice. The prayer ended and he shook hands with Martha and then Tim, a broad smile on his face. Tim and Martha, or Robert and Cindy, were, in the eyes of North Carolina, now married. The trio then walked toward the church, chatting and laughing. Tim and Martha looked happy, that postwedding glow settling on each of them.

As they approached the church, Tim's gaze caught mine. I stepped out into the sunlight. Martha looked up. Color drained from both their faces.

"Robert. Cindy," I said. "Bet you didn't think we would be here."

"Are these your friends?" Dunn asked.

"I'm Dub Walker," I said and shook his hand. "This is Claire McBride and Tommy Tortelli."

"Welcome," Dunn said. "I wish you'd been here earlier. We just finished the ceremony."

"We watched from here."

"Wonderful." Dunn rubbed his hands together.

"We're old friends of Robert and Cindy. Just drove up from Atlanta to surprise them."

I sensed Tim's wheels turning. Asking himself how we knew their new names, knew their cover story of being from Atlanta, knew where to find them. That's the thing about plotting the perfect crime, when it falls apart, it falls hard. The pasty whiteness of Tim's face suggested his world had just collapsed.

"You must be the ones Pastor Boles called about," Dunn asked. "He said you wanted to surprise them and asked that I keep it secret." He beamed at Tim and Martha. "It surely looks like you were surprised."

Surprise wasn't exactly what I saw in Tim and Martha Foster's faces.

"That's right," I said.

"Oh, my," Dunn said. "How wonderful." He turned to Martha. "I'll leave you to visit with your friends." He looked at Tim. "See you at next week's service?"

"We'll be there." Tim's voice sounded thin and broken.

Dunn looked back at us. "So nice to meet you. I've got a meeting in a few minutes, so I have to run." Back to Tim. "If you need anything my assistant, Debbie, will help you."

He walked into the church.

I turned to Tim. "We need to talk."

"We're done," Kyle said.

He and Cody were sitting in the rental. They had parked next to a huge SUV along the back edge of the church parking lot. They watched the Fosters, Walker, Tortelli, and Claire McBride climb into the Mercedes and the Fosters' car and drive away.

"Son of a bitch," Cody said. "JD ain't going to be happy."

"No, he isn't." Kyle keyed the car to life. "Let's head home."

Chapter 59

T-Tommy rode with Tim; Martha with Claire and me. We drove the mile and a half to their home in silence. A thousand questions rattled around in my head, but I held them, preferring to talk when we got there, wanting T-Tommy to hear anything said by either of the Fosters. I knew T-Tommy was doing the same.

Only took five minutes to get there. Seemed longer. It was as if every traffic light popped red just to aggravate us. To prolong the agony and pump up the tension that had already thickened the air. Finally Tim pulled into the garage. Claire parked in the drive behind him.

Now, seeing the house in daylight, I could tell the Fosters were already rooting in. Literally. Four large bags of potting soil and a cluster of black plastic nursery pots, containing roses and azaleas, sat on the lawn near the front porch. A shovel lay near by. They had begun prepping the brick-lined planting areas that flanked the walkway. The dark soil had been turned and appeared to have been mixed with mulch. It smelled rich and fertile as I walked by.

Inside, things were sparse. Easy to understand since everything they owned was still in their house back in Huntsville. A new sofa and two chairs sat on a thick area rug in the living room. Three empty packing boxes listed against one wall. No pictures had been hung; the window curtains looked new.

The Fosters settled on the sofa; T-Tommy and Claire in the chairs, facing them. I stood behind Claire.

Some color had returned to Tim's and Martha's faces, but the wide-eyed look of fear that had erupted back at the church remained.

"I take it you'll call the police?" Tim asked. He swallowed hard.

"Maybe," I said. "We want to talk with you first."

"How did you find us?" Tim asked.

"We'll get to that," T-Tommy said. "Tell us about Whitiker."

Tim glanced at Martha and then looked back to T-Tommy. "What do you want to know?"

"Everything."

"I guess we could tell you we don't know what you're talking about."

T-Tommy raised an eyebrow. "You could; we wouldn't believe you."

"Why not?"

"We found your car where you dumped it. We found tire tracks directly across from the prison that match the tires on your SUV. We found the clearing where you set up your sniper sight. Even the branches you snapped off to get a clear shot. You going to deny all that?"

Tim's shoulders sagged. He clutched Martha's hands with his, his fingers even whiter than hers. "Yes, we were there. Yes, we shot him." He looked at Martha. "I did anyway."

"Not both of you?" I asked.

He looked confused. "No, just me."

I glanced at T-Tommy and then back to Tim. "And then you shoved a screwdriver down the rifle's barrel and tossed it down the hill?"

His confusion deepened. "What are you talking about?"

"I'm talking about the rifle we found. The one that fired one of the bullets."

"What do you mean one of the bullets?"

"Walter was shot twice."

"No way. I fired one shot. Right to his chest. I saw it hit. Through the scope." He looked at T-Tommy and then back to me. "And it didn't come from any gun you found."

"Actually, it did. It came from the gun you bought down in Rome, Georgia. Same day you bought the cell phone."

"Not possible."

"Why would that be?" T-Tommy asked.

"Excuse me a second." Tim stood and left the living room. I heard a closet door slide open and then close. He walked back in, a rifle in his hand. T-Tommy jumped and reached for his gun.

"It's not loaded," Tim said. He extended the gun toward me. "This's the gun we bought."

A Browning BAR Safari .308 with a Nikon ProStaff scope. A mirror image of the one found at the scene. I took the gun and examined it and then handed it to T-Tommy.

"I used that rifle," Tim said. "I shot Walter Whitiker in the chest with it. One shot. That's it."

"And there wasn't another identical gun? One that Martha used?"

"No, absolutely not." He stared at me, gaze unwavering.

Was he telling the truth?

Tim went on. "Are you telling me that Walter was shot more than once?"

"Twice to be exact."

Tim looked at Martha. She had a shocked look on her face, too.

"There was one shot," Martha said. "Only one. Then we got the hell out of there. We didn't discard a rifle. We took it with us. That's the one we used."

"You didn't have your own gun?" I asked her.

"No. I don't know how to shoot. Don't want to know."

"Did you hear a second shot?" Claire asked.

She shook her head. "We were inside the tent and we had tissue stuffed in our ears."

"What tent?" I asked.

Tim explained about the tent they used to muffle the sound. How they collapsed it back into its cover and tossed everything into the SUV and hauled ass over a couple of dirt roads until they made their way back to Huntsville.

T-Tommy scooted up to the front edge of his chair. "You're telling us that you fired one shot from one weapon?"

"Exactly."

"Then, how do you explain the rifle we found about a hundred feet from where you say you were?"

"Don't know anything about it."

This wasn't going as I had expected. Everything was moving down a bizarre path.

"What I'm having trouble with," I said, "is that two people decided to shoot Walter at the same time from essentially the same place. Doesn't that strike you as an impossible coincidence?"

Tim took in a deep breath and let it out slowly. "Yes, it does. But I fired once. That rifle. That's it."

I nodded. "If I've learned anything about you two this past week, it's that you're very clever. Clever enough to almost disappear. Clever enough to buy two identical rifles, leave one at the scene, and bring one here to prove the one used in the shooting wasn't the one you bought."

"But—"

I raised a hand to stop him. "Buy one at a place you figured we'd find and the other even farther off the radar."

"Like where?" he asked. "What could be farther off the radar than a gun show in another state?"

He had a point.

I went on. "Damage the one you tossed so that a ballistic connection couldn't be easily made, leave it at the scene, and then if we did finally track you down you'd have your alibi gun right here."

Tim sighed. "I swear to God." He hesitated. His shoulders dropped and he reached over and squeezed Martha's hand. "I guess I shouldn't invoke God's name in this. Not after I betrayed everything I believe in."

I waited him out.

"We had one gun. I fired one shot. I'll have to live with that, but that's the truth of it."

Chapter 60

Tim and Martha explained in great detail how they created new IDs, emptied their bank and pension accounts, bought the rifle and the pre-paid cell phone, practiced shooting far from Huntsville in an isolated wooded area, sold their home and found this house, located the perfect shooting site across from the jail, used a tent to muffle the sound, dumped their SUV, everything.

Claire made notes; T-Tommy and I listened.

"How long have you been planning this?" I asked.

"Six months. A little more. Began when we learned Whitiker would be released."

"And you just up and decided to kill him and disappear?" T-Tommy asked.

"Not at first," Tim said. "Took a while to come up with that. At first we were simply going to move. Thought maybe if we put some distance between us and Whitiker, he would leave us alone."

"Makes sense," I said. "After all his threats."

"But what if he didn't?" Martha said. "What if he came after us? We'd live the rest of our lives looking over our shoulders."

Tim nodded. "So we came up with the idea of changing our names. Make it impossible for him to find us."

"That took a month or so," Martha said.

"When did you decide to take the next step?" Claire asked. "To kill Whitiker?"

"After we created our new identities," Tim said. "We thought about all that he had done to us. What he did to Steven. How he was going to walk free while we had to leave so much of our life behind."

Martha dabbed her damp eyes with the wadded tissue she had in her hand. "It was like he was getting out of prison and we were going in."

"It wasn't an easy decision," Tim said. "I laid awake at night for weeks. Every time I wavered on doing it, I could see the photos of Steven they showed in court. Hear the voice of Dr. Drummond explaining what Whitiker had done to my little boy."

A sob wracked him; tears streamed down Martha's face.

"I couldn't see him getting off more or less scot-free." He swiped a hand over his eyes and sighed. "What do we do from here? Are you going to arrest us?"

T-Tommy shrugged. "I'd rather not. That'd involve the locals and would make for a ton of paperwork and legal crap. Extradition and all that."

"What's the other option?" Martha asked.

"Come back to Huntsville," I said. "We'll test the rifle. Probably have a lot more questions to ask."

"We'll be arrested there?" Martha asked.

T-Tommy shrugged. "Probably."

"For murder?" Tim asked.

I glanced at T-Tommy. "Maybe not." Everyone looked at me. "Lou Drummond, the medical examiner who did Walter's autopsy, hasn't filed his final report yet. The issue as far as you're concerned is which bullet killed Walter. The one that likely did it, the one that struck his heart, was fragmented. It seems to match the weapon found at the scene though the ballistics aren't perfect. In fact, far from it. The other bullet hit his right lung, but that might not have been lethal in and of itself."

"So what does that mean?" Martha asked.

"That if the bullet that hit Walter's lung came from this rifle and if you didn't buy, fire, and discard the other weapon, you might not have been responsible for Walter's death."

"I still shot him," Tim said.

"And you'll have to answer for that, but it might not be a murder rap."

"But it's still a serious charge? Probably carry many years in prison?"

I nodded. "Maybe. A good lawyer and a sympathetic judge and jury might work in your favor. Walter killed your child. No doubt about that, and that will weigh heavily on any jury."

"Is there any other choice?" Martha asked.

"Not that I see," I said.

Tim and Martha both slumped into the sofa.

"I have a question." I said. They both looked at me. "If you did buy only one gun and fire only one shot, why didn't you get rid of it? Why chance keeping it in your possession?"

"We didn't want to dump it anywhere near Huntsville where if it was found it might be connected to the shooting and then traced to us. We hoped Walter's mur—" Tim swallowed hard, "murder wouldn't be solved." He looked at Martha. "And that we'd never be found." He sighed. "And then once we got here, the urgency seemed less and we simply haven't decided how best to get rid of it."

"If everything you say is true, then keeping it might be the only smart move you've made in all of this."

Chapter 61

It took a while to get out of Asheville.

Earlier, while the Fosters packed a few things, T-Tommy and I had walked outside and crossed the lawn to the curb, out of earshot.

"What are you thinking?" I asked.

"I'm thinking I believe them. To a point."

"Which point?"

"What I'm having trouble with is two people deciding to shoot Walter at the same place and at the same time. I mean popping him from a distance when he steps out of prison isn't a bad play, but two people doing it? Independently? What are the odds?"

"Big. Very big."

"Exactly," T-Tommy said. "And then there's the question of who."

"JD?"

"Good bet. Or someone he hired. But it still comes back to how would he have known about the Fosters?"

"Maybe he didn't."

T-Tommy shrugged. "Then we're back to a huge coincidence."

"Regardless, the first thing we have to do is get the Fosters' rifle in Sidau's hands and see if it matches the bullet taken out of Walter's chest."

T-Tommy nodded, his unfocused gaze traveling up the street.

"How do you want to play this?" I asked.

"I'm thinking off the radar. If we arrest them, it'll be a circus. I'd like to avoid that."

"Maybe put them up somewhere while we sort this out?"

"Something like that."

"What if they take off again?" I asked.

T-Tommy looked back toward the house. "I don't think so. I think settling here was the plan and now with this option gone, they have nowhere to go."

"Unless they have backup identities."

"You don't believe that," T-Tommy said.

"No, I don't."

"So we either arrest them or hide them until we get this sorted out." He shoved his hands in his pockets and rocked back on his heels. "And right now I'm thinking hiding them makes the fewest waves."

"I agree. Let's get rolling."

We walked back inside just as Martha brought a suitcase into the living room. Her color had returned and she looked as if she had simply packed for a vacation. Martha said she had to call her sister, Paige, and tell her all was okay.

"Not a good idea," I said.

"But she'll worry. She's knows we were getting married today, and we told her we'd call afterward."

"Okay. But nothing about us being here or about you coming back to Huntsville. You'll have to keep up your charade for a few more days."

She nodded and pulled the prepaid phone from her purse. The conversation lasted ten minutes. They talked mostly about the wedding and how happy they were, Martha ending by telling Paige she'd call her in a few days.

We then swung by our hotel to check out and gather our stuff. While there I called Philip Ponder, the Asheville PD officer we had bumped into last night in front of the Fosters' home. Got his voice mail. Probably off duty today. I left a message, telling him we had found the folks we were looking for and were heading back to Huntsville. I told him to give our regards to his chief and our apology for not contacting him when we first got into town.

It was nearly four thirty by the time I wound onto I-40. Fat-bellied pewter clouds had rolled in, blocking the sun, muting everything to a mostly monochrome gray. Rain battered the windshield. Traffic was heavy but moved at a brisk clip in spite of the conditions. I was amazed that Claire let me drive. She never let anyone strap in behind the wheel of her Mercedes. She sat next to me; Martha in back. T-Tommy and Tim followed in the Fosters' car.

We exchanged some small talk: weather, scenery, and things like that, but mostly we rode in silence. Soon, Claire dozed, her head lolled against the window. In the backseat, Martha adopted a similar posture. I had the radio tuned low to some country station. All I could find along this stretch of interstate. Not my kind of music. Not the blues. Major chords versus minors? I'll take the minors every time.

Kyle and Cody sat across from JD in a booth at Gibson's Bar-B-Q. They chowed on pulled pork sandwiches; JD having only sweet tea. Said he wasn't hungry. Wasn't happy either.

Kyle had given him the rundown on everything that had happened, assuring JD they were only minutes way from completing the deal when Walker and Tortelli showed up.

"Sorry," Kyle said.

"Not really your fault," JD said. "Shit happens."

"What now?" Cody asked.

"I'll have to refigure things. See what's happening. I still might have something for you boys."

"If they're in jail, there ain't much we can do."

"I know. But maybe they'll make bail. Maybe we'll get another shot at it."

"On a murder charge?" Kyle asked. "Bail might not happen."

"We'll see."

JD tugged a crumpled white envelope from his back pocket and slid it across the table to Kyle. "I don't think I have to say that no one, absolutely no one, can know about you guys going up to Asheville."

"We know."

"Not even in casual conversation."

"We got it," Kyle said. "You can count on it."

"I will." JD stood and tossed a twenty on the table. "Q's on me. Catch you guys later." He walked toward the door.

By the time I slid by Chattanooga on I-24, the rain let up some, and I could see the misty outline of Lookout Mountain to the south. A famous place in U.S. history. A history no Southerner ever forgets.

In 1863, in the shadow of this rich, green hillock and then on south to Chickamauga Creek, Confederate General Braxton Briggs' Army of Tennessee gave Union Major General William Rosecrans' Army of the Cumberland a spanking unlike any that a U. S. Army had ever received. Or ever would. It wasn't pretty and proved to be one of the bloodiest battles of the Civil War. It would also prove to be the last Confederate victory in the west. This series of battles ultimately opened the door to one of the greatest atrocities of that long and bloody conflict. William Tecumseh Sherman replaced Rosecrans, and the following year launched his scorched-earth March to the Sea, a genocidal destruction that even today raises the ire of true Southerners.

You want to piss off a Southerner? Mention two things: Reconstruction or William Tecumseh Sherman. The fight'll be in the parking lot.

For me, Lookout Mountain meant Rock City, its world-famous park. Though most of the old black-and-white signs and similarly painted barn roofs that dotted every corner of the southeast and shouted SEE ROCK CITY were long gone, I held vivid memories of my first visit there. I must have been ten, Jill about four. It was the greatest park I had ever seen. Cool places like The Enchanted Trail, The Stone Bridge, and Fat Man's Squeeze, where a narrow trail wedged its way between two massive rock formations. And, of course, Lover's Leap, with its sheer drop and vistas into seven states. Jill had been ecstatic, running from place to place as if she couldn't see all the wonders of Rock City quickly enough.

I yanked my mind away from Jill. Didn't want to go there.

I maneuvered through the spray kicked up by a convoy of six eighteen-wheelers and slid past them. Their huge tires whined against the road surface. I hated being on the same roads with those guys. Particularly rain-slicked roads. Any accident involving one of those rigs was more meat grinder than fender bender. For the other guy anyway.

Time for some food and coffee. I nudged Claire. She woke and gave me a groggy look.

"How long was I out?" she asked.

"An hour, maybe a little more."

"You okay?"

"Hungry. And some coffee would help."

"Want me to drive?"

"I'm fine."

I heard Martha stir in the backseat. In the rearview mirror, I saw her stretch and then rub her neck.

"How about some chow?" I asked her.

"That'd be great." She looked at the window. "Where are we?"

"Just past Chattanooga. On I-24."

"We must be near the Highway 72 turn off."

"Ten miles or so."

"There's a neat diner just after the junction," Martha said. "We stopped there on the way to Asheville."

"I see."

Martha sighed. "That seems months ago."

"You guys've been through a lot in the past few days."

"Longer than that, and I'm afraid it's not over."

I nodded.

She massaged one temple.

"Got a headache?" I asked.

"Yeah." She stretched and twisted again. "I can't believe I slept that hard in a car. I never can doze off as long as we're moving."

"Must've needed it," Claire said.

"Probably. Unfortunately, it wasn't all that restful."

"Probably Dub's driving," Claire said.

"Didn't keep you awake," I said.

"I'm used to it."

"It wasn't that," Martha said. "It was a bad dream."

"About what?" I asked.

She thought for a minute. "Steven was there—not sure where there was. No place I recognized. Very industrial as best I can recall. He was in danger, and I couldn't get to him."

"I understand."

"Do you?"

"I have the same dream. My sister. She was abducted over ten years ago. No trace of her since."

"I'm sorry. I didn't know."

"It's not something I talk about, and try not to think about."

She looked out the window as she spoke. "Ten years? Jesus. Steven's been gone for three and it seems like only yesterday he was taken." She looked back at me. "Will it feel this bad ten years from now?"

"I wish I could say it gets better, but it doesn't."

"At least we know what happened to Steven. I can't imagine not knowing."

There it was. The truth of it. The deeply painful part. The part that made me envy Martha and Tim. So many times I had wished we would find her body. So I would know. Then the guilt of wishing her dead would climb on my back and dig in. It was an endless loop and there was no way out. Not one that I could see anyway.

As I eased onto Highway 72, Martha said, " What's going to happen to us?"

"I'm not sure. If you're telling the truth about a second gun, then it'll be better."

"The police don't always find the truth."

"T-Tommy does," I said. "And he won't rest until he digs it up. The boy's a bulldog that way."

"But we're the only suspects. The ones with a motive. I mean, we planned it. We did it. Some of it anyway." I saw tears glisten in her eyes. "We have no one that can say otherwise."

"I'd've agreed with you until today. All the evidence definitely worked against you."

"What's different now?" Martha asked.

"I believe you."

"I do, too," Claire said.

Martha burst into tears.

Gladys's Roadside Diner emerged from the misty rain, and I pulled into the side parking lot.

Chapter 62

MONDAY, 2:00 A.M.

The dream arrived at two a.m. A bad one this time. One that seemed to go on forever.

I was underwater. Not the usual location for these adventures into insanity. Must have been in the ocean as I felt the to-and-fro action of the swells tugging against me. But oddly there were no fish, coral, or seaweed, and no signs of life anywhere. Only a flat and barren sandy seafloor interrupted by massive rock formations that looked like dark-gray cumulus clouds, one drawing me toward it with a soft mewing sound, as if the ancient sirens lived inside and called to me.

As I drew near, the mewing morphed to whimpers. Jill. I found an opening, a maw that led into a dark tunnel, currents carrying me inside, spinning me through a twisting channel. Jill's moans and cries pulled me deeper, the walls closing in, trapping my arms to my sides, movement impossible, lungs screaming for relief.

Then she was there. One of my arms somehow came free and I extended it toward her. Terror etched her face and her mouth gaped open as if screaming, yet only whimpers and moans escaped. Her arm snaked toward me, her hand opening and closing, as if searching for a lifeline. I stretched and twisted, willing my hand toward her, but only managing to brush her fingertips. As always.

She began to slide away. I struggled, but the rock walls held me. She faded into the darkness, her whimpers dying to total silence.

I jerked awake. My skin felt cold and damp. The sheets clung to me and seemed to be pulling me deeper into the bed. I kicked free and sat up. I looked to my left. Claire wasn't there. Where was she?

Home.

Last night after we had settled the Fosters in the Marriott, she had dropped me off and headed to her place. I asked her if she wanted to stay, but she said something about two days in a car with me was enough. I didn't have an argument for that.

I rolled out of bed and walked into the bathroom. Cold water on my face helped some. I pulled on the jeans that I had kicked into a corner last night, and headed to the kitchen. I snagged a bottle of water from the fridge and walked outside.

The air was cool against my bare, damp chest. I moved to the back edge of my property, the western crest of Monte Sano Mountain, the terrain abruptly angling downward toward the sleeping city below.

I remembered the last time I had stood here. Several days ago. As then, my thoughts went to the Fosters. Thoughts that were now very different. Then I had just learned about the tire track evidence. Then I believed they were the killers but didn't know where they were. Now I knew where they were but didn't know if they were the killers. My gut told me that Tim had gotten lucky. That his shot wasn't the killing one. That, as he and Martha both swore, he hadn't taken a second rifle up on that hillside. I wanted to believe that anyway.

I hated it when this happened. When you realized the tree you'd been barking up wasn't the only one you should have howled at. That you had followed only one path when there was another that you had ignored. It happened to every investigator, but that made it no less infuriating. We had spent a week focused on the Fosters, running them to ground. Thinking that once they were located, the case was solved. But now I wasn't so sure. Now I believed that Tim Foster didn't actually kill Walter.

He shot him. Sure. But someone else had fired the other bullet, the likely killing bullet. Who? Still, only one name came to mind.

JD Whitiker.

He definitely had a motive, now sole owner of the business, and the means—the business being a gun shop for Christ's sake. Did he have the opportunity? Did his wife lie for him? Wouldn't be the first time a spouse supplied cover.

What about Bo Hudson? He worked for JD, and, from what I saw the other day, was loyal. Loyal enough to help him murder his brother? Could he have been the shooter? At JD's request? Maybe JD paid him? Maybe he simply helped JD set it up? Where had Bo been that morning?

Okay, so if JD did it, with or without Bo's help, how do we prove it? How do we connect JD to the gun? To the sniper site? Did he have time to pull the trigger and then get down to the prison to confront T-Tommy and me? Without being seen?

I thought back to that morning. After Walter was shot, I performed CPR for at least fifteen minutes. JD arrived right after I pronounced Walter dead. Twenty minutes gave him plenty of time to clean, damage, and toss the rifle, drive the mile or so back down the dirt road to the highway, and then up to the prison. Not being seen was pure luck. Most crimes require luck. Otherwise they tend to blow up early.

Did JD know the Fosters bought a rifle? And did he know the make and model? According to Dale Bonner, owner of the Rome gun shop who sold the Fosters their rifle at the gun show, JD and Bo had been there. Bo had bought Dale lunch. Did Dale tell him about the rifle or show him the invoice? I made a mental note to call Dale Bonner and ask him.

JD would also have known that the Fosters were opposed to guns. Didn't own any, didn't allow them in their home. That came out in the trial and was repeatedly mentioned in the newspapers. Some reporters even postulated that if the Fosters had been armed, they might have been able to stop the abduction. Even if true, and that's a big if, I had thought that such speculation was cruel and unjust. Why heap more guilt on someone already drowning in it?

If JD knew the Fosters bought a rifle, he must have then concluded that they planned to use it on his brother. Some might think that a big leap. Not me. Seemed almost logical. People opposed to guns only buy them under duress. When they need them desperately. When they have a target in mind. The killing of your child's murderer would definitely qualify on all counts.

The nagging question was how JD knew when and where the shooting would take place? That one I didn't have an answer for.

I looked back toward the east. The sky showed no hint of dawn, which unfortunately was still hours away.

Patience isn't one of my virtues. I have a lot of them. Really, I do. That's just not one. I wanted to get to the lab and analyze the Fosters' rifle, now squirreled away in the trunk of T-Tommy's car. I wanted to sift through all the evidence Sidau had collected at the scene, now with different eyes, ones not focused on the Fosters, but on JD Whitiker.

Then I had another thought. That'd have to wait until sunup, too.

Chapter 63

Last night, our first stop on returning to Huntsville was to settle the Fosters into the Marriott under their new names. No one knew them as Robert and Cindy Beckwith and it was better it stayed that way. And their new looks—Tim's buzz cut and Martha's short, spiked, black hair—made them essentially unrecognizable as Tim and Martha. Maybe not to close friends and Martha's sister, but to any casual passerby.

While they checked in, T-Tommy and I discussed whether to have a couple of uniforms guard them but decided it was best not to risk attracting attention. We also decided that the probability they would take off again was virtually zero. If they couldn't hide after six months of preparation, they surely wouldn't try on the spur of the moment. Besides, Tim said he wanted to face whatever he had coming for what he had done, that it was the right thing to do. I believed him.

The fact that he was standing just outside the Marriott's entrance when I pulled up confirmed that belief. I had called him an hour earlier, telling him I'd pick him up. I wanted to visit where he had practiced with the rifle.

The morning was clear, not a cloud visible, yesterday's rainstorm having moved on, leaving behind a clean slate. I zigzagged over to Highway 53, the Ardmore Highway, and soon left the city behind. We slid past freshly plowed and planted fields, wads of native trees, and the small communities of Harvest and Maple Hill. Tim directed me off on to Macedonia Road, and we continued north for another couple of miles until he told me to turn right onto a dirt road, maybe three miles below the Tennessee border. A half mile later I pulled off onto the shoulder.

"Here's where we went most often." He pointed toward a stand of pine and maples about a quarter mile across an open field. We walked that way. The soil was soft and the grass still damp from yesterday's rain.

"Here," he said. "I used this stump as a target."

It had once been a sizable oak, the tree itself toppled onto its side, partially consumed by weather and grubs. The stump was punctured with twenty or so bullet holes that I could see.

"Where'd you shoot from?"

Tim turned and pointed toward a forested area in the distance. "There, in that stand of pines. It's exactly the same distance from there to here as it is from where we were to the prison gate."

"How'd you estimate that? Walk it off?"

"Better. I used my golf course range finder. It's exactly two hundred and eighty-three yards. The same distance between the prison gate and where we set up."

I knelt and began working on the stump. The bark was friable and easily pulled loose, revealing several bullet channels. I opened my pocketknife and began to chip away the wood along one of the bullet scars. The soft wood gave way to firmer wood, but I continued digging and soon felt the blade bump against something solid. Took another minute to free the slug.

I began excavating along another track.

"We appreciate what you and Investigator Tortelli are doing for us. We don't deserve it, but we're grateful."

I stopped digging and spun on my haunches toward him. "Truth is we think Walter got what he deserved and we'd hate to see the system grind you two up for doing something either T-Tommy or I, Claire, too, ,for that matter, would have done." I saw his lower lip tremble slightly and his eyes glisten. "And we'll stay on your side as long as you're truthful and as long as you don't take off again. If you do either, then all bets are off."

Tim nodded. "I understand. And don't worry, we aren't going anywhere."

I went back to probing into the tree stump.

"The truth is," Tim continued, "I'm not sure we could hold up. Not for decades. The planning, even the act was . . . what's the word? . . . not easy but maybe comfortable. Does that make sense?"

"Sort of."

"I mean, once we decided what to do, everything that followed was more or less robotic. I'm not sure we gave much thought to what things would be like afterward. How we would reconcile it all." He sighed. "I'm not sure we could spend our lives looking over our shoulder. We simply traded Walter for guys like you and Investigator Tortelli. Guys who would look for us forever. That's no way to live."

I looked up at him again. "That's a heavy burden for sure."

"In a way, I'm glad you found us. It's the only way to clear the air. So we aren't going anywhere. I'll face whatever I have to."

I returned to my excavating and over my shoulder said, "Can I ask you something?"

"Sure."

"Why? Why did you decide to kill Walter?"

"I told you. Knowing what he did to Steven, I couldn't see another way."

I kept digging.

"He not only killed our son, he killed us. Martha, anyway." He sighed. "She was so beautiful."

"She still is." I pried another bullet free.

"Yes, she is. But the light inside died. The glow that I saw in her eyes the first time I met her—" He swallowed hard. "It just faded. I don't know how to describe it."

"You don't have to. I know."

I had seen that dead reflection in my own mirror for years after Jill disappeared. Still did from time to time.

"I thought maybe if I cut out the cancer that was eating her, the light would come back."

"Did it?"

"I don't know. Maybe. She does seem a little more like her old self now that Whitiker's gone."

"Really?" I kept chipping away bark and wood.

"Maybe it was the excitement of the move and the wedding, but she's actually laughed in the past few days. Something that's been pretty rare lately."

I popped another slug free. It tumbled to the ground, settling into grass. I wormed it out and placed it next to the others I had removed.

"Look, this was my idea," Tim said. "I had to talk Martha into it. If payment is needed for this, it's on me."

"We'll know exactly what the bill is after we get your gun tested." I now had a half dozen bullets in my hand. I stood. "Let's go."

"What are you going to do with those?" Tim asked as we walked back toward my car.

"See if they match the gun you bought."

"What'll that tell you that you don't already know? I've already said this is where I fired the gun."

"Then these will show you're telling the truth."

"I thought you believed us?"

"I do. Just need to prove your story."

I dropped Tim at the Marriott, and then called T-Tommy and asked him to meet me at the Forensic Science Department. He said he was already there and that Sidau was working over the rifle Tim Foster had given us. I told him I had to swing by the lumber company but would be over in twenty or so.

I found Milk out back supervising the off-loading of a new load of sheetrock.

"How're things?" I asked.

"Great. Just got this order in, half of it presold. Got several big orders going out this morning."

"Sounds good. Need anything?"

"Copasetic."

"Check you later."

I went into the office where a stack of invoices awaited. Fewer than most Mondays, so I knocked them out in a few minutes. I then fished the card Lewis Brinkley had given me from my jacket pocket and called Bobby Poehler. His wife answered again. I apologized for the early call, but she said they were "always up with the chickens" anyway and put Bobby on the phone. After I told him what I wanted he took off, talked a mile a minute. He confirmed what Lewis had thought. JD and Walter had a love-hate relationship. Argued all the time, mostly over Walter taking half the money and doing little work. Said that Walter drank. A lot. Slept, actually passed out, in the back office at least once a week. Said it made working there difficult so as soon as he found something else, he left.

"Did either of them ever threaten the other one?" I asked.

"All the time. Hell, they went at it out back more than once. In the rear lot. Wasn't no slappy fight either. They would knock each other around. Always made up later, but it was a sight when it was happening."

"I know brothers fight and threaten all kinds of crazy things, but did you ever get the sense that any of the fights or threats were real? More serious than just two brothers acting like kids?"

"Mostly it was just that. Two juveniles butting heads. I do remember once hearing JD tell Bo that he was going to kill his brother someday. And it wasn't when he was all wound up. He and Bo were sitting in the office just talking. Walter wasn't there. The door was cracked, so I heard them. I remember Bo asked him if he was serious and said he was. Said he'd just shoot the bastard someday."

"Because he was a slacker?"

"That and the fact that he was a pedophile. JD said he couldn't forgive that and didn't want their mother ever finding out about it."

"Which, of course, she did," I said.

"Yeah, but this was months before Walter killed that kid. Before the whole freaking world knew what a real pervert he was."

"So it was only known around the shop? JD, Bo, and you but no one else?"

"And I never let on that I knew. I overheard conversations, but I acted like I didn't know nothing."

"Why?"

"I was an employee. I figured it was best not to involve myself in any family dramas. Or to even let on that I was aware of any."

"Probably a wise move," I said. "But what about Bo? He was an employee and he knew."

"Bo was more like family. Fact is he and JD were much closer than JD and Walter were."

"That right?"

"Sure is. As far as I could tell, Walter was a full-on alcoholic. Unreliable and unpredictable. A true asshole."

"I take it you didn't care for him all that much?"

"He was a hard man to like."

"Did you tell anyone about this? About JD threatening to kill Walter?"

"Like who? I wasn't sure if he was serious or not. Just that this time he wasn't speaking through anger like the other times he and Walter threatened each other."

"What'd you think when you heard Walter had been shot?"

"At first I thought JD must've done it. But then I heard tell he wasn't there at the time, so I figured someone else did. And Walter had his share of enemies. Like I said, he was hard man to like."

Chapter 64

Sidau Yamaguchi backed away from his Leica comparison microscope and glanced up at me. "Want to take a look?"

I sat, adjusted the twin eyepieces, and leaned into the scope. Sidau had mounted the crime scene bullet fragment and an intact one he had test fired with Tim Foster's rifle on the microscope's stage. Took only a minute to see this rifle wasn't the murder weapon. The rifle discarded at the scene we couldn't say yes or no for sure, but Tim Foster's rifle was easy. None of the striations matched. Not even close.

Sidau then replaced the fragment with the intact bullet retrieved from Walter Whitiker's corpse. The one that popped his right lung. This also took only a minute. They matched. Tim's rifle fired the non-lethal bullet.

Now Sidau mounted one of the slugs I dug out of the tree stump. Again a match.

I looked at T-Tommy. "Looks like Tim was telling the truth about this weapon. It's the one that he used for target practice and the one that trashed Walter's right lung."

T-Tommy sighed. "Still doesn't mean he didn't have two weapons."

"I don't think he did."

"Why?" Sidau asked.

"Too convoluted. Overengineered. I can see dumping both or taking both, just not one of each. Besides, I believe him."

"Then who was the other shooter?" Sidau asked.

"I'd bet on JD Whitiker," T-Tommy said.

"Me, too," I added.

"He killed his own brother?" Sidau asked.

I nodded. "That makes the most sense."

"But how would he know the when and where?" Sidau asked. "Know what the Fosters were planning?

"Don't know for sure." I stood. "Let's play a little 'what if.' What if JD knew they had a rifle? Knew they hated guns and wouldn't have bought one without some target in mind? Knew when and where they were going to use it? Couldn't he simply take advantage of the situation?"

"That's a lot of 'what ifs.' "

"Humor me."

"Okay," Sidau said. "How would JD know all that?"

"Dale Bonner," I said. "Over in Rome. The guy who sold the Fosters the rifle. It was JD who called Paul Twitty with that little tidbit. It was JD who told us. Said he just learned about it. That Bonner called him when he saw the Fosters' photos on the news. Yet JD and his boy Bo Hudson were at the show when the Fosters bought the gun."

T-Tommy gave a slow nod. "So, JD might've known the gun was sold to them months before he admitted he did?"

"Exactly."

"And he would have known the make and model. Right down to the scope and the ammo used."

"Which he could easily duplicate with his access to all things gun related," I said.

"Assuming that's true," Sidau said, "how did he know the when and where?"

"The when's easy," T-Tommy said. "They knew for months when Walter would be released. The exact day and time. That was in the news."

"And the prison on that morning would be logical," I said. "Walter was outside, unsuspecting, susceptible to a long-range shot."

Sidau shook his head. "They must've known there'd be cops there. That you two might be there. TV cameras and media types. Not to mention all the prison guards."

"True," I said. "But the woods provided cover and all those dirt roads up there offered a dozen escape routes." I propped one hip on the exam table. "An open-air shot from a distance would be safer than trying to take him at home or at the gun shop."

Sidau collected the bullets from the microscope platform and slipped each into a separate evidence bag. "They could've set up almost anywhere along that road. Shot from any angle."

"Yeah?" T-Tommy asked.

"The likely murder weapon was found only a hundred feet or so down the hill from where they were. How'd JD know exactly where they'd be?"

"The Fosters must have scouted the site before that day," I said. "Maybe he followed them, saw where they were going to set up, found his own spot nearby."

"Maybe he followed them there that morning," Sidau said.

I shook my head. "Tim said they were there by five. JD didn't leave home until well after that."

Sidau sealed and signed the evidence bags. "So he knew ahead of time."

"That'd be my bet. Then he wiped down the rifle, shoved a screwdriver down the barrel, tossed it down the hill near where the Fosters were, and drove away. He'd need a little luck to pull that off, but most crimes do."

Sidau gave a slow nod. "And if JD got really lucky, both of the bullets would be severely damaged as was the rifle he left, and we might not be able to match anything."

"Exactly. Then we would assume both bullets came from the tossed weapon and that would be that."

T-Tommy grunted. "And if the Fosters were never found, we'd write them off as the killers and life would go on. For JD anyway."

"Or—" I said.

"Or what?"

"Or JD could track down the Fosters and kill them. That would cover all the tracks."

"Twitty," T-Tommy said.

I shrugged.

"JD's GSR test was negative," Sidau said. "How could he have fired the other rifle?"

Ever have one of those thoughts that should've popped into your feeble little brain a lot earlier? Something obvious, like red brake lights snapping on in front of you, or pulsing blue police cruiser lights in your rearview mirror, or maybe a fist to your face?

"JD lives in a world of weapons and ammo," I said. "Wouldn't you think he'd have GSR on him all the time? Just from handling guns in his shop if nothing else. Not to mention he's a big time shooter and hunter."

Here's the deal on GSR: GSR or gunshot residue is all the stuff a fired weapon spits out along with the bullet. A cloud of gases and particles that result from the explosion of the primer and the powder within the cartridge, that contain elements such as lead, barium, and antimony, that spread out from the muzzle and the firing chamber, that settle on the shooter's hands, face, and clothing, that cling to anything in the area, including another person, a wall or other structure, a tree or shrub, anything. This GSR can also be passed from person to person with a handshake, a hug, a pat on the back, or to anyone's hands who simply handles a recently fired gun. Anyone who worked with or fired weapons often, like JD, would be expected to have traces of GSR on them. He didn't, so the question was, why not?

"Maybe he had someone else do it," Sidau said. "Or maybe he washed his hands between firing the rifle and arriving at the prison."

"I seem to remember a jug of water in his truck that morning," T-Tommy said.

"Too bad we didn't take it into evidence," Sidau said. "If he had any GSR on his hands it would probably have transferred to the jug. If he used the water to wash his hands."

"At that time we didn't have any evidence to suggest JD was involved," T-Tommy said. "We couldn't have taken anything from his truck without his permission."

"Too late now," I added. "Jug's probably gone, and even if it were still in his truck, it's been there a week so its value as evidence is nil. He could've laid down GSR at any time, not necessarily the morning Walter took the hit."

Sidau nodded.

"Let's look at all the evidence again," I said.

Chapter 65

The evidence collected from the two crime scenes, the sniper site and the prison parking lot where Walter went down, were packaged in an assortment of paper and plastic bags, each labeled and sealed, chain of custody forms attached, and stuffed into two cardboard boxes. While Sidau emptied each box and spread the packages out on a metal table-top, I told them of my chat with Bobby Poehler.

"So JD might have been serious about popping Walter?" T-Tommy said.

"Sounds that way," I said.

I began to rummage through the evidence bags again. I had done this the day after the shooting. Then I found nothing of interest but, now with a different suspect in mind, I hoped I'd see things in a different light.

Evidence collected at a crime scene, particularly an outdoor or publicly accessible one, was often an odd collection, some items connected to the case and useful, others not. Some might be the key to the case, others background noise that served only to confuse the issue. Crime-scene investigators always collected too much, simply because they had no way of knowing what was evidence and what was the flotsam of life.

I mean, the importance of packaging up a rifle or casting a tire track was obvious, but what about things like beer cans, fast-food bags, pieces of cardboard, torn and stained sheets of plastic and canvas, rusted lengths of chain, old shoes and clothing, chewing gum wrappers, old newspapers, and all the other things people tossed away without a second thought? These were the things that spread out before me.

Distinguishing what to test and what to simply hold in evidence is never easy. There are simply too many items and not enough time and money to do everything. On *CSI* and its clones maybe, but not out here in the real world.

Most of the items appeared old, dirt crusted, stiffened from being repeatedly rain soaked and then drying, matted with leaves and twigs, their time along that dirt road measured in months, not days. I picked up each bag, examined its contents, and set it aside, finding little that sparked a question. Until I picked up a plastic bag with a blue cotton cloth inside. Other than a couple of small stains that appeared oily in nature, it seemed fairly clean. I held it up.

"Where'd you find this?"

Sidau took the package from me, read the ID number, and then consulted the evidence logbook that sat on an adjacent table. "About a half mile south of the sniper sight. Just before the road swings left and heads back down toward the highway."

"On the road, or nearby?"

"In the brush along the edge."

"Which side?"

He hesitated for a beat, brow furrowed, gaze aimed upward, as if trying to recall an image. "Left side as you head down the hill."

"Driver's side," I said.

Sidau picked up a gray envelope, tugged out a stack of eight-by-ten photos, and shuffled though them. He found what he was searching for and handed me two photos.

The first was of the road. I recognized it as aiming south. Along the left side, the driver's side for a car headed that way, near the road's edge, the blue cloth was partially visible.

The second was a sharply focused photo of the cloth taken from a straight down, ninety-degree angle. It lay draped over what appeared to be an old hickory branch and a bread-box-sized stone, reddish in color, sandy in texture, a foot ruler at the bottom added to give scale.

"Have you done any testing on this yet?"

"No reason to."

"Test it for GSR."

Sidau nodded. "You thinking the shooter wiped his hands with it and then tossed it?"

"JD didn't have GSR on his hands. He had a water jug in his truck. He drove into the prison lot from the south, as if he had come from Huntsville."

"So maybe he made a brief detour up the dirt road," T-Tommy added. "Just long enough to pump a round into his brother and dump the weapon at the Fosters' feet."

I nodded. "Scrubs his hands as he heads back toward the highway, tosses the cloth, thinking no one would ever connect it to the scene he left behind, and then plays the outraged brother, ranting that HPD, or the Fosters, or anyone but him killed his brother."

"Like maybe me?" T-Tommy said.

"Like maybe you."

"I'll set up the electron microscope and have an answer for you later today," Sidau said.

"That'd be great."

"Are you sure JD killed Walter?" Sidau asked.

"No, but he had the most to gain."

"Derrick Stone sniffed around that business of JD's," T-Tommy said. "Grossed about six hundred thousand, netted half that."

Sidau scratched his chin. "So JD's annual income just doubled."

"That's about it."

"We just need to prove it," Sidau said.

I smiled. "That's what you're going to do. After you test this for GSR, see if you can get any DNA. If JD used this to wipe GSR from his hands, you might be able to get a DNA profile."

When someone wipes his hands with a towel or something similar, skin cells are collected by the material, particularly if the person is trying to scrub his hands clean. Like rubbing away GSR, or maybe like Lady Macbeth, endlessly scrubbing invisible bloodstains from her hands. With the PCR-STR DNA analysis technique, a profile can be generated from very small amounts of DNA, theoretically from a single cell.

Sidau nodded. "I still have Tim and Martha Foster's DNA patterns in my files from the abduction case, but I'll need JD's to do a comparison with him."

I glanced at T-Tommy. "We'll work on it."

Chapter 66

Bridge Street Town Center, the newest and most upscale shopping area in Huntsville, nestled along Old Madison Pike just a few miles from the Marriott hotel where Tim and Martha Foster had holed up. Open-air and European in style with broad walkways, park benches, and streetlamps, Bridge Street straddled an hour-glass-shaped, man-made lake. An arched bridge over the lake's central neck connected the two halves of the mall. A walking trail hugged the water's edge. Tenants included clothing stores such as Chico's and Ann Taylor, an Apple Computer store, a Westin hotel, and a dozen restaurants.

Tim lifted his sweat-soaked tee shirt away from his chest and flapped it. Barely nine and it felt as if the temperature was already nudging eighty. He and Martha were into their third and final lap around the lake when Tim spotted Adam Carlson, across the water, some two hundred feet away. Adam glanced their way but showed no sign of recognition, no wave, no change in his stride, and quickly turned his gaze back to the path in front of him. Tim nudged Martha with an elbow, and when she looked at him, nodded toward Adam.

"Look over there," he said.

Martha's gait hitched. She dropped her head and peeked over her sunglasses toward Adam. "Oh, my God. What should we do?"

"Nothing. He looked this way, but didn't recognize us."

"I can't believe I let you talk me into this."

"This what?"

"Being here. Out in public."

"You'd rather sit in a hotel room and stare at the walls?"

"No. But Investigator Tortelli told us to stay inside. Keep a low profile."

"We are keeping a low profile."

"What if we run into him again? Up close? Or someone else we know?"

They circled the far end of the lake, the path now curling back toward the bridge. "I don't think they'd recognize us."

"You think these lame sunglasses and ball caps will do the trick?"

"Don't forget your new hairdo."

She laughed. "What about you, Buzz Lightyear?"

Tim ran a hand over his head, the stubble rasping against his palm. "At least it's cool."

She slapped him lightly on the butt. "You're cool all right." She looked around. "But I'm getting uncomfortable here. I'm sure we're going to run into Adam again."

"He must've just started his walk, or we'd have seen him earlier. He's well ahead of us so let's slow our pace a bit, and by the time we get back up to the bridge, he'll be off to the other side of the lake and we can head to the parking lot."

He circled an arm around her shoulders and pulled her against him. They walked that way up the rise, turning right at the bridge, heading toward the front lot. Once back in the cover of the car, they decided to take a drive before going back to the hotel. Tim headed up the Old Madison Pike and zigzagged beneath I-565 and on to Bob Wallace until it crossed California Street. A few twists and turns and they were on their old street.

"Should we be here?" Martha asked. "After seeing Adam, we might be pushing our luck."

"We'll just drive by."

Tim slowed. As the house came into view, he saw that it was unchanged. He wasn't sure what he expected it to look like, but the sameness of it seemed odd. Like it should have changed in the past—what?—week?—had it only been a week? The grass needed mowing but that's it. It was as if they had simply been on vacation.

The new owner obviously hadn't moved in.

Tim stopped in front of the house.

"Don't stop," Martha said. Her head swiveled as she looked up and down the street.

"Your roses are still doing well," he said.

Her gaze followed his. Entering their fourth year and just now maturing, the thick, deeply green rose bushes were loaded with bright-yellow flowers and buds.

Tim saw Sandy Sechrest come around the side of her house. She wore shorts and a shirt, tied at the waist. She had obviously been working in her garden. Sandy picked up the hose that lay in the grass and twisted the faucet handle. She began to wash off her bare legs.

Martha must have seen her too as she took in a sharp breath. "Let's get going."

Tim eased forward. Sandy glanced toward them, gave a brief smile and a nod, and then returned to aiming the water down her legs. She didn't recognize them either. The smile and the nod were just her being friendly. Sandy would do that to anyone who happened by.

Tim headed back up California and turned onto Governor's Drive, a busy four-lane highway that climbed the southern shoulder of Monte Sano Mountain. He hung a left at Monte Sano Boulevard, a winding tree-lined, two-lane blacktop that rode the spine of the mountain. He slowed, switched off the car's AC, and lowered all the windows, the air being a good ten degrees cooler up here.

How many Sunday afternoons had he and Martha taken this drive? Too many to remember. They had always enjoyed cruising around the city, through Maple Hill Cemetery, south to the Tennessee River, north into the rolling, fertile farmland, and here, over Monte Sano.

"I love this," Martha said.

"Me, too."

"I thought you loved Asheville?"

"I do." He slowed further as a squirrel darted across the road and leaped onto a tree trunk, climbing rapidly, disappearing into the leaves. "But this is home."

They drove past the entrance to Monte Sano State Park, where they had often picnicked. Usually hot dogs and burgers cooked on a portable grill and served on one of the many tree-shaded picnic tables the park provided. Steven had loved playing baseball up here with the other kids that showed up on weekends. Or swinging on the giant swing, a wooden slat that would hold two eight-year-olds, attached to long, heavy ropes that hung from a thick pine limb a good sixty feet above. With the right pusher, you could soar scary high into the air.

Tim knew Martha was thinking about those days too. He sensed her tension and looked over at her. "What's wrong?"

She sniffed. "Nothing."

"Come on. What is it?"

"I didn't realize how much I missed everything." She laid her head back against the headrest. "I guess the excitement—the fear—of what we had planned—of escaping to North Carolina—I never really believed we weren't coming back." She extended a hand out the window and let it ride up and down on the wind. "But now that we're back here—"

"You want to stay."

She sat up and looked at him. "Yes, I do."

"I do too."

"Do you think we could come back? After all this gets settled."

"I was just thinking the same thing." He smiled, reached over, and took her hand. "Of course, I might be in prison."

"Don't say that. I'd die if that happened."

"But—"

"No, don't talk about it." Tears welled in her eyes.

"Okay. But, we'll have to face it soon."

"But not now. I don't want to think about that until we have to."

He turned onto the Bankhead Parkway and they rode downhill in silence, the road shadowed by trees, apple-green with spring growth. Bankhead plugged into Pratt Avenue, and then onto Five Points, where a left on Andrew Jackson Way, carried them uphill and merged them onto California Street.

Maple Hill Cemetery appeared on their left. Tim turned into the main entrance and wound his way along the narrow roads that criss-crossed the cemetery. Neither of them had spoken for twenty minutes, each knowing where they were headed. They remained silent as Tim eased to the curb. They stepped out of the car and walked hand in hand to Steven's grave.

Chapter 67

JD Whitiker looked up when the bell on the screen door jangled. Paul Twitty came in, wearing a tailored gray suit, white shirt beneath a deep-purple tie, cigar in his mouth, and a smile on his face. JD hissed open a fresh can of Dr. Pepper and knocked back half of it in several gulps. He suppressed a burp as Twitty walked up to the counter.

"What've you got for me?" JD asked.

"A location on the Fosters."

"Jail?"

Twitty shook his head. "Nope."

"They didn't arrest them?"

"Doesn't look that way."

"Don't tell me they're still in North Carolina."

Twitty smiled. "Nope. They're just a couple of miles from right here where we're standing."

JD took another slug of the Pepper and placed the can on the counter. "Where?"

"Over at the Marriott. Checked in under their new names. Robert Beckwith and Cindy Strunk. Actually they got married yesterday. In Asheville. So, I guess they're now the Beckwiths."

JD knew about the wedding, the Spraggins brothers having told him, but said nothing to Twitty. He wanted Kyle and Cody, his aces in the hole, completely off the radar. Twitty knowing about them could blow this whole deal up. But knowing where the Fosters were, knowing they weren't in jail, was better than JD could have hoped. Meant his backup plan was again in play.

"Any idea what Tortelli and Walker are up to?" JD asked.

"Not sure." Twitty scratched an ear. "But if they're hiding them out instead of arresting them, they must know something. Any idea what that might be?"

"What do you mean?"

"Just what I said. If they didn't arrest them, they must have some doubt about their guilt."

"I thought you said the evidence pointed at them?"

"It does." Twitty spread his spider fingers on the countertop. "Unless they dug up something that says otherwise."

"Like what?"

"Don't know. That's what I was asking. You know anything I should know?"

"How could I?" He took another gulp of Pepper. "Didn't I hire you to dig up that kind of shit?"

Twitty nodded. "Just don't want to be played."

"What do you mean?"

Twitty tugged the cigar from his mouth. "I get nervous when things don't mesh is all I'm saying. I don't like it that the Fosters weren't arrested. I don't like Tortelli and Walker having facts that I don't know. Facts that seem to have changed everything."

"Seems to me the question is exactly what those facts might be. And that's what I'm paying you to find out."

Twitty shrugged, clamping down on the cigar butt again. "I'll dig around."

"Good." JD eased from behind the counter. "Let me grab your new gun." He walked into his office and returned with a gun case and a plastic bag with the boxes of number eight-and-a-half shot, handing them to Twitty.

"You're all set for bird season."

"Thanks." Twitty settled the gun case on one shoulder. "I'll give you a shout later. When I know something."

JD watched Twitty head out the door, and then walked back into the office where Bo sat working on the books.

"You still know someone over at the Marriott?" JD asked.

"Yeah. My buddy Elvin. He works in maintenance."

"I need him to dig up some info on a couple of guests."

"I'll give him a call. What do you need?"

"Robert Beckwith. Checked in last night. I need his room number. Does he have a car? If so, make, model, and license number would be great. That should be on his registration form. Can your guy get me that?"

"Sure."

"Tell him there's a couple of hundred in it for him if he does this very quietly and keeps his mouth shut."

"I'm on it."

JD returned to the front counter, picked up the phone, and dialed. An answer came quickly and he said, "Kyle?"

"Yeah."

"That thing I mentioned the other night. I need you and Cody."

"We're in town. Got a stop to make and then we'll swing by. A half hour maybe. That work?"

"Yeah. Park around back."

"Will do."

Chapter 68

The light traffic on usually busy University Drive made for an easy left turn into the Whitiker's Rods and Guns front lot, the Porsche rocking over the uneven and cracked asphalt, loose gravel crunching beneath the tires. I angled into an empty slot, nose aimed at the front door, and T-Tommy and I got out. I looked up as the screen door snapped closed behind Paul Twitty, cigar in his mouth, a plastic bag in one hand, a cased gun across the other shoulder, out of place considering his sharply creased gray suit. He saw us and walked our way.

"What brings you guys here?" he asked.

"Bored," I said. "We were in the area and didn't have anywhere else to go so we thought we'd drop by."

"Right."

"And you?"

"Picking up my new shotgun." He tilted his head toward the shouldered case. "Remington 870 Wingmaster. Improved cylinder. This fall the doves better beware."

"What'd it set you back?" I asked.

He hesitated, obviously not expecting the question. "Uh, I don't know. JD just put it on my account." His weight shifted slightly from his right foot to his left.

"You get a chance to talk to JD?" I asked.

"Yeah."

"Anything interesting?"

"Can't say, him being a client and all."

"Anything on the Fosters?" I asked.

Twitty's weight shifted again. "I was going to ask you the same thing."

"Nothing yet."

"Me, either."

Was he lying? Did he know we had found them? We had told no one except Derrick Stone and he definitely wouldn't have leaked it. The crow's-feet at the corners of Twitty's eyes deepened slightly and his pupils bumped open a notch, but otherwise his face remained passive, giving away nothing. Paul Twitty was a good poker player. Not perfect, but good.

"Got to run," he said. "See you guys later."

We watched him cross the lot to his Navigator. Gunmetal gray, fat tires, blacked-out windows. He popped open the rear boot and placed the gun and the plastic bag between two canvas duffels. His surveillance tools no doubt. He gave us a brief wave as he turned on to University and accelerated.

We walked inside. Bo stood behind the counter, chatting on a cell phone, turning away slightly as he saw us, JD nowhere in sight. As we approached, I picked up what Bo was saying.

"Yeah. Soon as you can." He listened for a beat. "Can't really say right now." Another beat, Bo's head giving a slight bob. "Tell you what, I'll swing by and we can talk about it." Pause. "I'll bring the money I owe you." Another wait. "See you in twenty."

Bo closed the cell, laid it on the countertop, and looked at us. "What can I do for you?"

"Need to see JD," I said.

"Can I ask why?"

"You can ask."

"He's busy."

"So are we," T-Tommy said.

"What do you guys want?" It was JD. He came from his office and moved behind the counter, sliding past Bo.

Bo picked up his cell. "I'm heading over to take care of that thing. Should be back in an hour, tops."

JD nodded. Bo headed out the front door.

"So this is where I left this," JD said, picking up the Dr. Pepper. He drained it and tossed the empty into the trash can near his feet. "I'll ask again. What do you want?"

"Just a couple of questions."

"I don't think so. I got nothing to say." His eyes narrowed and his chin came up. "Not to you anyway."

"I thought maybe you'd heard something else on the Fosters."

He looked at me and shook his head. "Is this the state of police work now? You have to come to the victim's family to find the killers?" He looked at T-Tommy. "This what I pay my fucking taxes for? So they can hire a moron like you?"

T-Tommy's jaw tightened, chin rising, eyes narrowing, fists curling at his side.

I honestly thought T-Tommy was going to take his head off. Wouldn't be the first time he'd laid out someone who jumped in his face like JD just did. In fact I'd seen him go off with much less provocation. I must admit, I'd love to see it, love for T-Tommy to flatten this jerkweed, love to do it myself, but since that wouldn't help things and would drag T-Tommy into a world of crap, I jumped in. "Since you found out about the rifle they bought, we thought maybe you'd heard something else."

"Like what?"

"Maybe where they are?"

"That's your job." He leaned on the counter. "So why don't you run along and do it."

"That's what we're doing," T-Tommy said. "So answer the question and your precious tax dollars won't be wasted."

"What question is that?"

"Do you have any news on the Fosters?"

"Why would I?"

"You have a network of gun sellers all over the area," I said. "Maybe they bought a new rifle to replace the one they left near the prison."

"You mean the one they used to kill my brother?"

I nodded. "I mean, you were lucky enough to hear about their last purchase. We thought maybe if they'd picked up another one, you might've gotten a call on it, too."

"Nope."

"Maybe Twitty uncovered something?" I asked.

"Why don't you ask him?"

"He didn't have much to say."

"Neither do I."

The screen door squeaked open. A man entered, carrying a large square cardboard box, SHIMANO SPINNING REELS stamped on the side. JD nodded to him and then said to me, "Why don't you two go do something useful? I got work to do."

The man placed the box on the far end of the counter. "Got those reels you ordered."

JD nodded. "Great. I got a couple of guys chomping at the bit for them."

The man unfolded a one-page yellow invoice, handing it to JD. JD looked it over and placed it on the counter.

"I'll get you a check," JD said, and headed into his office.

I glanced at T-Tommy.

He moved toward the guy and indicated the box. "Mind if I take a look?"

The man smiled. "Sure." A pocketknife appeared and he deftly sliced through the packing tape and opened the flaps, pulling out one of the boxed reels inside. "Best you can get." He opened the smaller box and removed a polished reel, handing it to T-Tommy. "This is our newest. The Sidestab 4000RE."

T-Tommy leaned one elbow on the counter, partially blocking the man's view down the counter. "Feels good. Nice weight." He worked the crank. "Smooth."

The man beamed. "They don't come much better than what you got right there."

While he and T-Tommy went back and forth on the merits of Shimano spinning reels, I squatted as if tying my shoe, the trash can behind the counter just out of reach. A couple of duck steps to my left fixed that. I lifted the Dr. Pepper can JD had tossed, careful to avoid the rim near the opening, and slipped it into my jacket pocket.

Your tax dollars at work.

Chapter 69

T-Tommy and I swung by the Forensic Science Department. Before going inside, we stood in the lot while I called Dale's Cheap Guns over in Rome. Wanted to ask Dale Bonner about his phone call to JD, telling him about the Fosters buying a gun. He wasn't in, and the guy that answered said he would be out all day, back tomorrow.

We found Sidau in the DNA lab, a long, narrow, beige room with counters along each side. Blinds, twisted close, covered the narrow windows, the only light source banks of overhead fluorescents. Arrayed on the countertops were the tools of DNA testing: a GeneAmp PCR System 9700, an ABI PRISM 310 Genetic Analyzer, an ABI PRISM 7000 Sequence Detection System. All new and improved since I worked here.

Sidau looked up as T-Tommy and I came in. "Sometimes you're a genius, Dub."

"Why would you doubt that?"

Sidau rolled his eyes. "That cloth was loaded with GSR and it looks like there's DNA. I'll have it extracted soon and then I'll start the cycling process."

I pulled the can from my jacket pocket, fingers gripping the rim on each side, avoiding the opening, and handed it to Sidau. "Here's JD's DNA."

"That was quick. How'd you pull that off?"

"JD's got a Dr. Pepper jones. Must knock back a dozen a day. We managed to lift this from his trash."

"Inside or out?"

"In."

"So, this isn't really evidence?"

"No. But it'll tell us what we need to know."

Had the can been outside in a trash bin it could be collected and tagged as evidence. Once it was tossed out it became more or less public property and could be lifted without a warrant. But inside, behind JD's counter, a judge would rule that it was still in his possession and therefore couldn't be legally obtained without a warrant. That didn't matter for this little exercise. We only wanted to know if the DNA on the cloth belonged to JD. If so, we'd find a legal way to get JD's DNA, maybe rummage through his outside trash, maybe get a warrant.

"How long?" T-Tommy asked.

Sidau scratched an ear. "Extraction and purification and say thirty cycles of PCR amplification. That'll take three or four hours. Then the STR analysis and building the ladder—later tonight or early tomorrow."

"Call as soon as you know."

"Will do. Now get out of here so I can work."

We left.

JD didn't really trust the Spraggins brothers. No one did. But he knew that they were greedy and for money would do just about anything. Maybe actually anything. He wasn't sure the brothers had any boundaries. To say they were criminals was an insult to criminals. They dabbled in robbery, intimidation, selling stolen property, moonshine, crystal meth, and if need be could be as lethal as rattlesnakes. Best to avoid them if possible. Until you needed them.

Their first mission had failed when Tortelli and Walker grabbed the Fosters before they could do them. Maybe this one would work out. It had to. If not, the Fosters could sink them.

Most people believed the brothers were twins, but JD knew Kyle was older by a couple of years. Couldn't tell that by looking at them.

Both six two, lanky, sinewy arms, a shock of dirty blond hair that swept across their foreheads just above ice-blue eyes, and a constant smirk as if disdain was the only thing they ever felt, which was probably true.

They came through the back door, both in jeans, work boots, and tee shirts, Kyle's navy blue, Cody's dark gray.

JD took them into the office, closed the door, and explained the situation and what he needed. The pair nodded, but said nothing. Didn't ask a single question, didn't flinch, simply took the envelope with two grand inside, said they'd get right on it.

Tim Foster opened the door to my knock. He wore jeans, no shirt, a towel around his neck, hair damp, feet bare. I could hear the shower running in the bathroom.

"Come in," Tim said. He stepped back and let T-Tommy and me enter. "Martha's in the shower. I'll tell her you're here."

He slipped into the bathroom. His voice smeared with the sound of the shower, so I couldn't make out what he was saying. When he came back out, a cloud of steam followed him.

"She'll be out in a minute."

"How're things?" I asked.

"We went for a walk. Over at Bridge Street. And then drove up over the mountain."

I glanced at T-Tommy. "Anywhere else?"

The shower fell silent.

He hesitated, and then sighed. "We went by the house."

I started to say something, but he held up a hand.

"We didn't go inside or anything like that. Just drove by."

"Didn't we talk about keeping a low profile?" T-Tommy asked.

"Yeah, but I didn't think we were under house arrest."

Martha came out of the bathroom. "Who's under house arrest?"

"No one," I said. "Tim was just telling us about your adventures this morning."

Martha shrugged. "Neither of them recognized us."

I looked at Tim.

"I hadn't gotten that far yet."

"Oh," Martha said.

"Tell me," T-Tommy said. He didn't look happy.

"We saw an old friend at Bridge Street. And then saw Sandy Sechrest, our neighbor. They both looked right at us, but neither recognized us."

I nodded. "And you went by the cemetery."

"How'd you know?"

"I didn't, but it's what I'd do."

"I'm sorry," Martha said.

"Look, I don't blame you, but you have to be cool. If anyone discovers you're here, it could create a frenzy. Drag in the media. T-Tommy might have to take you into custody then." That seemed to sober them a bit. I went on. "We completed the ballistics examinations. The rifle you had matches the bullets I took from the stump this morning and, more importantly, the nonlethal one that hit Walter."

Martha almost jumped up and down. "That's good, right?"

"That's very good. And even better, we might have some evidence that puts the onus on JD Whitiker."

"What evidence?"

"Can't say, but we should know something by tomorrow."

Martha looked at me. "You're saying JD killed Walter?"

"Maybe."

"And you can prove that?" Tim asked.

"We'll see."

Tim looked at Martha. "I think we can handle room service for a day or two."

I nodded. "That'd be best. But tonight, why don't you come over to my place for dinner?"

"We'd like that," Martha said.

Chapter 70

Thick smoke and the aroma of the Tabasco-marinated brisket I was cooking rose from the grill as I led Tim and Martha out onto my rear deck. Claire and T-Tommy were seated at the table, glasses of Biale Black Chicken Zin before each. I poured Tim and Martha glasses and they sat.

Kramden and Norton must have followed them up the mountain, because they swooped in, squawking, demanding attention, Norton settling on the back of an empty chair, Kramden bolder, hopping across the table, stopping in front of Martha, head angled to one side, examining her with a single black eye. Martha seemed fascinated, and a little afraid.

"It's okay," I said. "They're annoying but harmless."

"They're your pets?"

Claire laughed. "Other way around. They've got him trained."

I introduced the boys to the Fosters and then told the story of how they came to be my—whatever they were. "Go ahead," I said to Martha. "Pet him and he'll be a friend for life."

"Feed him and he'll go home with you," Claire added.

Martha tentatively extended a finger. Kramden looked at it, bobbed his head a couple of times, and then ducked, presenting the top of his head to her. She smoothed his crown feathers with a finger, Kramden rubbing back, now a friend for life.

Claire went into the kitchen and returned with a bowl of corn, leading Norton into the yard. Kramden hesitated, not wanting to give up the attention, but food won out and he flitted over to the bowl Claire placed on the grass.

We sipped wine and made small talk until the brisket was ready. I carried it to the kitchen, sliced it, and then served it along with T-Tommy's famous squash risotto, and the salad Claire had tossed together. I opened a bottle of Sapphire Hills Winberrie Zin and we dug in.

"This is delicious," Claire said, taking a bit of brisket. "And it has a little bite to it. What is that?"

"Tabasco."

"Really?" Tim asked.

"Pretty easy. Put the meat in a plastic bag, dump in a bottle of Tabasco, marinate it a few hours, and then grill it."

"How did you ever come up with that?" Tim asked.

"My dad used to make it all the time."

Everyone fell silent as we ate. The boys, now filled to capacity, hit the air, heading west where the sun balanced on the horizon and painted the sky red orange. A squadron of chimney swifts, swirling black silhouettes against the sunset, briefly scattered, abandoning their gnat catching as the boys plowed through. They quickly re-formed and continued their sunset feeding ritual.

After we finished dinner and cleared the table, I served strawberry shortcake and chilled glasses of late-harvest Riesling.

"What's this new evidence you have?" Tim asked.

"Can't say," T-Tommy said. "It might be nothing or it might blow this whole thing open."

"But if it is good, it'll implicate JD?"

I nodded. "Put him right in the middle of it."

Martha reached over and grasped Tim's hand. "What about us?"

"We know you didn't fire the lethal bullet," I said. "That'll help, but what happens after that is up to the judge."

"Could be as bad as attempted murder or as light as aggravated assault," T-Tommy said.

Tim nodded. "Then there is the IRS to deal with."

"We might be able to help you there," I said.

Tim raised an eyebrow.

"We know the regional director. From an old case. He's a reasonable guy, and I'd bet he'll cut you some slack."

"Let's hope."

"I hope all our friends will be as forgiving," Martha said.

"They will," I said. "I spoke with several of them. My impression is that they all cared for you great deal. I think they'll understand."

Tears glistened in Martha's eyes. "It's Pastor Boles that I dread seeing."

"Why?" Claire asked.

"We committed a sin," Tim said. "A mortal sin."

Claire leaned forward, elbows on the edge of the table, her gaze directed at Tim. "But you didn't kill Walter."

"I intended to. I tried to. Same thing in God's eyes. The sin was as much the thought as the action."

I shrugged. "Maybe the Big Guy will cut you some slack too."

"Maybe." Tim gazed up toward my neighbor's pecan trees. "But right or wrong, I'm glad Walter Whitiker is no longer on this planet."

I couldn't argue with that.

Chapter 71

JD Whitiker sat in the passenger seat, Bo behind the wheel of his dark-blue Chevy Tahoe. Bo had backed into a slot at the far end of the Marriott's front parking area, beneath a tree that shaded them from a nearby light standard. The Tahoe's deeply blackened windows added another layer of concealment.

In the next row over, the Spraggins brothers waited in their black Lincoln Continental. They were there for backup if things went sideways. JD prayed that wouldn't happen. Better if this went smoothly and quietly and didn't turn into something chaotic and bloody.

JD felt edgy. As if his nervous system was plugged into a high-voltage transformer. It was that more than the warm night that caused sweat to collect on his forehead and the back of his neck. He wiped his moist palms on his jeans.

Hurry up damn it.

They had been in the same spot for over an hour and had seen only sparse activity. Mostly people returning from dinner or a movie or whatever. No sign of the Fosters.

He watched as three business types, suits and ties, probably here for meetings with one of the many aerospace companies in the area, climbed from a rental Taurus and walked toward the hotel entrance. The third such group they had seen since arriving.

"Your guy sure they went out and aren't back in their room?" JD asked.

"Yeah." Bo said. "They left around five thirty and haven't come back since. Besides, their car isn't here."

"Any idea where they went?"

"Dinner, I suspect."

JD glanced at his watch. "Getting late. Maybe they aren't coming back. Maybe they moved to another hotel."

"Elvin says not. They're still registered. Their stuff is still in their room."

"He went into their room?"

"He works maintenance. He has a master key. If they showed up, all he'd have to say is that all the thermostats were acting up and he was checking on theirs."

JD sighed. "I wish they'd hurry up."

Bo glanced at his watch. "It's going on eleven. They'll be along soon I'd bet."

"I got to piss," JD said. He stepped out and moved to the rear of the truck, where sandwiched between it and the row of hedges that marked the back edge of the lot, he was hidden from view.

Tim saw the Marriott off the left side of the freeway, maybe a half mile ahead. Just beyond the hotel, the night-lit rockets of the adjacent U.S. Space & Rocket Museum loomed over the trees, their whiteness stark against the black sky.

"I wish we could turn back the clock," Martha said.

"Three years?"

"That would be nice, wouldn't it? Make all of this go away."

"Wish it were that easy."

Tim exited I-565 onto the feeder road, past Sparkman Drive, and hung a left at Old Madison Pike. Up and over the freeway it became Tranquility Base, a short road that slid past the hotel and plugged into the Space Museum parking area.

How long had it been since they had visited the museum? Had to be at least five years. Tim could still see Steven's wide-eyed wonder at the virtual forest of military missiles and space rockets that towered overhead and the excitement and pleading in his voice when he asked to go to Space Camp, a six-day program for aspiring astronauts.

Steven never made it to Space Camp.

Tim felt tears collecting in his eyes as he turned into the Marriott lot.

"There they are," Bo said.

He pointed toward the Fosters' car as it moved along one of the rows of parked vehicles. Apparently unable to find an empty space, they continued to the end, looped around, and headed back, now only two rows from where JD and Bo were parked. Tim Foster swung their car into an empty space.

"Let's go," JD said.

Bo cranked up the Tahoe, but didn't turn on the headlamps, and maneuvered over to the row where the Fosters had parked. Bo pulled in behind their car, blocking any escape, just as Tim shut off the engine. As planned, the Spraggins brothers eased up near the rear of the Tahoe, the Lincoln's headlights also dark. Helped block line of sight from the hotel. Put the brothers in position to jump in if necessary.

JD checked the lot, saw no one moving around, and climbed from the passenger seat, his nine millimeter in one hand, two pairs of handcuffs in his jacket pocket.

The overhead light popped on as Tim opened his door. Martha appeared to be rummaging in her purse.

JD shoved the nine against the side of Tim's head. "Not a word, hands on the wheel."

"What the—" Martha started.

"Shut the fuck up," JD said. "Hands on the dash."

Martha hesitated, looking across at her husband and JD.

"Unless you want me to splatter his brains all over that pretty little dress of yours."

Martha flattened her palms against the dash.

"That's better."

"What do you want, JD?" Tim asked.

"Did I stutter? Didn't I say shut the fuck up?"

Tim nodded.

JD glanced toward the hotel entrance. Quiet. He leaned down and looked at Martha. "If I see your hands leave the dash, or if I hear a peep from you, he's done. Clear?"

Martha nodded.

"That's better." He took a step back and leveled the weapon at Tim. "Now out of the car."

Tim stepped out. JD grabbed Tim's shoulder and spun him around, pushing him against the car. "Hands behind your back."

"You can't do this," Tim said.

"Really?" He pressed the muzzle against the base of Tim's skull, grinding it into the flesh. "Don't you doubt for a minute that I'll kill you right here, right now." He rapped the gun barrel against the side of Tim's head. "Now put your fucking hands behind your back."

Tim complied.

JD stuffed the gun beneath his belt and cranked a pair of handcuffs around Tim's wrists. He walked Tim backward toward the Tahoe, yanked open the rear door, and shoved him inside, nudging the door closed with one hip.

He then moved around to Martha's door and pulled it open. He ordered her out. She hesitated so he grabbed her hair and pulled her from the car. She struggled. JD shoved the gun muzzle against her chest.

"Want me to blow your nipples off?"

"Please. Just let us—"

His other hand closed around her throat. "I don't want to hear any crap from you, lady." His fingers tightened, digging into the soft flesh on either side of her windpipe. "Now I'm going to let go and you're going to turn around. Clear?"

She managed a half nod.

He released his grip, she turned, and he cuffed her. As he led her around the SUV to the other rear door, a car turned into the lot and moved their way.

"Hurry up," Bo said.

Martha tried to pull away, but JD grabbed her by the back of her neck, pushing her forward. "Move it." He forced her along the side of the Tahoe and shoved her into the rear seat just as the car turned down the row. He jumped back into the passenger seat. The car moved by. Three middle-aged Japanese dudes, suits and ties. The one in the backseat looked right at JD as the car passed.

Bo put the Tahoe in gear and drove away. The Spraggins brothers followed.

At the lot's exit, Kyle pulled the Lincoln up next to the Tahoe. Cody let the passenger's side window down. "We'll go take care of that other thing. Talk to you later."

The Lincoln spun out on to Tranquility Base Road and headed toward the interstate.

Chapter 72

I lay on my bed, staring at the ceiling, Claire's head resting on my chest. After the Fosters left, we had sent T-Tommy home, saying we'd clean up. He didn't argue.

"They're good people," Claire said.

"I know."

"I'm glad Tim didn't actually kill Walter."

"He tried to."

"So he'll be charged with attempted murder?"

"Probably."

She raised up on one elbow and looked at me. "You're talkative tonight."

"Just thinking."

"About?"

"About the DNA. If what Sidau found on that cloth doesn't match JD, we're screwed, blued, and tattooed."

"How's that? He had motive, means, and opportunity."

"None of which puts him at the shooting site. The DNA will."

She pressed her cheek against my chest again. "So JD's the shooter? No one else could have done it?"

"Sure, someone else could have. They just didn't."

"No other suspects?"

"Most of the possibles have been cleared. T-Tommy and Stone are looking into a couple of guys. One had sued JD and Walter. Something about not paying him the full freight on an order of ammo a year or so back. He doesn't have an alibi. Lives by himself out toward Gurley."

"Sounds like a suspect to me."

"Except I don't think a couple of hundred bucks is much of a motive for all this. Especially with a year lag time."

I could feel her head nod slightly. "True. And the other suspect?"

"A guy Walter got into a fight with at a bar about six months before he went to jail. Not only beat on the guy—he needed two dozen stitches in his face—but Walter also humiliated him in front of his wife and a roomful of people. Apparently said some awful things. The guy said he'd get even."

"Another good suspect."

"Possible. If so, like the Fosters, JD beat him to it."

"You're convinced he did it, aren't you?"

"Yep."

"And if the DNA isn't his?"

"Like I said, we're screwed."

"Speaking of which—"

By the time Bo worked his way onto I-565 and got up to speed, JD had pulled pillowcases over the Fosters' heads. He made Tim stretch out on the rear floorboard and Martha on the seat.

Now JD settled back into the passenger's seat, head lolling against the window, and watched the scenery roll by. He went over his plan. His new plan. He wasn't wild about it, but it was all he had. He had had a better one. Twitty finds the Fosters. He sends Kyle and Cody there and the Fosters disappear. Far from home. Far from where anyone would miss them.

Simple and clean. Here in Huntsville, the story would go something like the Fosters killed Walter, disappeared with new identities, and were never heard from again. Up in North Carolina, or wherever Twitty tracked them to, a different story: new couple moves in, moves out, never seen again, must not have liked it and decided to move on. No one knew them. No one would miss them. Perfect in every way.

But now? With Tortelli and Walker finding them and bringing

them back to Huntsville. With them now being living witnesses. Maybe able to unravel everything. If they fell away as suspects, who would that leave? Who would the police turn their attention to?

The only saving grace was that the cops had no evidence against him. He'd been careful not to leave anything behind. Except the murder weapon, which he dropped right under the Fosters' noses. Pretty smooth move he had to admit.

At least this little wrinkle had gone well. He had planned to have Bo's buddy Elvin go knock on their door and tell them there was something wrong with their car and they should hustle down to the parking area. Nab them then. But this worked out better. The Fosters came right to him. No need to involve Elvin in the actual abduction. One less loose end.

Maybe luck was on his side.

"You'll never get away with this." It was Tim Foster's pillowcase-muffled voice, coming from the back floorboard.

JD twisted in his seat. "Looks like I already did. Getting you guys out of the hotel was the hard part."

"Not really."

"What does that mean?"

"The police have evidence that proves you shot your brother, not us."

"Just what might that be?"

Tim twisted his shoulders and rolled his body a little as if looking for a more comfortable position. "I don't know, but from what I've heard, it'll put a noose around your neck."

"Heard? From who?"

"Investigator Tortelli. Dub Walker."

Bo swung the Tahoe south on Memorial Parkway.

"Don't believe everything you hear from those two," JD said.

"Maybe you should."

"Right. Look where it got you."

"Where are you taking us?"

"Someplace you won't like."

Chapter 73

I had awoken at five thirty, tried to go back to sleep, couldn't, gave up, and rolled out of bed. So did Claire. She headed home, so I went for a run along Monte Sano Boulevard and then hit my gym, a glass-walled shed I'd put in near my back property line. I pumped some weights and pounded the heavy bag. Needed to release some steam. Needed to think. Through all this I lost track of time, so was late arriving at Sidau's office. We had planned to meet at eight. T-Tommy wasn't late. He sat in a chair, facing Sidau across his desk, a Starbucks cup in his hand.

"Sorry I'm late." I sat down. "What've you got?"

"You're going to love this," T-Tommy said.

"It matched?"

Sidau nodded. "The cloth contained what looks like gun oil, but definitely GSR and JD's DNA."

"Good call on testing that rag," T-Tommy said.

I shrugged. "Sometimes you get lucky."

"Yeah, I'm sure that's what it was."

"Maybe a little common sense," I added.

"Pretty much puts the old boy right there," T-Tommy said.

"Based on what I found," Sidau said, "I'd say someone fired the rifle and then used the cloth to wipe it down and scrub his hands. That'd explain the oil and GSR. The DNA says that someone was JD Whitiker."

"How strong is the match?" I asked.

"Very." Sidau handed me his report. "Twenty billion to one."

"That'll work." I looked at T-Tommy. "Want to go pick JD up?"

T-Tommy stood. "This should be fun."

"One thing," I said to Sidau. "Don't file your report yet. In fact, don't tell anyone about this."

"You thinking it might get into the wrong hands?" T-Tommy said. "Maybe hands attached to Paul Twitty?"

"And JD Whitiker." Sidau said.

"Exactly," I said. "JD not knowing we have him dead to rights might come in handy."

On the way out to my car, T-Tommy had called Derrick Stone, brought him up to date, and told him to grab a couple of officers and meet us at JD's gun shop. I tried the Fosters' room and Martha's cell, but got no answer from either. Maybe they were downstairs having breakfast. Maybe Martha's phone was in her purse and she couldn't hear it. Maybe they'd ignored what I said and gone for a walk again.

By the time we reached Whitiker's Rods and Guns, two squad cars sat out front, Derrick Stone and three uniforms nearby. I didn't see JD's truck. Stone walked up as we climbed out of my Porsche.

"Nobody's here." Stone nodded toward the front door.

A handwritten sign, a white rectangle with blue block letters written with a marker, said: CLOSED FOR INVENTORY.

How convenient.

"Front and back doors are locked up," Stone went on. "Nobody inside that we could see."

T-Tommy forked his fingers through his hair. "Okay, get on an arrest warrant for JD and put out a BOLO on him."

Stone nodded. "Will do."

"Get search warrants working for this place and his house." T-Tommy turned to the three uniforms and said, "Two of you stay here and keep the shop locked down. No one gets in. Who knows, maybe JD'll show up."

"Do we arrest him if he does?" one of the officers asked. He was young, rookie written all over him.

"Absolutely."

"Even if the arrest warrant hasn't come through by then?"

"That shouldn't take long, but don't worry about that anyway. If JD shows up, hold him here and call me."

"What if he tries to leave?"

"You got a gun and handcuffs?" T-Tommy asked.

"Yes, sir."

"Then use them."

The officer gave a nod. I could tell he was still unsure.

T-Tommy turned back to Stone. "Follow us over to JD's house. Maybe he's still there."

Chapter 74

JD's wife, Priscilla, answered my knock. She wore jeans, a pale-blue shirt, sleeves rolled up, yellow rubber gloves covering each hand. A single strand of her pulled-back hair had escaped and hung across one eye. Looked like she was in cleaning mode. Her face darkened and her hackles went up when she saw us standing on her porch.

"What do you want?" she asked.

"Looking for JD," T-Tommy said.

"He ain't here."

She started to push the door closed, but T-Tommy took a half step forward, his shoulder blocking it. She took a step back.

"Know where he might be?"

"Gone fishing for a couple of days."

T-Tommy nodded. "Any idea where?"

"No. Now get off my property."

"Who is it?" The raspy voice came from behind Priscilla.

The door swung wide open and JD's mother, Lula, appeared. She was about a big as a minute, easily in her eighties, shoulders slumped forward. She wore a pink-and-gray housecoat, skinny legs extending out the bottom, feet shoved into oversized fuzzy pink slippers. Piercing blue eyes jumped from her deeply wrinkled face, now arranged in a look of defiance. Her gaze settled on T-Tommy.

"What the hell do you want?"

"I'll handle this, Mama Lula," Priscilla said.

"The hell you will." Her chin rose and she pointed it at T-Tommy. "You kilt my boy Walter. Sure as I'm standing here. Now get off my porch or I'll go get my shotgun."

"Don't think that'd be a good idea," T-Tommy said.

"You gonna shoot me too?"

Stone's cell phone sounded behind me. He pulled it from his pocket, stepped off the porch and out into the yard, walking a good twenty feet away.

"Mrs. Whitiker," I said to Lula, "we need to talk to JD. You sure he isn't here?"

"What'd she say?" Lula jerked her head toward Priscilla. "Don't you hear so good? He ain't here and we don't know where he's at."

I shoved my hands into my pockets and nodded. "We went by the shop. Had a sign on the door saying he was closed for inventory. Which is it? Is he fishing or doing inventory?"

"It's none of your business," Lula said.

"Actually it is," Stone said as he stepped back up on the porch. He looked at T-Tommy. "Got the arrest warrant."

"What arrest warrant?" Lula asked.

"For JD," T-Tommy said. "For the murder of Walter."

For a little old lady, Lula packed a wallop. She lunged forward, slamming both palms into T-Tommy's chest. He staggered backward a couple of steps. I'd never seen anyone back up T-Tommy.

"Liar, liar, liar," Lula screeched. "You kilt Walter. You did it."

I grabbed her from behind, my arms wrapping her in a bear hug. She tried to bite me, tried to kick me. Damn, she was strong. I lifted her off the ground. Her legs churned the air.

"Take it easy, Mrs. Whitiker," I said.

She twisted and turned and tried to break free from my hug. I was afraid I'd break something, so I let her go. She whirled on me, fists balled at her side, her entire body vibrating with anger.

"I'll sue you for assault."

"You want to go down to the station?" T-Tommy asked.

Her head whipped toward him.

"Take a breath," T-Tommy said. "Relax or I'll arrest you for assaulting a police officer."

Priscilla grabbed Lula's arm and pulled her back into the doorway. Lula yanked her arm free, but didn't go back after either T-Tommy or me. Thank God. I had a mental image of us wrestling her to ground and cuffing her. Not a pretty picture. Worse, I imagined Claire showing a video of the takedown on her report. That would be just like her.

"Where does he usually go fishing?" I asked.

"All over," Priscilla said.

We weren't going to get anything here. Maybe if the search warrants for his home and business came through, we could sniff around and find something, but these two weren't going to give him up. No way.

We apologized for bothering them, said our goodbyes, and T-Tommy asked them to call if they heard from JD. Lula responded by using one of her fuzzy pink slippers to kick the door shut.

Chapter 75

Unlike the Whitiker women, the Fosters didn't answer our knock on their door. I had again tried Martha's cell and called their room as we drove over. No answer on either, but we decided to swing by the Marriott and see if they were in their room anyway. They obviously weren't.

"Where do you think they are?" T-Tommy asked.

"Who knows? Maybe they went back over to Bridge Street for a walk. Maybe out to breakfast. Maybe—"

Behind me, I heard the door across from the Fosters' room open. I turned that way. A Japanese man stepped out. He wore a gray suit, red tie, thick-rimmed glasses, and carried a well-worn and over-stuffed black leather briefcase. Definitely an engineer type. Probably here for some NASA-related business. He nodded sharply and headed toward the elevators.

"Excuse me," I said.

He stopped and turned toward me.

"Do you know the couple that are staying in this room?"

He hesitated.

T-Tommy flipped open his badge. "Huntsville PD."

The man's brow furrowed. "What's this about?"

His English was perfect. Not a hint of an accent.

"Just routine," T-Tommy said. "Have you seen them?"

"A couple of times."

"This morning?"

He shook his head. "Last night. Not today."

"Where were they? Last night?"

"In the parking lot. They got into a car with two men."

I glanced at T-Tommy as my pulse ramped up. "What time was that?"

"When I came back from a dinner meeting." His eyes deflected up and to his right. "Around ten thirty. Maybe eleven."

"What kind of car?" I asked. "The one they got into?"

"A big SUV type. Dark colored. I don't know what make it was."

"The two men? What'd they look like?"

"One was tall. The other, the driver, was big. What I could see. He had very big biceps anyway. Had one arm propped on the window frame. He never got out of the vehicle, so I didn't see him well."

"Tell us what you did see," T-Tommy said.

The man, who said his name was Patrick Takada, works for the Jet Propulsion Lab out in Pasadena, California. He was here for meetings and had a late dinner last night. As he and his colleagues drove into the lot, he saw the big man behind the wheel, the man from the room in the backseat, the tall man helping the woman climb through an open back door.

"Did the woman seem to go willingly?"

He hesitated again. The furrows in his brow deepened. "I'm not sure. The tall man had one hand on her head. Like he was preventing her hitting her head as she got in. Now that I think about it, it was a little odd. Like they do on those cop shows on TV. When they're putting someone in the back of a police car."

"Then what happened?" I asked.

"Nothing. We parked and walked into the hotel."

"Anything else unusual?"

"The vehicle had its headlights off. The other car too."

"What other car?"

"There was a black car behind the SUV. They both had their lights off. Then they drove away together. Both cars' headlights came on as they left the lot."

"You sure?"

He nodded. "Seemed odd, so I remember."

"Did you see where they went? What direction?"

"Not really. I know they both turned toward the highway, but after that I don't know."

"What did the black car look like?"

"That one I know. It was a Lincoln Continental. One of those mid-sixties square-looking ones. Looked at buying one myself a few years ago." He smiled. "My wife vetoed that idea."

We rode down the elevator with Patrick, thanked him for his help, and T-Tommy got his cell number in case we had any other questions. We then found the manager, not in his office but in the restaurant where he was chatting with a couple who appeared to be finishing breakfast. We stood back, near the reception deck at the restaurant's entrance, waiting for him to look our way. I heard him thank the couple for staying at the hotel and saying he hoped their breakfast was satisfactory. They assured him everything was fine.

When his gaze finally landed on us, T-Tommy nodded to him. He excused himself, telling the couple to let him know if he could do anything for them, and then walked toward us.

We introduced ourselves. His name was Joe Carrick. He looked to be thirty-something and wore a blue suit, white shirt, and a geometrically patterned dark-blue tie.

"What can I do for you?" he asked with a smile.

His smile weakened a notch as T-Tommy showed his badge and completely collapsed when we explained why we were there and that we needed to look inside the Fosters' room. He hesitated until I said the Fosters might have been abducted from his property by a killer. That settled it.

On the elevator ride back up, Carrick said nothing, his gaze locked on the row of numbered buttons, number five the only one lit. I saw the tension in his jaw and his stiff posture. His only movement was to flick an imaginary bit of something from his jacket lapel. I could tell he had a pile of questions he wanted to ask but was afraid of the answers, his brain rapidly creating scenarios that wouldn't reflect well. The job of manager probably didn't seem so plum about now.

As we stepped off on the fifth floor, he finally asked, "Are you sure they were abducted?"

"No," T-Tommy said. "But it's a possibility."

"You think someone took them from their room? I don't see how—"

"Parking lot," I interrupted. "We believe they were taken from the lot."

We reached the door to the Fosters' room. Carrick had his passkeys out, but hesitated as if still unsure.

"Looking around their room might help us figure out what did happen," I said.

Carrick opened the door, standing aside and letting us enter.

The room was neat, except for a few dirty clothes draped over a chair, an open suitcase on the floor near the window, and used towels flung over the shower door. They were dry. Hadn't been used today. The bed was still made.

Nothing looked out of place. No signs of a struggle. It looked as if the Fosters would return any minute. They wouldn't.

An ugly scenario wormed around in my brain. Patrick Takada had described JD and Bo and Bo's SUV. Not much doubt there. No way the Fosters would willingly go with those two. Meant they were taken by force.

And then there was the other car, the Lincoln. Who was that?

We easily found the Fosters' car in the lot. Doors unlocked. Key in the ignition. Martha's purse on the passenger floorboard, on its side, contents partially spilled. I flashed on Jill's purse in the lot at the medical center, but jerked back from that. This wasn't the time or place.

But the worst thing I saw? The dashboard. Someone, probably Martha, had fingernail scratched "JD" into the vinyl.

The scenario that fluttered in my brain became officially ugly and was joined by even uglier questions. Where had JD and Bo taken the Fosters? What were they going to do to them? How did they know the Fosters were in town and where they were staying? The answer to the last question was easy. Twitty. Not sure how he found out, but if JD knew it could only have come from Twitty.

Chapter 76

Tim sat next to one of the two painted metal support poles that rose some fifteen feet to the top beam of the A-framed ceiling. Handcuffs bound him to one and Martha to the other. They had spent the night like this, unable to reach each other, comfort each other. The hard floor had made sleeping difficult and the thin blankets JD had given them did little to ward off the night's chill.

Exhaustion pulled at Tim, and when he looked at Martha, he saw the same fatigue on her face. Lack of sleep and the stress of their predicament hung dark bags beneath her eyes.

He had no idea exactly where they were but believed they were in a cabin on the banks of the Tennessee River, which cupped the southern border of Madison County.

Last night, as he lay in the rear floorboard of the SUV, head covered with the pillowcase, he had listened to the road sounds, felt the swaying of the vehicle, and tried to create a mental image of where they were going. The high-pitched whine of the tires suggested that they had traveled along a highway for thirty minutes or so. They then turned onto a rougher road. Some loose gravel pinged against the undercarriage. Not as much as a gravel road would have picked up, more like a rural road peppered with a few loose stones. The road also had its share of wiggles. Another ten minutes and the SUV slowed, turned right onto a heavily graveled surface, and came to a stop.

As Tim stepped out, the pillowcase over his head snagged the door frame and lifted a bit, just enough for him to catch a quick glimpse. Even though it was dark, he managed to capture a few impressions. Wooded area. Fairly large cabin. River. Short pier with a corrugated-metal boathouse at its end. That's all he saw before Bo tugged the hood back down.

Once inside, they pushed him and Martha to the floor, removed their pillowcase hoods, and handcuffed them to the support poles. JD and Bo then walked outside, closing the door behind them.

The cavernous room had knotty pine-paneled walls, thin brown carpeting, a wide stone fireplace, a cheap, plaid-patterned sofa, and two wooden ladder-back chairs. A small TV perched on a wicker stand in one corner.

Tim could hear JD and Bo talking out on the porch, their voices too muffled for him to make out what they were saying. Then he heard the sound of shoes on gravel followed by the SUV's engine coming to life. Then tires crunching across the gravel, engine noise fading in the distance.

At first he thought they had simply left them there, but the door swung open and JD came in. He retrieved a pair of blankets from a closet near the back door and tossed one to each of them.

"Get some sleep."

"What are you going to do to us?" Martha asked.

JD ignored her and headed up stairs. Tim heard the commode flush, JD's footsteps move around for a few minutes, and then silence. They heard nothing else until earlier this morning when the sun began to lighten the room. More footsteps, another flush, and then JD's voice, very faint, probably on the phone. Twenty minutes later the crunching of the SUV's tires returned. JD came down stairs, walked through the room, and out the door. Not a word. The SUV drove away. An hour later it returned. JD and Bo walked in, JD with two McDonald's bags. He dropped one near each of them.

"Don't get used to it," JD said. "We ain't running a bed and break-fast here."

JD and Bo went back outside. Tim had heard the sound of a chain rattling and the boathouse door squeaking open.

Inside each bag was an Egg McMuffin and a bottle of water.

"Any new ideas?" Martha asked around a bite of McMuffin.

Last night they had passed most of the time trying to come up with an escape plan. They thought of several, the problem being that each required they get free of the metal poles that held them. They had no plan for that.

"Nothing," he said.

"In the movies they always find a way."

"James Bond maybe. Not any of the *Halloween* movies."

"Not funny," Martha said.

"Wasn't trying to be."

"Do you think they know we're missing yet?"

"I hope so."

"How will they find us?"

"As soon as they search our car, they'll know JD did it. That was a clever move on your part. Scratching his initials into the dash."

"If they see them. It was dark and that dash is pretty stiff vinyl. I pressed as hard as I could, but I'm not sure it took."

"They'll still figure it out. Who else would harm us?"

"That's true but—"

The door swung open and JD came in. Outside the SUV came to life.

"What's true?" JD asked.

"That you won't get away with this," Tim said.

"You said that last night and now look where you are."

Tim wanted to punch the smirk right off his face. Hard to do bound to the pole.

"The police know the truth."

"What truth might that be?" JD moved closer and looked down at him.

"That I didn't kill Walter. That you did."

"How you figure that? You shot him too."

"But my bullet wasn't the one that killed him. Yours was."

Tim saw a slight wrinkle of concern at the corners of JD's eyes.

"How do you know that?" JD asked.

"I just do."

"You're wrong. I happen to know the ballistics exams didn't show shit."

"And you'd be wrong. The truth will come out."

JD shrugged. "Truth ain't got nothing to do with it. It's all what you can prove."

"The police know you did it."

"Really? Wonder why they haven't arrested me?"

"Maybe they're looking for you."

He laughed. "And tomorrow they'll find me. Soon as I get back from my fishing trip. I'll play completely ignorant about you guys. Last I heard you took off, leaving no forwarding address. I should thank you for that. You did a good job of dropping out of sight."

"But we're here," Martha said. "We came back with Investigator Tortelli and Dub Walker. They know we're here."

"What they know is that you changed your identity, took all your money, and ran away. Now you've disappeared again. If you ran once, why not twice? I mean if you're going to go to all the trouble to create new identities, why not make two or three? Just in case? See how neat it all is?"

"It's not that neat," Martha said. "Our car is still at the Marriott. They'll find it and know we didn't leave."

"Really?" JD gave her a smirk. "The last time you took off you did the same thing. Left your vehicle right on the street." He laughed. "I think I see a pattern here."

"They told us last night that they have proof you did it," Tim said.

"I don't think so. I covered all the bases."

Now Tim laughed. "The prisons are full of people who pulled off the perfect crime. Best laid plans and all that."

"But I have a good lawyer."

"The truth is hard to defend against," Tim said.

"There're quite a few truths in play here. There's the one that says you changed your names and emptied out your accounts and took off. There's the one that says you bought a gun over in Georgia and left it at your shooting site. There's the one that says you left behind your tire tracks, dumped your car, and took off in another one. A car that's sitting over at the Marriott." He laughed. "You see, I'm way ahead of you. Way ahead."

"How did you know what we were planning?" Martha asked.

"Simple. You bought the gun from a friend of mine. I was there. At the gun show in Rome."

"So? We bought a hunting rifle."

"Which got me to thinking. Why would two people who didn't own guns, didn't care for them, suddenly buy one?"

"You don't know anything about us," Tim said.

JD walked over to the front window, pulled the curtain back, peeked out, and then let the curtain fall back into place. He turned toward them. "I know a great deal. I made it my business to find out."

"Find out what?" Martha asked.

"At my brother's trial, you both told the judge that you hated guns. Never kept them around your boy. Wouldn't have one in the house. And then you go buy one a few months before my brother gets cut loose." He pulled one of the ladder-back chairs away from the wall, spun it around backward, and sat down, resting his forearms on the back. "So me and Bo took an interest in your activities. The practice sessions? Learning to shoot stumps at three hundred yards? Made putting the rest together pretty easy."

"How'd you know that? That we had practiced?"

He laughed. "I'm a pretty good hunter. Tracked smarter creatures than you two."

Tim ran everything through his mind. They had gone way out of town. He was sure no one had followed them. Yet somehow JD had.

Tim felt a hollowness creep into his stomach. Their careful planning hadn't been so careful after all. The possibility that JD might get away with this settled over him. For sure, they were in no position to take him on — handcuffed to metal poles in an isolated cabin that was — where? He had no idea. More importantly, neither did Walker or Tortelli or anyone else who might be searching for them. They were on their own.

Tim knew that hoping for mercy from this man didn't offer even a glimmer of hope. Any man who would kill his own brother wouldn't hesitate to kill them and, with all the rivers and isolated forests around, getting rid of their bodies would be easy.

Something else settled over him, too. Maybe this is what was owed them. Maybe this was payback for their sin. For planning to kill someone. A sin in the heart is as much a sin as performing the act.

"How did you know where we were going to be?" Tim asked. "That morning."

"That was easy. If you were practicing a long-range shot, where else would you use it except at the prison when he came out? Actually that was pretty clever. The trees kill and scatter the sound. A ton of roads up there to get away." He shrugged. "Of course those same roads allow a man to follow you without traveling the same path. Easy to park out of sight and sneak through the trees and watch you scout out your little sniper site. Piece of cake. So on the morning my brother died, I knew exactly where you'd be."

"Still, the truth will come out," Martha said.

JD stood. "I got something better than the truth."

"What might that be?"

"Reasonable doubt. The possibility that you two did do it and that you slipped away yet again. No one knows where you are or where to look, and they never will. Reasonable doubt trumps the truth every time."

Tim had no comeback for that. What he knew of the court system was that truth was often the first casualty. That what JD said was completely plausible.

"Why did you shoot Walter?" Tim asked. "If you knew I was going to, why even get involved?"

JD laughed. "Call it insurance. I saw where you practiced. Took a good look at all them stumps you tried to kill. You ain't very good. That rifle you bought tends to shoot a bit to the left and, obviously, you didn't know how to correct it."

"I see."

"Truth is most people don't know how to properly sight a gun. Anyway, the worst thing that could of happened would be for Walter to get winged. Not killed. Then he'd have been made a goddamn hero. Look at poor Walter. First he was framed for murder. Then he got put away for a bullshit charge. Then someone tried to kill him."

"I don't think anyone thought Walter was innocent," Martha said.

"You don't know Mama Lula. She thought he could do no wrong. Thought the police framed him. Planted all that stuff on his computer and the DNA, the whole thing."

"Mothers always believe the best about their children," Martha said. "It comes with being a mother."

JD shrugged. "Been that way all our lives. She always took his side. When we fought, it was my fault. When Walter got drunk and did something stupid, it was my fault for not taking care of him. When I complained that he wasn't pulling his load at the shop, she always said that was my job, being the older brother. She never saw that it was me that ran the business. Paid her bills. Never saw that Walter screwed up time and again and spent money like crazy. Walter, her baby boy, could do no wrong."

"So this was all some childhood mommy-loves-you-better-than-me problem?" Tim asked.

JD stood, moving the chair aside. "You better watch what you say, smart boy. You're in no position to get mouthy."

"Leave him alone," Martha said.

JD walked over to where Martha sat. "Want to hear something really hysterical?"

"What?"

"I wasn't even going to tell you. Let you die in ignorant bliss, but now that you've pissed me off, I'm rethinking that. You'll love this. Remember that Sunday morning when your boy was took? When you saw my brother drag him away?"

"Vividly. I'll never forget."

"Got the memory all ingrained in there, do you? Well, what if it was all wrong? You know how unreliable eyewitnesses are."

"I know what I saw. And I saw Walter take Steven."

JD laughed. "See what I mean." He hooked one thumb on his wide leather belt. "It wasn't Walter. It was me."

"What? No."

He laughed harder. "I wish you could see your face." He looked toward Tim. "Yours too."

"It was Walter," Martha said. "I know it was."

"Since you're all big on the truth, here it is. Walter was passed out drunk over at the shop. It was closed, it being Sunday and all. So I took his van and snatched the boy."

"I don't believe you."

"Me and my brother look a lot alike. From a distance. Same height, same build. And with me in his van, well—what you saw wasn't what you thought you saw."

"But Walter was the pedophile. All that stuff on his computer."

"Which made framing him for a child murder a piece of cake."

"Why?" Tim asked. "Why would you frame your own brother?"

"Because he was sick. All that child porn he was into? Mind you, he never once touched a child, just collected pictures off the Internet. I tried to get him help, but he refused. I was the only one in the family that knew, but things like that get out. It would've stained our entire family. Probably hurt the business. No one wants to deal with that kind of sickness. We'd all be suspect of the same disease. Guilt by blood. Besides my brother was a worthless loser. Never worked, drank all the time, yet took half the money I made. I made. Not him."

"It always comes down to money, doesn't it?" Tim asked.

JD walked over and kicked him in the ribs. "Ain't you listening?"

Tim felt his breath rush from his chest. He grabbed his ribs and rolled to his side. A wave of nausea cascaded over him.

"Stop it," Martha said.

JD whirled toward her. "You want some too."

Martha cowered against the pole as Tim struggled to grab a breath.

"My brother was a worthless and sick son of a bitch. The world is better off without him. I first thought about shooting him while we were out hunting. Make it look like an accident. But my mother would then blame me forever. It'd be all that poor Walter crap. I didn't want to deal with that. So I had to make him the villain."

Tim had righted himself and now sat against the pole. "So you killed our son and framed Walter."

"And it was perfect until that asshole judge threw out the DNA evidence and Walter went in for some lesser bullshit. I wanted him away for life. Maybe get killed in prison as pedophiles often are. Either way he'd be out of my hair. Forever."

Tim saw tears collect in Martha's eyes, her breathing heavy.

"Why Steven?" she asked. "Why did you pick Steven?"

"He picked himself. I was just looking for a kid. Any kid. I only had a couple of hours before Walter woke up from his alcoholic stupor. I had to get back, drop off the van, and clear out. That way I couldn't be his alibi. He'd be alone at the shop and wouldn't have anyone to vouch for him." He walked toward the door, but stopped and turned back, his gaze locked on Martha. "So in a way, you picked Steven. You sent him out to play on his own. So there he was. All by himself, walking down the street. Made my job easy."

The wail that rose from Martha's throat was like nothing Tim had ever heard. Her face a mask of twisted pain.

Tim jerked against the chains. "I'll kill you, you bastard."

"Don't rightly see how."

JD walked out the door.

Chapter 77

We found Paul Twitty in his office. Second floor of an office building just across the intersection from the famous Schiffman Building, the birthplace of the one and only Tallulah Bankhead. 1902. Second floor apartment. Her father, William Bankhead, later a U.S. representative and Speaker of the House, was practicing law in Huntsville at the time of Tallulah's birth.

I loved Tallulah. Her daddy did too, even though she never made that easy. Her antics, rumored bisexuality, and drug use in a time that neither was even remotely acceptable, and her foul mouth were a constant embarrassment to William and the entire Bankhead clan.

Her quotes are legendary:

If I had my life to live again, I'd make the same mistakes, only sooner.
It's the good girls who keep diaries. Bad girls don't have time.
I'm the foe of moderation, the champion of excess.

And to a prospective lover:

I'll come and make love to you at five. If I'm late, start without me.

What's not to love?

Twitty looked up as we came in. He pulled a well-chewed cigar from the corner of his mouth and rested it in an ashtray near his left elbow. The ashtray was clean, white with some kind of red-and-yellow resort logo along the edge. Probably lifted on some past visit.

"What brings you guys by?" Twitty asked.

"JD Whitiker."

"What about him?"

"Where is he?"

Twitty lifted the cuff of his shirt and glanced at his watch. "Probably over at his shop."

"It's closed for inventory."

Twitty looked confused. "Then he's probably there doing inventory." He picked up the cigar and settled it back between his teeth. "Why are you asking me all this?"

I stepped forward and leaned both hands on his desk. "Because JD abducted the Fosters last night."

Twitty's eyes moved back and forth between T-Tommy and me, finally settling back on me. "What are you talking about?"

"We believe JD and his buddy Bo grabbed the Fosters outside the Marriott last night. We want to know where he took them and what he's planning to do."

"Or what he might've already done," T-Tommy said.

Twitty's confused look deepened. "I don't know anything about this."

I straightened and turned toward T-Tommy.

"You sure?" T-Tommy asked. "You didn't tell JD where they were?"

"How would I know where they were? Last I heard they'd disappeared."

"Twitty, don't get stupid," T-Tommy said. "If you know anything and don't tell us and something happens to the Fosters, it won't be just your license this time. I promise. It'll be a trip up the road."

Twitty removed the cigar and sighed. "I knew they were here. At the Marriott. I told JD."

"When?"

"Yesterday."

"Did you know what he was planning?"

"Of course not. I'd've called if I'd known."

"What about client privilege?" I asked.

"That only goes so far, and doesn't include me sitting back and letting a felony take place."

"You better pray that's true," T-Tommy said. Now he took a step forward and looked down at Twitty. "Here's your chance. Your only chance. Tell me everything you know, everything you told JD."

Twitty knew a lot but not everything. He knew the Fosters had gone to North Carolina. Knew their new names. Knew their address. Knew they'd gotten married. Told JD all of it.

"So that gets us to the million-dollar question," I said. "Do you know where JD took the Fosters?"

"Not a clue."

"Any ideas on possibilities?"

"I don't know JD. Just to buy guns and fishing gear from time to time."

"And track down runaways for him."

"That's business. As I said, I don't really know him. Don't know his habits or where he goes when he heads out of town."

I nodded. "So he headed out of town?"

Twitty smiled. "Nice try. I don't know where he went. Just saying that if I'd grabbed someone, I'd want to put a few miles between me and you guys."

T-Tommy shoved his hands in his pockets. "I'll remember that. Just in case."

Twitty came up from his chair. "Wait a damn minute. I didn't—"

I stopped him with a raised hand. "Relax, Paul. We believe you got played like the rest of us."

"Of course, if you hear anything from JD, you'll give us a call," T-Tommy said. "Right?"

Twitty's face and shoulders relaxed and he settled back into his chair. "Of course."

Chapter 78

By the time we walked down stairs and outside, my anger was boiling. Literally. I could actually feel the blood bubbling in my brain.

My anger had several targets.

I was angry with JD for targeting the Fosters, for setting them up to take the heat for his greed-driven murder of his own brother.

I was angry at Twitty for being an arrogant prick who knew more about JD than he was willing to admit. Until he was cornered anyway. He must have known that JD didn't want the Fosters found for any altruistic reasons. Truth, justice, and the American way. None of that was operative here. It must have crossed Twitty's mind that JD might want to harm them. But a paycheck is a paycheck.

Mostly I was angry with myself. For sniffing along the easy path. The one that bread crumbs like tire impressions, ballistics examinations, and cell phone traffic led me down. Never stopping long enough to see the big picture. The one that said the Foster's revenge motive wasn't the only thing in play. That greed and family feuds were much more powerful motivators for acts of violence and murder. I mean, I write books on this stuff for Christ's sake.

I let the evidence overwhelm my common sense. I didn't stop and think. Look at all the players involved. At who really had the most to gain.

The real tragedy was that Fosters were good people and didn't de-

serve all this. Hadn't they been through enough? Sure, they wanted
Walter dead and did indeed try to kill him. Even thought they had. And
that changed things a bit. There are no innocents here.

Except for young Steven.

But if Tim's attempt to kill Walter was a sin, then that would be between Tim and God, not Tim and JD.

Was what they did a sin? Was wanting Walter dead and taking steps
to make it happen an affront to Christian thinking? Probably. But I
couldn't blame them. If I ever found out who took my sister, Jill, I'd
kill them. No questions asked. Whoever snatched her from that rainy
parking lot over a decade ago set in motion events that destroyed my
parents, and nearly me. Sure, they died in an auto accident, but the
light in their lives went out when Jill disappeared. Nothing was ever
the same. For that and for the pain that still haunts me, still creeps into
my dreams, I would extract an eye for an eye if I ever found who did it.
No doubt in my mind.

And it wouldn't be pretty.

I knew T-Tommy sensed my anger because as we walked along the
sun-dappled sidewalk that bordered the south side of the square, he
clamped a hand on my shoulder and said, "We'll get him. And we'll get
him before he does anything to the Fosters."

"You know what really pisses me off?" I asked.

"Lots of stuff."

"Yeah, but I'm talking about this whole JD thing. The only way all
this makes sense, the only way all the evidence fits, is if the "what-if"
scenario I outlined the other day is exactly what happened. JD stumbled on the Fosters' plot to kill Walter. Saw a way to get his brother out
of his hair, out of his business. Figured out the when and where of the
Fosters' plan, tagged along, and did the shooting himself."

"Sort of an insurance policy in case Tim missed?" T-Tommy asked.

"That'd be my bet. He probably figured this was a one-shot deal.
Take Walter down there when he had someone to toss the blame at or
he just might not get another reasonable chance."

"And now JD's trying to eliminate the only witnesses who can make
things a bit sticky for him."

"Bingo."

We waited for a couple of cars to pass and then crossed the street to where my Porsche sat. I hesitated, looking at T-Tommy over the roof.

"Smart money would then go with JD planning to use Twitty to find the Fosters before we could, and then taking a road trip to whack them. Then they'd simply be two murderers who shot a man in broad daylight, tried to disappear, and ended up dead. Random act of violence. Karma. News story for about a day, then life would go on. JD free and clear."

"Pretty damn clever actually," T-Tommy said. "Until we trashed his perfect little plan and found them first."

"It won't matter if we don't find them again. Soon."

We climbed in the car.

"But for JD to take all the steps needed to latch on to the Fosters' plot he had to first know that they had bought a rifle," I said. "Without that knowledge he would never have gone down that path."

"Dale Bonner?" T-Tommy asked.

"Dale Bonner."

I pulled my iPhone from my jacket pocket, scrolled through the recently called numbers until I found Bonner's, and pressed dial. I punched the speaker option so T-Tommy could hear the conversation.

"Dale's Cheap Guns. This is Dale."

"Mr. Bonner, this is Dub Walker. I'm here with Investigator Tortelli. We were in your shop the other day."

"Yes, I remember. What can I do for you?"

"Got a couple of questions."

"Fire away."

I ignored the pun, doubting Dale even caught it. "The couple we talked about? The ones that bought the Browning?"

"Yeah?"

"You said that Bo was there around the time they bought it but that you didn't see JD."

"That's right. Bo offered to buy lunch."

"You also said that as far as you know, Bo didn't see the couple. Right?"

"That's right."

"So, how did JD Whitiker know they had bought it?"

"Not sure I follow you."

"JD said you called him and told him you had seen them on the news. After JD's brother Walter was shot and the couple was reported missing."

He hesitated for a beat. "What's this about?"

"Just a routine follow-up."

Another hesitation. "Can I get back to you?"

"The question is pretty simple, Mr. Bonner. Did you call JD or not?"

The pause this time was longer.

"Look, Mr. Bonner, we don't want to bring any trouble your way, but if we have to we will. And it will get very ugly."

"I'm thinking. Trying to remember if I called him or not."

"Let me make this easy for you," T-Tommy jumped in. "Last night JD abducted the couple. Maybe he's going to kill them. Maybe he al-ready has. Maybe that makes you an accomplice of sorts. Maybe I can make your life miserable. Maybe I can call your sheriff and have a little chat with him. Maybe you need to search your memory a little more thoroughly. Maybe you should answer the fucking question. Did you call JD or not?"

"No. I didn't."

"You never called JD about them?"

"No."

"Then I'll ask again," I said. "How did JD know they had bought guns from you?"

"I don't know." His voice was weak and unconvincing.

T-Tommy snorted. "Listen up, Dale. The jails are full of people who think cops are stupid. Do you think I'm stupid?"

"No."

"Glad to hear that. I don't think you are either. Don't try to protect JD. Trust me, he'd never return the favor. He killed his own fucking brother."

I heard Dale sigh.

"Okay," Dale said. "This is what happened. JD did see them. Came over just after they left. Asked what they'd bought. I showed him the sales slip."

"He say anything about them?" I asked.

"No. I figured he was just making small talk. I never figured—Jesus."

"This story's a little different than the one you told us the other day," I said. "Fact is, you said JD didn't know they were there. Why'd you lie?"

"I don't know. Didn't want to get him in trouble, I guess."

"Why would you think he might be in trouble?" T-Tommy asked.

"You're a cop. From another state. Asking questions."

"Have you heard from JD recently?" I asked. "Maybe the past day or so?"

"No. Not since the gun show actually."

"Any idea where he might be? A favorite place to hunt or fish? A place he visits often?"

"Not really."

"That sounds like a qualified no. Anything you know might help."

"I know he likes to fish over on the Paint Rock River and down at Smith Lake. He used to have a cabin down there, but I think he sold it."

"Do you know exactly where it is?" T-Tommy asked.

"No. Never been there, if that's what you're asking."

"Do you know who he sold it to?"

"Sure don't."

I thanked Dale for his time. Told him we might have more questions for him later, and disconnected the call.

I suddenly realized we had screwed up. Big time. We had taken JD at his word, so when we drove over to chat with Dale, we never asked if he had called JD. We assumed he had.

T-Tommy realized it too. I know this because I'm smart and intuitive, and I know T-Tommy better than anyone. Of course it helped that he said: "We fucked up."

"Sure did. It would've helped to have known this earlier."

"It does explain how JD knew exactly what they had purchased. Made duplicating it easy."

"JD ain't as dumb as he looks."

"Jury's still out on that," T-Tommy said.

Chapter 79

We headed back over to JD's shop. Not that we thought he'd be there, but we had no place else to look right now. A helpless feeling. The Fosters were in JD's hands, and we had no idea where his hands were.

Desperate people do desperate things and JD was desperate. His best laid plans had gone sideways, and he was now searching for an exit. If he could kill his own brother, the Fosters would be a snap. And making them disappear was his only play. Without them JD just might walk on both Walter's murder and the Fosters' kidnapping and murder. To have any shot at that, he would have to kill them and hide the bodies where no one would ever find them. Couldn't let them talk; couldn't let their corpses pop up.

Then a clever attorney could argue that the Fosters killed Walter and simply took off again. Bamboozled us. Looked like they were co-operating while putting into play their backup escape plan. Why not? They had planned an elaborate disappearing act before.

If it went down that way, it could end T-Tommy's career. He, actually we since much of it was my idea, didn't involve the Asheville PD but brought the Fosters back in the dark of night. We didn't arrest them, but rather put them up in a hotel. We didn't guard them. Gave them more or less a free rein to come and go as they pleased. There is no way this would look good.

That would leave JD's DNA that we found at the scene as the only way to connect him to Walter's shooting. A judge could toss it like Kleinman did with Steven's DNA in Walter's van. Or a defense attorney could attack it, and if that was all we had, a jury just might not think that was enough for a murder conviction.

All this meant that the Fosters might not still be alive. We had to assume they were, but we had no proof of that.

T-Tommy had uniforms running all over the county, searching for JD, for Bo and his truck, and surveilling JD's house, even though I knew he wouldn't show up there, but maybe, just maybe, his wife or mother would head to wherever he was.

As I drove along University, I saw clouds gathering to the west. Looked like more rain was headed in. Smelled that way too.

T-Tommy called his office and got someone looking into any cabins JD might own or have owned down at Smith Lake. I didn't hold out much hope that that'd help, even JD wasn't dumb enough to take the Fosters to his second home, but you just never knew.

The two uniforms T-Tommy had left at Whitiker's Rods and Guns sat in their patrol car in the otherwise empty front lot. They got out as we pulled in.

"Anything?" T-Tommy asked.

"Nothing," one of them said. He looked too young to be a cop.

I walked to the front door and peered through the front window. Empty and quiet. As I turned away, I heard a sound. Like something heavy hitting the floor. I looked back and saw Bo, near the back, bending over and moving around as if picking up objects from the floor.

I rapped a knuckle on the window. Bo's head snapped around. We looked at each other. He made no move, so I waved him toward me. He hesitated and then lumbered toward the door.

"Bo's in there," I said to T-Tommy.

T-Tommy walked toward me, pulling his Sig from the small of his back, holding it at his side. The two uniforms moved up behind him.

Bo worked the lock and then pulled open the door. "We're closed," he said.

T-Tommy lifted his gun. "Keep your hands where I can see them."

Bo raised his hands. "Whoa. What's this about?"

T-Tommy told the uniforms to stay put, and he and I stepped inside, Bo backing away to give us room.

"What the hell's going on?" Bo asked.

Either he was ballsy or stupid. Maybe both.

"Turn around," T-Tommy said.

Bo did, looking back over his shoulder. "What's this all about?"

I frisked him. Clean. Seemed odd frisking a man in the middle of a gun shop. Why carry one when the walls and cabinets were filled with just about any weapon you might need?

"Where's JD?" I asked.

"Can I put my hands down?"

"Sure," Tommy said. He holstered his gun and waited for Bo to lower his hands and turn toward us. "Now where's JD?"

"Don't know. Said he was going fishing."

"Where?"

"He didn't say."

"When'll he be back?"

"I don't know. Couple of days."

"And you're running the shop until then?" I asked.

"We're closed. He left me here to do inventory."

"Just you?"

"Shit runs downhill. He's the boss. I like my job. I do what I'm told."

"You do whatever JD says?" I asked.

"More or less."

"Let's talk about the more," I said. "He want you to do anything else? Other than the inventory?"

"Like what?"

"That's what I'm asking."

"Look, I got work to do. This inventory ain't going to get done by itself."

I moved past him toward the rear of the store. A box lay on its side, its contents spilled onto the floor. Two spools of yellow ski rope, a pair of rain ponchos, a pair of rubber hunting boots, a large bag of potato chips, and a six-pack of Dr. Pepper. Well, well.

"This part of the inventory?" I asked.

"My stuff. Getting it out of the way before I begin to take stock."

"You a Pepper guy?"

"Yeah. Not like JD, but I like it."

"Where you going with this?"

"To my truck. Out back."

I noticed the rear door was cracked open and moved that way. Bo followed, T-Tommy behind him.

Bo's deep-blue Tahoe, rear gate pushed up, sat in the narrow alley that ran behind the store. The third row of seats had been removed and in the cargo area I saw a dark-brown hunting jacket, two gun cases, a small plastic storage container filled with green-and-yellow boxes of Remington shotgun shells, and four cinder blocks, pushed back up against the rear seat backs.

"This your stuff too?" I asked.

"Yeah. It is." Bo twisted his neck back and forth. "You guys want to tell me what this is about?"

"Where were you last night?" T-Tommy asked. "Say around eleven?"

"Who wants to know?"

"Bo, don't go all tough guy. Okay?" T-Tommy said.

"I ain't saying nothing until I know what this is about."

I was getting the impression that old Bo wasn't as dumb as he seemed. He surely looked confused. Wouldn't go all the way to innocent looking, but he didn't have the demeanor of someone who was panicked either.

"Someone saw your truck over at the Marriott where a crime was committed," T-Tommy said.

"Wasn't me. Wasn't my truck. I was home and it was with me."

"You sure?"

"Of course I am." Bo closed the Tahoe's rear gate.

"Anyone with you?"

"Yeah. All the Victoria's Secret models. We had a real good time."

T-Tommy didn't flinch. "Can one of them vouch for you?"

Bo shook his head. "And no one can say I wasn't there, so that ought to do it."

"Except the person who saw you at the Marriott."

"This person get a license number?"

"No. Just saw you and your truck."

Bo shook his head. "Wasn't me. Told you I was home with the girls. They do this little lingerie show. You should see it sometime."

"Maybe I will."

He stared at me, but I wouldn't let go of his gaze. Wouldn't back down. Finally he did and glanced toward the back of the store. "Unless you got something else to say, I got work to do." He pushed past T-Tommy and went back inside.

I nodded to T-Tommy. He followed Bo, pulling the rear door closed behind him.

I slipped my iPhone from my pocket and turned the ringer and the vibrate mode off. I opened the passenger's door and settled it among the wad of maps Bo had stuffed in the door pocket.

As I straightened up, I heard a car coming. Low guttural engine in lope mode. I turned toward the sound. A sixties black Lincoln came toward me. Two men inside. They slowly drove by, the guy riding shotgun looked at me. He had ice-blue eyes and an unhappy smirk. I watched as the car went by and turned at the end of the alley.

I had no doubts that that was the car Patrick Takada had seen at the Marriott.

I mentally repeated the license number to lock it in my memory.

Chapter 80

JD had changed the arrangement. Tim and Martha were no longer handcuffed to individual poles, but rather JD had looped a ten-foot length of thick-linked chain around the support pole a couple of times and attached Tim's and Martha's handcuffs to it, one on each end. This allowed them to comfort each other and gave them a little more free-dom of movement but still offered no way to escape.

Not that they hadn't tried. During the night, while JD slept and again this morning every time he went out, they attempted to dislodge the lower end of the pole. They pulled, pushed, jerked, kicked, and even attempted to loosen the flooring that butted against the pole's base. The pole ignored them. It became apparent, after they had managed to loosen a couple of the floor planks, that it was bolted to the underlying concrete slab. With the top firmly fastened by a metal bracket to the ex-posed roof ridge beam, dislodging the pole wasn't going to happen.

Now Tim lay on the floor, Martha next to him, and stared up at the ceiling. JD had left again about an hour earlier, saying he'd be back shortly.

"He's going to kill us," Martha said.

"We don't know that." Tim knew that was a lie, but it seemed that consoling Martha was all he could do. Wasn't he supposed to protect her? Wasn't that his role in the family? Of course he hadn't protected Steven and that had been his job too. And now he had failed again.

"Yes, we do," she said. "If we live, we can tell the truth. He'll go away for killing Walter. If we disappear, maybe not." She sighed. "He wouldn't have confessed to us if he wasn't going to kill us."

Tim rolled to one side and looked at her. She lay on her back, gaze aimed upward. She looked beautiful. He could find no fear in her face. Maybe anger, but no fear. She was strong. Stronger than him. Always had been.

"I mean," she went on, "it's like he said. If we disappear, he'll have reasonable doubt. We did do all those things. We bought a gun. We changed our names, emptied the accounts, and ran away."

"We didn't kill Walter."

She looked at him. Her eyes looked sad and tired. "We tried to."

"I tried to."

"We, Tim. We. Don't try to take all the blame here. I'm as sinful as you."

He took a deep breath and slowly blew it out. "Maybe this's what we deserve."

She rolled toward him. "Maybe. But not here. Not like this. We'll answer to God for what we did. We don't deserve JD's justice."

"What are we going to do about it?"

"If his plan is to kill us and get rid of our bodies, he'll have to move us. He'll have to uncuff us. We might have a chance to overpower him then."

"Unless he shoots us before he takes the cuffs off."

"Too messy," Martha said. "He wouldn't want to leave any evidence here. He'll kill us where he's going to bury us. Or dump us in the river."

"You've really thought this through."

She gave a little explosive laugh. "Got nothing else to do. Might as well focus on our deaths."

"Don't say that."

They lay silently for a minute and Martha said, "Overpowering him is the only option I see."

"He's a pretty big guy."

"We're motivated. We've got nothing to lose by going for it."

"What if Bo is here?"

She sighed and rolled to her back again. "Then we'll need a plan B or C or Z or something."

"Like what?"

"I have no idea."

They lay quietly again, this time for several minutes. Tim heard crows cawing in the distance. Something scurried across the roof. Probably a squirrel. Then the sound of tires on gravel. JD was back.

The front door swung open. JD came in, followed by a cool breeze and the aroma of rain.

"Looks like some rain's coming in," JD said.

"Can I visit the bathroom?" Martha asked.

"Sure." JD reached in his pants pocket, pulled out the cuff key, and tossed it to her. "Unhook yourself and toss the key back." He pulled a gun from his jacket pocket. "Don't try to be cute or I'll shoot old Tim here."

She unlocked the cuffs and threw the key at JD's feet. She stood, twisted her back one way and then the other, and then headed down the hall toward the bathroom.

"What's the plan?" Tim asked.

"What difference does it make? You got no say in it."

"Just want to know what to expect. For Martha. She's scared. I want to reassure her."

"I wouldn't be doing that."

"Why?"

"Because you'd be lying to her."

"I don't want her anymore scared than she has to be. Can't you understand that?"

JD looked down at him and shook his head. "Okay. I've got a couple of guys joining us later. And Bo, of course."

"What guys?"

"A couple of dudes you'd never want to meet. The worst kind. The kind that will make your death painful."

"Death is always painful."

"Some more so than others. My idea is to shoot you both in the head and dump your bodies in the river. In deep water near the dam. Weighted down of course. But these guys, they might do anything. Maybe work you over for fun. Maybe add the weights and toss you in alive."

Tim jerked against the chain. "Don't you dare. Not Martha."

"Relax. That's not in the plan. Unless you try something stupid. Just do what I say. It'll be easier that way." JD squatted so that he looked Tim in the eye. "If you make it hard, if you try to fuck with me, I'll feed you both to them."

Tim felt the blood drain from his head like a deflating balloon. Fear gathered in his gut and swelled to a cold dread. He thought he might vomit. Or faint. He took a couple of ragged breaths.

"We clear?" JD asked.

Tim could only nod.

JD walked to the window and looked out. A few raindrops tapped against the glass. "Here it comes." He turned back toward Tim. "That'll make tonight's boat ride a little less comfortable. Of course, yours won't be round trip."

Martha came back into the room. "What won't be a round trip?"

JD ignored her question. "Fasten the cuffs."

Tim's gaze caught Martha's. She obviously sensed his fear.

"What's the matter?" she asked. "Are you okay?"

Tim nodded. "I'm fine."

JD laughed. "Old Tim and I had to come to an understanding, didn't we?"

"What are you talking about?" Martha asked.

"Nothing," Tim said. "Just do as he says."

Martha sat down and ratcheted the cuffs back onto her left wrist.

"Tighter," JD said,

"They hurt."

"Two clicks more." He pointed the gun at her. "Or maybe you want me to put them around your neck?"

Martha clicked the cuffs down.

JD then allowed Tim to visit the head. Once he had returned and recuffed himself, JD headed toward the door.

"Got some work to do in the boathouse." He laughed as he closed the door behind him.

The rain continued to pepper the window.

Chapter 81

I sat at T-Tommy's desk and booted up his computer while Derrick Stone told us he had located the cabin JD used to own at Smith Lake, near Cullman, an hour south down I-65. JD had sold it three years ago to a retired school principal and his wife.

"Guy named Ben Lester," Stone said. "I called him. He said he hadn't seen or spoken to JD since the sale."

"He sound sincere?" T-Tommy asked. "Like he wasn't hiding anything?"

Stone smiled. "Yeah. But I called the chief over at Cullman PD and he's going to stop by and say hello. Make sure all is as advertised." He shrugged. "Ain't going to amount to nothing though. Dude sounded old and ill."

"Ill?" I asked.

"Kept coughing. One of those death-rattle coughs. I had an uncle with the black lung so I know what it sounds like."

"Great," T-Tommy said. "Now we got nothing."

"Except Bo," I said. The computer completed its booting process, and I logged into my account and activated the "Find My iPhone" link. Took about ten seconds for a map to appear. The blue locator circle showed that my phone was still parked behind Whitiker's Rods and Guns.

"Got it," I said. "He's still at the shop."

I scribbled the Lincoln's license plate number on a piece of paper and handed it to Stone. "Can you run this?"

"Give me a minute." He headed down the hall.

So we waited. Something I hated, but we had no other options. If Bo didn't lead us to JD and if JD didn't still have the Fosters, we were definitely screwed. T-Tommy went to grab us some coffee. I called Claire.

"What are you doing?" she asked.

"Waiting."

"And you do that so well." She can be such a smart-ass. "What are you waiting on?"

I explained everything to her.

"You figured out that phone thing all by yourself?"

See, what'd I tell you? A smart-ass to the core.

"Sometimes I'm brilliant that way."

"Yeah, I can count those times on one hand."

"Glad you noticed."

"I'm coming over," she said.

"Why?"

"I miss your face."

"You're looking for a story."

"That, too. See you in ten."

She didn't even wait for a reply before she hung up.

T-Tommy returned with two cups of coffee. I moved and let him take his seat behind his desk.

"How do you work this thing?" he nodded toward the computer screen.

"Just refresh it every few minutes. If Bo moves, we'll know."

I heard him click the keys, and then grunt. Meant Bo hadn't moved in the last two minutes. He clicked again. Another grunt. T-Tommy was getting impatient. I understood the feeling.

"Now that we have Bo tagged," I said, "why not call off the tail? Make him comfortable. Think he's free and clear."

T-Tommy nodded. "Maybe lead us right to JD."

"And the Fosters."

Stone came in. "The car's registered to Kyle Spraggins."

T-Tommy looked up. "You're kidding?"

"Wish I was."

"Who's Kyle Spraggins?" I asked.

"Kyle and Cody," T-Tommy said. "Both with rap sheets from here to Montgomery. Assaults, extortion, robbery, drug manufacturing and distribution, and maybe a murder or two."

"Any connection with JD?"

"Not that I know."

"Just cruised his alley out of boredom?" I asked.

T-Tommy sighed and looked at Stone. "Pull the Spraggins brothers' sheets and get someone to come monitor Dub's phone." Stone nodded. "Pull everyone off Bo and get them to finding the Spraggins brothers."

"Will do."

As Stone left, Claire came in. She looked at us sitting, coffees in hand.

"Ah, my tax dollars at work," she said.

I rest my case.

Chapter 82

Took about twenty minutes to find the Spraggins brothers. They were home. We headed that way. Claire said she was coming with us. I said no. She didn't even flinch. T-Tommy drove, I took shotgun, and Claire the backseat of T-Tommy's city-owned Crown Vic. Someday I'm going to win an argument with her. Someday.

The wind had kicked up a notch and the rain slanted across the windshield, lacquered the streets, and accumulated in low spots on the roadway and along the curbs.

"Tell me about these guys," Claire said.

I had their files with me and now twisted in my seat and handed them to her. She flipped the top one open.

"They've been in the system for about ten years," T-Tommy said. "Started with petty theft and then climbed the ladder from there. Each of them's been arrested twelve times. Eleven of those were together."

"Got to love a close family," she said. She held up their photos. "Are they twins?"

"No. Just look like it," T-Tommy said. "Kyle's a couple of years older."

"You think they had anything to do with the Fosters' abduction?" Claire asked.

"From what the witness said, the guy that saw the abduction, they were there," I said. "And they cruised JD's shop. Took off when they saw me. From what I read in those files, kidnapping would be a step down for them."

"The file's not the whole story," T-Tommy said. "They were part of a big meth operation up in Tennessee. Near Pulaski. Feds took the place down, but had nothing on Kyle or Cody. But they were in it. No doubt about it."

"Sounds like you know them pretty well," Claire said.

"I worked one of their suspected murders. Couldn't quite put it together. They're a slippery pair."

T-Tommy turned onto 4 Mile Post Road/Cecil Ashburn Drive.

"Where're we going?" Claire asked.

"The Spraggins' farm is out in New Hope," T-Tommy said. "Old man Spraggins lives in the big house and the brothers have a cabin on the east end of the property."

"So you've been there?"

"Oh, yeah. I've had this chat with the brothers before."

"How much land they got?" I asked.

"Don't know exactly. A few hundred acres."

We crossed the southern edge of Jones Valley where the road made a sweeping S curve and became Sutton Road. A few minutes later, we reached Highway 431 and T-Tommy turned south toward Owens Cross Roads and, beyond, the small farming community of New Hope.

"Remember that judge that got whacked over in Albertville?" T-Tommy asked. "Couple of years ago?"

"Yeah," Claire said. "Some big divorce case. Involving a huge chicken farm."

"That's the one. I went over and helped the local PD with the case. The Spraggins were the triggermen."

"Really?"

"Couldn't prove it. No witnesses and the weapons fell off the earth."

"Good thing I brought a gun," Claire said.

She had a permit. Carried a gun everywhere now. Since she was taken hostage by Rocco Scarcella's goons. She owned three handguns and a short-barrel 12-gauge pump, and could use all of them.

"Which one?" I asked.

"The little one. The thirty-eight. The others won't fit in my purse."

"I don't want you shooting anyone," T-Tommy said.

"Wouldn't think of it."

"I don't have a gun," I said. "I feel naked."

"Stay behind me, then." Claire said.

Jesus.

By the time we turned off 431 onto Main and reached tiny downtown New Hope, the rain had let up. There were even patches of blue sky visible through holes in the cloud cover. T-Tommy veered off on to College Drive, also known as County Highway 9, and after a couple of miles, the Spraggins' farm came into view.

Wilmer Spraggins lived in a white frame house near the highway. His property spread out behind, rolling green grass with a few cows munching lazily. Near the far end, where the land lifted into a wooded hillside, another white frame house stood. That would be where Kyle and Cody called home. Since we had to pass Wilmer's house on the single dirt road that cut through the property to reach the boys' place, we decided it would be best to stop and see the old man first, let him know we were there, maybe save a load of buckshot into the rear of T-Tommy's car. According to T-Tommy, Wilmer didn't like uninvited guests and had been known to take shots at trespassers.

T-Tommy turned into the gravel patch that sat near the front door and parked near the old man's pickup. The house looked freshly painted, but the sloping green shingle roof needed some work. To the left of the house, an open-doored, weather-beaten shed exposed a red Pontiac GTO. A 1966. Jacked up on cinder blocks. The hood was raised and wires hung out. Looked like someone was restoring it.

Wilmer sat on the front porch swing, a wad of tobacco in his cheek. A shotgun leaned against the porch railing to his left.

As we climbed out of the car, Wilmer leaned over and fired a wad of tobacco juice into a coffee can that sat on the floor beside him. He wiped his mouth with the back of one hand and looked at us.

"What brings the law out here?" Wilmer asked

"Just wanted to chat with your boys," T-Tommy said.

"About what?"

"Looking for a friend of theirs. Thought they might know where he is."

He scratched his arm. "Coulda called. Saved you the drive."

"We like road trips," T-Tommy said. "You know, get out of the city, smell the fresh-cut grass."

Wilmer gave a dismissive grunt.

"Besides, I like to ask my questions face-to-face."

"You saying my boys are liars or something?"

T-Tommy shook his head. "Just saying I'd like to look them in the eye."

Another salvo of thick black spittle, another hand swipe across his mouth. "So go look at 'em. Instead of standing here and bending my ear."

"Wanted to let you know we were on your property."

"That's real neighborly."

"That's what we thought."

"Go ahead on." The swing began to rock back and forth.

The road that cut diagonally across the property and led to the boys' house was actually two worn tire lanes that flanked a grassy strip, overgrown with weeds that slapped against the bumper and scraped along the undercarriage as T-Tommy gyrated over the uneven terrain. Muddy water splashed up from the low spots.

The boys' house was an exact copy of Wilmer's. Kyle and Cody came through the front door as we pulled up and stepped out. Kyle had what looked like a Glock in his hand and Cody had a similar model stuffed beneath the waistband of his jeans.

"What the hell are you doing here, Tortelli?" Kyle asked.

"Want to put the gun away?"

"Not till you tell me what you want."

"Just a couple of questions."

"You have to bring a posse for that?" He looked at Claire. "Or is it pussy?"

Kyle and Cody both snickered.

"Funny," Claire said. "You guys should go to Hollywood. Get your own sitcom."

Kyle moved forward and sat on the steps. He placed the gun on the porch beside him. Cody leaned against one of the porch roof support poles, scraping beneath a fingernail with a pocketknife.

"Go ahead," Kyle said. "Ask away."

"We're looking for JD Whitiker."

"So?"

"Just wondering if you knew where he might be?"

"Why would I know that? We ain't cousins or nothing."

"Since you cruised by his shop earlier," I said, "we thought maybe you and him were buddies."

"Free country," Cody said. He closed the knife and slid in into his back pocket. "We got a right to shop where we want."

"That what you were doing? Shopping?"

"Maybe. Don't see that it's any of your concern."

"It ain't," T-Tommy said. "Unless you know where JD is."

"We don't." Cody hooked a thumb in his belt.

T-Tommy stared at him for a minute and then looked at Kyle. "JD's got himself in a bit of a spot. I'd hate see him drag you boys into it."

Kyle rolled his eyes. "Your compassion is touching. Really. It is."

"Going fishing?" I asked. I nodded toward an electric-blue dually pickup that had a boat and trailer attached.

"We might do a little night fishing," Kyle said. "If this weather breaks up."

"Where you going?"

He looked up at me, hesitated a beat, and then smiled. "Ain't decided yet."

Chapter 83

TUESDAY, 2:16 P.M.

By the time we passed back through Owens Cross Roads, the rain had returned. A soft drizzle, but I could see nasty clouds gathering to the west. Looked like some serious weather was moving in.

T-Tommy's cell phone rang. He answered, putting it on speaker. It was Derrick Stone.

"Where you at?" Stone asked. "Been trying to reach you."

"Just leaving the Spraggins place. Cell reception is spotty out here. What've you got?"

"Bo's on the move. Went by his house and then stopped at a service station. I sent a guy by to talk with the manager. After Bo left. Bo bought two one-gallon jugs of water, a bag of Cheetos, four Snickers, a pound of beef jerky, and a case of beer. PBR longnecks. He also filled his truck and a pair of ten-gallon gas cans and bought a couple of bottles of marine fuel additives."

I looked at T-Tommy.

I heard Stone say something to someone else. Couldn't quite make it out, his voice low and muffled as if he had turned away from his cell phone. Then he was back. "Looks like Bo's back at the shop. What about you guys? Anything up with Kyle and Cody?"

"Probably. Not sure what. They did have a boat trailered and hooked to their truck."

"Interesting," Stone said. "Boat, marine fuel additive, I'm smelling a conspiracy here."

"We're headed that way. Keep an eye on Bo. He's our only connection."

"Want me to get someone on the Spraggins boys?"

"Don't see how. Out there in the country they'd see anyone a mile away. Let's stay with Bo."

Tim stood over the toilet, urinating. JD had let Martha go to the bathroom and now him. He finished and then washed his face in the sink. Looking up in the mirror he saw the toll of the last fifteen hours. Had it only been that long? He looked pale. Dark circles hung beneath his eyes. If he and Martha were going to get out of this alive, he had to do something.

But what? Overpower JD? Not likely. JD had fifty pounds on him. But right now it was just him and JD. Soon Bo and the other guys JD had mentioned would show up. That would be an impossible situation. With JD alone it wasn't impossible, just improbable.

Improbable trumped impossible every time.

He walked out into the living room. Martha sat on the floor, chained to the support pole. JD stood near the window, curtain pulled back, looking up as if checking the weather.

Tim didn't hesitate. He grabbed one of the bar stools and rushed JD. JD turned. Tim raised the stool and swung it as hard as he could in a broad arc aimed at JD's head. JD blocked it with his forearm and stepped to the side. He grabbed one leg and twisted the stool from Tim's grasp.

Jesus he was strong.

JD tossed the stool aside. Tim froze. JD didn't. He stepped forward and landed a right hand against the side of Tim's head. Tim went down. Pain shot through his face. A loud ringing erupted in his ear. The room twisted into an odd shape.

Tim shook his head, trying to clear it.

JD kicked his ribs. Hard. The point of his boot digging in. Then he kicked Tim again.

Tim felt as if his lungs had collapsed. He tried to inhale, but his chest seemed frozen. His eyes watered and he covered his ribs and rolled into a ball. He waited for the next blow.

It didn't come.

He looked up into the muzzle of JD's gun.

"Want to try that again?" JD asked. Cool and calm, like nothing had happened.

Tim didn't say anything. Actually he couldn't, his lungs still searching for a breath.

"Didn't think so." JD moved to his left and pressed the barrel of the gun against the top of Martha's head. "Want me to redecorate her skull?"

"Leave her alone," Tim said, his voice weak and raspy.

"Clamp those cuffs back on."

Tim hesitated. If he did, it was over. JD would have complete control again. But didn't he anyway? Tim had had one chance and he blew it. He was no match for JD. The way the stool bounced off JD's arm, the way JD didn't even flinch. The power of JD's fist to the side of his head was like a two-by-four. He didn't really have a choice. He crawled over and ratcheted the cuffs back on his wrist.

"That's better." JD stuffed the weapon back into his waistband and rubbed his arm. A red welt had appeared. "You'll pay for that one."

Martha gave a short, nervous laugh. "What? You're going to kill us? What could you do worse than that?"

"There are lots of ways of dying. Ain't that right, Tim?"

She started to say something, but stopped. She looked at Tim. "What is he talking about?"

"Nothing."

"Come on, Tim," JD said. "Don't get all bashful on us. Tell her what we talked about."

"Shut up," Tim said.

"What is it?" Martha asked.

"I told you—nothing."

JD laughed. "You see, old Tim and I had an agreement. If he behaved himself, then I'd make sure the Spraggins brothers would too."

"Who are the Spraggins brothers?" Martha said.

JD looked at Tim. "Want to tell her?"

Tim felt his entire body sink. A wave of nausea rode over him. He couldn't talk, so he simply shook his head.

"You sure married a winner here," JD said. "What a pussy." He looked down at Martha. "Kyle and Cody. They won't kill you quick like I will. They'll make a game out of it." He shook his head and walked back to the window and looked out. "Those boys sure love games."

Chapter 84

Our big break came at 6:11 p.m. Bo had left the gun shop just after 4:30, driven by his home, stayed only ten minutes, and then headed south on Memorial Parkway, Highway 231. The GPS in my iPhone followed his every move. Derrick Stone had stationed a rookie uniform at the computer, and he was keeping everyone informed virtually minute by minute.

Bo continued on 231 over the Tennessee River bridge, the Parkway now carrying the moniker Heart of Dixie Highway, to the small town of Arab, where he exited onto Guntersville Road, State Highway 69. He drove east for several miles and finally reached Guntersville Lake, a broad expanse of water created by the Guntersville Dam, part of the TVA system. A mecca for boaters and fishermen. Cabins and boat-houses lined much of the lake's shore.

Bo had turned south near the lake's edge onto Diamond Road and then slanted off onto Point of Pines Road, which followed the curve of the shoreline and provided access to a collection of lakeside cabins. A mile later, at exactly 6:11 p.m., he came to a stop. Bingo.

The GPS signal revealed that Bo had settled next to a waterfront cabin about a mile south of Highway 69. Google Earth showed that the property was mostly wooded. A driveway spurred off Point of Pines, cut through the trees, and ended at a parking area on the north side of the house. The only open area on the property was a grassy front yard that stretched between the cabin and the boathouse and dock at the water's edge.

T-Tommy contacted the owner, William Dawson, at his home in Atlanta. He said the property had been on the market for nearly a year and that no one was authorized to be there. He said he'd drive right over, but T-Tommy suggested that might not be a good idea.

Now, just after eight p.m., we stood among a stand of trees that lined an RV rental lot near the intersection of Highway 69 and Diamond Road. There were thirty of us: HPD officers, Madison County Sheriff's Department deputies, six guys from SWAT, and a couple of Marshall County deputies, since we stood on Marshall County soil. And then there was Claire with her .38. No way she was going to miss this story so she had called in the *Channel 8 News* van and her cameraman Jeffrey Lombardo, now sitting in the back of the van, keeping himself and his equipment dry, the rain pelting the roof like a snare drum.

The rain had been squirrelly all afternoon. At times, like now, a steady rain, at others a light drizzle, and at still others hard lightning-and-thunder driven sheets of peppering spray.

Sheriff Luther Randall arrived. Pulled up in his Tahoe, his personal car, and stepped out, wearing jeans and a plaid shirt beneath a Sheriff's Department windbreaker. He'd obviously been at home when he got the call.

Luther was Madison County's first black sheriff. He had held the job for four years and his tough stance on criminals and smoothness with the press made his reelection virtually a sure thing. The electorate loved him. I had worked cases with him several times, the most recent being the Brian Kurtz murders.

I knew Luther had worked out all the jurisdictional stuff. The Marshall County Sheriff was away at a law enforcement convention in Chicago, so he gave Luther the authority to run the operation in his county. He and Luther went way back.

"Luther," I said as he walked toward the gathering.

"Dub." We shook hands and then he looked at T-Tommy. "What's the plan?"

T-Tommy ran through it. We weren't sure if the Fosters were alive or not. We didn't know how many people were holed up in the cabin, but Derrick Stone had earlier done a quick drive-by and, through gaps in the trees, had seen three vehicles in the parking area next to the cabin: Bo's SUV, JD's truck, and the Spraggins brothers' pickup, the attached trailer now empty. That would pencil out to four people and a missing boat. And, hopefully, the Fosters.

The plan was for SWAT and the other officers to move into the trees that separated the point of land where the cabin sat and Diamond Road while T-Tommy and I tried to get close enough to see if we had a hostage situation or not. If the Fosters were alive, we'd have to move carefully. If not, we could simply storm the Bastille.

"How do you plan to get close without them knowing?" Luther asked.

"From the water," T-Tommy said.

"Roy Kim has a place just up the river," I said. "We'll use one of his canoes."

Luther nodded. The rain peppered the leaves above us. "Roy cool with this?"

"Yeah. So long as we don't get holes shot in it."

Luther looked out toward the road for a beat and then said, "Might work."

"This rain will actually help us," I said. "Good cover. Muffles the sound."

"Okay. Get moving and I'll get everyone else down the road and into position."

Roy Kim was sixty-five years old and now ten years removed from his two-decade stint as an HPD homicide investigator. A Korean father and Italian mother, he had a round face, narrow, quick eyes, and thick black hair, no hint of gray. He'd worked with T-Tommy on several cases and had been a close friend of my father's. I'd hunted and fished with Roy and my dad many times growing up, including this part of the lake.

Besides being a good homicide investigator, Roy was an artist. After retirement, and the death of his wife of twenty-two years from breast cancer, he'd settled deeply into his painting. Mostly watercolors. He had won awards and his artwork had been shown in galleries all over the south. I had a pair of his paintings on my walls. Yet for all his skill with a brush, he was best known for his duck and goose decoys. Hand-carved and painted, these were true works of art. Collectables. Each signed and numbered by Roy. I had three on my mantle: one a gift from Roy, one I purchased, and one I inherited from my dad after his death.

We found Roy in his studio, a generously windowed room that faced the lake. He sat on a stool, snugged against a worktable, a bare-bulb overhead, a partially painted decoy in one hand, a paint brush in the other. He looked up as T-Tommy and I came in.

Roy set the decoy aside and stood. "So you got some bad guys hiding out down the river?"

"At least four," I said. "Maybe a couple of hostages."

His brow furrowed. "Not a good situation."

A man of few words, Roy always seemed able to distill a problem down to a simple truth. This qualified. This was definitely not a good situation.

He snagged a rain jacket off the nail beside the door and led us out to a dock that extended along one side of a weather-worn wooden boathouse before nosing out into the lake. Rain ticked against the boathouse's corrugated-metal roof. Roy pushed open a side door and we followed him inside, where a powerboat sat in the water, two canoes hung from the rafters, and a third canoe, the largest of the three, hung on the far wall.

"Better use this one," Roy said, indicating the one on the wall. "It's a little choppy out there and this is the heaviest of the bunch."

Roy undid the chain that locked the lake-facing double doors and shoved open one side. Rain slanted through the opening. T-Tommy and I lifted the canoe from its bracket and settled it in the water.

"Don't get it shot up," Kim said.

The canoes were handmade. By Roy. Another of his many talents.

"We'll do our best," T-Tommy said.

We climbed into the canoe, and Roy handed us a pair of paddles.

"Wish I could go with you," he said. "Sometimes I miss chasing the bad guys."

Chapter 85

Roy Kim's place was half a mile north of the Highway 69 bridge, our destination a mile south. We paddled twenty yards or so out into the lake and then turned toward the bridge. I heard Roy closing and chaining the boathouse door behind us.

The water was rough, the rain steady, but we made good progress, what little current there was this close to the shore pushing us along. The headlamps of the few cars that moved across the bridge, smudged by the rain and mist, emerged from the darkness, and then faded along with the wet whine of their tires behind us as we moved on south. The cabins that lined the shore were mostly quiet, only a couple with visible inside lights.

I figured we were halfway to William Dawson's cabin when the wind kicked up, sheets of heavy rain pounding us. Lightning streaked the sky off to our left and the short delay before the thunder arrived meant it wasn't far away. The wisdom of being on the water in the middle of this seemed weak about now. At least the canoe was wooden.

We pressed on, digging our paddles into the water. Soon the backlit windows of Dawson's cabin came into view. A powerboat, the one I had seen earlier at the Spraggins' place, sat against the short dock. I didn't see any signs of activity near it.

The house just this side of Dawson's place was dark and quiet. Probably someone's weekend retreat. Shielded by its boathouse, we slid the canoe to shore and dragged it from the water. We scurried into the trees. The rain battered its way through the leaves and ran in rivulets down my windbreaker and face.

We wound our way between the trees until we reached the gravel lot next to the cabin. The two pickups and the SUV Stone had seen on his earlier drive by hadn't moved. Through the cabin's side window I could see movement but couldn't make out who was inside. Or how many.

The cabin was two stories and, except for the parking area and the grassy yard that stretched from its porch to the water, was surrounded by a thick envelope of cedar and pine. The porch extended the width of the house and was embraced by railing and covered by a roof that served as the floor of an upper deck. I could see two rockers and a bench on the porch.

T-Tommy pushed aside a cedar branch and studied the house. "Can't tell how many are in there."

"Not from here. Hold the fort, I'll try to get closer."

Staying low, I darted across the lot to the rear of the SUV, the rain and wind muffling the sounds of my steps against the gravel. Stone had given me a .357, his backup piece. I checked to make sure it was still in my jacket pocket as I eased past the SUV and crept up to the window. Now I could hear them talking.

"Let's get this done." I didn't recognize the voice. Probably either Kyle or Cody.

"When the rain lets up," JD said. His voice I knew.

I looked through the corner of the window. Kyle, Cody, and JD were standing, Bo lounging on the sofa, beer in hand, the Fosters sitting on the floor, handcuffed to a chain that wrapped around a metal support pole.

That answered our major concern. Tim and Martha were alive, and so far seemed unharmed.

Kyle squatted near Martha. "Maybe me and my brother can amuse ourselves while we wait."

He reached out and smoothed her hair. She jerked away from his touch. Tim lunged at him, but Cody grabbed him by his hair and pulled him back. He drove a fist into Tim's stomach. Tim balled up on the floor, trying to wheeze in a breath. He convulsed as he dry retched against the pain.

"What'd I tell you?" Cody said. "You try to fuck with us and we'll fuck you up."

Tim finally grabbed a breath. "Leave her alone."

"What difference does it make?" Kyle said. "You're both going to be dead shortly. Why not let the little lady have a last fling?"

He reached out, fisted the front of Martha's blouse, and yanked. The material resisted. He yanked again. This time the fabric gave up, the blouse ripping down each side, coming free in his hand. Martha crossed her arms over her chest and kicked at Kyle. He grabbed one ankle and pulled. She slid toward him, on her back. He wedged one leg between hers. She tried to scratch him, but he deflected her hands.

"I love a woman who puts up a good fight."

I had to do something. But what? I looked back toward T-Tommy but couldn't see him among the trees. I needed something to distract without letting them know the cavalry had arrived. I didn't want this to turn into a hostage standoff. Right now we had somewhat of an advantage. They didn't yet know they were surrounded.

The light from the window shed a twisted rectangle of illumination onto the gravel. I squatted and scratched around until I found a suitable rock. A little larger than a golf ball. I picked it up and moved to the front corner of the house. The metal boathouse was a hundred feet away. As a kid I'd played a lot of baseball, some center field, some shortstop, some third base. This was just like throwing out a runner heading toward home plate. I hurled the rock, clanging it against the boathouse's metal door.

"What was that?" I heard JD ask.

I scurried toward the rear of the house, staying low beneath the windows, and then veered right, back into the protective cover of the trees. I knelt behind a cedar tree, secreted by its drooping, water-laden branches.

Kyle and Cody burst out the door and into the open yard, heads swiveling, guns extended before them. Kyle walked a straight line toward the boathouse, each stride confident and unhurried, as if he thought he was bulletproof, maybe invisible, as if he had no fear that someone might be out there pointing a gun in his direction. Ballsy son of a bitch. He yanked open the side door and disappeared inside. Cody walked to the end of the pier, looked around, and walked back.

The brothers finished their search of the boathouse and now stood on the walkway that stretched between the pier and the cabin. They chatted for a minute and then Kyle waved his gun toward the house. They moved that way but split before reaching the porch, Kyle heading my way, Cody circling the opposite way. Kyle searched around the vehicles, even looking underneath and opening them to look inside. He moved to the back of the SUV and scanned the trees.. Cody finished his lap around the house and joined him.

"See anything?" Kyle asked.

"Nope."

"Maybe a limb or pinecone from one of the trees?"

"Didn't sound like that to me."

Kyle looked up. The rain had softened to a drizzle and the droplets peppered his face. He looked back toward the house. "Don't look like this rain is going to stop and it's getting late. I say we get this done and get the hell out of here."

Cody nodded. "Let's go chat with JD."

Chapter 86

"Anything?" JD asked when Kyle and Cody came back inside.

"Didn't see nothing," Cody said.

"This rain ain't going to let up," Kyle said.

"What, you a weatherman all of a sudden?" JD asked.

Bo laughed. Kyle glared at him. "I'm just saying it's late and we got work to do. Let's dump these fuckers and get out of here."

JD nodded. "You got everything ready?"

"Yeah. The cinder blocks, the plastic sheets, and the rope are in the boat." He pulled his Glock from his belt. "And I got this."

The rain continued to hammer against the roof. JD walked to the window where water streamed down the glass. Nothing worse than being out on the lake with rain and wind and lightning, but he had to agree with Kyle, this wasn't going to let up anytime tonight. Just like that fruitcake doofus on Channel 8 had said. Of course, as often as not, that moron was wrong.

I heard movement behind me and turned. T-Tommy, Derrick Stone, and Luther pushed between two cedar trees and walked toward me.

"What's the story?" Luther asked.

I told him what I and seen and heard: the Fosters were alive; Kyle had ripped off Martha's blouse; the rock I tossed had bought some time, a few minutes anyway; the Spraggins brothers were getting a bit nervous.

"We've got everyone in position," Luther said. "And close. These trees and the rain make good cover."

"Sometimes you get lucky," I said.

"You see any way of getting in there without putting the Fosters at risk?" Luther asked.

"Not really. All four of the bad guys are armed."

"Any idea what their plans are?"

I glanced back toward the house. I saw JD standing at the window, his gaze directed skyward.

"Kill them and dump them in the lake." I looked at Luther. "Why else bring them here? Why else would Kyle and Cody trailer their boat here on a night like this?"

"Not to mention the rope and cinder blocks Bo had in his truck," T-Tommy said.

Luther nodded. "So they'll have to bring them out to the boat?"

"That'd be my guess."

"Unless they kill them first," Stone said.

"Too messy," I said. "I'd bet they'll do them on the water and dump them. Easier to clean up a boat."

"Makes sense," Luther said. "You think of that?"

"Claire."

Luther smiled. "Figures."

"Our best bet will be to intercept them as they're taking them to the dock," T-Tommy said. He looked at Stone. "Move some guys down near the water, flanking the yard area and in the trees over past the boathouse. Quietly."

"Will do."

"Get a sniper on either side," Luther said. "Clear view of the walkway and the dock."

Stone disappeared into the trees.

I looked at T-Tommy. "Want to get wet?"

"Don't you mean wetter?"

Chapter 87

The water was chest deep and not too cold but the silty bottom made traction uneven. T-Tommy and I had shed our jackets and slipped into the lake about halfway between the docks to Dawson's cabin and his neighbor's. We held our weapons near our heads and trudged along parallel to the shoreline. The plan was to get near the boat, maybe disable it, but at least be close enough to take down a couple of the bad guys if they made it that far. The one thing that couldn't happen was to let them get Tim and Martha on board and out into the lake.

Vulnerable was the word. We were twenty feet from shore, no cover, easy targets if any of the kidnappers stepped outside and saw us. The darkness and the rain were our only allies here. I followed a few feet behind T-Tommy as we worked our way toward the Spraggins brothers' boat.

Suddenly T-Tommy stopped. I heard the cabin's rear door slam shut. Kyle crossed the porch, hesitated a beat, looking around, his gaze passing over us a couple of times. We sank more deeply into the water, only our heads above the surface, weapons now against our cheeks, hearts fluttering in our throats. At least mine was. I assumed T-Tommy's was too. I expected Kyle to pull out a weapon and start blasting away. Instead, he bounced down the three steps, hurried along the walkway that bisected the grassy yard, stepped up on the dock, and climbed into the boat. He sat in the driver's seat and seemed to be searching for something. He stood again and shoved his hands into the pockets of his jeans. Front and then back. He rummaged in his jacket pockets and patted his shirt.

"Damn it," he said. He climbed out of the boat and headed back toward the house.

Once he was inside, we moved quickly. T-Tommy settled into the shadows at the end of the dock, me alongside the boat. I hoisted myself up, resting my stomach on the gunwale. I found the fuel line to the huge Evinrude 225 and yanked it. The connection broke. Then I pulled it free from the gas tank and tossed the tubing into the water. I slid back into the water and trudged to where to T-Tommy stood, nearly chest deep in the water, the dock shielding us from view.

"Any problems?" he asked.

"No boating tonight."

The door slammed shut again. Kyle walked our way. I could hear keys jangling. He climbed back into the boat and cranked the starter. It whined, ground, and coughed, acted as if it might start, but fell silent. Again, he tried the starter. More whining and grinding, but the engine refused. A lack of fuel will do that.

"What the fuck?" Kyle said. Again he tried to crank it.

Now things began happening fast. The cabin door swung open. I heard Cody say, "Move it."

I raised up just enough to see over the length of the dock. Cody held a gun in one hand, the other gripping Tim's upper arm as he led him to the boat. Tim's hands were bound behind his back.

"Get in," Cody said.

Tim hesitated, looking around, obviously searching for some way out of this.

Cody grasped the nape of his neck. "I said move it, asshole." He shoved Tim forward. Tim tumbled into the boat, his head thudding against something. He groaned but managed to rise up on his knees and then regain his footing. Not easy with your hands cuffed behind your back.

Behind him, JD and Bo flanked Martha as they led her down the walkway. Her hands were also restrained behind her back.

"What's wrong?" Cody asked.

"Fucking thing won't start," Kyle said.

Cody stepped into the boat, stooped to examine the fuel tank, and then suddenly stood. "Somebody trashed the fuel line." His head swiveled, the gun following his gaze.

Kyle pulled his gun.

"What's wrong?" JD asked. He stopped, yanking Martha close to him.

"Somebody messed with—"

Kyle's forehead exploded. The crack of the sniper rifle echoed among the trees. Kyle staggered to his right and tumbled over the gunwale into the water.

T-Tommy's gun exploded behind me. A black blossom appeared on Cody's chest. He wavered.

Now gunfire erupted from every direction. Bullets pinged off the metal boathouse and splashed into water behind us. Three more bullets thudded into Cody, and he collapsed into the bottom of the boat.

I waded around the dock and to the side of the boat. Tim stood next to Cody's body, frozen in shock from what had happened. A bullet whizzed by, then another. I planted my feet on the lake bottom, coiled my legs, and leapt upward, grasping Tim's belt, pulling him from the boat and into the water. He hit flat on his back, a solid slap, a spout of water, and a wave that smacked me in the face. I lost my grip. Tim sank from sight. I could almost feel his underwater thrashing. One foot and then the other broke the surface, each churning, Tim now in full-on panic mode. I guess being disoriented in dark muddy water, hands bound behind your back will do that.

I grabbed one of his feet, yanked him toward me, clutched a pant leg, and finally got an arm around his waist. I pulled him tightly against my chest and righted him. He came up sputtering, coughing, wheezing.

"Relax, I've got you."

More coughing.

"The water isn't that deep. Get your feet on the ground."

He did.

"You okay?" I asked.

He coughed again and then said, "Where's Martha?"

I looked toward the house just in time to see JD drag her through the door and back inside the cabin. Bo followed, but didn't make it. He caught a shot to the shoulder as he climbed the stairs and one to the neck as he stepped up on the porch. He stopped, standing stark still. His gun fell from his hand. Two more bullets slapped his back, high near his left scapula. He fell backward down the stairs.

Chapter 88

A full-on hostage situation. That's what we now faced.

Bo, Kyle, and Cody were done, now property of the coroner's office, but JD had Martha in the cabin. Every HPD officer and sheriff's deputy had now emerged from the trees and surrounded the cabin, some taking cover behind the vehicles in the lot, others plastered against the cabin's walls near windows and doors, but out of the line of fire in case JD wanted to make this a real shootout.

I could see shadows moving inside the cabin but had no visual on either JD or Martha. Luther shouted to JD, suggesting he might want to give this up. In response, the cabin went dead. Dark and silent. JD had obviously flipped the master circuit breaker.

I walked over to where Tim sat in the open door of the SWAT van, shivering, more likely from fear than from his wet clothing and the chilly night air. One of the SWAT guys had given him his windbreaker and Tim had zipped it up to his chin.

"What are you going to do?" Tim asked.

"Sheriff Randall's trying to talk him out," I said.

"He's desperate."

I nodded. Yes, he was. And desperate people do desperate things.

"And he killed Steven."

"What?"

Another shiver racked Tim's body. "He told us. He's the one who took Steven. Not Walter. Walter was passed out drunk at their shop so JD took his van. Since Martha saw him from so far away and they are about the same size, she thought it was Walter." He sighed. "Probably because they told her it was Walter's van that had the DNA. And in a photo lineup they look enough alike that she was mistaken."

That changed things. If this was the case, JD would never give up. Shooting his brother was one thing, but killing an innocent child another thing altogether. This was getting very ugly, very fast.

"Dub?"

I turned. It was Luther.

"He wants to talk to you. Says he won't talk to any cops."

"Why me?"

"Because you're so charming. Who cares? Just keep him talking while we figure this out."

I told Luther what Tim had said. That JD killed Steven.

"Jesus." Luther massaged his neck as he looked toward the cabin. "That thickens the stew a bit."

Tim grabbed my arm. "I'm coming with you."

"No, you're staying here."

"But—"

"But nothing. We want him calm, focused. You being there might confuse him, make him more angry or impulsive." Tim started to say something, but I raised a hand to stop him. "I don't know what he'll want or what he plans to do but it's best if you're out of the equation. Let him think you're dead or off to the hospital. One less bargaining chip he can use."

Tim hesitated a beat and then nodded. "Dub, get her out of there."

"I'll try my best. Sit tight, and I'll see what he wants."

What JD wanted was for all of us to go away. And a boat. Or a car. I didn't bother arguing the point that neither would get him very far. Rather I let him talk. Sometimes, like in JD's situation, a bad guy's best laid plans go off the rails and he freaks. Can't think clearly. Can't see that he's in a corner. Can't see that there was no way Luther would let him take Martha and leave.

If you let him talk, pretend you really give a rat shit about what he's saying, the flaws in any escape plan begin to loom larger. Sometimes the bad guy will give it up after he talks it through.

But JD was a double murderer. One victim a child. In my gut I knew he'd never give up. But I had to give it a shot. Maybe, just maybe, JD would waver.

"I want a fucking car," JD said.

JD had opened the window, the silhouette and a few ghostly details of him and Martha now visible just inside the window frame. JD held Martha snug against his chest, his gun touching the side of her neck near the angle of her jaw. She still wore only her bra. I could see her shivering. I stood in the parking lot, twenty feet away, partially shielded by JD's SUV.

"To go where?"

"Away from here."

"That's not really a place."

"I'm not going to tell you where I'd go. I'm not stupid."

"Didn't say you were. You know, JD, I'm not stupid either, but for the life of me, putting myself in your pickle, I can't think of a single place I could hide from this."

"Well, I can."

"Really?"

He hesitated for a minute and then said, "Just get me the car and nothing bad happens to her."

"JD, Sheriff Randall already told you that that couldn't happen."

"He better fucking reconsider."

"Think it through, JD. There's no place you can go."

"You don't know what I can do."

"I'm not exactly a virgin in this sort of deal. I've seen how these situations go. The guy in your position usually loses."

"Not me. I don't lose." He raised his Glock above Martha's head and gave it a waggle. "I'll kill her if you don't do what I say."

Tim felt panic rise in his throat. He sat in the open side door of the SWAT van that was parked on a bed of pine straw just off the drive and near the back edge of the parking area. Maybe a hundred feet away from where Dub Walker stood, trying to talk reason into JD. He could clearly hear everything that was said.

When JD said he'd kill Martha, Tim believed him. In fact, he knew that JD wouldn't give up and if he wouldn't do that, he'd definitely take Martha down with him. He couldn't simply sit here and let that happen. He had to do something.

But what?

He stood. The rain, now a soft drizzle, ticked against the SWAT jacket he wore. Before him, HPD officers and sheriff's deputies surrounded the house, some in the trees, others behind the vehicles in the lot, others covering the rear door in case JD decided to make a break that way.

Tim didn't believe that was a possibility. JD wasn't going to run. JD would go down first.

Then he saw movement to his right and turned to see Claire McBride and her cameraman come down the drive and walk toward him.

"You doing okay?" Claire asked.

"Anxious would be the word."

"Any progress?"

Tim shook his head. "Dub's trying to talk him out." He sighed. "Doesn't sound to me like it's going well."

"I'll see what I can find out." She walked along the perimeter of the lot, hugging the trees, ducking beneath a few low-hanging branches. Her cameraman followed.

Chapter 89

"Where's Tim Foster?" JD asked. "I want him here."

"He's on the way to the hospital," I said. Lying to kidnappers is definitely allowed.

"I don't believe you."

"Want to take a ride over there and see for yourself?"

"I want him here."

"Not going to happen, JD. He was shot in the crossfire. Looks bad."

I heard Martha take in a breath and murmur, "No." A sob jerked across her chest.

I hated to do that to her, but I had to convince JD that Tim wasn't part of this anymore. That his only real option was to give up Martha and himself. Or not. It was the not that was the problem.

"Look, JD, so you shot your brother. He was a jerk and a pedophile. Not saying you'll get off on that, but there were mitigating circumstances. And the kidnapping stuff isn't as bad as a rap for murder one, which is what you'll face if you harm Martha."

JD laughed. "You're something else, Dub. You think I don't know Tim talked."

"I told you he's on the way to the hospital."

"Don't play me. Not now while I hold all the cards. He told you I was the one that killed Steven. And if I give it up, Martha will tell the same story. So, it's murder one already. I don't see you have much to offer, and I don't really have a choice here."

"You always have a choice, JD."

"The only one I see is whether I shoot Martha here in the right side of her head or the left."

Tim sat in the door of the SWAT van listening to Dub and JD as well as Sheriff Luther Randall, who stood near the rear of the van, talking to the four SWAT team members.

"We're going to go in," Luther said. "There's no way JD is coming out."

"No," Tim said, jumping to his feet. "Martha's in there."

Luther turned to him. "That's why we have to end this now. He'll kill her and then himself. That's the truth of it. Our guys might take him down first."

"But she would be in the line of fire."

"Possibly. If we do nothing, definitely."

"Please."

"These guys train for this. They have the best night-vision equipment, which gives them advantage in there. Just let them do their job. It'll work out." Luther turned back to the team. "Okay, you know how this goes. Two through the back door; two through the front. Don't hesitate. First one with a clear shot, take him down."

Luther looked back at Tim, nodded, gave a grim look, and walked away. The SWAT guys headed to their positions.

Tim paced. Panic rose in his chest. He knew how these things went. In books and movies the hostage was always, always rescued. In real life, almost never.

He had to do something.

He looked back into the van. Two sniper rifles leaned against the far wall. Both had massive scopes. He crawled inside and lifted one of them. He quietly worked the bolt and seated a round into the chamber.

He stepped out of the van and looked around. No one was paying attention to him, everyone focused on the cabin. He slipped into the trees.

• • •

"JD, Tim didn't tell us anything, and if your attorney was here he'd tell you to shut up. Not confess to anything."

"Too late for attorneys."

"It's never too late. You never know what they'll figure out."

"Get real. I'm a dead man anyway this goes."

"That'll definitely be the case if you do anything stupid. But if you just listen, things might not be so bleak."

"Bleak? That one of those fancy words you use in your books? Bleak? This ain't bleak, it's fucking pitch black."

"Doesn't have to be."

"Actually, it does because that's exactly what it is."

Tim examined the rifle and then the scope, which was a little more complex than the one he had practiced with. The first knob he tried seemed to do nothing, but the second one changed the scope to night vision. He settled the rifle on the limb of a pine tree, wedging his shoulder against the damp trunk for stability. He pressed one eye to the scope and scanned the house. Everything had an eerie green hue. He found the window, and then JD and Martha. Her face filled the circle. He could see tears on her cheeks and fear in her eyes. His jaw flexed.

JD's forehead and the right side of his face appeared just above and to the left of Martha's head. He planted the crosshairs on JD's right eye.

Could he pull this off? The last time he tried something like this he had missed. Not completely, but enough. His target had been the center of Walter's chest. He had missed it by half a foot. Here he had only a couple of inches. The fact that this rifle was finer tuned than the one he had used and the distance here was maybe a hundred and fifty feet and not three hundred yards added little comfort. The stark truth was that a mistake here, a six-inch miss, could kill Martha. Or miss JD altogether, in which case he'd kill Martha.

His mouth cottoned and his hands shook. Exactly as they had done the day he laid in that tent and placed crosshairs on Walter's chest. Hot sweat trickled down his back and leaked from his forehead, seeping into his eyes, blurring his vision. He wiped his forehead and eyes on the jacket sleeve. A sob caught in his throat.

He couldn't do this.

Now he used a hand to swipe the tears from his eyes. He thought of Steven. Heard his laughter, his insane giggling at something Martha said. She always teased him, made him laugh. He heard her laugh too. So wonderful, musical, alive. Their home, their life, had been so perfect. Steven had been so perfect.

This is the guy that killed Steven.

He pressed his eye against the scope again. Martha's face was contorted into a grimace, her eyes scrunched closed, tears streaking her face.

Dear God, give me the strength to do this.

Asking God to help him kill someone seemed odd but right here, right now, he didn't care. All he cared about was saving Martha. And bringing justice for Steven.

He took a deep breath and rested his finger on the trigger.

Please give up, JD. Don't make me try this.

"So you think a jury's just going to let the killing of my brother and a kid slide?" JD said.

"Not completely but maybe enough to keep the needle out of your arm. A good attorney can convince a jury to do all sorts of things."

"Somehow I don't see that as very likely."

"Let's say I can get you a car. Then what?"

"You can't. We both know that. You're just buying time. I suspect so the SWAT guys can bust in here and kill me. I'd rather do that myself."

"No one's going to crash in on you, JD."

I saw JD's grip on Martha's hair tighten and he pulled her head back, her chin angling upward. "The way I see this going is the first bullet in her head and then I swallow the second one." He ground the gun's muzzle into her neck. "Dub, tell my mama I'm sorry."

"JD, you don't have to—"

The rifle crack came from behind me. A black hole snapped into view where JD's right eye had been. His head jerked back and he fell. Martha screamed. The SWAT guys splintered the front and rear doors.

I turned. Tim came from the trees, both hands raised, the rifle in one. Three officers descended on him, one taking the gun, the other two grabbing his arms. He didn't resist.

"Let him go," I said.

They hesitated.

"He's not going anywhere."

Luther appeared, one arm around Martha. She pushed away and ran to Tim, locking her arms around his neck. The dam broke and she collapsed against him, sobbing.

Chapter 90

Deputy DA Carol Barton-Higgins looked across her desk at Tim and Martha Foster. I sat to one side on a sofa with Claire and Martha's sister, Paige Baker. The Fosters had asked that Claire and I come with them, for moral support if nothing else. That's about all we could offer at this point anyway.

Since the Fosters hadn't hired an attorney, Carol felt it would be best if HPD didn't have anyone there either, so T-Tommy wasn't present. Tim and Martha had decided they would take whatever punishment was given and only involve attorneys if the DA came down hard. I advised against that, but they were adamant.

Yesterday, T-Tommy and I had talked with Carol and explained the entire case. The motivation behind Tim shooting Walter, the fact that it wasn't his bullet that killed Walter, and that the Fosters had returned to Huntsville on their own. The fact that Tim shot JD to protect Martha seemed clear self-defense to me.

She countered that they returned only after they were tracked down and their elaborate disappearing act blew up on them and that while the killing of JD didn't bother her, the planning and attempted murder of Walter did.

I couldn't argue with that, so I talked about their community service, their ties to the church, the fact that the murder of a child, particularly an only child, could knock anyone off balance and lead to poor choices. I argued that this was definitely an isolated case. The Fosters weren't killers, just two distraught and damaged parents.

She said revenge didn't make a good defense.

She also wasn't happy that T-Tommy had decided not to arrest the Fosters, but rather let them return to the Marriott. He said he didn't want a media circus and didn't want to put them through a perp walk. He said he'd take full responsibility and that he now had guards outside their room.

Carol said she would chat with the DA and have a verdict today. So here we were, waiting for her pronouncement.

She closed the folder on her desk and held it up. "This is your file," she said to Tim. Her face appeared hard. "Pretty thin. Most of the ones that land on my desk are measured in inches, not pages." She dropped the folder on her desk. "Part of me wants to throw the book at you. Attempted murder, conspiracy to commit, and a handful of other charges. All the gymnastics you went through to plug Walter Whitiker goes far beyond premeditation. Hell, I've seen murder one filed when the killer did only twenty minutes of planning."

I saw Tim stiffen and Martha close her hand over his. I could smell their fear. This woman literally held their future in her hand.

"The other part of me understands what you did and why you did it," Carol went on. "I'm a mother. I have an eleven-year-old son." She looked at Martha and gave a half smile. "I couldn't sit right here and promise you that I wouldn't do exactly the same thing under the same circumstances." She stared at Martha for a beat and then sighed. "The DA and I spent most of yesterday and well into the night wrestling with what to do and we came up with something that we're both comfortable with."

Tim and Martha sat wide eyed. Deer in headlights came to mind.

She looked at Tim. "You plead to attempted murder for Walter and we'll let JD Whitiker's shooting slide. That'll translate to an eight-year sentence, possibility of parole after five and half, maybe only four with good behavior." She looked at Martha. "And you plead to conspiracy of the same. No jail, but six-years probation."

Tim and Martha looked at each other. Martha nodded.

"That's very generous," Tim said. "And probably better than we deserve."

Carol smiled. "That was part of our decision. We believe that you're truly remorseful, and that goes a long way."

Martha sniffed and dabbed a tear from one eye with the tissue she held wadded in one hand.

"When does this happen?" Tim asked. "The jail part?"

She rested her forearms on the edge of her desk and leaned forward slightly. "Two weeks. I suspect you need some time to straighten out your financial mess. We'll draw up the papers. I suggest you get an attorney to look everything over before you sign. But, no leaving the county. That would be considered a breach and the deal is off."

We walked outside into a perfect spring day. Crystal-blue sky, a soft breeze, and a new life—again—for Tim and Martha.

"Thanks for everything," Tim said as he shook my hand.

"Don't forget I was one of the ones that tracked you down."

"That's actually a good thing," Martha said. "I'm not sure we would've been able to keep up the charade the rest of our lives." She hugged Paige. "Not seeing Paige and talking to her all the time was too painful."

"Where are you going now?" I asked.

"First stop?" Tim said. "A visit with Pastor Boles. We have a great deal to rectify."

I nodded. "I think he'll be forgiving."

"But will God?" Tim asked.

"Isn't forgiveness what it's all about?"

Tim nodded and a faint smile appeared. "Yes, it is."

I watched as Tim, Martha, and Paige walked toward their car.

"What do you think?" Claire asked.

"I think they'll do just fine." I threw an arm around her shoulder. "Let's call T-Tommy and head over to Sammy's for lunch."

"That's one of your better ideas."

Author's Note

Every author has been asked: where do you get your ideas?

The short answer is: everywhere.

That is indeed the truth of it. Something you see or read or an overheard conversation or a couple arguing at a nearby restaurant table or an odd character you pass on the street or simply an idea that pops into your head from wherever those thoughts are born raises the questions: What if? What if this happened? What if that person did this? What if that couple was actually planning a murder? What if that briefcase contained state secrets? Or an explosive device? Or a deadly virus?

From those two words—what if—stories arise.

What if a good, God-fearing couple are threatened by the man that killed their only son, forcing them to plan the man's murder and their own disappearance?

That's the question that drives this story.

It didn't begin as a novel, but rather as a short story. My first, and to this date only, short story. A story that appeared in International Thriller Writer's anthology *Thrillers 3: Love Is Murder.*

After the story was completed, I sent it to my older sister, a retired schoolteacher and accomplished storyteller herself. After she finished, she asked me: what happens next? My response was: what do you want to happen next? She laughed, saying she wanted to make sure that I intended for the story to have an ambiguous ending. I did.

But then over the next few weeks I asked myself: what does happen next? The answer to that question is this novel.